C000143402

Stories for

Homes

To Barbara

Best wishes

Mandy Berriman

Edited by

Sally Swingewood & Debi Alper

Stories for Homes is a project to raise funds for the housing charity Shelter and to raise awareness about the housing crisis in London and beyond. Known and emerging writers were invited to submit stories of up to 3,000 words on the theme of Home.

The housing crisis is urgent and action needs to be taken now. The aim of the project has been to publish a world-class anthology of short stories, with all profits going to Shelter.

The Shelter website address is:

www.shelter.org.uk

The Stories for Homes website is: storiesforhomes.wordpress.com

Shelter is a registered charity in England and Wales (263710) and in Scotland (SC002327)

ISBN-10: 1493534246

ISBN-13: 978-1493534241

Stories for Homes

Stories for Homes

DEDICATION

To everyone who knows what it is to struggle and to those who work to make a difference.

Stories for Homes

CONTENTS

FOREWORD

Home is a funny, emotive sort of word. Each person on the planet has their own concept of what it means and their own battles to secure it.

My own story is common place. It isn't tragic or dramatic. I simply found myself starting again as a single parent, wanting to do the right thing and not knowing quite how. Money never went far enough, housing was over-priced and under-maintained and, no matter how well-intentioned, those in a position to help never could. Home stopped being something I took for granted and became a quest. But I'm one of the lucky ones: I have an income, supportive friends and family and the ability to fight, through education and language. Which is pretty much how this book was born.

It was a sunny April afternoon, a housewarming for the simple, freshly painted, clean, dry, two-bedroom flat which we now call home, and I shared a possibility with a new friend, Debi Alper. What if we could make a difference? What if we, as writers, could begin something that would help ease other people through the journey of finding a home? What if we sent out word that we wanted to create a fantastic collection of short stories which could both raise awareness of just how tough it is for people in the UK to get and keep a decent home and along the way raise money to ease that struggle?

A conversation led to a Facebook status, to a Tweet, to a blog. Two people shared a dream over a glass of cheap red and their dream went viral. Hundreds of writers responded to a ludicrously tight deadline and sent in stories which made us weep one minute and laugh uproariously the next. Editors, proof readers, designers, technical gurus, PR professionals – we had a team within a week of going public and a book in less than three months. The creative energy everyone involved has put into this project has meant that no corners were cut and no compromises were made. This collection is nothing short of outstanding. Thank you all.

All money raised from the sales of this book will be donated to Shelter, the charity which works relentlessly to improve the UK's housing situation. With that in mind I have no qualms in asking you to tell everyone you have ever met to contribute by buying a copy. If you enjoy it – and believe me, you will – tell random strangers to buy copies too.

A lot of coffee and cake was consumed in the creation of this collection. Keep up the good work by arming yourself with something similar, then get comfortable and enjoy.

Thanks for supporting Stories For Homes.
Sally Swingewood

MANDY BERRIMAN

A Home without Moles

Eyes open.

Dark.

Dark *and* quiet.

Not the quiet like when I jam my fingers in my ears and quiet-noise leaks past them so I can still hear the busy-ness and the veekles and the door-slamming and the yelling and the thump-da-thump-da-thump music. This is Real Quiet like if I was a caterpillar curled in a cocoon or a deep-sea diver explorating the bottom of the sea or a princess sleeping at the top of a giant*nor*mous tower. This is Magic-*Amazing* Quiet.

I look and look and look into the dark and it stops being so dark and starts making the shapes of everything in the world, like the wardrobe and the rainy-hater and the door with our dressing gowns hanging on it and the stripy bars on Toby's cot.

Does quiet stop being quiet if you listen hard and hard? I hold my breath and send messages from my brain to my ears to tell them to open as wide as wide and ... oh! The Quiet grows into Mummy breathing slow and Toby snuffling cos he's got another cold and the swish-ROAR-swish of cars whizzing by downstairs, but there's not many of them, and in the spaces atween our building clicks and clanks and sighs, like it's talking to me. Probly telling me to get out of bed and play in the Quiet afore it gets Noisy again.

I roll over and lift my head to look over Mummy's hilly bump. The clock says four; it's not Getting-Up-Time unless it says seven. How much counting does it take to get from four to seven? Maybe if I count to a-hundred-a-thousand-a-hundred-a-hundred, then it'll be seven. Our building clicks and clanks and sighs some more. Silly Jesika. If I wait for four to count to seven, there won't be any Quiet left; it's never quiet at Getting-Up-Time.

It's lighter in the living room. There's a crack where the curtains don't meet and silver-grey has sneaked in and painted everything in the room so it's hardly dark at all. But it's shivery-cold so I creep back into the bedroom for my dressing gown and my Peppa slippers and wrap myself up all snugly-buggly.

Baby-Annabelle isn't snugly-buggly; she's lying on the floor next to her pram all nudey-dudey. Poor Baby-Annabelle. I fetch my doctor bag and put Baby-Annabelle on the hopsital bed. *Let's listen to your chest.* The stefscope listens to Baby-Annabelle's heart. *Oh dear, you have a chesty fecshun. You need some special medicine. Here you go. All better now.* I dress Baby-Annabelle in her woolly trousers and woolly cardigan but the buttons are tricky-fiddly so I wrap a blanket around her to cover up the gap down her middle and then tuck her into her pram. She goes to sleep without rocking. Her eyes are always closed when she's lying down, not like Toby who has to be picked up and rocked and put down and picked up and rocked and put down again and again and again til Mummy gets tired arms and a tired voice. Sometimes I'm asleep afore Toby and I'm a big girl and he's only a baby.

I leave Baby-Annabelle to sleep and fetch my colouring book and my bag of pencils and pens and I lay down on the carpet on my belly and turn the pages til I find a girl on a horse next to an apple tree. Horses are my fayvrit animals. When I'm growed up I'm going to have a horse called Velvet and my house will be like the yellow house in my fayvrit Tilly books and have lots of windows and a green door, cos green is my fayvrit colour, and we'll each have a bedroom, me and Toby and Mummy, and in the garden there'll be a slide and a swing and an apple tree and a ginger cat and a pond with some tadpoles.

I start to colour the apples on the tree but the silver-grey has even painted all my pencils and pens, and the apples could be red, which is good, or purple, which is very silly. I can't switch on the light cos it's still not seven and there's a hole in the bedroom door and the light will fly through it and zap Mummy's eyes and she'll wake up with her cross face and her grumpy voice. But I can't colour my pictures in the silver-grey either. I need to turn on my thinking cos

Mummy always says you can find answers with thinking. When Mummy turns on her thinking she's good at finding answers. That's how she knew to squish a bit of chewy-gum on the rainy-hater pipe to stop it dripping.

I turn on my thinking, and think and think ...

The telly! It's not telly-time and I'm Not-Allowed to watch telly when it's not telly-time but that's ok cos I'm not achully going to watch it. I turn it on and press the quiet button til the big blue line shrinks to a teeny blue dot making the people's voices small so I don't isturb the Quiet or Mummy and Toby sleeping. Then I press 7 and 1 for CBeebies, cos all the other numbers are For-Grown-Ups-Only. CBeebies is still in bed but that's OK cos even asleep, CBeebies makes light and it's not bright, zapping, Wake-Up-Mummy light but small light that only shines in front of the telly and when I hold up my pens and pencils right in front of it, I can see my colours almost proply.

I've coloured in the girl on the horse and a pirate on a treasure island and a dog with a big spotty bow round its neck and a fierce tiger hiding in a jungle, and now the light creeping through the gap in the curtains is orangey which means the Sun is waking up. And it must be almost seven cos I'm starting to hear busy-ness noises outside and through the wall and there's a sizzly-cooking smell that means someone's having breakfast and it makes my tummy growl like there's a big, brown bear inside me.

I turn the page and it's all covered in little black

dots and I can't do these ones without Mummy cos you have to know all your numbers and I only know one-two-three-four-five-six-seven-eight-ten-leven-fifteen-sevteen-tenty, but it remembers me bout my secret dot pichers and I've not done one for a-long-a-long time and they're much better than these dots cos I can do them all by myself and make any picher I want.

I take my fayvrit green pen and squeeze ahind the telly and find the peeling-paper. It feels soft and soggy and when I lift it up, there's even more black dots than afore and my pichers of the house with lots of windows and the horse and the apple tree and the slide and the swing have dribbled down the wall a bit. There isn't a pond yet so I join some dots up in a pond shape and then add tails to the dots inside the pond so they look like tadpoles and then I think bout which dots will make the best cat cos it won't be right til the cat's there too.

But afore I can decide, Mummy is there yanking my arm hard and the telly is hitting me on the head and Mummy is screaming, *Moles! Moles! Dirty, Jesika, dirty!* and my head's gone all spiky and hot and my eyes are all stingy, but Mummy keeps dragging me til we get to the bathroom sink and the light's on bright and hurty and she's scrubbing my hands and my fingers with the scrapy-brush that's apposed to be for cleaning nails and now I'm crying and telling her they're not moles, they're *tadpoles* but she's not got her listening switched on cos now she's being cross bout the telly wasting lectristy and it's not fair cos even if my tadpoles were moles, only real moles that dig in the earth and make muddy molehills are dirty; picher moles are just pichers.

After breakfast, Mummy puts my shoes on tight with tuggy fingers cos she's still cross bout the moles and now she's also cross cos Toby coughed and coughed and sicked up his breakfast milk all over his clean clothes and the bag for the washing machine shop is very heavier. We're going to the doctor after the washing machine shop so Mummy can tell the doctor off cos Toby's chesty fecshun medicine isn't working proply.

On the landing, Mummy fights the door shut and I do my job holding Toby's buggy cos the brake doesn't work proply. Next-door-lady huff-puffs up the stairs and walks straight past us not even saying, *hello,* which is achully very rude, and I'm still thinking this when she opens her door and I forget to hold my breath quick and her house-smell is all eggy-yucky in my mouth and my nose afore I can stop it. Then Mummy's finished fighting and we're bumping and banging down the stairs and round and down some more stairs and Mummy remembers me to be quiet past the door at the bottom cos the other day a nasty man opened it and said scary-words. But he's not there today and then we're out on the street in the middle of the busy-ness, stopped next to the smelly-stairs that go down to the door-that-never-opens cos Mummy's got her bags tangled on the buggy. I'm

Not-Allowed to go down the smelly-stairs cos they're dirty and daynjrus but I always look cos sometimes there's people down there and I wonder why they go down to the-door-that-never-opens cos that's just silly unless it's cos they're thinking for an answer to open it.

There's nobody down there today but I look and look while Mummy gets cross with the bags and I see something intresting right at the bottom of the stairs. It looks like a jection, not like the one in my doctor bag for Baby-Annabelle, but a proper jection like the one the real doctor scratched my arm with so I don't get nasty-bugs. My thinking's still turned on and I say to Mummy, *look, there's a jection for Toby to make his chesty fecshun go away*, but she's still fighting with the bags and I know I'm not apposed to go down the smelly stairs but Toby is coughing and crying and this is a mergency and it's ok to do Not-Allowed things when it's a mergency. I hold my breath to make the smells go small and I hold on to the handrail and I count the stairs down and there's scary feelings jumping in my belly cos it's quite dark at the bottom and it remembers me that there might be monsters hiding where I can't see them.

One-two-three-four-five...

Jesika! Get back up here now! And Mummy has run down and is squeezing my hand so tight and pulling me up the smelly-stairs so my feet almost fly and her voice is all shouty. *What do you think you're doing? You hold the buggy and you don't let go! That's the rule!* And I tell her bout my thinking of getting the jection for Toby to make him better and I think there really must be a monster down there cos when she looks down the stairs her face goes all scary-wide-eyes and she's pressing her hand to her mouth like she's holding a scream in and she's so scared that we have to run away very quickly and she even forgets bout the washing machine shop and then she forgets the doctors and she forgets to say, *scuse me*, to all the busy people on the pavement and some of them make cross faces as we push past them and I want to stop and explain that Mummy's not achully rude, she's just running away from the monster but I have to hold tight to the buggy and make my legs go fast and fast so Mummy doesn't leave me ahind.

We run all the way to the house-lady. We sit in a boring line for a-long-a-long time and Mummy's not in a talking mood with me or Toby but when it's our turn to see the house-lady, she talks and talks and talks at the house-lady bout moles in the wall and Dirty-Needles and Noise and Toby's chesty-fecshun but the house-lady doesn't look very intrested cos she keeps looking at her computer not at Mummy. Then Mummy stops talking and the house-lady says, *A tempy roof is better than no roof*, and I think bout asking what a tempy roof is but Mummy is pointing at Toby and telling the house-lady that if we don't move to a house without moles, Toby will keep getting chesty-fecshuns and I miss what the house-lady says to that cos I'm turning my thinking back on but Mummy gets very shouty and then it's time to go.

We're waiting for the green man to say, *go,* and a van drives by with bricks on and I'm still thinking for answers and it remembers me bout the three little pigs and I get excited and say to Mummy, *Why don't we find a man with bricks and then we can build a house and it won't have moles in the wall cos moles can only dig through mud, they can't dig through bricks.* And the green man starts beeping us across but Mummy doesn't move. I say, *Come on Mummy, the green man says go,* but she just bends over the buggy with all the busy-ness going on all around and people showing us cross faces again. I think she's checking Toby but then her shoulders start shaking and she's covering up her face like she's laughing cept water leaks atween her fingers and I know she's crying, and all the busy people just keep walking past and the cars and the buses and the lorries don't stop and I think someone should stop to check what's hurting cos something must be hurting; you only cry when you're hurting.

And then I feel a sore-hurt in my belly cos I think maybe it's my thinking for answers that's made Mummy sad cos maybe I thinked the wrong answer like with the telly and the jection and Mummy's really sad cos I can't think answers proply and I say, *I'm sorry for thinking the wrong answer, Mummy, I'm sorry.* And I'm thinking that I better stop thinking for answers and I only say that bit inside my head but Mummy must hear it cos she turns to me and wipes the wet off her face and looks all tiger-fierce and says, *Don't you ever stop thinking for answers, Jesika. Promise me, not **ever**. Not even when the answer is really, really hard to find, you just keep thinking.* And she crouches down and hugs me as tight as tight and says, *Promise me,* again.

And the words are in my mouth but they won't come out cos there's a lady with a mean face tutting cos we're right in her way and my special words are just for Mummy, so I turn my mouth right into Mummy's ear and let the words whisper from my mouth. *I'll not ever **never** stop thinking for answers.*

And then I have to tell Mummy to stop hugging so tight cos it's getting hard to breathe.

FRANCES GAPPER

Babylon

This is nothing against my brother Bernard, who we're both very fond of. He acted from the best of motives throughout, I'm sure. While visiting the UK and staying at our house in Acton, he presented us with a green teapot. Just as an ornament it was fine, but he insisted on us using it. I sensed my sister-in-law's influence and sure enough. Lucinda says it's unsociable not to use a teapot, Bernard told us.

But the problem here was my husband Joe likes his tea very weak. Just show it the teabag. The thought of tea stewing in a pot gives him the willies. So he pretended he didn't really like tea and he'd have Nescafé instead. I'm afraid I'm a bit of a snob about coffee, Bernard said. He bought us a grinder, a filter machine and some Guatemalan coffee beans. We sipped politely, trying not to wince.

Laura phoned: Mum, you've got to stand up to him, you know Dad won't. I re-entered the lounge to find Bernard criticising our flowery wallpaper, our curtains and our carpets. You're only in your forties, not your eighties. But I liked the sense of continuity and connection with the previous owner (she died here). Patterned carpets are coming back into fashion, I told Bernard. It was true, I'd read it in a colour supplement. Not these ones, he said.

Joe's parents rang: their usual weekly call. His mum is very nice. His dad harrumphs in the background. They used to live in Africa and Joe's father remembered a tribal saying: feast your guest as a prince for two days and on the third morning, hand him the hoe. I laughed, but thinking of my plants I thought no. As it turned out, this was prescient of me.

Then, Bernard shipped us off to a country house hotel. How generous of him, we thought, to show his appreciation. Only we both felt it was a bit peculiar, him staying in our house while we're in a hotel. But he said only those dates were available. A sense of dread prevented me from fully enjoying the swimming pool, the health club and the extensive grounds. When we got back, the first thing I noticed was four skips outside the house. The second thing – which Joe saw first – was the house itself had been painted turquoise over the pebbledash, with gold window sills and frames, and gold guttering. It looked dreadful.

A surprise makeover. The TV designer people like to have a theme and in our case it was Babylon. The garden was covered in glittery plastic decking. Our old shed had gone, replaced by a temple. Back indoors, the stripped floorboards looked cold. The lounge was where they'd really gone to town, with a mural of Babylon – more temples – and hanging baskets everywhere. It struck me at once these were impractical, because of the watering. But nobody had thought of that.

Faced by the TV cameras, of course we told them how wonderful it all was. Modern and yet linked with an ancient civilisation. The old place was due for a bit of a change, Joe said, and we all laughed.

We waved from the door then went back inside. No sofa, only an uncomfortable metal thing. By the mural of Babylon we sat down and cried, remembering our lovely home.

Stories for Homes

JO LIDBETTER
The Edge of the World

The edge of the world. That's how she thought of it. She sat in the doorway looking out to a life that wasn't hers. Children shrieked, naked in the sunshine, holding their swollen bellies like trophies. They'd be tired soon. The worms taking their energy. Occasionally, someone would get a break, maybe enough to buy medicine. Then their bellies would flatten out and they'd lose the dullness in their eyes. In the hot season, no one got lucky.

It was too hot for luck. Too hot for anything. Actually, she preferred it. At least in the heat, people would come around more. They couldn't travel so they came by for a chat and a smoke. The creaking from below was comforting too: a slow rhythmic groan from the wooden struts that kept the house away from the ground and dry when the rains came. Someone was on the hammock below the house, swaying gently, keeping the air moving. She listened for a moment, her head on one side. There was a gentle snoring but that was probably just one of the dogs. She could picture the hammock. When threads

17

snapped it'd be brought up to her and she'd twist some cotton into twine and knot it back into shape. The kids would come and sit at her feet while she did this. Well, not at her feet, obviously, but next to her, teasing each other before leaping back out into the sunshine. Into their world and out of hers.

Her world was now this little house. Her eyes took a moment to adjust to the gloom. A checkerboard of light criss-crossed the floor where the sun found its way through the gaps in the bamboo walls. A shaft lit up the pale dust as it danced and landed on a strip of faded pattern on the mat.

She tutted and made a mental note to ask someone to rearrange the grass of the roof, maybe even tie on a few more lengths. There wasn't any hurry but she'd need it done before the rains came. She'd ask the boy from next door when he came round with her food. He'd grown quite tall lately. It should be fairly easy for him now.

She leant over to the bag of charcoal, took out a chunk and scratched a rough arrow on to the doorframe, pointing upwards towards the gap. She wouldn't forget now.

Next to the bedding was a pile of her clothes, the sarongs folded neatly and kept in place by a plastic bowl containing a bar of soap, now just a sliver, a toothbrush and a half-finished tube of toothpaste. A piece of rope stretched across the room from bed to door and there was a knife, stuck in the wall within easy reach. Between that and the bag of charcoal were matches, leaves and a pile of tobacco. This gave the heat of the late afternoon a musky sweetness. The only other item in the room was her potty. She scrunched up her face. Oh, how she missed being able to go to the toilet properly. It wouldn't be so bad if she had any family left but having to pass her potty to others to deal with, that was humiliating. They were kind about it, of course, but it still made her feel ashamed, every day. She glanced once more around the room. There weren't any cooking pots now. No plates, bowls, cutlery. Just that one knife. Everything else she'd given away after it happened. She didn't like to remember it. That awful day. When was it now? She didn't know. Many full moons had gone by.

It had started as such an ordinary day. Not long after the water festival. The kids were still in high spirits after three days of throwing water. They didn't understand the religious significance of the festival yet, the purification and hope it inspired, but there was time for that. At least she'd thought that there was time. They were just children. They wanted to swim away the heat so they'd gone for a picnic. The whole family. And they'd taken a goose. She'd carried it herself, holding the sack tightly as the creature squirmed inside. It had settled as they'd walked along one of the hard crusts that checkered the paddy field. The children had headed off into the trees alongside the field and had come running back, yelling. The noise they made. It had set the goose off so she'd had to put the sack down and was only half listening to the kids, her back to them as she soothed the bird. She caught a word or two, but wasn't really paying attention.

'I think it's a toy pineapple.'

'Can we keep it, Dad?'

'Can we?'

Then nothing. No pain, noise, light or heat, just nothingness. It would have been better if the nothingness had gone on forever. It had for the rest of her family. An eternity of nothingness. No more pain, or sorrow, no knowing that the whole family was gone, forever gone. No trying to survive. No pity or charity.

A tear darkened her sarong, where her legs used to be. She grabbed the rope and pulled herself over to her bedding, the wheels of her trolley squeaking below her.

She looked around her home, her entire world, and wondered what had happened to the goose.

SARAH EVANS

Motherhood

Post thudded through the door and Doug clattered up from the kitchen chair. 'I'll get it.' Two seconds later he handed an off-white envelope to Marjorie.

'Looks like it's from our Katie,' she said, thinking how it was ages since either of them had written; these days it was all email, texts and phone. Not much of those either. She drank the remains of her coffee and wiped her hands on a napkin before opening the envelope.

The letter was written on a piece of lined A4. She got up to find her glasses, but even with them on it was difficult to decipher Katie's scrawl.

'Well?' Doug said.

'Just a moment.' She laboured through the letters, words and sentences. It was like a jigsaw puzzle with missing pieces.

'Is everything alright?' Doug asked.

'Yes. I mean, I think so.' She handed it to him, though she doubted he'd decode it any better than her. 'Sounds like things haven't worked out with Jason.' Not that that was any loss; on the one occasion they had met, she'd disliked his eco-warrior look and constant stream of innuendo. 'And she's packed in work.' Abandoning the tills at Tesco wasn't exactly tragic, but at least the job had been something. 'She wants to come home for a while.'

Just until I get myself sorted, she had written.

'Well,' Doug said. 'That's nice.'

Marjorie looked up at him. 'Yes.'

'A bit of company.' He went back to his toast and newspaper. 'Don't suppose she says how long for?'

'No.'

Later she rang Katie's mobile. *Voicemail.* 'Hello, darling,' she said into the electromagnetic void. 'Lovely to hear from you. Yes, of course that's fine, you coming to stay.' Not that it had been posed as a question.

Days passed in agitation. She turned her PC and mobile on far more frequently than usual. She followed up her voicemail message with an email then a text.

'Perhaps she's changed her mind,' Doug said and Marjorie could not detect whether his voice betrayed hopefulness or disappointment. 'She'll be in touch sooner or later. Not as if we're going anywhere.'

Marjorie's legs kept itching to be out of the house. She invented shopping trips then found herself scuttling back to ask, 'Has she rung?'

'Who?' Doug said. 'Oh Katie. No, not yet.'

A week passed and another two days. In the middle of an evening watching television Marjorie heard the front door open. Her heart thudded. *Intruders?* But burglars could not simply waltz in.

'Hello?' Katie's voice echoed through the house. 'It's just me.'

Just wasn't the word Marjorie would have chosen.

Katie smelt of stale cigarette smoke and sandalwood as they embraced. She was wearing low-hanging jeans and a skimpy top. She'd gained a little weight, Marjorie thought, or else her clothes were more revealing than the last time they'd met. That had been when? She froze in a second's amnesia.

Six months ago. It must have been all of that. Katie had dropped by for lunch with hardly a breath of notice. Only a fleeting visit, its purpose mainly, as far as Marjorie could deduce, to cadge a certain amount of cash. *Just to tide me over*.

Doug was smiling broadly. 'Don't you look well,' he said. It was what he always said. Marjorie looked at her daughter. Her face was drawn and the tinting of her hair didn't reach the roots. Her clothes had a grubby sheen.

'Tea?' Marjorie offered.

'Or something stronger?' Doug added.

'Oh, yes please,' Katie said as she settled into the sofa in the space Marjorie had just vacated.

'Which?' Marjorie asked.

'Or both?' Doug said.

Katie shrugged. 'Oh, whatever.' Her hand stirred the air as she beamed at Doug.

Fine! Marjorie left the room. She'd make tea. It hardly mattered if it remained untouched.

She came back three minutes later with a tray laden with mugs and a plate of plain biscuits.

Doug and Katie were drinking whisky. The TV had been switched to a soap which Marjorie and Doug never watched. Katie was mid-flow. Marjorie didn't need to tune into the words to pick up their meaning. The world was custom-designed to thwart her daughter. Jason was the current topic. Six months ago, he'd been God's gift and Katie had flamed with fury when Marjorie dared to suggest that perhaps he might like to find a job. Now he was being fed, bit by bit, to the lions.

Marjorie picked up her mug. Katie deigned to notice she was in the room, or at least noticed the plate of biscuits. 'Is there anything else?' she asked.

'If you'd let us know -' Marjorie started.

'Weren't there some fancy chocolate ones in the cupboard?' Doug said.

'Perhaps you could get them.' Marjorie smiled tightly. She'd bought them for her weekly book-reading club.

Katie smiled just as tightly back as Doug left the room.

'So,' Marjorie said. 'How long did you think you wanted to stay for?' She hadn't intended to sound so brusque.

Katie's eyes opened wide with six-year-old distress. 'I've only just got here,' she said. 'You're already trying to get rid of me.'

'Don't be silly. I was only asking.'

But Katie was crumpling up in tears.

Marjorie and Doug had just sat down for breakfast. After years of hurried toast, it was pleasant now, in their retirement, to treat breakfast as a proper meal, to linger over coffee and the daily paper, to chat about this and that.

The door opened in a rush, letting in a draught from the hallway. Katie stood there, wrapped in Marjorie's newest dressing gown, which had been washed and left in the airing cupboard to warm. Katie raked a hand through her hair and yawned.

'Is that coffee?' she asked and walked over to where the cafetière had been left to brew. She had pushed the plunger down before Marjorie could ask her to wait a minute. She had poured herself a mugful, before Marjorie could point out that if it was going to stretch three-ways they'd better use the cups not mugs. She had headed back to the door and was squeaking up the stairs before she had so much as said, *Good morning*.

Doug smiled indulgently and raised his eyebrows at Marjorie.

'I'll make some more,' she said. She felt irritated out of all proportion. It was a faff to scoop out the steaming grains, rinse the jug and start again. Morning rituals usually left her feeling mellow and ready for her day. Today, she had the beginnings of a headache.

An hour later and there was no further sign of Katie. She couldn't sit around all day.

She had her coat on and was double checking that her key was in her bag when she heard the door upstairs. She fought the urge to simply go.

'Did you have a good night?' she asked as Katie slouched down the stairs, still wearing Marjorie's dressing gown.

'Yeah. OK,' Katie said.

'I'm just popping out to the shops. Anything I should get?'

'Whatever.'

'Anything you're allergic to these days?'

'It isn't a question of *these days*.' Katie's voice slipped into irritability and she proceeded to list a whole host of things that surely by now her mother ought to be aware she couldn't eat.

Marjorie wouldn't mind hunting round for goats' milk if she didn't already know that most of it would lie festering in the fridge. If she didn't know that the intolerance to cows' milk ceased to apply when it came to overpriced coffee in Starbucks. She very much doubted Katie was scrupulous about buying organic chicken when the cost was on her.

She felt mean and petty to resent an extra few pounds. She felt irked at being made to feel that way.

Days accumulated into weeks. Katie slept late. She mooched around, half-dressed and yawning. She could be discovered in all corners of the house, talking with loud emotion on the phone. She adopted

Marjorie's favourite dark-red jumper. Face-cream disappeared, and it was less the absence of the jar that Marjorie minded than the fact Katie considered nothing odd about wandering into her parents' bedroom and picking up whatever came to hand. The house filled with unsettling aromas of exotic oils and, while Marjorie never actually caught Katie with a cigarette, stale smoke lingered here and there. Katie declared she would manage her own cooking and then she'd appear just as Marjorie was dishing up and say, 'That looks good,' leaving Marjorie obliged to stretch it out. When she did cook for herself, the kitchen was abandoned in utter chaos.

'I'll deal with it,' she promised, but Marjorie could not abide the mess for the time it might take Katie to actually do so.

'So how long is she staying?' Doug said one morning, his voice low. They seemed reduced to whispers in their own home.

'I don't know any more than you do.' The question felt trickily out-of-bounds.

'Can't you ask her?'

'Can't you?'

There was a click somewhere and they both started guiltily. It was their house, but they felt like guests. Katie was the one who seemed to feel at home.

'It would be better coming from you,' Doug said.

Doug had always left the difficult conversations to Marjorie, reserving for himself the rôle of adored father.

Marjorie thought about protesting. But Doug was so soft, he simply wouldn't see any conversation through. She felt a gathering of her inner forces and determination. After weeks of inaction, she would *do* something.

She hung around, cleaning out cupboards in the kitchen, her ears alert for Katie's emergence. Time passed and she went out into the garden and pruned with vigour. By the time she returned, the house was silent. No trace of Katie or of Doug.

An hour later, she heard the door and went to greet them, finding the pair of them in a happy, smiling mood. Typical Doug! Abdicating all responsibility.

'Where've you been?' she asked, sounding fractious and not caring.

'Katie fancied a coffee out,' Doug said.

Katie yawned. 'I'll just …' she said and gestured up the stairs.

Which could have meant she was about to occupy the bathroom for the next two hours, or monopolise the computer in the spare room, or disappear behind the door of her bedroom for half a day with eerie music thumping out.

'Actually,' Marjorie said. 'I wondered if I could have a word.' She heard how she sounded: ridiculously formal.

Katie looked at her. Her eyes moved over towards Doug who was busily retreating to the kitchen. 'Now?' she asked.

'Yes, why not?' Not as if her daughter had pressing engagements.

Katie shrugged theatrically. 'OK.'

Marjorie turned into the living room and sat down on one of the armchairs, sitting on the edge to remain upright. Katie slouched into the sofa opposite and stared down at her fingernails like a sulky schoolgirl.

'I just …' Marjorie started, trying to bring back the opening lines she'd practised. 'Your dad and I just wanted a better idea of how long you think you'll be staying.'

'Like I said, I need some time and I don't really know how much. Not yet.'

'When might you know?'

Katie's eyes were wide and serious. 'That's not something I can predict. Not really.'

Marjorie's knees were twitching with impatience. *But why?* Surely the failure of a relationship was something Katie had learned to deal with by the age of forty. Not as if she hadn't had lots of practice.

'Your dad and I …' This type of conversation never got any easier. 'It's just … I suppose we're used to having the house to ourselves.' Not unreasonable, surely. 'And while you're welcome …'

'It doesn't sound like it.'

'… to stay for a while …'

'You want me to go.'

'I didn't say that.'

'Well, you did. I mean, that's exactly what you're

saying.'

'Your dad and I ...'

'Don't bring Dad into this. *He* hasn't said anything.'

Well, no, he wouldn't have done. 'I've discussed this with him.'

'Talking about me behind my back.'

Well, yes, that's what parents do. 'Discussing the situation.'

Katie sniffed loudly. 'I thought I could count on you. I thought my parents – my mum, my dad – would be the people I could rely on ...'

'And you can.'

'Instead, you just want me out the door. You're as bad as everyone else, except it's worse, because you're my parents and I thought, well, aren't parents supposed to look out for their kids?'

The volume of sniffles increased and Katie's protestations emerged as a semi-coherent cloud of accusations out of which familiar phrases surfaced.

You've always been cold. You should never have had children. It's your fault I've ended up like this. Everything's always about you. You're so selfish.

Marjorie clamped herself tight, trying to resist being drawn in.

She hated this.

Confrontation.

Argument.

Conflict.

She hated the way she was left exposed, torn

between the desire to express her own feelings and the sense that her feelings must be wrong, unnatural, that they were better kept private and dealt with on her own. Was she in the wrong? Was it wrong for her and Doug to want their home to themselves, with visits, of course? Her own needs – for space, for routine – sounded so nebulous and self-centred.

She tried to break through Katie's monologue to explain. She tried to give concrete examples of what the difficulty was, to be specific.

Each point sounded petty and Katie had its counter.

'But I said you didn't need to cook for me,' Katie wailed. *That wasn't the point.* 'I don't see why it matters to you when I get up.' 'You can ask me if you want to use the computer.' Those didn't get to the heart of the issue either. 'Have the bloody jumper.' She tore it off and threw it in Marjorie's direction; it landed on the floor, lying on the carpet like a bloodstain.

'You're an adult,' Marjorie said, her voice losing control. 'Adult children generally leave home.'

Silence fell.

It lingered on between them, allowing time for reflection, for retraction, for one or both of them to say, *I didn't mean that.* Marjorie felt dreadful. Yet at the same time she was not prepared to simply pull back, to say, *Sorry, of course you're right, of course you can stay here for however long you want.* She believed completely in the reasonableness of her own perspective, whilst recognising the utter impossibility of communicating it to Katie.

Finally, Katie stood up and, in a high-pitched voice, she said, 'All right. If you don't want me here, I'll go.'

It was meant to be the trigger for Marjorie to say, *Don't take it like that, of course you mustn't go*. The way she had done all those other times, through all the years.

She sat and gazed at the carpet and listened to the patter of Katie's feet across the floor, the open and heavy slam of the door, the rapid pounding up the stairs.

She closed her eyes and kneaded the tension between them. Time passed. Her circling thoughts did not bring clarity.

Eventually, she heard Katie clattering down the stairs and the scratch of canvas against the wall. Heavily, she stood up and opened the door to the sight of Katie with her bulky bag slung over her shoulder, bits of cotton clothing trailing down.

Just go. Marjorie longed to say that. Katie's happiness was not her responsibility.

Then she swallowed down her thoughts, just as she always did. Motherhood did not allow such options. She swallowed down some essence of herself.

'Of course you can stay, Katie,' she said. 'For as long as you want. This is your home.'

MARK ARRAM

Home

Home is where the heart is
or isn't
Home is where the heart longs to be
or not to be
Home is spoons
Home is her
Home is him
all in dreams
or flesh
memories to warm
or chill in regret
Home is where you are wanted
or not
in or out
in the woods
or on the street
Home can follow you around
like a friendly cat
or a heavy rucksack.

SONJA PRICE

Dreamtime's Legacy

It was nothing special. Just a stone in the middle of the Outback. All around, dry shrubs and parched red earth. The view north, a clean sweep to Stuart highway, better known in those parts as Drought Trail, serving the road trains rolling in a straight line from Adelaide to Darwin. Break down there and you'd be in real trouble, with temperatures nudging the hundreds. Don't know how many times I drove past it without taking my eyes off the sweltering river of tarmac in front of me.

It sure never crossed my mind to take a break there until, years later, I hired an aborigine to clean up our yard. When I offered him a fag, we got talking about the routes I covered in my days as a trucker. He looked a bit shifty and then asked, 'You ever stop at the stone?'

'Not me,' I replied. 'Why would I want to leave my load of cattle or cars to walk all the way to some dirty rock that didn't even hold much promise of shade? Far as I know, no white ever came within two miles of it.'

'Exactly,' said the man as he leaned on his broom and took another drag at his cigarette. 'Which is why the place was perfect.'

'Perfect for what?' I asked and then there was no stopping him.

He told me that the stone's secret had been kept for a thousand years, passed on from elder to elder, generation to generation. He talked about Moqo, a boy with bat ears and frizzy, rust brown hair, who lived deep in the bush with his ma, pa, two brothers, a sister, cousins, aunts, uncles and his grandpa, in Wailpi territory. Moqo's folks kept to the old ways, he said, looking up to Moqo's grandpa, who was their elder. When they gathered around the fire at night, the old man would tell them stories about Dreamtime and the spirits who had given them the land. One night, Moqo had his own dream and as soon as he told it to the others, his grandpa knew it was time to take him walkabout.

The chief, tall and straight with a wooden staff in his hand and the boy, with a smaller one in his, set off at dusk and walked through the night and most of the next day, only sheltering under a gum tree at noon. Moqo fell asleep the moment they sat down, while his grandpa kept watch. They finally reached the red and dusty rock at dawn on the second day.

The elder pointed with his long knobbly finger. The boy threw down his stick and ran. Up close, it still didn't look much different but, when he rubbed away the dirt, the warm surface glistened like nothing he'd ever seen before. As big as a white man's shack, he was up on top before his grandpa could say *gumiri*. Nothing much to see: just endless outback and the thin ribbon of a highway. No gum tree, not even a fence in sight. When he next looked for his grandpa, the old man had vanished like a wombat in the morning light.

Moqo scrambled down and walked all around the stone. Behind a small boulder was a real *gumiri*, a hole in the ground. He crawled into it and felt his way down the dimly lit passageway to find his grandpa waiting for him in front of a small stretch of water. Moqo drank in the deliciously cool air as faint light spilled out from under a low hanging rock. To one side, a canoe floated in the water. The old man gestured to Moqo to climb in before getting in himself and pushing it away with his staff. They paddled, heads bowed, into a second cavern. Moqo gaped up at the black ceiling, lit up by thousands of glow-worms, sparkling and reflecting in the water like stars. They moved slowly across the lagoon to the splash of the oars. Once they reached the other shore, the chief pointed to several piles of bones. Moqo gasped. It was just like in his dream. His grandpa nodded.

'One day you will follow me. You have been chosen to guard our most sacred treasure. The burial grounds would only appear to a future elder.'

I thought the *abo* must be making this up to get another cigarette but I gave him one all the same because by this time I wanted to know more about

Moqo. He rewarded me with a toothless smile as we sat down on some old tyres stacked beside the tool shed.

He told me that Moqo's people never stayed in one place for long but that it wasn't a big deal for them, so long as they were all together, helping each other to survive in a place no white would last a week. The kid learnt how to spear wallabies sleeping in the shade of a banksia tree and kill yellow thornbills with his pa's beautifully carved boomerang. His ma taught him how to gather seeds, nuts and juicy fern roots and, if they were lucky, to find the occasional nutty-tasting snake's egg. He would forage in ant heaps with his sisters with thin sticks, or play football with a ball made from hide and feathers with the other kids. There was always someone around to do something with.

Moqo dreamed of the lagoon, long after he had been recruited by the National Programme for the Promotion of Indigenous Australians, or NAPPIA. The whites didn't exactly kidnap him, like they did with the Stolen Generation, but they plucked him from his family and sent him to one of their schools, all the same.

Moqo, you see, loved numbers and could do sums quicker than anyone he ever met and that included grown men. The boy didn't want to go until the whites told him there were other kids who played with numbers at their school. It would only be for a year, after all. His ma cried and his pa gave him his boomerang when the jeep came to get him.

The concrete and glass maze, complete with swimming pool and cricket field, lay four hundred miles away, just outside Adelaide. Moqo looked about as out of place as a cane toad on a bonfire. A couple of rich kids arrived in helicopters and they sure weren't used to having a black around. Called him *wog* behind his back and wouldn't let him join in.

No one helped him with his homework and he always sat alone in a corner of the great dining hall, while they laughed or whispered to each other whenever he caught their eye. There was no grandpa nearby anymore to look after him and tell him about the old ways, and what was right and wrong for his kind.

Then a letter arrived, telling him the old man had finally gone to Dreamtime. When he woke, all tears and snot one night, and told his roommates that he had seen his dead grandpa waving at him from across the water, they walloped him with their pillows. He clammed up about his folks after that.

He sure showed those white fellahs, though. Beat them at maths every time and bagged all the sports trophies to boot, because he was stronger and faster than anyone his age.

Slowly, very slowly, things changed for Moqo. Kids started inviting him home, like some funny mascot, and picking him for their cricket and rugby teams, and somehow he landed up staying.

Ten years later, the government really had

something to shout about. Moqo graduated from the Melbourne School of Business with distinction and went on to have a career that would turn your average Aussie green with envy. Earned his first million a year after he left college and then went on to join the Tasmanian Coal Company's board of directors. Their stocks and shares soared as soon as they started mining on the mainland, said the aborigine.

'Did he ever go back to his people?' I asked.

The man shook his head, stubbed out the butt and carried on sweeping. I knew there was no point in being pushy; that was all I was going to find out about Moqo and the stone from him.

I can remember going inside to catch up on the test match results but somehow I couldn't get that boy out of my mind. The way you do when you finish a book that keeps you wondering.

Last year, I drove back to find the stone and see if the bit about the lake was true. This time, there was no way I could miss the place. The orange glow of the lights broke the darkness, like a false dawn before I even crossed the horizon, and there was a wide, new road that led off Drought Trail to take me there. In daylight, you could spot the black ventilation shafts in the flat, unchanging landscape from miles away.

It's unbelievable how much business a mine generates. Makeshift blocks for the miners, who spend a good part of the month in the middle of nowhere, a massive car park, a gas station, a supermarket, two bars and even a motel. Truckers flock to the place like swallows to a waterhole since word got round that it was a good place to take a break, having driven a third of the journey in one direction or two thirds in the other.

'A cold beer is heaven after a long drive in the sun and it's no fun being alone when the dingoes start howling in the dark,' said the bartender as I sipped at my pint of Fosters.

Then I asked him about the lagoon.

'Can't have water near a mine, can you?' he answered. 'First thing they did was drain the lake. They found a load of bones. It wasn't easy but no worries. The boss oversaw the entire operation himself. I bet you've heard of him. First black to be named Executive of the Year in the papers. We're real proud of Mr Moqo Doodaroo.'

RACHAEL DUNLOP
Drowning in Fresh Air

I

Ruth and Pete met waiting outside the bathroom at a party. She noticed the way his smile went all the way up to his eyes and wondered how many other girls had felt that he was smiling just for them. He liked her dimpled arms, pliable and soft against the fabric of her summer dress. She twirled the syrupy dregs of her punch around the bottom of the plastic cup she was holding and wondered how to start a conversation with him. He thought she was probably a little drunk and let her go into the bathroom before him, pretending not to notice the disappointed look on her face. He didn't like girls who drank.

They were sixteen.

II

By the time Pete started going out with Ruth's best friend the next summer, he had got over his prissiness.

'Hello, bathroom girl,' he said when first they met again.

She pretended she didn't recognise him and made him look foolish for remembering a girl he had met once, a year ago, at two in the morning. He turned away from her, and she was sorry.

'What's up with you two?' the best friend asked.

Ruth shrugged and walked away.

Pete called Ruth one day, out of the blue. 'We broke up,' he said. 'Can I see you?'

'When did you break up?' she asked.

'About ten minutes ago.'

'Come on round.'

III

The best friend announced that she was pregnant and Pete decided to stand by her, even though he couldn't be sure the baby was his.

When he came to tell Ruth he was getting married, she refused to let him in the door.

'I wouldn't love you if you weren't the sort of guy to do the right thing,' she said, and closed the door before he could see her cry.

'She loves me,' he said to himself as he turned to go. He couldn't help but smile.

Ruth applied to universities as far from home as possible. The night before she left, Pete threw grit at her bedroom window until she let him in, afraid that her parents would hear him. She pulled him into the bathroom and locked the door. They made love on the bathroom floor, the thick pile of the white bathmat embossing her back with a lace of loops as she smothered her cries in the crook of his neck. It was her first time.

Getting up from the floor, Pete caught the edge of the fish tank with his elbow, nearly knocking it off its stand. The fish bobbed and swayed in the unexpected current, their faces eternally blank. His still-shiny wedding ring clinked against the glass as he steadied the tank.

'Strange place for a fish tank,' he said.

IV

When Ruth came home for the Christmas holidays, everything seemed different, although it was her that had changed. The fish were gone.

'It wasn't long after you left,' her father said. 'I got up one morning and all the water had drained from the tank. There was a hairline crack right down the side of the glass.'

She looked at herself in the mirror but all she saw were those fish, drowning in fresh air.

V

Ten years later, Ruth returned home once more, to be married from her parents' house. Pete watched from the far side of the street as Ruth entered the church. He saw her milk-white shoulders framed by the stiff fabric of her wedding dress and remembered how she had shyly loosened her bathrobe and stepped into his arms. She had tasted of soap and cotton, cool and clean and good. Beside him in the car, his son checked his watch, anxious to get to football practice.

VI

Ruth decided to take her parents out to dinner to break the news to them. Better done in a public place, she thought. Not that they were likely to make a scene, or even be surprised. A decade of marriage to a good man hadn't made her happy, and they knew it. But they were old-fashioned enough to think that divorce must mean the beginning of unhappiness, not the end of it.

It was as Ruth was scanning the restaurant to find the toilets that she saw Pete at a table on the other side of the room. The young man with him was talking to the waitress, giving her a smile that the girl clearly felt he had been saving just for her. He turned to speak to his father but Pete was gone, heading for the toilets.

In the tight, dark lobby at the back of the restaurant, Ruth took Pete's hands in hers, turned them palms up. She ran her thumb over the hard callous at the base of his ring finger, then over the polished skin where his wedding ring used to be.

'She left me,' he said, 'Left me and the boy, five years ago.'

'I'm getting a divorce,' she said.

He stepped forward, cupped her face with both his hands, and kissed her as he should have done, more than twenty years ago, outside another bathroom door. She closed her eyes and thought she could smell again the musty scent of the bathroom floor, damp and talc and hope combined.

It was like coming home.

CHRIS NICKSON

The Joyful Return

Revenge. He savoured the word on his tongue, letting it run like an infection through his veins, thinking it remarkable what a fire burning in a man could do. It could keep him alive all these long years away and then bring him back home.

'Nicholas Andrews, I sentence you to seven years' transportation,' the judge had intoned, allowing himself a merciful smile at keeping another felon from the gallows dance, and all for the crime of cutting a few purses. He could still hear the words with their smug inflection and feel his hands gripping the polished wood of the dock.

He'd expected things to be bad, but the truth proved far more cruel than anything he could have imagined. Puking his empty guts out in the hold of the ship, fettered hard and helpless as the guards and sailors taunted him. Then, in Jamaica, a heat so harsh and hellish he thought it might burn the skin from his back, so intense he thought the devil was pricking his lungs. They'd set him to work, cutting the sugar cane, day after day, out in the steaming, stinking fields, wounds from the machete festering on his hands and arms, healing slowly and painfully as he prayed with quiet fury for his preservation.

He survived two bouts of fever, raving off his head and swearing murder, so they told him later as he lay in bed, thin as a pauper's dog and so weak he couldn't even raise his hand to take the drink they offered.

It was education that saved him, those brief years he'd hated of sums and making his letters. After the clerk died, the plantation owner had needed someone who could read and write and Nick had pushed himself forward, grovelling and despising himself for his arse-licking words, but knowing it was better – that anything was better – then serving the rest of his sentence in the cane.

The job became his life, and he was good at it, quickly trusted for his accurate accounting and good hand. The master never suspected the occasional coins he filched and buried in the dirt beneath a tree.

Every single morning, he formed his lips to spit the name of the man he hated – Richard Nottingham, Constable of Leeds, the man who'd caught him, put him in gaol and landed him here. He'd have his blood for that. Seven deep cuts from the knife, one for each year he'd been gone, the last, gentle and loving across the throat, so he could watch the man's life bubble away in hopeless breaths. And tell him why just before he died.

When his freedom finally came, the days ticking slow like a clock running down, the ticket of leave in the pocket of his threadbare coat, the owner asked him to stay. Nick looked at him as if the words made no sense. All he knew now was home and the flame burning, strong and hot, in his heart.

The ship landed in Liverpool in January 1732. The money he'd stolen at the plantation had paid for his passage and food, hard tack riddled with weevils and small beer turned sour before the gale-ridden crossing was halfway complete.

He arrived penniless to an England that seemed like a foreign land, in the grip of a bitter, bruising winter which had no mercy. It was no work at all for him to cut the purses of a pair of drunken sailors, the skills of his old life still sharp. He ignored the port whores, all pox-ridden, rowdy and consumptive, and bought a hot meal and a bed for the night instead. In the mirror, he caught a glimpse of himself, his shoulders stooped, face burned dark and lined, hair matted and hanging to his shoulders, thin and grey though he wasn't yet thirty. He pulled the worn blanket over his body. There were fleas in the sheets, but at least the bed didn't rock and shiver in the waves. The next morning, without a second thought, he turned his back on the coast and began walking east.

By the time he reached Winnat's Pass, the pain from the cold weather had seared to his bones and his old boots were ribbons of leather, feet flayed and bloody from the stones and ice on the roadway. But he was lucky, finding a stranger for company whose corpse at least provided new shoes, even if it added nothing to his small supply of coins; when the snow melted in the spring they'd find the body and never know what happened.

From Sheffield, he made his way north, face set tight against the snow and the chill, the ragged coat held tight around his body as the gusts tore at his cheeks more brutally than any overseer's whip.

He passed Wakefield in the early dusk. His money was running precious thin and he was looking at a hungry, freezing night burrowed in a copse when he saw the farmer, a florid man with ugly, fat thighs jiggling in his breeches as he walked briskly home through the fields.

It took little to slice him, pull the body into the trees and take the rich, warm coat. There were coins in the waistcoat, enough to see him to Leeds.

Back to his home.

Back to Richard Nottingham.

Back to kill.

He crossed Leeds Bridge in the late morning, blending with the market crowds, and heard the traders shilling their wares up on Briggate. The snow piled, soot-blackened against the houses and walls, the slush, icy and treacherous, in the streets. He could smell the tannery on Swine Gate and the rich earthiness and piss of the dye works down by the river. For a small moment, he stopped to stare up at the bulk of the new, graceful Holy Trinity Church. Soon, he was at the top of Kirkgate, watching silently as people lurched and slid around him.

He'd been standing there for nigh on two hours,

his feet feeling as though they were still shackled and his hands numb from the wind's frigid tongue, when the Constable emerged. Slowly, Nick followed, unnoticed and invisible in the throng, beyond the Moot Hall with its bloody, metallic tang of butchers on the ground floor, up to the Head Row. He watched through the window as Nottingham entered Garroway's Coffee House, hailed some men and sat with them. Steam blurred his view through the glass and he walked on.

He'd seen what he needed and closed his eyes as a smile creased his lips. The man was still alive, still here.

He could do it tonight; he could watch in the darkness as the blood stained the snow; then he could breathe out and live again.

His fingers twitched.

No, not tonight.

He wanted the act to last, for each moment to fill him so the memories could tumble over him in all the evenings to come.

Slowly, almost carelessly, he strolled back down Briggate. He passed the Ship, once his haunt, and walked on to the Talbot.

Inside the door, the noise overwhelmed him like a wave and he stood still, eyes flickering with suspicion across a press of faces. Fire leapt in the large hearth, the heat inviting and irresistible. He pushed his way onto the corner of a bench near the blaze. As one of the serving girls swept by, he ordered ale and stew, the cracked, awkward sound of his own voice surprising him.

Tomorrow, it would all be done. The debt would be paid; he could leave Leeds and finally feel like a free man.

The warmth of the food and the sharp crackle of the logs left him weary. He needed a bed, he needed sleep; in this city that would pose no problem. First, though, he needed a woman.

The last time had been two years before. As a present to celebrate Christmas, the master had presented him with a slave for one night. She lay, brown eyes wide and empty, silent as he forced himself on her. When he woke the next morning, he was alone, and only the heady smell of her in the thick dawn assured him that it hadn't been a dream.

Outside, the air was cold and the sky had stilled with early darkness. His breath clouded the air and his soles crunched over ice as a few flakes of snow fluttered half-heartedly.

She stood half on Briggate, at the corner of a yard whose name he didn't recall. Her face was in shadow, a pathetic, patched shawl drawn across her shoulders, moonlight picking out the pale skin of her bony arms. He moved closer, astonished to find his heart pumping fast.

'Looking to warm yoursen up a bit, are you?' She tried to sound cheery but her voice quavered with the chill.

He nodded.

'Down here then, love.'

He followed her into the tight entrance to the yard, still in sight of the street. As she turned towards him, a sense of relief in her smile, her hands already hoisting her skirts, he rested his blade lightly against her throat so that a paint line of red drops bloomed on her skin.

He didn't need words; she understood. He pushed her back against the wall, tore at her clothes and entered her. Her eyes opened wider, the blank, hopeless stare an echo of the girl in Jamaica. It was only seconds later that his backhanded blow sent her to the floor, still mute, and he dashed back into Briggate, tying his breeches.

It was God's joke, he decided, that he'd end up in a rooming house in the same yard where he'd been a boy, before his parents had died of the vomiting sickness and he'd made his way on the streets. He glanced at the old door as he passed, but any memories were held like secrets behind the wood. It was just one night then he'd be finished here, on his way to York or London, to anywhere a man could disappear and start life anew. There was only one tie here and he'd loosen it soon enough.

The dank room already held two men with ale heavy on their breath, their sleeping farts sweetening the air. He lay on the straw pallet, fully clothed, the wretched rag of a blanket over him, and drifted away.

Something cold and metallic was pushing against his mouth. Confused, still sleep-drunk, he thought it was a dream and struggled to open his eyes, pawing at his face with one hand.

'Sit up.'

The words came as a command, colder than the bitter air in the room. Without even thinking, he sat up. Thin, early light came through a window covered by years of grime.

The man towered over him, seeming to fill the space, his presence full of menace. He was tall, with unkempt grey hair, his face lined, but his back was straight and his chest wide under dirty clothes. One large fist held a silver-topped walking stick.

He knew who this was; it was impossible to have lived on the edge of the law in Leeds and not know. Amos Worthy.

'I hear you were with one of my girls last night.' The man's eyes were dark, his voice slow, as deep and resonant as any preacher. 'You didn't pay her. I can't allow that.' He paused, letting the words hang ominously in the air. 'But then you had to cut her, didn't you? So now I have to make an example of you.'

Nick started to reach for the knife in his pocket. The man simply shook his head once and gestured over his shoulder. A pair of thickset youths, their faces hard and scarred, arms folded, stood inside the door. The two other beds were empty.

'I know who you are,' the man said, speaking softly and conversationally. 'Oh aye, you've got the Indies burned on your face, Nick Andrews. Seven years is a long time away from home.'

All he could do was nod. Whatever words he'd once possessed had deserted him. Worthy was offhand, easy in his certainty, and Nick felt the piss burn hot down his leg as his bladder emptied. He was going to die here, in this room, in this bed, before he could finish his work. And all for a few short seconds with a whore.

'All that time doesn't seem to have made you any wiser, laddie. Just back, are you?'

Nick nodded again.

'A short homecoming then.' He raised his thick eyebrows. 'You crossed me. You can't do that here.'

He brought his stick down hard. Nick saw it fall, quick, effortless, but it burst his nose, the shock of pain hard and sudden, blood gushing chokingly into his mouth.

'You can kill him now, boys. You know what to do with the body.'

IAN SHINE

Sparrows in a Coal Mine

'You know how sometimes you can sit with someone and it feels … I don't know, just like, comfortable?'

'Yeah.'

'And you feel like … thanks for the drink by the way … you feel like you could talk about anything at all, and say anything, or maybe even say nothing, like, just sit there in silence, and the atmosphere would never become … tense.'

'Yeah.'

'But with other people, you just feel uncomfortable straightaway, and when you talk to them it's uncomfortable, and when you have nothing to say it's even more uncomfortable?'

'Yeah.'

'Well, if you ask me ... I mean, I know people say we're all humans, and we're all the same, and there is some sort of connection between us all ...'

'Go on.'

'But I mean, to me, that sort of thing, with feeling, like, automatically uncomfortable with some people, just shows that we're … well … some of us are a totally different species from each other.'

'What do you mean?'

'Like … we're all humans, but isn't that a bit like saying everything with wings is a bird? I mean, it's a bird, but it's not just a bird, is it? Because it can be a sparrow, or a kestrel, or a penguin, or … an eagle, or a vulture, or something else.'

'That's true.'

'And if you put a sparrow and a vulture together, in the same nest, I mean, there'd obviously be trouble, right?'

'Right.'

'And even if you put a sparrow and like … I don't know, some other small bird like a blue tit together, they still might not really get on, right?'

'Right.'

'But if you put two sparrows together, then it's like, bingo, everyone's happy. And two sparrows could just sit together in their nest forever, and they'd never stop feeling comfortable, whether they were chirping or not.'

'Hmm.'

'And it wouldn't even have to be in their nest. I mean, you see them sitting together all over the place: on chimneys, telephone wires, lamp posts, fences. They're happy anywhere, as long as they're together.'

'I think I heard once that there was a sparrow that lived in a coal mine.'

'In a coal mine?'

'Yeah.'

'Where did you hear that?'

'Dunno. Can't remember.'

'You can't remember?'

'No.'

'I mean ... hold on ... what are you talking about? Why would a sparrow live down a coal mine?'

'I dunno. Maybe it liked it there.'

'Yeah, but ... how did it get down there in the first place to find out that it would like living in a coal mine?'

'I dunno. It just flew down there one day and thought it was all right.'

'And how did someone find out that this sparrow lived down there and hadn't just gone down there one day by mistake?'

'I don't know. Presumably there was a nest or something.'

'In a coal mine?'

'Yeah.'

'That's bollocks.'

'It's not.'

'It is.'

'Well, fine, you don't have to believe me.'

'I'm not going to believe you.'

'OK by me.'

'It's just ... I mean, I don't see what it would be doing there. I mean, it can't be natural for it, right? Like ... birds like open air, don't they? And what the hell would it eat if it lived in a coal mine? Coal?'

'I don't know. Maybe the miners left it bits of food. Like crumbs from their sandwiches and stuff.'

'This is bloody ridiculous.'

'Why?'

'I think you're thinking of a canary.'

'I am not thinking of a canary.'

'Are you sure?'

'Yeah. If it was a canary, why would I bother telling you, and why would I have even heard about it? Everyone knows that canaries live down coal mines, so there's no need to talk about it.'

'But they don't live down there, do they? The miners just take them down for a bit.'

'Same thing.'

'No, but it's not really, is it? Because the canary gets to come out, and have light and air and bird seed and water, and it gets to live in a cage, and that's why it doesn't die. Whereas this sparrow you're on about, it was presumably stuck in this coal mine all the time, and it lived off absolutely nothing, apart from maybe some sandwich crumbs, and I don't know how the thing didn't die.'

'Maybe it didn't give a shit.'

'What do you mean, *Maybe it didn't give a shit?*'

'Well, if we go with your theory, maybe it was down there with another sparrow, and they just sat there not chirping so no-one would find them, and they felt comfortable and were dead happy because they were together, and they were also dead happy because if a sparrow lives in a coal mine, it means it doesn't have to worry about all these other birds, like vultures and blue tits or whatever, who want to steal its nest and eat its babies.'

'…'

'Like, what I'm saying is, maybe these sparrows were just chuffed to be sitting in this coal mine, getting no hassle from anyone. And even if the other birds thought it was a stupid place to live, these sparrows didn't give a fuck, because they lived there, and they thought it was great.'

'What?'

'…'

'What are you on about?'

'I don't know.'

'Like, you think a sparrow makes a conscious choice about where it's going to live? Like it goes to the sparrow estate agent and says, I'm looking for somewhere dark where I'm not going to get any shit off the neighbours?'

'Ah, shut the fuck up.'

'You total dunce. A sparrow in a coal mine. It was a fucking canary.'

'I was just having a chat, trying to have a conversation.'

'You call that a conversation?'

'Fuck off.'

'Idiot.'

'…'

'Sparrowman.'

'…'

'I'm going to call you Sparrowman from now on.'

'…'

'You done with that drink, Sparrowman?'

'Yeah.'

'Want to move on to another place?'

'Don't mind.'

'Or we can go to mine for a couple of beers if you want. I've got some in the fridge.'

'Don't mind.'

THOMAS McCOLL
The Keys to the House

Even in stock photography world, where life is always exaggerated and skewed, it was clear that my wife-to-be was definitely out of my league.

We'd been briefly introduced at the start - then we'd each had about fifteen minutes to think about it while we both went separately to make-up - and now we were about to be joined together.

'Right, you two are married,' pronounced the photographer - and, just like that, we were: a two second ceremony on the pavement of a dull suburban London street, in front of a house with a sign saying 'Sold'. I expected at least a kiss from my new bride, but Debbie didn't even deign to look my way.

'OK, Donna, if you'd just like to stand there ...'

Oh yes, Donna - I knew I'd forget her name. But then our courtship - all too brief - had simply consisted of my now wife giving me the once over and a frown in response to my smile. We didn't actually even speak to each other - other than to just say 'Hi' (and I then overheard her complain to a friend on her phone: 'He's a right dork - I'm meant to be married to him') - yet, ironically, this was a marriage that was guaranteed to last forever, for both of us had signed the release forms, which meant we'd now be held together indefinitely on the agency's files. There was no chance of divorce - or even annulment - from that. In stock photography world, a signature meant forever.

But still, even if I wasn't the coolest guy on the planet, the agency had asked for an 'everyman' kind of guy, and I was the one they chose - a dork. My new wife was just going to have to open up her eyes to the beauty within. And even if she wasn't impressed with me, I was rather impressed with her. She definitely wasn't Donna the Dork - she was actually very attractive - though repeating 'Donna the Dork' to myself a few times was at least ensuring I wouldn't forget her name again.

So here I was, married to someone way above my station - or at least I was in stock photography world, which was just like the real world, yet nothing like it at all. Here, outside on a street in Streatham, Donna and I were about to be transported, via a camera click, to a parallel universe that existed only in adverts.

It was the only reason Donna was allowing herself to be seen with a dork like me - but it wasn't like I wanted to be in her company particularly either. Quite apart from the fact that she clearly didn't like me much, she wasn't my type as it happened: I was more into brunettes than blondes, and she was far too perfectly proportioned, like she went to the gym every day for hours at a time, whereas I preferred a girl who didn't mind going on a date to McDonalds once in a while …

… or was I just bitter?

Well, anyway, Donna and I had just been given the keys to a new home. I was the one who'd actually been given the keys, to dangle in my hand with my best delighted face directly in front of a three-bedroom detached house - newly-built at the end of a street of mainly old Edwardian houses. We were stood at the foot of the garden path, where there were two steps, and the photographer asked my wife to stand on the first one to bring her up to my height.

'OK, Tom, place your arm around Donna's waist and raise your other arm in the air with the key in your hand.'

I did as I was told. In stock photography world, the agency photographer is God - a person able to create, manipulate and bend all life to his will - and when Donna was asked to place one hand on my shoulder and raise the other hand in the air as a fist, she obeyed without question too.

Of course, it was only natural - now we were linked together, arm-in-arm - that my brand new wife and I would begin, at last, to talk a little.

'Don't hold me so tight,' hissed Donna under her breath.

'Sorry, I didn't realise,' I whispered, mortified, but though I immediately loosened my grip, Donna, with an exasperated sigh, made it clear, beyond doubt, that the honeymoon already was over.

Well, at least our new home was nice - not that we were going to get to see inside it, as all that was required were shots outside in front of the 'Sold' sign. The sun was out but its rays weren't shining on us enough, so one of the two assistants came up and stood just left of us with a light-reflecting disc, while the other kept watch behind the photographer to ensure that no-one passing by inadvertently walked into shot.

'OK, you two, give us your best big smiles. Show me how delighted you are to have finally got the keys to your brand new home.'

So I gave the photographer my best cheesy smile (and, no doubt, so did Donna with her beautiful pearly white teeth), but I was starting to realise now that it wasn't just my brand new wife who was making me feel uncomfortable, nor even the stares I was getting from passers-by - first an old lady, then straight after that a middle-aged office worker and, following him, a couple of smirking teens - it was the shoot itself, and how it was bringing into sharp relief how desperately hopeless my life was here in London.

Here I was, turning up to some photo shoot I was getting paid peanuts for, just to make out I was delighted to buy a place I'd never in real life have the slightest chance of paying the deposit for, let alone obtaining any kind of mortgage to pay off the rest of the exorbitant asking price …

… and nor could anyone else in London now,

unless they were earning huge amounts of money.

Thinking about the bedsit I lived in, and how much I paid for a tiny room with damp on the walls, and knowing that this shoot was the nearest I'd ever get to owning any kind of home - let alone a huge three bedroom house - I felt depressed and even a little ridiculous. With my big cheesy smile about to be plastered all over adverts, it was like I was going to be laughing in people's faces.

And now my discomfort was compounded by a passer-by who wasn't passing but deliberately making a bee-line for our spot - a homeless man with matted hair, soiled clothes and tatty shoes, and a can of Kestrel in one hand, his other hand outstretched.

He'd stumbled on to our street from the main road and, seeing that a professional photo-shoot was underway, had presumably decided we had money to give away.

'You got some change?' he said in a croaky voice, as he dodged the assistant guarding our spot and stood in front of the photographer, who lowered the lens of his camera and frowned.

'We're on a shoot,' God snapped. 'So you need to get out of the way.'

But the homeless man, who knew there'd never be any place for him in stock photography world, didn't feel at all compelled to obey the Almighty's command, and simply ignoring him - and ignoring Donna too who, no doubt, was grimacing at him - came up to me with his outstretched hand.

'You got some change?'

And I don't know why, but I gave him the keys.

For a moment, the homeless man was confused to see these shiny new keys in the palm of his calloused, grubby hand. But, hearing the photographer asking for them back, he closed his hand and held them tight.

It was now the photographer's turn to beg with an outstretched hand. 'Give the keys back, please,' he said, doing his best to remain calm, but looking as if he was going to explode at any moment.

The homeless man, though, refused to budge, and nodded in my direction. 'He gave them to me.'

The photographer shot me an evil look then put his face right up to the homeless man's. 'They're not his to give you, mate.'

The homeless man stood his ground and refused to loosen his grip on the keys. He smiled, revealing his missing teeth, and looked over at the house we were standing in front of.

The photographer rolled his eyes. 'They're not the keys to that house,' he said, with a sigh. 'This is all just make-believe. They're just keys. They're worthless.'

But clearly they weren't, and the photographer, knowing this, said, 'OK, I'll give you some change.'

He rustled up some coins from his pocket, but the homeless man just shook his head. With his fist still clenched, it was clear he was holding out for notes.

The photographer offered him a fiver. 'Look that's four cans of Kestrel at least.'

'Ten.'

The photographer looked confused for a moment then, realising the homeless man wasn't on about the number of cans but the amount of money he wanted, shook his head. 'I haven't got time for games.'

But the homeless man had the upper hand. 'Ten,' he insisted.

The photographer shook his head again – but, this time, as someone who knew he'd been defeated - and, digging deep inside his pocket, brought out a tenner. Face-to-face, each man in the stand-off held out his hand, and the money and the key were swapped simultaneously.

Satisfied - and lit up momentarily by the light reflecting disc which the assistant was adjusting - the homeless man walked off, leaving stock photography world to return, once again, to the real world.

Meanwhile, the photographer glared at me. 'I'm taking that off your fee - and I'll make sure you never get to work with this agency again.'

Donna looked like she could hit me.

And maybe I should have apologised, maybe I should have tried to explain myself, but all I could think to do at that moment was give them both my best cheesy smile.

JULES ANNE IRONSIDE
Mayflies

It was a Dawning day. Finally, the choice, light or dark? Dania couldn't wait to see the hot, pink sky for the first, maybe the last time. It had been two years since she was a naiad. Two years of waiting as an imago. Finally, she would stand under the creamy sun and choose a mate and a home. If her compound eyes were strong enough. If the light didn't dissolve her chemical bonds too quickly. Except … what if she couldn't do it? What if she couldn't walk into the light? She would be in the dark forever …

Shaking her spiky, dark hair out of her face, Dania shoved those thoughts aside. She wouldn't end up a gremma, living on and on and tending the new born hatchlings until they became naiads and then imagos like her.

She made her way down the lightless corridor without error. She had grown up here, for nearly twenty years, and underground Phregia was home. When she was seven, she was told that it took thirteen years for the planet to complete its revolution of Phregia's sun. As it was too cold to survive up there, she would have to wait that long before she could surface. Sometimes Dania had been tempted to peek, but the entrances were well guarded and, now she was of mate-able age, she was expected to take on more duties in the colony. Just in case.

It won't happen, Dania told herself grimly. I want adventure. And light. Even if that means a shorter life. But part of her was terrified that she would loiter on the edge of the gateway to the surface, minute by minute, growing more frightened of moving into the sun until, finally, a kindly guard would explain to her that she was better suited to a long life underground. That the darkness was her home. And take her back.

'Nervous, Dania?' Herkal had a teasing note in his voice.

He and Eska were gremmas, assigned to care for her and three other naiads until they became imagos. Dania supposed they were content enough as gremmas. They had always been kind. Secretly, she couldn't help feeling a little scornful of anyone who hadn't wanted to risk that glorious light. Her own parents had. So had Herkal and Eska's. None of them would be here without those who walked into the light. Dania's people, the Nerrids, were only fertile in sunlight, after all.

Dania realized that she had gone too long without answering Herkal. She tried anyway. 'Of course I'm not nervous. It's what I've always wanted!' She tried to sound assured. Her voice sounded woefully young and unsure to her own ears. Her heat sense showed her that Eska was walking over with the morning porridge.

'Pay Herkal no mind, Dania. We will be proud of you, no matter what you choose at the opening.' She kissed Dania lightly between her antennae.

Dania gave a faint smile. It was all very well for Eska to say that but she'd chosen to play it safe, hadn't she? Or had Eska just known where *her* home really was and not been plagued with restlessness like Dania?

'Eska, how old are you?' Dania had never thought to ask this question before. Both she and Herkal seemed ageless. Fit and strong. As though they could go on forever.

Herkal snorted with laughter and Dania blushed. She had just been unbelievably rude. 'I'm sorry! Forget I asked ...'

'I am one hundred and twenty years old.' Eska drew herself up very straight then collapsed into helpless laughter. 'Forty years younger than Herkal, actually.'

Herkal stopped laughing and made a *hmmmph* noise.

So old! Dania reflected on her own scant twenty years. If I stayed, I could live on and be safe here at home with Herkal and Eska and ... and be bored and trapped for the rest of my life. No. She had to get outside. This was her only chance. Twenty was the age of opening and dawning. There would be no second chance. Much as she loved them, her gremma guardians and their coombe weren't home. Not really.

Dania dropped her spoon into her empty bowl with a clatter. 'I'm ready,' she announced.

She could feel Eska moving to take Herkal's hand for comfort through her heat sense. They must have grown very close in the last hundred years, despite not being mated. No-one was mated underground.

'OK, Dania, we'll see you when you get back.' Eska said the traditional farewell softly.

They would see her too. She just might not see them. The two gremmas kept any grief they might feel to themselves. This was a joyous occasion, after all.

Dania hugged each of them in turn and kissed them both on the cheek. 'Thank you,' she whispered. 'I would like my hatchlings to go to you!'

Eska nodded. They both knew that even if she walked into the light, Dania might not last long enough to have hatchlings.

'Off you go then, girl.'

Dania suspected that the gruff note in Herkal's voice covered tears. She waved in the dark to them as she turned away. Their heat sense and the disturbed air flow would show them her gesture.

Heart climbing into her throat, Dania joined the long line of prospective candidates. They were all too nervous for much talk. The guards lined them in pairs to allow a more effective exodus into the opening. Dania found herself next to a boy she didn't know.

'What do you think pink looks like?' he whispered.

'Huh?' Dania was distracted.

'The sky. They say it's pink. What do you think it looks like?'

'Oh.' Dania had never talked to a boy who wasn't a member of her nest before. 'I always pictured it as a huge warm blanket, sort of tented over the ground. Pink. It sounds as though it should be warm, doesn't it?'

'You're good at describing.' The boy sounded admiring. Dania blushed again and hoped his heat sense wouldn't register it. 'I'm Effric. What's your name?'

'Oh. Uh. Dania.'

'Dania. Pretty,' Effric murmured. 'So what else, Dania? What else do you see?'

'Well, puffy clouds crossing the creamy sun and picking up the warm colours. And the spiky-leaved bushes will have burst into flower. I've heard they're white, so very pale. And they are supposed to smell amazing. And, of course, the wild Antles, who migrate after the path of the sun, will be there. Grazing and flicking their tails in the warm air ...' Dania blushed again. 'Sorry. My gremmas always say I talk too much.'

'No. Not at all. Now I feel like I've already been there.' Effric sighed. 'It makes me less afraid to go.'

'You're afraid?' Dania tried to pick up teasing or falsehood through her heat sense but couldn't find any sign of it. Could he really understand?

'Terrified? Aren't you?' Effric was matter of fact.

'A little.' Dania smiled. He did understand. He was leaving a home he'd outgrown too.

'Dania. Brave and pretty and good with words.'

'You don't know what I look like yet!' Had she ever blushed so much in one day?

'You're pretty. I can tell.' Effric paused. A very faint line of dim light was ahead. 'Looks like we're next.'

'Already?!' Dania felt something close to panic.

'Shall we go together?'

The faint grey light was bathing them now. Dania's almost unused eyes could make out Effric's faint silhouette. It was more frightening than Dania had ever imagined. Minute by minute, she held back, too afraid to step any further.

'You go on. I'll be along ... in a little while ...'

She wasn't going to be able to do it. She just wasn't. Any second now, a kindly guard would lead her away and she would have missed her chance. She would be in the dark forever. And what if she was missing her chance at belonging? Of being home?

'Dania?' Effric was holding out his hand. 'Dania, I think I might be able to keep going if ... well ... if you could hold onto my hand. Just til we get outside?'

'OK,' Dania agreed weakly and clasped his hand with hers. She barely noticed the gentle fizz of her nerve endings as their skin made contact.

Step by slow step, they moved forward. Hand in hand. Comforted and comforting. The darkness receded before a rising tide of lesser darkness then what Dania could only assume was light. She had no words now, no matter what Effric had said. It was pale, this light, it looked the way it sounded when two metal spoons chinked together. A ... a silvery sound. A silvery light. It grew warmer, creamy pale like the taste of butter, then a true gold with a rosy tint, like her heat sense showed her when someone was being affectionate. She was seeing all of this, all of it with her eyes. Her real eyes! As they stepped out on to the rich blue grass, cool as its colour around their bare feet, they were both gasping and sobbing in wonder at all they saw before them.

Light seemed to fill Dania, making her feel weightless and full of possibility. She wasn't one of those whose ability to stand light was measured in minutes. She felt strong. Alive. Beautiful because the light touched her. And she wasn't dying at the door to paradise. She was going to live in the light. She felt drunk on it all. Intoxicated on the flooding of a newly used sense with so much ... so much ...

A stab of anxiety tore through her, shredding the dreamy feeling of lightness.

Effric! Dania felt his hand still in hers. Almost fearfully, she turned to look at him. Was he OK too?

Effric gazed back at her. Grinning, wide and wondering. His inky hair was the only scrap of dark in the world. Despite all the beauty of the light, Dania realized that darkness was beautiful too. She smiled at him. Effric tightened his grip on her hand and Dania knew she had already found her mate.

And for five days, ten if they were very lucky, the world was a new born paradise and made for them. Home.

REBECCA SWIRSKY

The House with Eight Windows

Night curls like smoke around the House with Eight Windows.

At 6pm sharp, Celia and John sit at their scrubbed wooden table to eat boiled eggs and buttered toast. Each loves the other with the vagueness of years of cohabitation, of temporary sharing of toothbrushes when the other needs replacing, of reciprocal nursing through winter flu and summer colds. They neither mind nor are excited by the years which have amassed like dust-balls behind the guest room furniture. The House with Eight Windows is big enough to hold Celia and John both.

This evening, Celia will watch a play written by her friend and lover. She is alert with anticipation. The play tells the tale of a young man who loses his leg in the Crimean War. Celia has little knowledge of the Crimean War, nor of what it would mean to lose a limb. But it is her friend and lover who has written the play, and so she will travel across town to see it, making sure to place her ticket and bus pass safely in her purse. Having hollowed out the last of her egg-white, she leaves the egg-cup and plate on the table for John to clear. Once her coat has been fetched from the stand in the hallway, she is ready. Celia has no need of lipstick, nor adornment of any kind.

John rubs his forehead with one calloused thumb. He hasn't been invited, and thinks with pleasure on a BBC documentary of the building of Egyptian pyramids scheduled for that evening. Still, smooth lips are placed on Celia's forehead in much the same way a child deposits two-pence in a piggy-bank. With care, but soon forgotten. A silence filled with plays and pyramids and boiled eggs passes between Celia and John. They offer silences often, like the many cups of tea they make for each other.

When Celia closes the front door, the two bottom windows shudder and sigh in her wake. John returns to the table to butter the last slice of toast on both sides. He feels only steady satisfaction. The evening ahead will be a slow unfurling of waves pushing him from shore to shore. All around the house, the wind can be heard looking for old, forgotten cracks where it might steal its way in and warm itself by the radiators. As always, it will be unsuccessful.

Pushing his chair from the table, John leaves the kitchen. Through the living-room's modest bay window, the television can be seen as a blue-tinged fire with images flickering at its centre. When John sits down, the old couch whistles, telling a breathy story of many evenings spent this way. The House with Eight Windows is very probably a house meant for children, filling its rooms and corridors with shrieks of laughter and spilled sugary drinks. But Celia and John have no children, and the House with

Eight Windows is a concrete and mortar boat built of brick, moored securely in its jetty, sailing nowhere.

Having watched the documentary on the building of pyramids, John draws heavy green curtains and checks the radiators are turned up for the cleaner, sharper hours dawn will surely bring. Celia likes being warm at night. He clears the kitchen table, stripping its pockmarked surface of spoons stained with egg yolk and plates smeared with globs of butter. Having brushed his teeth and washed his face, John now settles himself in the big double bed to wait for Celia. It has been a fine evening. Nothing more, nothing else, could have been asked of it, other than Celia be returned to him safely. He closes his eyes and waits.

Celia, on the other side of town, is kissing the tiny, sweet brown moles which dot her lover's chin like a constellation. It was a thoughtful play that her lover has written, and although it will make her lover neither rich nor famous, the playwright and Celia don't mind. They lie in each other's arms having received an orgasm each, bodies trembling after such gifts. Celia has also learnt much she did not know about the Crimean War, and as she strokes her lover's forehead and smoothes her lover's rumpled shirt-front, she tells her so. When she finally rises, adjusting tights over thighs, she invites her lover for afternoon tea and banana cake the following week. Celia's lover nods as she reapplies brick-red lipstick and brushes out long, fine hair before her mirror. Celia looks on admiringly. Gradually, Celia's lover is becoming John's friend too. Guilt has not been allowed to enter the House with Eight Windows. Like the wind, it fends for itself under the watchful moon, tapping for ways to enter through hidden cracks and gaps.

Perhaps John will recognise Celia's friend for what she is. Perhaps he will not. Whatever his thoughts, nestled inside the softly shining dome of his head, he will be a genial host, discussing the challenges of researching, writing and directing a play. If the tea goes well, as it almost certainly will, John will invite Celia's friend and lover to watch a well-reviewed documentary with him. If Celia's lover refuses, he will not be affronted, for the pleasure in watching will remain the same.

Now, leaving her lover's flat on the other side of town, Celia feels a certain safety that soon she, too, will be tucked in bed, hot water bottle coddled between her feet, she and John in matching flannel pyjamas. It would be foolish to imagine a world beyond the House with Eight Windows. Celia is too old to find another to spread itself around her with arms of crumbling brick and mortar, creaking wooden joists and mismatching crockery. She will turn 75 this July, and is looking forward to the frosted icing chocolate cake John traditionally bakes for her birthday.

By the orange-sodium flare of the street lamps, Celia notices the honeysuckle and jasmine need cutting, and the front door could do with another coat of paint. In the morning she will discuss these tasks with John, whom will do what, and when. But now, under the hallway mirror, Celia hangs her keys on the little yellow hook. Steadying herself against the flocked-papered wall, she eases shoes from stockinged feet. Her shoes, made of good leather, have a dainty heel like a secret. Slowly, luxuriously, Celia climbs the stairs. John, having heard the front door close from his bed, falls into a light sleep which deepens as he registers Celia sliding under the covers. He is safe to wander in his dreams because Celia has returned. Soon, Celia too is adrift. Dentures removed, she snores gently into the darkness, mouth slack with release.

Throughout the night, the wind pushes against The House with Eight Windows, inspecting for cracks, howling its frustration at the moon. Yet the House with Eight Windows holds tight, allowing its occupants to sleep soundly, with no dreams to interrupt them.

PETE DOMICAN
A Room with a View

Last month, I came home from school but it was no longer home. We'd lived there for as long as I could remember, which isn't that long for an adult I suppose, but a long time when you're nine. I just assumed it was our house and that we'd live there forever, but it wasn't and the people who owned it wanted it back very quickly.

Mum made it all sound as if we were going on a fantastic holiday but I could see her wiping away the tears and trying to smile. That just didn't seem right. Holidays are meant to be happy things, aren't they? And aren't you only supposed to go away somewhere during the school holidays? Not that we've had a going-away holiday since Dad left.

We packed my suitcase with as many clothes as we could and then had dinner. Mum was quiet and I knew not to ask more questions. She didn't seem to know the answers to the ones I'd asked.

'Go to bed. We've a long day ahead tomorrow.'

'But it's not my bedtime,' I replied.

I wish I hadn't said anything. Mum looked as if she were about to burst out crying again. I decided not to be any more trouble.

I tried to sleep but the sound of voices and things being moved around downstairs kept me awake until very late. I peered out of my bedroom window and saw my mum hugging her friends in the street below. They climbed into a white van and drove away, leaving my mum standing alone under the streetlamp. I watched her from behind the curtain for a while until I began to shiver, then I climbed back into bed and pulled the blankets over me. When I woke in the morning, the house was empty except for a few pieces of furniture and our suitcases in the hall.

From our window, you can see the pier and sea. There's a film called 'A Room with a View' and that's what we have. Except it isn't ours. It belongs to the hotel we stay in now.

Most people think living in a hotel by the seaside would be fabulous, like being a film star, but there's nothing good about living here. We have a bedroom with a TV, a kettle, a cupboard to put our clothes in and a desk (although I don't go to school here) and that's all we have. We share a bathroom with three other families and there's just one kitchen. There's one little cooker and there are twenty-five families, so it's impossible to get a chance to cook anything and, if you leave something in the fridge, it will be gone the next time you look. So we live on sandwiches and other things from the corner shop that won't go off in the room.

It's really noisy in the hotel. The TVs are on too

loud or someone's arguing with someone else. Sometimes you can hear people hitting each other. My mum will cover my ears and hold me tightly as it's quite frightening, but I can still hear them. I asked one day if Dad hit her but she said nothing and turned away to look at the sea. I never asked again.

When the sun shines, we walk along the seafront to get out of the hotel. It's nice to walk on the beach and play in the sand rather than watch TV all day. On those days, it feels like we're really on holiday, except when the rude people try to spoil it.

In London, everyone is different yet here almost everyone is white. We stand out a mile. Most of the people here don't seem to mind but some stare as if we shouldn't be here. One or two shout at us to go back home. I wish we could. Mum misses the job that she lost just before we had to move and I want to be back at school with my friends. I tried to tell one of them that one day but my mum just dragged me away and told me not to speak to them again. She says they won't understand but they must know that we don't want to be here either.

We're waiting now. Mum says we'll get something soon but she doesn't think it'll be in London. It's too expensive, she says. In the meantime, at least we have each other and our room with a view.

SALLIE WOOD

With Hindsight

Dear Rose,

I hope this letter finds you well. My apologies for not putting pen to paper sooner, but life has been a bit hectic of late.

It is close to midnight and I am surrounded by a sea of boxes, on what will be my last night here at 16 Garden Close. In just a few short hours, I will be walking down that little winding path for the last time. 'On to pastures new' – as they say.

'You're moving?' I can almost hear you gasp, when you read this unexpected news - particularly as my previous letters have expressed my contentment at living here.

Well, it's a long and rather complicated story, so I'd better start at the beginning.

As planned, I spent my birthday with Diana, Tom and the grandchildren (thank you for the lovely card). We had a lovely weekend together in London; the hotel in Mayfair was as you would expect – pure luxury. Although the highlight of the trip was a surprise ride on the London Eye. It was a wonderful experience and something that I will always remember.

I returned home the following weekend to an unexpected visit from Richard. I opened the front door to find him ashen-faced and flustered on the doorstep. Something was clearly wrong - as he would usually knock three times before letting himself in.

'Come on in,' I said, ushering him into the kitchen. He sat down at the table but barely said a word. I put the kettle on, hoping that he would open up and start to talk. But he said nothing, other than to ask about my stay at Diana's. 'Whatever is the matter?' I finally asked, as I sat down opposite him. 'Is it Sarah?' I knew that he and Sarah were having problems, but hoped that they could work things out for the sake of the children.

He nodded, his troubled eyes avoiding my gaze. I looked at his unkempt hair and bristly face with unease. It had been a while since he had used that Gillette Razor I bought him for Christmas. He fiddled with his hands as tears began to trickle down his cheeks. I hadn't seen Richard cry since we lost his father, six years ago. Yet this wasn't a look reminiscent of grief but utter panic. It was the same look that he had as an eighteen-year-old lad, when he admitted that he had written-off our Vauxhall Cavalier while we were on holiday in Greece. And then again, a year later, when he made the shock announcement that Sarah was pregnant. They were still kids in my eyes and had only been together for a few months. So, mother's instinct told me that a confession of sorts was coming. I braced myself and waited – knowing that in time he would break his silence.

While I was away at Diana's, Richard had been made redundant. But that wasn't all. He had discovered that Sarah had got herself into debt and owed thousands on a handful of credit cards. They were in a mess. He explained that re-mortgaging their house wasn't an option as Richard would soon be without an income. Similarly, a loan from the bank was a non-starter. I gulped at the news of my eldest child's plight, wishing that I was in a position to help. But he hadn't finished, there was one final bombshell that was about to be dropped.

Richard and Sarah had agreed on what they believed to be the only solution to their financial woes, and that was to sell the house. Not the house that they lived in, as it was stuck in negative equity. It was the house that I had lovingly called home for all these years. I nearly choked on my digestive.

'I'm really sorry to do this to you, Mum,' Richard sobbed. 'If there was any other way...' He could barely look at me. I just sat there staring at my tea, wishing that I could disappear into the sweet swirling liquid. I wanted to scream and shout at him, at Sarah, at anybody - but the words just wouldn't form in my mouth. It was probably just as well - as all the obscenities under the sun wouldn't change the fact that it wasn't my house to hold on to. Not in the truest sense of the word anyway. The house belonged to Richard and Sarah and, by all accounts, they could do whatever they wanted with it.

After Richard had gone, I rang Diana. She was furious and ranted on about how she had never liked Sarah and how Richard should be ashamed of himself for putting his mother out onto the streets. 'Go and see the council or Citizens Advice in the morning,' she said to me. 'You must have rights.'

So the next morning I got up early and caught the 49 bus into town. I arrived at the council offices as they were opening.

'I've lived in that house for over ten years,' I said to the woman at the desk.

She smiled at me sympathetically. 'Has the landlord served you notice in writing?'

'No,' I replied, dabbing my wet eyes with a tissue. I told her that I didn't have a tenancy agreement as the house belonged to my son and his wife.

'I see,' she replied. 'Do you pay them any rent?'

'No. I have always lived there rent-free. Does it make any difference?' I asked.

'I'm afraid it does.'

She explained that as I don't have a tenancy agreement and have never paid rent, I don't have any rights to stay – none whatsoever.

I should have listened to you, Rose. You warned me not to rush into things without getting some legal advice. 'Safeguard your future, just in case,' you said. But I didn't listen. It never crossed my mind that I could be made homeless by my own family.

It's ironic, isn't it? Ted and I were happy in our council house, but Richard wanted to buy a second property as an investment. He suggested that his dad and I moved in. It seemed like the ideal solution for everyone.

'Where am I supposed to go?' I asked the woman, as the reality of the situation began to sink in.

'That's what I'm here to help you with, Mrs March,' she confirmed.

I reached into my bag for another tissue and my keys fell out onto the desk. Harold's big brown eyes on the key ring photo looked up at me, pleadingly. 'What about Harold? I can't part with him after all these years,' I asked her in a panic.

'Who's Harold?' she asked me, with a look of surprise.

'Harold is my dog.' I turned the tiny photo to face her.

She smiled, looking intently at the photo. 'Ah, a King Charles Spaniel - he's lovely.'

'Yes he is. But he's old and suffers with arthritis like me. I can't get rid of him. I just can't.'

'Don't worry about Harold, Mrs March. I'm sure we can work something out.'

So we spent the best part of an hour filling in a form on the computer. It would have been quicker, but I couldn't remember my phone number. I'd never forgotten it before, so didn't feel the need to have it written down. Fortunately, I had Diana's mobile number written down on a card that I carried in my purse. It was all very embarrassing. I know that I should get to grips with that mobile that Richard brought me last Christmas. And I will - if I can find it again after the move.

Finally, the form-filling was done and the lady advised me that they would be in touch. She was very kind and told me not to worry - but that was easier said than done. She wasn't the one losing her home, was she?

That afternoon, I gathered some flowers from the garden and visited Ted's grave. I picked out the stray weeds while I told him all about it. I found myself scolding him for not being there to sort it all out for me. And then I cried for blaming him. Ted died in this house, so I've always felt close to him here. There's a part of me that feels like I'm deserting him by leaving this place. I hope he understands that I had no choice. I told Ted that his shed would have to be sorted out. It had remained as he left it – a cluttered museum of joinery. I asked Richard to see to it and he did.

The weeks that followed passed quickly, as I started preparing for the inevitable big move. I did as the lady at the council suggested and asked Richard to put the details in writing. She also advised that I should contact my doctor and ask him to write a letter - to confirm that I would benefit from living in a bungalow. I was reluctant at first, as I'm not one to make a fuss. But Diana talked me into making an appointment at the surgery. My heart and joint problems have been getting progressively worse and I've been struggling with the stairs for a long time. I just didn't want to admit it.

The week after Richard's shock announcement, the house was valued. A Mrs Bright came from Cooper and Brown, the new estate agents on the High Street. She measured up, took some photographs and it was put on the market. I dug my heels in and refused to show any prospective buyers around - so Sarah had to do it. It was the least she could do. I generally made myself scarce while they looked around - poking their noses in all my drawers and cupboards.

A couple of months later, I received a phone call advising me that a bungalow would soon be available. It only had one bedroom but there was a little garden. And I could keep Harold. I made an appointment for a viewing the following week. It was better than I expected. It needed a lick of paint and a good clean, but I couldn't afford to be fussy. So I gratefully accepted it.

To be honest, Rose, I felt guilty that something came up so quickly and that I didn't have to wait for years like some poor souls.

But, I was in need, wasn't I?

So everything is packed and I'm ready to go. Richard and Sarah found a buyer for this place (a young family) and they move in next week. I hope they will look after my lovely little garden. I will miss whiling away the hours out there on my vegetable patch. This year's strawberries are proving to be the tastiest yet after the miserable spring that we had. I said a tearful goodbye to my neighbours today as well. They have become really good friends over the years. Apart from Enid of course, who lives at number 12. She stopped speaking years ago. All because my hanging baskets received more compliments than hers. I won't miss her or her lame *Petunia Surfinia*.

Richard has got another job. It's less money than he was on before, but at least it's an income. And Sarah will be able to pay off her debts from the proceeds of this house. I hope she's learnt her lesson. Time will tell whether they make it as a couple. I have my doubts, if I'm honest. But it's got nothing to do with me. Richard seems happy enough, although I can still see the guilt in his eyes for the turmoil that he has put me through. I've told him I'll be okay and not to worry. It was a shock at first but I've accepted it now.

I just hope that, one day, this little bungalow will feel like home too.

Best wishes from your dear friend,

Lillian x

ZELAZKO POLYSK
Nadzieja Dreams of Nowhere

There are Poles stuck in airports all over the UK as words ring out like spells, conjuring up people and places that have never existed.

Young Jaroslaw runs frantically from gate to gate, searching for his plane to Wroclaw, oblivious to the final call skirting over his head for the flight to Rocklaw, a city where God knows what happens and who lives, but where a man dozing near duty-free imagines Neolithic people perhaps still rule. And when the tannoy asks Jar-oh-slore to report to his gate for boarding, the flight crew picture an uncouth old pig whose dumpling of a stomach pushes the cotton threads clinging to his shirt buttons to breaking point, and who they'd rather not have onboard.

Elsewhere, Zdzislaw dashes for his long-gone flight to Lódz, while a shadow called Zedsi-slore with a giant moustache and an envelope full of probably untaxed and ill-gotten sterling, sits on a flight to Lods, a city of nothing but snow, nothing but Catholics, nothing but vodka and potatoes, nothing but plumbers or nothing but beautiful women, depending on your predisposition.

And then there is Nadzieja, who waits to fly to the grey industrial shell she left two years ago, and which her parents and memories still echo around, but which has since become a building site of shining metal and glass at the heart of something called New Europe. When she speaks to her parents on the phone, they say she's lost her Polish accent, but customer services pick out Nadzeejar's foreignness straight away, and as she joins a queue moving nowhere across the departure hall, she wonders if she'll ever make it to the place she once called *dom*, but now calls home.

KATHERINE HETZEL

Homeland

Councilman Tartris slammed his fist into his saddle. 'We will not go into this wasteland. Look at it!'

Anna's gaze swept over the barren expanse which lay in front of them. Withered grass stretched as far as the eye could see, as far as the strange, flat-topped mountain in the distance. 'The heart leads me - and we must continue,' she answered, with a calmness she was struggling to maintain.

'No. I have had enough - we've all had enough.' Tartris shook his grizzled head and gripped the reins more tightly; Anna wondered, fleetingly, whether he wished it were her neck. 'We began this futile search twenty years ago and are no nearer a homeland now than we were at the start. The Council have decreed that the exodus stops, my lady,' he growled. 'Right here.'

She had expected it - there had been rumbles of dissent for weeks as they drew nearer to the plains. But to finally hear it was more painful than she'd imagined. Tears prickled Anna's eyes, but she refused to let them fall - not in front of this arrogant fool. 'So you would betray the heart?'

Tartris laughed, a grim sound with no mirth in it. 'Has it not already betrayed us, by leading us on a wild goose chase? The years have been filled with nothing but women's dreams and heartsickness. It is time we listened to reason and common sense instead. We go no further, my lady.'

With a click of his tongue, he turned the horse and galloped away, towards the tented city that had taken root where there was still grazing for the animals, wood for cooking fires, and water.

Anna stared, unseeing, at the acres of scorched grass swaying in the breeze.

'I must continue,' she whispered. 'We are so close - I can feel it calling …'

'I do understand, my lady - but this is madness!'

Anna watched as Councilman Draygon paced the floor of her tent. He reminded her of the caged lions they'd seen beside the pools of Tra-manth.

'The Council cannot forbid a priestess to continue searching,' she told him. 'I will take six of our best hunters and plenty of provisions and water in an ox-cart.'

'And what if it's not enough? What will you do if you run out of water, or fall ill, or the wheel drops off the cart?' Draygon ran his fingers through his hair and sighed deeply. 'Perhaps they were right about the heartsickness. It seems to affect every lady of the heart in the end.'

Anna rose swiftly from her chair, two spots of livid colour on her cheeks. 'Even you doubt me?' Her entire body quivered with rage.

'I didn't mean - My lady, you know I - Bah!' Draygon took a steadying breath, struggling to control his frustration. When he next spoke, his voice was soft. 'Anna, we were both children when we began this journey. Your head - and plenty of others beside - was filled with the idea of discovering our ancient homeland. Spending aeons in captivity robbed us of our identity - of course we long to rediscover who we are and where we came from. It's perfectly natural - but we do not need to spend even more years on a fruitless search to fulfil that dream. We can make anywhere our home now.' He reached to take the priestess's hand, but she snatched it away.

'It is a dream that our people have clung to for centuries,' she snapped. 'How do you explain the heart in all of this?'

Helpless in the face of her anger, Draygon shrugged.

'I will not give up on the heart. It is part of me, Councilman, part of who I am and what I represent. And we are so close. I can feel it, here.' Anna pressed the first two fingers of her right hand against her heart and glared at him. 'I will find our homeland, with or without your support. Or I will die trying.'

Draygon watched Anna and her hunters as they crawled away across the scorched brown land. She had insisted on going, even though he had begged her

103

to stay. At least he had managed to persuade the Council to allow her a single lunar cycle before the people began to retrace their journey in search of more hospitable surroundings. Determined for some reason to reach the mountain at least, Anna had seemed confident that she would be back well before then. Draygon hoped she was right. Time was running out.

It was a lookout who spotted their return, two days before the Council's deadline.

'They're back! Anna's back!' the man yelled as he ran through the tented city.

Equal measures of fear and hope surged through Draygon's body as he leapt onto his horse and galloped out into the wasteland to meet the caravan.

'We found it!' Anna called, as he drew closer. A great city!'

'What?'

'Inside the mountain!'

'Inside the -'

'Aye - and the heart is everywhere!'

Draygon pulled alongside the ox-cart, where Anna sat beside the driver. 'My lady of the heart, is it true?' he asked, suddenly in awe of his priestess and a little ashamed of having ever doubted her.

'Yes.' Anna's eyes twinkled mischievously. She had never looked more jubilant. 'Do you want to be there when I tell Tartris?'

'My lady? It is time.'

Anna remained by the window and gave no sign

that she had heard Councilman Tartris. She could feel the impatience radiating from the rest of the Council, but decided to make them wait a little longer while she drank in the reality of their new world.

Deep within the dormant crater, a great city was rising from the ruins of one which was millennia older. Just three lunar cycles after the Great Descent, and already there were the green shoots of wheat and corn colouring the fertile inner slopes. The people and animals, which had been dying of hunger, were now full-stomached, and the new-built watermills were drawing fluid of such clarity into the well-pools, they rivalled the turquoise waters of Tra-manth.

Anna sighed as Tartris tried again.

'My lady of the heart, the people are waiting.'

'Our people have waited for centuries already, Councilman. What are a few more minutes, when added to that greater measure of time?' As she turned towards them, every member of the Council bowed, placing the first two fingers of their right hands on their hearts as they did so.

'Rise.' Anna's silver-grey gaze swept over them, resting for a moment longer on Draygon before moving on. 'Our forefathers hoped and prayed for this moment. They waited lifetimes - and yet it is we who are to see the fulfilment of their dreams. Let us not forget what we owe to those who kept the faith before us.' She took the arm that Draygon offered. 'As you say, it is time.'

As they walked along the corridor, trailing the rest

of the Council in their wake, Draygon was intensely aware of Anna's cool hand, resting lightly in the crook of his arm. Today, she was very much his priestess. He glanced sideways at her.

Her hair had been brushed till it shone like copper, the thin silver band which represented her exalted position resting lightly on her brow. Like many, she had chosen to wear red today – the colour traditionally associated with the heart – and the fabric of her gown hung loose from her shoulders, hiding her form within its folds. Over the dress, she wore a sleeveless surcoat of white silk, shot through with threads of silver, so that she appeared to shimmer in the torchlight.

'Do I have a smudge on my nose?' Anna asked quietly. 'Only, you are staring so hard, I fear I must have applied the paint wrongly.'

Draygon felt the heat rise in his cheeks.

'No, my lady - I find the patterns strangely enthralling.'

He always had - the green swirls across her cheeks and around her eyes enhanced rather than marred her beauty.

A smile flickered across Anna's lips. 'As did I, when I tried painting them the first time. Do you remember?'

'How could I forget? You insisted on practising on me!' Draygon chuckled.

They walked on through the crumbling temple in silence, each lost in their own thoughts.

When they finally emerged onto the balcony, high above the people, a roar rose to greet them. Draygon released Anna's hand, content to remain in the background with the Council while the priestess stepped forward to receive the adulation of her believers. The silver robe shone more brightly still in the light of the twin suns, and Anna dazzled all whose gaze fell upon her. She raised her arms, calling for quiet.

'Centuries ago,' she called, her voice carrying over the masses and echoing back from the sides of the crater which surrounded them, 'our people were enslaved and taken far from their ancestral homeland. Yet their heart remained strong, hidden from its captors and continually whispering to the priestesses of home. Over the years, memory faded until we were left with only the heart and our belief that there was somewhere in this world that was ours - that we could truly call our own. Since we left captivity, we have travelled many leagues; we have experienced hardship and seen many of our loved ones pass over, their souls now carried with us in our heart.'

Anna's voice wavered as she recalled all whom she had reassured that they would find a home - soon. But it hadn't been soon enough for some. She breathed deeply before continuing.

'We have experienced the joy of marriage oaths and births, and seen our children grow into adults. I, myself, was no more than a child when we began this journey, and I thank the heart that I have lived to see the rediscovery of our homeland. This is the place where our story began!'

Tears sprang into Anna's eyes and she smiled through them.

'My people,' she called, her voice rising high into the circle of blue sky above them all. 'My people, we are home!'

JACKIE BUXTON
A Life with Additives

Shelley laid out the ingredients in a strict line on the tatty, wooden work surface as she did every day at 5.15am: 1kg of wholemeal, strong, plain flour, delivered personally from one of the few working mills in the country; 30g of fresh yeast; the same of honey; a flask of water, boiled and cooled just before she fell into bed late last night, and 30g of salt.

She set the yeast and honey with the water to dissolve in the brown, porcelain bowl her mother had left to her for the purpose. She sifted the flour and salt then tossed the sieve into the stained Belfast sink which made her back ache. In the early days, she'd have marvelled at how much quicker she was at carrying out this procedure but, today, Shelley simply added the yeast, pushed and prodded and rolled and folded the dough and hurled it intermittently onto the work top.

She glanced up at the clock. It was 5.30am. Of course it was.

She forced the dough into a ball, struck it a couple of times with a knife and threw it onto a baking tray which she shoved onto the flat top of the boiler.

What would she do, she wondered, if she didn't bake bread every morning? Finally learn Salsa? Revisit her flute, which lay yellowing in its battered leather case in the junk room, lamenting the lack of silver polish and a dose of elbow grease? Or she could write a novel. She'd said she'd make a story from her mother's diaries.

'Go ahead,' her mother had said, 'but,' she'd added, her eyes down, knotted fingers playing with the ring which had long since become welded to the joint, the cruel extra flesh of age grown around it, 'wait until I'm gone.'

'Stop it,' Shelley hissed as a tear planted itself in the corner of her eye. She wrestled the *Born to Bake* apron from around her neck and flung it onto the stool behind her. 'You owe it to her!' she reprimanded again as she stomped off to the shower.

The television Shelley wished they didn't have in the bedroom boomed out that the government was launching a campaign to Get Britain Baking Again. She tutted, pulled on her dressing gown - inside out - tugged the towelling turban from her hair and marched back into the kitchen. While the kettle boiled, she retrieved the dough from its place on the boiler and gave it a second bash. She strangled it in the worn muslin, returned it to its warming place and put the oven on to heat.

'We should spend more time together,' Morris said when Shelley placed the two mugs of tea down onto the bedside tables without a word. He pulled her into bed beside him, kissed her on the lips, ruffled her damp hair. 'Like we used to,' he said.

Shelley shrugged her shoulders. If only it were that simple.

From the screen, bacon popped, crackled and spat from a sparkling frying pan, prodded by a grinning husband. A crispy curl of bacon peeked out from between two slices of white bread, tomato sauce oozed out of the sides. The happy wife took a perfect bite from the middle of the sandwich and belched as her beloved winked to camera, the bag of long-life bread held tightly behind his back.

'Just think of the additives in that!' Morris said, shaking his head a little over enthusiastically.

Shelley crouched down to manhandle the bread into the oven. But she didn't stand up, rather turned on her haunches to gaze at the pile of washing up, the splats of sticky dough on the work top, the dusting of flour over the quarry tiles. It was 6.15am. Morris had left for the day and the children wouldn't be awake until the bread was baked.

'Wait until I'm gone,' she'd said.

Shelley bounded up the stairs towards the junk room and forged a path through the voluminous memorabilia of a family's younger days. The idea of opening any of the journals had been too painful before. Today, she'd happily read them all but she only had an hour. Her pulse quickened. This was right. She'd wanted her to read them.

Shelley took the top diary from the stack in the plastic crate and flicked through the first few pages. She settled on a picture of the grandfather she'd never met, dressed proudly in air force uniform, but snapped the book shut before she could read more. She would look at them all and devour every word, examine every brown-edged photo, held in place only by aged Sellotape, now dry and cracked like a fly's wings. But not now. Carefully, she lifted each of the fourteen journals out of the crate and placed them purposely in a pile to her side. Only one remained in the bottom of the box. The newest book. She held it above her head by its spine and let the pages spill open. An old, brown envelope, only big enough to house a wage slip, fell onto her lap.

Shelley gasped and clamped her hand to her mouth but quickly let it drop again. She smiled. It was typical of her mother to hide something so obviously. With an incongruously measured movement, she unsealed the underside of the envelope with her thumb nail. Inside was a hand-written note on a piece of quality parchment paper cut to size.

Shelley examined the paper, then turned it over, but there was nothing more. She read it again, kissed the script, jumped up, picked up her flute case, a pair of discarded dance pumps and a pink taffeta tutu.

'No bread and jam this morning, my beautiful children,' she said, relishing the incredulity on their faces as they watched the Sugarplum Fairy lift a tired-looking flute to her lips.

'Rory, you're on egg duty - scrambled, please.' Shelley failed to raise a sound from the instrument. 'Stacey, we'll have crackers.'

'Wicked!' Stacey said.

'Mum?' Amy scrunched up her button nose. 'The bread's burning.'

Our family has been baking bread for two centuries. More people than my 87 years have been nurtured and grown on our simple recipe. Well, I hate it, she'd written. *I've baked bread every day of my adult years but I only did it because I had to. There*, she'd finished with a more exuberant, loopy script, *finally, I've admitted it*.

'Amy,' Shelley said, 'Let it burn!'

She lifted the flute to her lips once more, savoured the noisy silence of her children and finally managed a string of notes, before saying, 'Dance, anyone?'

REBECCA L PRICE
A Sign of the Times

My face may now be a mess of lines and cracks, more than I ever had in the early years, but I am still told that I am beautiful. My hands ache in the bitter chill of winter, but I find that if I keep them flexed and moving, slowly but surely, then they carry on doing their job well enough. I have never been a great mover and shaker in the world, but from my vantage point, I am able to see secret things that are hidden from others' view and overhear snippets of stolen conversations: protestations of love, hisses in anger and whispers of jealousy and hatred. I have no companion, but I have lived a useful life, helping those who need me and guiding the lost. I hope I have done my job well.

I see every morning dawn, beautiful and bright, throwing splinters of sunlight through glass. The silence resonates as the introduction of the pattering of pigeon's feet just goes to show how empty this place is of human life in the early hours. The silence echoes through rafters and the occasional bird squawks at an unknown foe and heaves itself up and away from its grubby resting place, leaving a ruffled feather floating to the ground.

At first, it is just light footsteps but, as the crucial time of the morning approaches, it begins to build like a slow crescendo. The doors to the main entrance swing back and life bubbles forth through its opening: heels clacking and wheeled suitcases rattling over the stone floor, mobile phones buzzing and everyone's affairs made public as they shout into the receiver. A man in black hurries past – pointy, shiny shoes glistening, carrying a briefcase that surely contains plans for making millions on the stock exchange. An early morning buggy appears, accompanied by the usual screams and placating murmurs. People queue for coffee, slurp coffee, spill coffee and rush through a hurriedly bought croissant for breakfast, wrapped up in a skimpy napkin that gets hastily thrown to the floor. Women in suits stare ahead, never meeting the eyes of their co-walkers, arms swinging, thoughts in the office, all neat coats and tightly held handbags. Clip clip, beep goes the barrier and through they go and onwards into the rest of their day. But not me. I will be here to see their less hurried, more wearied, languorous return through those same gates later on, when it is dusk.

The noise eventually recedes and the footsteps ease and the rhythm of the middle of the day begins.

It was a Tuesday when he came, shuffling through the carved iron doors. His face was bearded, through lack of care rather than design, and his blue eyes were empty of life from exhaustion, fuelled by the need to rest and breathe easy. I thank God that he found me because, on closer inspection, his forehead and hairline were crusted with old blood and he was smeared with days' old dust and grime. He was hurt. His arm hung loosely and his right shoulder sloped dangerously low. He had strips of brown cloth wrapped around his feet, shoved into ill-fitting shoes, as if some previous injury was being treated in the only way he knew how. My heart flew out to him as he lay down near me and sighed like a dying man. He had no money for food so he lay down and breathed in the fumes of other people's hot food, because that is free, after all. He often looked at me, as the day limped on, and I think he knew that I was aware of his desperation. I called him Michael.

At noon, he slept, a bundle of dark clothing, taking the lull in the footfall around him as the peace and quiet he so needed. He was woken an hour later by a voice, a loud voice, extolling passers-by who weren't plugged into their music systems to accept that the end of the world was nigh and that Jesus was the only way to salvation.

'Don't burn,' he exclaimed, 'Embrace the love of Jesus and be saved.'

I was elated by this man. Surely, he would save this poor Michael, whose pain I could feel like a stab through my being. Surely, the preacher's evangelism extended to the shabby creature curled up only metres from his feet? Michael stretched painfully and saw the man in front of him. As the Christian man realised that the distasteful smell that had slowly crept up on him came from the man on the floor, he picked up his megaphone, shuffled his bright green pamphlets and walked away, crossing to the other side of the station and beginning again his tirade, this time to a new audience.

The shadows were beginning to lengthen into the middle of the afternoon when I first saw the small, brown-haired woman, dressed in a red tabard, headed straight for me. She was wearing a red plastic badge and held a white collection bucket that jangled with people's loose change – well, the few coins people spared, just enough for their guilt to be appeased and for them to be seen to be 'giving.' Michael was no longer asleep, just sitting, slumped, with head down and shoulders low. He didn't speak, just sat, lost in his own strangled thoughts of hope and despair. The woman came forward slowly, looking straight at me. She didn't speak to me but shook her bucket at the row of people occupying the plastic seats outside the newsagents next door.

'Any spare change for disabled children?' she asked, shaking, shaking, shaking and smiling her 'good person' smile.

She would have been a fool not to notice the man sat near her feet, but she seemed at once to see him and not see him, as she stepped over his outstretched legs to reach the prosperous-looking gentleman who had begun to open his wallet over at the other side of the seating area. As she crossed over, she sneered and wrinkled her nose, passing by without another sound.

The early evening's commotion came and went, as it did every day, and the same faces worried their way through the barriers, through the gates and onwards into the dark evening's cold. Michael wrapped himself more tightly in his threadbare coat and looked more longingly than ever at the hot drinks and food in the hands of the bystanders, those waiting for trains, waiting for loved ones, waiting for time to pass. As the night time freeze sank into his bones, Michael passed into a state of numbness and closed his eyes against the biting draught.

The only person that could be seen, shivering in her light blue tunic dress, was a young nurse, in her mid-twenties, hair tied in an orderly bun and shoes worn with sensible laces. She was waiting for her husband and young son to arrive from a trip to see grandma near the sea. She wrapped her arms around herself and looked from a barrier in the distance, to me, then back to the barrier and back towards me. She bounced slowly up and down on the balls of her feet to keep the blood moving in her veins.

It took her a full five minutes before she realised that Michael sat as quiet as a whisper only a few steps away. She was wrapped in her thoughts of home and the feeling of small hands holding tightly to hers. It was when she glimpsed the first sight of her beloved ones that she first saw Michael. His sad, blue eyes stared straight into hers and she looked, ashamed, and mumbled 'sorry' into her chest as she lightly ran over to the other side of the station floor, to be greeted with loving shouts, big dark eyes and warm embraces.

The tiny boy with the big, dark eyes walked across the echoing floor and with one outstretched hand, gave Michael his lifeline. A single, prized coin, a gift from a child, a chance for a new start. One phone call to a brother who may still care was all he needed. A new day would begin in a few hours and it would all begin again. But I will never forget the voice I heard, rasping into that phone booth receiver.

'Hello. It's Michael. I'm at Waterloo. Under the clock.'

My face may be worn, and my hands may be old, but my heart breaks just the same as yours.

HELEN HARDY

Fathom

They make the perfect cruise image, windswept in the setting sun – my husband against the rail with our daughter Ellie, tall at his side, shielding her wide-eyed baby from the spray. I press the button to preserve them then linger to watch the waves, while they head inside to get ready for dinner.

The sun drops and suddenly the sea sounds louder, closer. Marbled with fatty, white froth, it heaves like a troubled heart. My great aunt is in there somewhere, still younger than I am. I can't remember her name, but I get goose pimples as I think of her.

On the voyage out, did the new bride watch the sea at night, like me? Did she already guess that her marriage was built on water? She set out home, alone with her fears. No-one saw what happened; no-one heard a splash over the suck and crash of the waves. I wonder how long she struggled in the sea's muscular arms before they rocked her unconscious and she drifted, breathing fluid like the baby inside her.

Turning, I heave at the door against the salt wind to open a crack of shelter and slip inside. I want to stroke the hair of my lovely, abandoned daughter as she nurses her baby.

Most of all, I want to bring them both safe home.

DAN MAITLAND

There was this bloke, right,

started to get messages from God. First one came in through the letter box. It said: Dear Derek, you are doing a lot of things wrong. Sort it out. Lots of love. God.

God had quite nice handwriting and wrote, as you would expect, in rather old-fashioned, capital letters. Derek was a little perturbed about this letter but he also had a lot of other mail that morning and one of the other letters told him that the phone company would stop allowing him to talk to his friends if he didn't pay them the money he owed within seven days. God's letter, as you will remember, was far less demanding than that.

He rushed to the post office and paid the money. He also sat down in a café to have a coffee as he didn't actually, normally, do anything at all during the daytime. This was because he didn't have a job and there was nothing in particular that he felt like doing on his own account. What he *would* do, is wander around trying to get rid of as much of the day as possible, in as painless a manner as possible, until his few remaining unmarried friends returned home from work. At which point he would sort them through in his head and then pick the one he had bothered the least in the recent past and offer him out for a drink - and a 'laugh'.

Today, while he was having his coffee, it occurred to him that it was probably fairly unusual to get an actual letter from God, and he felt a little swell of gladness, because he knew now that, when this evening's particular friend came out to the pub with him, he, Derek, would have something interesting to say. Something, for once, to tell the other fellow, about *his* day.

The next morning, he woke up at about nine with an aching head and a throat sore from smoking too many cigarettes. He opened his eyes and stared at the bedroom ceiling whilst considering the previous night's revelries. His friend had been impressed with the God letter and they had spent some time discussing the beautiful handwriting and checking out the postmark, which said Cricklewood. Derek's friend (whose name was Norman) was of the opinion that God had merely got a colleague to post it who lived locally, whereas Derek saw no reason why God could not be a West Londoner. Norman (who worked and, therefore, had time to do things) had promised to check the electoral register today. Derek closed his eyes again. It was far too early to be awake; there was too much left of the day.

He awoke again at about eleven, which was more

respectable and, after lying for a while giving the ceiling further attention, rose and walked into the kitchen. He was dressed only in his crumpled boxer shorts. He turned on the radio before heading toward the bathroom as he found the silence made him feel guilty.

Whilst brushing his teeth, he realised that he had forgotten to check his post and walked back into the hallway of his flat - from the kitchen there came the sound of the kettle clicking off - to check. Sure enough, there was a letter. Derek couldn't remember the last time he'd had two consecutive days of post. He walked back into the bathroom to put down his toothbrush and swill himself out, then went back to the hallway and picked the letter up. He checked the postmark: Cricklewood. He opened it as he made his way once more to the bathroom, pulled out the single page inside and with his free hand put it to his face as he stood, spread-legged over the toilet, and began to urinate.

Dear Derek, the letter said, Thought I told you to sort it out. Lots of love. God.

Derek made a cup of tea and sat to wait for Norman's phone call - which was the next thing that was going to happen to his day.

He placed the letter in front of himself and looked at it as though it meant something. He would have something else to talk to Norman about now. God was making him an interesting person. He pondered also upon who amongst his remaining friends to let into his club, that he would be the hub of. He decided, upon much reflection, that the inner circle would comprise only all of them. He would wait for Norman's information before setting the ball rolling though, as he would then have three different offerings.

Norman rang at twelve thirty; it was his lunch hour. He had asked an ex-girlfriend who worked for the government to check the Cricklewood electoral register for God. She had informed him that this would only work if God was a respectable citizen and was properly registered for his council tax. Norman had assured her that He almost certainly was. She had found no one called God, though there were a couple of Goods. Norman had then advised her to look under Jah - nothing, and Yahweh - nothing, and finally Jehovah (he knew there were many other names for God but couldn't remember them) - nothing.

Derek was a little disappointed and said so before telling Norman about the new letter. Norman was impressed again, though Derek felt a little less so than the first time, and promised to keep up with his search.

Derek put down the phone. It was lunch time; his belly growled in happy anticipation of an event.

The phone rang again. Derek sighed and said, Fuck me, in an aggrieved sort of manner, as though he really was the sort of person who has things to do and is fed up with endless interruptions.

It was Norman again.

'Send it back,' he said.

'What?' said Derek.

'The letter,' said Norman. 'I've got an ex-girlfriend who works for the post office - she can tell me if it gets delivered and if so, where.'

'Good idea,' said Derek, also wondering how it was that Norman seemed to have so many ex-girlfriends - and useful ones at that.

'Goodbye,' said Norman.

Derek went out for lunch. He bought a paper and read about last night's football games. He smoked a cigarette. He was allowed one, after eating.

The afternoon dragged on. Luckily there was a film on TV that he liked and hadn't seen too many times, though the period between 5.00 and 6.00 was a little bare. He decided he would write an email and send it to his friends; that way, he would save on unnecessary phone calls and would be able to present his story in precisely the right way. It would also imply, once again, that he was now the sort of fellow who is a little too involved with something else to be able to waste time in idle gossip

After the emails were sent, he checked his messages. He was affiliated to a couple of websites that sent you mail, consisting of lists of women who were evidently looking for casual sex though, none of his previous inquiries having borne fruit, he'd begun to doubt their physical existence. This, of course, had been the case with God up until the previous day so he justifiably approached that day's deliveries with a little more optimism.

Once he had picked his candidates and posted them the sex-email (he had a template), he found there was another message waiting in his inbox. He opened it. It was headed 'Untitled'. It read: This is not what I meant. Lots of love. God.

He downloaded the email onto his desktop and saved it under *Letters from God*. He would print it out and bring it along to the first meeting, with the others.

Throughout that evening, he received a gratifying amount of phone calls - his friends obviously *weren't* too busy for gossip - and a meeting was arranged for the following night. In the morning, he was awoken at 9.00am precisely by the telephone. He obviously was not going to get out of bed and lay listening as the answer machine cut in and told the caller that Derek was unable to get to the phone at the moment as he couldn't be arsed.

After the tone, a deep and portentous voice said, For fuck's sake! and hung up.

The following night, all the friends met up in a pub in Camden called The Moon under the Water. The beer was cheap and there was no piped music; this was why it was a perfect pub - though some of the younger members felt uncomfortable at the lack of attractive women and the surfeit of unattractive men.

Derek, by this time, had a third letter and second email from God. The new missives said: Am I not speaking English? Lots of love. God. And: I don't know why I bother sometimes, I really don't. Love God.

It was pointed out by one of the younger members of the group that God had forgotten to quantify his love at the end of the last email, which broke the ice of the evening rather nicely - the fact that even God makes mistakes. In fact, one of the wittier members put it rather admirably.

'Oh well,' he said. 'He's only human.'

Further discussion was put on hold as the newest of the fellows, who had not understood the 'Lagging behind upon entering a pub with a large group' rule, collected orders at the bar. They all ordered a whisky chaser with their pints as it was cold outside and the fellow had to learn.

Once pints and chasers were placed in front of appropriate recipients, the meeting was started in earnest. And, as Derek had predicted, his stock had definitely risen since the last similar assemblage. He was invited, upon hushed attention, to deliver his personal account of things, and then to act as arbiter in the following dispute upon the meaning of it all.

One friend, who had once played football for the first team at Derek's school, mentioned rather cautiously that he seemed to remember a similar incident occurring to another mutual acquaintance. This led them up half an hour's worth of blind alleys, and incurred the necessity of a further trip to the bar, before it was remembered that the gentleman in question had been playing Judas in an amateur production of *Jesus Christ Superstar*, and that the communications in question were in fact from the director. It was pointed out, however, and Derek thought a little irrelevantly, that the fellow in question wasn't a very good Judas and hadn't, by consensus recollection, finished the run of the play.

The evening wore itself away in the aforementioned manner, until a bell sounded at the bar and the, now somewhat drunken, quango was firmly ejected from the premises. One of the friends attempted a rebellion; but upon finding his erstwhile comrades in attitudes of unmistakable capitulation, was forced to revoke previous threats and in fact offer a humble apology to the humanity-wearied barman, who had been quite looking forward to taking out his life's disappointment upon a meeting between the friend's head and Camden Council's paving stones. They adjourned, as is the custom, to somewhere that would both feed them and provide further intoxication. At this point, Derek, and his right hand man Norman, assimilated all suggestions and forced a consensus decision that they would continue in their efforts to track God down. It was decided, after more than a little buffoonery with the Indian waiters - who managed to smile thinly - that the very next morning (that being Saturday) they would each stake out a Cricklewood post box and pounce upon any bearded gentleman with a righteous gleam in his eye. This decided they all took taxis home - the evening done.

Derek awoke at about 9.00am the next morning

and, much to his annoyance, found that he was unable to return to sleep. This he found a constant irony; in that he had no trouble sleeping until midday when the rest of the world was working, but come the weekend he has to be the early bird. It seemed, no matter how late the night before, he was always a Saturday morning 9.00am man. Of course, he had plans for this particular morning, and, of course, he had no intention of seeing them through - drunken pub talk.

There was another letter on the mat. He ignored it and proceeded to take his slight nausea into the bathroom, where he evacuated his bowels. He exited quickly, deciding to clean his face and mouth at a later stage, and headed back to the bedroom, grabbing, almost as an afterthought, the new letter as he went.

He muttered to himself as he sat beneath his covers and opened it. He should have made a cup of tea. Too late now.

You do realise that you're going to die? the letter asked. There was no signature this time; God was obviously getting busy too.

Derek felt a bit offended. He decided to try for more sleep, reflecting as he lay down that 9 o'clock in the morning was a hell of a time of day.

Later that day, after Derek had joked on the telephone with Norman and a couple of others from his crew about no-one doing the post box thing, God rang. Derek picked up the phone.

'Hello,' he said.

'Do you know who this is?' asked the deep portentous voice.

'God I suppose,' Derek said, perhaps a little sulkily.

'Well,' said God, 'Aren't you amazed?'

''Spose so,' said Derek, knowing that he wasn't really behaving himself.

'You don't *sound* amazed,' said God, sounding a bit amazed himself.

'Mmm,' said Derek, then, making an effort, 'You sound a bit amazed.' As though that may help.

'I do, don't I?' God agreed then went on, 'I suppose I am a bit.'

'Mmmm,' said Derek. He wasn't really very good with new people, never had been. 'What you up to?'

'Oh, you know, this and that ... Yourself?'

'Oh, this and that,' Derek said, 'You know ...'

There was a bit of a silence whilst both of them tried to work out whose turn it was to speak next, and also what to say when doing so. Derek, meanwhile, realised that unless he was going to make up the things he'd said when he told his mates about this, he better at least say one important thing.

As is the way in films, they both broke the silence at once:

'You're not really doing very well'/'What do you think about Allardyce as new West Ham manager?'

Derek was actually a Chelsea man himself and couldn't believe he'd had the balls to tell God that He wasn't doing very well. Again, they did it like the films:

'He's doing okay, I suppose, though letting Lampard go was -'/'Did you just tell me I wasn't doing very we- Look, STOP! One at a TIME!!'

God's voice was actually a little bit scary when he got angry so Derek stopped talking and waited.

'Well ...' said God.

'What?' said Derek.

God sighed and said, 'I'm really not sure I've got time for this ... What did you want to say?'

'Oh, nothing really. You?'

God paused, as though thinking. 'Nothing really, either,' he said eventually. He sounded a bit sad.

'Oh well,' said Derek.

'Oh well,' said God.

'See ya,' said Derek, for whom the cafe was calling.

'Oh, yes, right you are then ... Oh by the way sort -'

Derek had hung up.

That didn't go too badly, he thought to himself over his fry up. He also spent a little time thinking of things he could have said but hadn't (this had all the makings of a great pub game), then caught sight of a paper left by a previous patron and buried himself in it. One cigarette. As he flicked over the sports pages, he decided that Allardyce was probably going to do all right at West Ham, as long as Nolan stayed fit.

ANDY SZPUK

Home Brew

I walked up the steps and found home
It was a few years ago now
I took my place next to fine spirits
And swapped stories with souls old and new
We uncorked bottles of borrowed faith
And poured warmth onto cold terrains
We gave cheer to the lost and the lonely
And chased our own frayed nerves through
everyday mists
We still join hands to intoxicate
Potency pulsing through our golden glow
We reach parts others cannot reach
While the wheels of history turn
So, throw me down in the mix once again
To do battle with ghosts, to unlock cages
Our minds together make a fine brew
And it flows from the heart of this home

SUSMITA BHATTACHARYA
Going Home

'Your mother's gone,' my father said.

The telephone line crackled and I wondered if I had heard right. I rubbed my eyes and peered into the darkness. The red digits glared at me. 4.15am. Oh God, it dawned on me. Mamma's dead?

'Dad,' I said. 'How? When?' I squeezed my eyelids shut. She seemed perfectly well when I spoke to her last week. No, she seemed a bit depressed, now that I think of it. She had refused to cook Dad's tea, and that was odd. I paced around the room, bumping into furniture, unsure what to do.

My father's voice took on a petulant tone. 'Left a note on the table. Yesterday morning. Going home, it says.'

'What?' I shouted. 'Where did she go?'

I slumped down on the bed. Thank goodness, she was alive. But she had left him? Left the house? After all these years?

'So you have no idea where she's gone?'

'No,' Father said.

'What did she mean, going home?'

'God knows. I have more important things to do than encourage her loony ways.' He sounded distracted.

He's probably working on his 'very important paper' while talking to me, I thought. I didn't want to continue this conversation. I'd have to find her myself.

'Why are you calling me at 4.00am when she left yesterday morning?'

He hesitated. I could hear him shuffling around.

'I thought she would come back. I couldn't sleep.'

'Did you call the police?' I asked and walked into the bathroom.

Where could she be? The bathroom light dazzled my eyes. An image of my mother flashed: thin. Tired. Despondent.

'No,' he said, 'I didn't want to bother ...'

'Call the police *now*,' I said. 'I'm coming over.'

I banged the phone down. It would take me hours to get to Edinburgh from London. I remembered how Mamma always wanted to leave. I was very young then. Father was too busy doing important things, like doing a PhD and lecturing at the university in Edinburgh. Travelling around the world, attending seminars, conferences. He was too busy for us.

She always talked of another place, one that would be ideal for us. Mother and daughter only. This place did not exist on a map. It was a fairytale kingdom where families lived happily ever after. There was always plenty of food and relatives and friends to share it with. There was laughter, and sunshine and babies. She sucked me into this secret world of hers and we lived there, far away from Father's corrosive tongue and condescending attitude.

Mamma never finished school. When her father died, she sat with two hundred other women in a dark, damp basement room, and embroidered underwear all day long. The strain made her eyes weak and, before her eighteenth birthday, she couldn't see beyond a few feet. She was beautiful and vanity prevented her from wearing glasses.

She used to laugh and tell me that she didn't see her husband's face until the day after the wedding, when she peered down very close to his face while he was sleeping. Perhaps I wouldn't have married him then, she'd say and her laugh would dry up.

Mamma had been busy, sewing underwear, when the owner of the factory chanced upon her. He was a rich merchant and of the same caste as Mamma's. On talking to her, he discovered that she was his Sanskrit teacher's daughter and that she had been sent here to work out of desperation. He pulled her out of the line and got her married to his orphaned nephew. This nephew had got a scholarship to study in Edinburgh and would need a wife to cook and clean for him there.

She was all of seventeen and he was twenty-three. They sailed to England on the HMS Mary and Mamma always talked about how she loved her days at sea.

What carefree days, she'd say. The weather was balmy, the sea calm. She was never sea-sick and looked after her poor husband, who couldn't bear even the slightest pitch and roll of the ship. The other passengers were kind and friendly. The voyage lasted three weeks and father was very attentive to her. He was so polite and kind. He spoke such good English, and taught her how to speak the basics. She was so proud to have a husband whose nose was always in a book.

Edinburgh was a big shock. It was grey. It was wet. It was full of cobbled streets and old buildings that were cold and damp. They had to live on the meagre scholarship money, which meant wearing coats and scarves indoors and making do with candles when they couldn't afford electricity. Not a single brown face, she would tell me. I'd be afraid to step out of the house. I couldn't read, not because I was without spectacles, but because everything was in English. And men wore skirts. It frightened me.

Kilts, I'd giggle. In India men wear *lungis*, so why are you so surprised here?

She'd click her tongue in exasperation. In India, it was okay. But here? *Baap re baap*. But we had so much fun together. While Father was busy, Mamma and I would skip down to the Scott Monument and watch these kilted men play their bagpipes. We'd share an umbrella and splash in the puddles in the gardens below the Castle. We'd walk down Princess Street, window shopping. Sometimes she'd buy me an ice-cream, as a treat. She never had any though. She said nothing compared to the *kulfi* from back home, but really she couldn't afford a second one.

We never visited India. Father had no family there. He didn't have the money to send Mamma home. Mamma had asked once, begged him, when a letter came from her home saying her mother was ill. But Father had exploded. Where did she think the money would come from? Why hadn't she married a businessman or a prince? Going abroad on a lecturer's pay? Then her wheedling family would ask her for the treatment. And the funeral. He went on and on. She listened to him, without saying a word. Then she walked away and never mentioned India again.

That summer, the three of us went on a holiday to France. Paris. Versailles. Brittany. The weather was beautiful. Everything was green and blue and golden. I fell in love with every young man I passed. My skin got a sun-kissed glow. Father laughed a lot and gorged on chocolate crêpes. I tasted my first glass of champagne. Mamma, as well. Her lips puckered as she took a sip. Her throat contracted sharply and, when she smiled, it was like ice, and it could have frozen those bubbles in her glass.

Her brothers did call her once. They said their mother had died. She had wanted to see her only daughter, her first-born, once before she died. Now that wish remained unfulfilled. She could at least contribute to the funeral arrangements. So father had been right. They did beg, after all. Their sister was a rich *bilayeti*. She had hung up on them. Later, she had hugged me close to her, as if I too would disappear one day and never be seen again. She pressed her nose into my new breasts, inhaling deeply. Her fingernails dug deep to leave her marks behind. I held her and wiped her tears. My grandmother was dead, and I didn't even know what she looked like.

I looked at my parents' wedding photograph. It was yellow with age and heavily photo-inked. My mamma's eyes were painted black and my father's moustache looked fake. It must have been a cheap studio shot. I took this photo with me when I moved to London. I wanted it as a keepsake. To remind me that I had parents. I had a lineage because, for me, it was only them. I had never seen any other family member.

Mamma was gone. But where? Was she on her way to see me? I checked my mobile phone. No missed calls. What if she didn't know my number by heart? How would she get in touch with me? I got into my car and started towards Gatwick. I would get to Edinburgh by mid-morning at best. My mobile phone buzzed. I grabbed it and pulled over. It was the police.

Mamma was at Heathrow Airport. She had bought a ticket to India, but she didn't have a visa. The airline authority had raised the alarm when she had turned hysterical. She wanted me to come and get her. I changed course and headed towards Heathrow instead.

I was there in an hour's time. I was led to a tiny room where she was waiting. I studied her through the glass door. She looked so frail, so old. She kept wringing her coarse hands and clenching her fists. Her purse lay on her lap, along with the air ticket. Her duffel bag was by her feet. She was wearing a sari. Mamma had given up wearing saris the day her mother died. My past is dead for me, she had said. This is my present, and I shall live like the *goras*. I will become one myself.

I smiled, despite myself. Mamma had done well. She had learned English. She had learned to appreciate her adopted country. But looking at her now, clumsy in a blue silk sari, sneakers on her feet, she didn't belong anywhere. She was what her marriage had intended her to be. The housekeeper. Looking after my father. Cleaning up behind him. She was never his equal. She would always be the factory worker he had brought to this country to be his slave.

I opened the door and walked in.

She looked at me and smiled wearily. '*Chalo beta,*' she sighed. 'Take me to your flat. I am very tired. I'm sorry for all this headache.'

She stood up, tears flowing down her lined cheeks. She took off her glasses and wiped her face. She looked old, my beautiful Mamma. How defeated. I made up my mind then. Old maybe, but defeated, certainly not. She had taken the first step, I would follow it through.

'Good you left him,' I said, smiling. 'You should

have done it years ago, and taken me with you. Then we could have watched men wearing *lungis* and eaten *kulfis* all day.'

She laughed, delighted that I remembered. 'Shameless girl,' she said.

'Mamma, let's go to my place now. Didn't you know you needed a visa to go to India? You are a British citizen.'

Her face fell. 'I never believed that I would be refused. I wasn't thinking. My country, not my country anymore? I couldn't believe that for a minute.'

I nodded. 'Tomorrow we shall apply for a visa, OK?'

'We?' she asked.

'Yes, we.' I smiled and pulled her to me.

She straightened and linked her arm through mine. 'When we return home,' she said, 'I will buy you the best ice-cream in the world. The shop in Bara Bazaar, Kwality Ice-creams, the best *kulfi* in the world. I used to spend all my pocket money there.'

I smiled as I guided her out of the room. I'd call Father later and tell him. I held Mamma's hand as we walked towards the car. The sun had come up and was bathing its pale light directly on us.

ROB WALTON
A Letter to Jennifer

Dear Jennifer,

I must jump straight in and tell you about the towel rail. It's not – that's NOT - connected to the central heating system. It works independently via the switch near the bathroom door. The switch has a smiley face sticker and my son, Aaron, has written his name on it ('ANRON' – he was four at the time).

So, Jennifer, sorry about that opening – felt I had to get that down before I forgot. For us the countdown clock is tick-tick-tick-tick-tocking! I don't usually start letters or conversations with towel rail tit-bits. Maybe it's my age. I feel if I don't get something down it will go for ever. I could run after it with a butterfly net or a fishing rod or some sticky tape wrapped round my hand but I'd never get it again. It would be gone-gone-gone!

Thank you very much for your email. Thought I would put my fountain pen (a strange wedding present from his strange mother, and don't get me started on the strange hat she was wearing on that very strange day) to the notepaper for a change. I will, of course, keep up the emails too – and maybe even Facebook! I've certainly been thinking about it of late, getting in touch with a few old friends, thinking about how things could have worked out. Do you have ifs and buts over there?

I thought you could bring this letter with you as a handy reference guide. I'm really looking forward to this exchange and have hundreds of questions to ask – but they can wait.

First, I need to share a few little quirks about our humble abode.

There are two locks for the front door and, as I already detailed in my email of the 16th (sent at 4.03am – do all wives have these crosses to bear?) John at number 16 (a number coincidence – do you believe in those sort of things? There's a book about it in the small room downstairs if you do) will have the keys. You'll love John. (Any problems go see him. He can turn his hand to almost anything. Literally.)

Quirk numero uno. When our heating was installed the switch for the water was problematic. The man I married, Antony, claimed to have 'solved' it, but the switch is now set to OFF when the water is ON (ie constantly heating) and is set to ON when the hot water boiler is lying idle, ie is OFF. Please don't worry about any of this because John – why didn't I ask him to do it in the first place? - will pop round to make sure it's all OFF (ON!) before you arrive. You'll probably end up having an ON/OFF relationship with

John. You wouldn't be the first.

Oh, I'm jumping about. He gets me like that.

When you walk in the house – before the bathroom! – you will see a photo of Aaron and his sister (Daddy's girl!). There's also another photo face-down. Please leave it. Really. That's not an example of the British sense of humour. Leave it.

In the dining room please do not stand any of the photos up. Just leave them as they are. I would appreciate it if you did not move them. Thank you, Jennifer. Thank you very much. I feel you'll be on my side. I feel, whatever happens, however things pan out, you'll be there for me.

Also on the hall table is a list of potential visitors – the postman, who's a woman usually, will come Monday to Saturday. Well, if there's post. (You've got mail!) The window cleaner comes every Friday when he isn't doing other things and I haven't yet told him about your visit, so don't be surprised to get a few questions. He has quizzed me about things in the past.

So – the kitchen. I could write a book! (It would be a book about the kitchen. Not sure how clear I made that. An illustrated book, I suppose, and I guess you'd call it non-fiction, though I have been known to *make up* some recipes! John says I can be very inventive.) The basic rule is Help Yourself. Please replace anything you finish, but also feel free to use our condiments, oils, etc, etc, etc. Again, John will pop round before your arrival – when he's turning the water ON/OFF – and will bring milk and bread and butter for you. I'll ask him to put a bottle of white in the fridge – he'll probably not need asking – and some red on the workbench.

(If you find yourself out of wine when the shop is closed, my husband has a supply in the corner cupboard. There are some lovely bottles. Feel free. 'Fill your boots' as some Brits say. But please leave your actual boots in the utility room. There's a rack with brushes, shoe horns and so on and so forth.)

The taps (faucets?) in both kitchen and bathroom are colour-coded. It's simple. The towels are on display. Well, maybe not on display, but you can certainly see them.

Now on to the master bedroom. (What a phrase – don't take it too seriously! The master has lost his voice.)

The two singles become a double very easily. The instructions are under the counterpane. I know nothing of your preferences re sleeping with your husband – and you don't need to tell me (but I think I'm a good listener and if you did want to tell me I'd be all ears, if you can understand that phrase). Sort the beds as you wish, but please put them back in their original positions. We don't want anyone getting any ideas about anything, do we?

I've made some space in one of the wardrobes. It's the empty one. If you need any clothes for a male middle manager look under the bed (please don't!).

The children's toys and games are in the cupboards

in their rooms – again, help yourself. A makeshift bed has recently been set up in my daughter's room.

Please do whatever you want with it. Some of the games, such as Scrabble, with score cards and score sheets, may have silly comments John has written. Feel free to ignore them! Or add your own! In green pen!!

And if there are any messages left by John on the answerphone please delete them. (I realise that might be asking a lot, but it might be of help. Let me know if there are any little favours I can do for you.)

So, Jennifer, I hope you'll be very happy in this house. It's not impossible. I'm looking forward to visiting yours.

I always think of a holiday as being a fresh start. 'Who knows what tomorrow brings?' as the song says. Someone somewhere might get a taste for something new, something different.

Rest assured I will be back in touch before the swap and if there are any further changes here I will let you know.

Oh – I remembered! There's a neighbourhood cat who may make an appearance. He is 'welcomed' here depending on who is in at the time, so what might seem like an out-and-out personality disorder is really only a bit of uncertainty. I can understand that. Ha!

Your new acquaintance/friend by letter,

Michaela

P.S. Don't go worrying about that stain on the

patio. It might look a bit macabre but would you believe it's from a vegetarian marinade?!

.

JODY KLAIRE
Fields of Gold

Alina heard the words, 'Not guilty', and her heart dropped into her stomach. Two years of hard work, sacrifice, long hours, and the jury had found a guilty man innocent.

She looked over at the defendant, who was smiling, his supporters cheering. Alina looked at the family of the victim.

What could she say?

The rain hammered her windscreen, as she drove the 300 miles from the city to the tiny fishing village where she had been born and raised.

The one she hadn't visited in five years.

She felt sick. Her own personal failure stung, but failure to get justice for the family - her body trembled with it. She gripped the wheel. She was going back to her parents for the summer. She'd promised her mother that she would at the end of the case - whatever the outcome.

Alina couldn't help but see the faces of the family; they had lost so much and now there would be no justice.

The motorways became country roads, and the

towering buildings became hills, covered in patchwork green. Alina wanted to turn around. She wanted to go back to her apartment, her *empty* apartment, and crawl into bed.

Anything not to face the people she barely knew anymore.

The road narrowed again and she made her way down the little cobbled street, her car suspension juddering. Brightly-painted, little fishing cottages were on either side, their lights twinkling against the puffs of mist coming off the sea.

It was a forgotten village, on a forgotten part of the coastline, the houses not reaching twenty, the population as small.

Alina pulled up to her father's shop. The lights were still on and it was nearing midnight; nothing changed. She *should* go up to the farm, to see her mother, but Alina had rented the little apartment above the pottery shop for the summer.

She needed the space.

Alina didn't want to face her father and her head throbbed at the thought. 'Get out and get this over with,' she muttered to herself.

She took a deep breath and braved the torrential rain. The mist was now fog, the sea gale stealing her breath as she dragged her luggage from the boot. Her heel caught on the cobbles: snap.

She looked down; they cost most people's monthly wage. Stupid cobbles, stupid place. Why couldn't they have tarmac like the rest of the world?

Alina fought with the heavy shop door which slammed behind her, nudging her inside, and stood in the empty space: wet, freezing cold, with her hair smattered across her face, covering her eyes and mouth like seaweed.

Why the hell was she here?

'Can I help you?' came an oddly familiar voice from somewhere beyond her hair.

Alina laughed. Help? She needed more than help. 'Who are you?'

'I work here,' came the amused reply.

Alina frowned; she knew that voice. 'Frauke Bärbel?' Pulling her hair from her eyes she looked at the woman who used to be her childhood friend. 'Since when have you worked here?'

Frauke smiled. 'Only five years.'

Frauke, the girl, had been a mass of brown, wavy hair, charcoal eyes and a lopsided smile; she had been all legs and arms and adventure. Frauke, the woman, was so different that Alina hardly recognised her: burnt copper hair, shaved, weather-tanned skin, an earring in her nose and a seashell necklace. Frauke had grown into her frame, but she was still slim, and still had mischief in her eyes.

'You left,' Alina stated.

Frauke nodded.

'You didn't call.'

Frauke shook her head. They stood in awkward silence, Alina soaked and starting to shiver.

'I'm renting the flat,' she finally said.

'I heard - it's open,' Frauke answered.

Alina nodded and started to pull her bags but Frauke took them off her.

'I don't need help.'

'Didn't say you did,' Frauke answered.

Alina followed her up the back stairs into the flat. It was not the dingy place she had remembered from childhood. Now, it looked like they'd hired an interior designer.

'The lights were on,' Alina said as Frauke set down her bags.

'Yeah, it's easier than working in the dark.'

Alina frowned. Frauke shoved her hands in her jeans. She was covered in clay, a pencil shoved behind one ear. Alina saw the memory: Frauke leaving in a car after her grandparents died. Her tear-stained cheeks and her wild, brown hair.

A year later, Alina left herself, headed to the city and never came back.

'So, here's the key - home sweet home, huh?' Frauke said.

'Not even close.'

The smell of freshly-baked bread drew Alina into the shop the next morning. Frauke sat at the design table, with a baguette in one hand and her pencil in the other. Alina looked around. Her father was still nowhere to be seen.

'Didn't you go home?' she muttered. Did Frauke live here?

'Yup.'

Alina put her hands on her hips and Frauke laughed.

'Where is my father?'

'In the house. I would guess feeding the chickens, like he always does at this time.'

'How the hell do you know?'

Frauke shrugged. 'I listen.'

Alina growled. 'Fine. If you know him so well, you can introduce me!'

She yanked open the shop door and flipped the sign to 'back later'.

Frauke raised her eyebrows then got to her feet, baguette still in hand. 'Only if we walk,' she said.

Alina looked up the steep hill. Could she be bothered? She hadn't been for a run in months. Maybe it would help keep her temper in check. 'Fine.'

The sun oozed warmth into her bones as they walked up the little cobbled path. The villagers all waved to Frauke, exchanging greetings, but no one recognised Alina. Clearly, fifteen years in the city had rendered her a stranger.

'Want some?' Frauke asked, offering her baguette.

Alina's stomach rumbled but she was too tense - too wound up - too nauseous at the decision in court to eat.

'It's good - you used to love it,' Frauke offered.

Alina shook her head. 'I'm not fifteen anymore.'

Frauke sighed. 'You always this mad?'

'With you, yes.'

That wasn't the entire truth. No one made it to the

top of the legal food-chain without learning to battle and argue for every point. She worked hard, she went home. Smiling was for people with time.

'What the hell are you doing back anyway?' Alina snapped.

Frauke walked on, forcing Alina to catch up with her. 'City changes people,' she said. 'My brother lives in the city. He's a cop now, by the way - hates it - but there's no money here.'

Alina nodded. 'A bunch of pensioners and the past.'

Frauke laughed. 'I look pretty good for a pensioner, don't you think?'

She forced herself not to smile, not to laugh. She was still mad. No way was Frauke getting away that easy. 'You didn't answer the question. Why are you here?'

'Some things are more important than money.'

'Like?' Alina was expecting some drivel about tradition or the sea air.

Frauke almost whispered her response, as though to say it aloud would mean breaking the illusion. 'Home.'

'You seemed pretty happy to leave it behind before.'

Frauke stopped, her eyes narrowed. 'You can't be that cold. My grandparents died, Alina. I *had* to go.'

Alina turned to look at her parents' farm. A red painted door, cream walls splashed in the vivid colours of summer in full bloom.

'You forgot me soon enough,' she said and before Frauke could reply, she stomped to the door. She almost knocked. She didn't live here anymore.

'Ada, the prodigal daughter is here to see you,' Frauke called out before Alina could turn and bolt.

'Hmmm ... What did you say, dear?'

Alina's breath caught. A little old lady stood in the kitchen, candyfloss white hair and eyes like bottled sunshine. They were almost amber - like hers.

'Hi, Mum.'

Her mother touched her hand to her mouth, her eyes drifting over every inch of Alina.

'Hello, sweetie. Welcome home.'

She tensed at the words. Home? No - home was the city, home was a grey power-suit and a courtroom.

'I heard the verdict,' her mother said. 'The media said the jury were scared.'

Alina nodded. 'Scared and I didn't do my job properly.'

Ada turned to Frauke. 'Still a perfectionist, like her father.'

'A guilty man got away with murder!'

Her mother tutted. 'He was convicted on two other counts, Alina. He's behind bars.'

'Until he appeals - or his sentence for assault ends.'

Her mother smiled, throwing Alina off her argument. 'The family said you worked wonders to get them that. You did your best.'

Alina rubbed the bridge of her nose.

'My best wasn't enough.'

Her mother walked forward and planted a kiss on her forehead. Alina's inner child wanted to be wrapped up in the warm, soft arms of her mother, smell the scent of fresh washing and sea air. The adult in her detested the needy response; she was a grown woman.

At a loss how to act, Alina hugged herself instead.

'I'll go check on the old codger. Leave you two to catch up,' Frauke said, sauntering out the kitchen door.

'So, how long has she been running things?' Alina asked.

'Three years. You know how much your father loves her.'

'She must be good if he's left the workshop.'

Her mother smiled, touching Alina's cheeks with her hands. 'She's a very shrewd business woman too - we're in safe hands.'

'What happened to her?'

Alina's mother shook her head. 'I don't know. She turned up on the doorstep, not long after your last visit. Bought the Bärbel farm from us, outright. It's as though she never left.'

Alina heard laughter and looked out of the kitchen window. Her father, with a chicken under his arm, chuckling with Frauke. What the hell was so funny about chickens?

'She seems happy. You, my girl, do not.'

Alina shrugged. 'Just tired.'

'Nonsense, I'm your mother. I know better. Was it – well -'

'Jana? No - it didn't work out.'

Her mother fiddled with her glasses, taking them off and cleaning them. Alina sighed. Why was she here? Everything was so awkward.

'Is that why you're so unhappy?'

Alina shook her head and walked over to the breakfast bar. She lifted herself up onto it, like she had as a child. 'I don't know what it is. I wanted to reach the top. I have - and now I'm there -'

'It's not enough?'

Alina nodded. 'Sad, isn't it?'

'No, I would say you're lonely. You can go to all the glamorous parties, and get awards, but if all you go back to is an empty apartment, is that really success?'

'Maybe I should get a cat.'

Before her mother could answer, Alina's father strolled in. Her heart hammered in her chest. She'd been his little girl. He'd adored her. Her 'other life', as he called it, had separated them.

All her fault, of course.

'Come on. I'm starving and you're not getting any younger,' Frauke piped up from behind him.

His eyes warmed at Frauke's words then he turned and walked off to get cleaned up. No hello, nothing. He didn't even look at her.

Lunch was eaten in silence, speckled with Frauke and Alina's father chatting about business. Alina didn't eat much; she didn't breathe much either. Her mind was too busy, replaying his stinging words. Years passing hadn't dampened the pain.

As Frauke and Alina walked back down to the shop, she stopped and sat on the dry stone wall running between Frauke's farm and her parents'.

'You seem more laid back than you used to be,' she said.

Frauke smiled. 'I have all this. The city makes you think success is instant - the future all that matters, life online - success, popularity.' She grabbed hold of Alina's hand and dragged her through the wooden gate. 'Take off your shoes,' she said, pulling her boots off.

Alina sighed, the days of following Frauke's next whim rippling through her mind. There had always been some adventure.

'Come on,' Frauke said.

Alina took off her flats and followed Frauke to the centre of the yellow field, the earth, drying from the downpour, soft beneath her toes.

Frauke ran her hands through the barley. 'Life here is about patience - about today, not tomorrow. Success is measured in how happy you are - in simple things.'

'You sound like a hippy.'

Frauke waved away the comment. 'I sowed this field myself - like grandpapa did. Every single glint of gold is here because I tended it - my work - and nature's.'

Alina looked around the massive field. The barley swayed in the gentle sea breeze.

'I give some to the bakery. He gives me baguettes.'

Alina slumped onto the ground, feeling lost. 'My father disowned me,' she stated.

'Yeah, and he was an idiot - but he's human.'

'He told me I was sick, Frauke!'

Frauke nodded and sat beside her. 'Five years of dealing with me. He's pretty OK now.'

Alina rubbed her head; trust Frauke to sweep in and save the day. 'Wouldn't surprise me if you'd rode in on a horse.'

'It was a Suzuki, but close.'

Alina laughed. 'I missed this.'

She didn't even realise it until the words fell from her mouth. Had she? Days spent wandering, talking, laughing... Hiding from lightning under the oak tree, and lying in the forest of golden barley.

'Me too.'

'Where did you go?' Alina asked. She was fifteen again watching Frauke leave, not one word.

'Convent.'

Alina raised her eyebrows. 'Convent? That sounds awful!'

'Don't believe everything you read. I stayed on after I finished school there. I nearly took final vows too.'

Alina laughed. Frauke didn't. 'Really?'

'Really. I saw so much through the outreach, y'know? The pain. The things people do to each other.

I wanted to get in there and help.'

'So what happened?'

Frauke pulled her T-shirt up, showing a nasty round scar on her side. 'Got caught in the crossfire.'

'Why did you come back?' Alina asked, trying not to look at the wound. The thought of Frauke lying hurt nearly suffocated her.

'Are you that dense?'

'Are all nuns this irritating?'

'Are all prosecutors as unperceptive?'

Alina growled.

'So why did *you* come home?' Frauke asked.

Alina looked around. She didn't know where the hell home was anymore - if it even existed.

The days moved fast, too fast. The hot summer sun baked the fields; the little village filled with tourists. Alina spent her days helping in the shop, watching Frauke work. The routine fell into place so easily ... Too easily.

The world started to fill with colour; Alina didn't even realise it was happening. It was only when the scent of late summer filled the air, and the nights cooled, that she felt the tension returning.

She was leaving. Her career, the city, her life beckoned and, a few hours later, Alina closed the boot of her car as Frauke stood in the doorway of the shop, hands shoved in her jeans.

'Let me know when you get there?'

Alina nodded and Frauke's eyes filled with unspoken words, with confessions, with heartbreak. It tied a knot around Alina's heart to know it was her doing, but this, here, wasn't her life.

'I promise,' she answered and, before she could say something stupid, got in the car and sped off.

Her head was filled with memories: the sky grey, tears soaking her shoulder, her life ripped out from her as Frauke was driven away, the driving rain, years of silence, of emptiness filled with work and endless ambition. The fields swayed, vibrant swathes of colour against blue skies, charcoal eyes that filled her soul.

It all vanished that day. It just wasn't home any more.

Alina fled, fled to the city, in the hope of finding someone, *anyone* who knew her. She found loneliness. She had been emptier than ever. The city wasn't home and, as she pulled into her parking space, the truth hit her.

Home wasn't a place. Home was a seashell necklace and a soft laugh.

She spun the car around but it took her until nightfall to drive back. Her heart hammered the whole time in her chest, like the sea hammering against the rocks.

By the time she pulled up to the little village, the lights in the shop window twinkled. She tried to calm herself. Did she really want this?

She looked up to the hills; the fields of gold against a saturated sky; the smell of salt in the air; all of it resonated Frauke. Every seagull's cry, even the crackling of the pebbles dragged out by the tide. Everything was her.

Alina was so terrified by the time she reached the door that her hands trembled. What if Frauke didn't feel the same? Had Frauke come back for her?nShe walked in and heard the bell over the door but Frauke was nowhere to be seen. Instead, her father stood there.

'Forgotten something?'

Alina shook her head.

He beamed and handed her an envelope. 'She's gone to the farm - said to give you this.'

Alina cocked her head. There was mischief in his eyes. 'You know, don't you?'

'Of course. Not even I'm that blind. Go.'

She walked over to her father and hugged him tightly. No words needed.

She drove up to Frauke's farm, down the lane lined with apple trees. She sat in her car, her head dizzy with thoughts, and opened the envelope.

'A key. That's it?'

Alina got out of the car. Frauke was lounging on her swing bench, cutting an apple with a knife. She smiled and patted the seat beside her.

Alina sat down and looked out over the fields, right through the village to the sea. 'It's to the farm, isn't it?' she asked, taking out the key.

Frauke nodded and handed her half of the apple.

'Welcome home.'

OWAIN PACIUSZKO
Leaving Home

It's funny, no matter how familiar I have become with this place, I still find myself missing a step on my walk downstairs. I guess you could say that the house does change. Now that the children have left, it isn't the same. It comes back to life at Christmas, like moving from black and white to full colour.

That's not to say that this isn't a home anymore; no, it's just different. Peter and I, we've found ourselves almost back in our courtship days; that's nice, that we have that back. In many ways, we're starting to discover one another all over again. I must admit, I was worried that without the hustle and bustle of a full house we might realise we'd lost all commonality, but we fell in love because we always were the best of friends.

Peter always told me that nobody could make a cup of tea as good as I could; not even he could make a tea just the way he likes it but, somehow, I had the knack. Water, up two-thirds of the way, a generous splash of milk, and just a sprinkle of sugar. I call his name, hear him move; he's upstairs, tidying Joshua's room; we're thinking of making it into an office.

But, then, there's silence, a confused quiet.

I call his name again and, in response, get a questioning and quizzical cry of my own name back.

Stepping out into the hallway, cup of tea in hand, I walk past the coat rail and telephone cubby towards the base of the stairs, except - and it takes me a moment to notice - there aren't any stairs. I follow their absence with my eyes up to the landing, where Peter stands, hands on hips, looking down at me.

Peter, chewing his bottom lip, contemplating the void. The perfect lack of staircase is baffling. There's no rubble, no damage, no conceivable way by which it could have been removed, but, undoubtedly, the stairs are not there.

Tentatively, I step into the space they inhabited, expecting to encounter an invisible staircase, but, almost disappointingly, there is nothing other than the unkempt foundation they once sat upon.

I continue forwards, reaching up to hand Peter his tea, lest it go cold.

To reach it, Peter has to lie on his stomach, stretching out his arm and just about clasping the top of the mug with his fingertips.

I move a chair in from the lounge and place it at the foot of the drop. Peter decides to take a bed sheet and tie it to the banister, so we can climb back up; this would undoubtedly be necessary if either of us were to need to use the bathroom.

Once Peter is safely downstairs, we call a construction firm, asking for a quote on building a stairway but, unfortunately, it is a little out of our budget. So, Peter brings in a ladder from the garden, which does the job just as well. In fact, it's quite fun; it makes it feel like we're living in a tree house. It is a bit of an inconvenience, but there are far more terrible things that could befall us, and I'm forever grateful that, all told, we've lived a nice, pleasant life.

A few days pass and, as I'm setting the table for dinner, I notice something strange about the dining room. It has always felt quite cramped, but that had lent itself to cosy Sunday lunches, with everyone squeezed in as best they could yet, today, it seems oddly spacious. Though there is no more room around the table itself.

With evening drawing in, I move to the light switch and, as I press the button, nothing changes. There is no illumination but, now, looking up, I realise that the room is extending up to twice the height it had before. Except, halfway, the wallpaper changes from the calm, vanilla of the dining room into the stripy pattern of my daughter's bedroom walls.

Quickly, I leave the room, climb the ladder, walk down the landing and edge, tentatively, into my daughter's room. Sure enough, I can now stare right down on top of the dinner table.

Below me, Peter walks in, about to settle himself for dinner. I flick on my daughter's bedroom light, which draws Peter's attention upwards. He looks through the missing ceiling, and I look through the missing floor.

The following morning, I wake up. It had been an uneasy night's sleep as I'm unsure about what we can do about the vanished floor in my daughter's room. I walk out onto the landing and round into the bathroom.

I pull down my pyjama bottoms and sit on the toilet, rubbing my sleepy eyes. I turn to the wall and, instead, see my husband, to my left, in our room, lying asleep in bed.

I leap off the toilet, pulling my bottoms up with me, and race through the opening where the bathroom wall should be, dashing back into our bedroom, jostling Peter awake.

He stirs, the alarm on my face working better than that of any clock. He says he'll call the council straight away, to see if they know what's going on, and he hurries towards the bedroom door.

Fortunately, spurred on by some unexpected concern, I manage to grab him before he steps out onto the landing, because the landing isn't there anymore either. Peter teeters precariously, eventually managing - with my help - to brace his hands on the doorframe and ease himself back into our bedroom.

We both look down into the hallway below as a breeze blows leaves in off the street, through an opening where our front wall used to be.

Peter takes action, disassembling the bed covers, and we both push the mattress out of the door into the downstairs hall. He then uses the duvet to lower me down onto the mattress, and, having shimmied and dangled from the edge, drops down afterwards.

Sure enough, the front wall up to the living room is no longer there and we can stare onto the street outside. It's a chilly morning, so I slip on some shoes and wrap a coat around me on top of my pyjamas.

We walk out into the street to see if we are the only ones affected, but there are others, quite clearly, people who are missing walls in front of their bedrooms, who have suddenly been woken by a gust of wind and are now screaming at one another as if their family members were to blame.

There are people trying to contain a flow of water that is gushing out of an opening where their toilet used to be.

A young couple have found their house besieged by pigeons, setting up roost and redecorating what floors remain.

There is a family now imprisoned in a stack of disconnected rooms, trying to carefully pass a toddler from floor to floor, towards the safety of the ground.

We turn back to our house, which is now merely a handful of walls, a gap between the two other, rapidly evaporating, houses on either side. We can see straight through, down to the end of our small garden, but we can also see beyond that, through where the back wall should have been in the house behind our own, down across another road towards a lack of facing buildings and on and on.

What walls, floors and ceilings that remained, continued to vanish, and then everything else began to disappear: the streetlights, the paving stones, the cars and the bicycles, the train lines and the hospitals, the shops and the offices, until all that was left were the people.

BERNADETTE STEADMAN
The Scent of Violets

Violets and death. Call me a cynic, but I thought lilies were the appropriate flowers for a funeral. Tall and elegant and white. It seems disrespectful, somehow, to have flowers at a funeral which are so much about life springing up from winter's little death.

It's cold. Fittingly cold for a funeral. It never feels right when it's warm. I never know what to wear. So much easier when you can wear your good, black coat and a pair of boots.

Trust Marcia to be different and get buried in a field. She even had a wicker coffin, of all things. Looked like she was going to her grave in a massive cat basket. Meowing her way into the next life.

All her hippie friends are here, weeping and wailing and wiping their noses on their sleeves. Makes my skin creep. They need a good wash, the lot of them. She didn't have a vicar, of course. Some bloke in a shroud read from the Bhagavad something and they sprinkled holy water over her. It probably wasn't holy water.

Of course, I loved her. She was my sister, after all. I just couldn't understand her. Why give up a house and a job to be a white witch in Glastonbury? She could have stayed married to Colin, and kept in touch with the children, but she gave it all up, for what? A tent, in a field with chanting, and 'vegan' food, and 'helping in the community'. Dear God.

Did she think she could stop the cancer? That she could make herself well with all this nonsense?

Well, she couldn't. The doctors couldn't fix her, and the hippies couldn't fix her, and me? I couldn't fix her either.

At least the chanting has stopped. I suppose we'll have to eat some of that unspeakable food in a minute. I'd prefer a ham sandwich and a cup of tea.

Oh no, they're all coming over to hug me. I'll drown in their weeping. I can't stand this.

'Elizabeth?' says the first one. 'Marcia's sister?' I nod and she clamps onto my arm, face crinkled into care and concern. 'D'you need a tissue, lovey?' she says and drags a crumpled wad from her pocket. She sees my hesitation. 'Go on, take one. They've not been used before, you know.' The others smile their crinkly smiles.

So I take one and blow my nose and dab my eyes and still she stares at me. 'You look so like her, you could be twins.'

'We were born less than a year apart,' I find myself saying. 'I'm the youngest. Marcia was always there.' But my heart hardens. 'At least, she was until she gave everything up to live in squalor in a tent with a bunch of old hippies. No offence.'

'None taken, lovey,' says the woman. 'I can see

you're suffering. But Marcia *wanted* to join us, to live a wholesome life in the bosom of nature. No-one forced her to make her home with us. You should be glad that she passed her last months, living at peace in our community. It was the end she chose.'

She's leading me towards a table set up in the orchard, next to the natural burial site. I've never eaten vegan food and I'm not about to start now. Out of the corner of my eye, I see Colin with the rest of the normal people: my almost grown-up niece and nephew, Hattie and Callum, Colin's mother, a couple of Marcia's friends – the ones who didn't give up on her when she gave up on them. I remove the wrinkly woman's hand from my arm. I know she means well, but enough is enough. I join the family. They are drinking mead. At least it's warm. And I have to admit, it tastes good.

'All right, Liz?' says Colin, and I nod.

'At least that part's over with. Just got the wake to survive now.'

'You know what,' he says, looking around at the orchard decorated with rushes, hops and early spring flowers. Faint sun warms our backs. 'Maybe this *was* the right thing to do. It's so peaceful here. I can see that it would suit Mar. She always hankered after a simpler life. A place where she felt at home.'

I'm shocked that Colin thinks this is an acceptable way to carry on. I look at Hattie and Callum. They are smiling and chatting away with some of the younger ones. Callum looks to his dad for approval then follows a young man with disgusting dreadlocks over to a tree stump, where they play on a bongo drum. Hattie wanders over to a small group of children who are weaving beads into each other's hair. I find my feet have moved a yard and my hand is reaching out towards her.

'No, Liz, let them go,' Colin says. 'They're trying to understand, too. They want to know who these people are who took in their sick mum and looked after her until she died.'

He stops then and I see something flash in his eyes. Anger, I think. 'We were wrong to shut her out, Liz. To shut all this out. I was wrong to listen to you. Because of you, my kids spent hardly any time with their mum at the end. I deserted her when she needed me most.' Tears spring to the corners of his eyes and roll down his cheeks. He doesn't wipe them away.

I don't know where to look. Because of me? The crinkly woman appears at my side again. I won't be able to bear it if she smiles at me again. But she doesn't. She passes tissues from her wad to Colin and strokes his arm while he sobs.

It's then that I notice that all the mourners have a member of the community with them. That they are talking quietly, laughing or crying. Someone has brought a chair for Colin's mother, and she seems to be drinking tea.

No-one has been left alone. Except me.

I can't accept what Colin says. He's a grown man and can make up his own mind. Anyway, he agreed with me that it was a ridiculous decision. I remember us discussing it with Marcia. I said she should stay for the children. She said they were fifteen and thirteen and could go with her if they wanted to, but they hardly needed her anyway. I said she needed palliative care. She said she could get all she needed from whole food and fresh air. It was a painful discussion and, in the end, Marcia did exactly what she liked, as per usual, and Colin stayed at home with the kids.

Crinkly Face comes back. 'My name's Alice Penfold,' she says. 'I'm a midwife at the local hospital.' I stare at her. I work at the hospital. 'Don't recognise me out of uniform? We're not all scroungers, you know, lovey. Strikes me you need to open your mind a bit. Might make you a bit less lonely. No offence.'

Offence taken. Cheeky old bat. Alice Penfold? Now I remember, part-time midwife. I altered her salary when she changed her hours. Of course, it's difficult for me to remember every face on the payroll.

'Oh, yes. Alice. I remember you now.'

'Another mug of mead, or would you prefer a cup of tea? And there are some lovely veggie pasties just coming out of the oven. They'll warm us all up. Come on, let's join the others.' She tugs at my arm again. She doesn't give up easily, does Alice.

I want to go along with her and just endure the rest of the day, but I can't stop myself from blurting out, 'What did you mean, it might make me less lonely?

I'm not lonely.'

But the hollowness of those words rings around the orchard like a church bell in an empty tower. I feel a sort of vertigo, where the grass seems to be slipping and sliding from under my feet. Alice leads me to a wicker chair but I can't speak. I try so hard to stop the tears, but they crash through my careful barriers and engulf me, until I'm sobbing and gulping for air. I know people are staring but I can't stop until it's all out. I keep my head down and make inroads into Alice's tissues. I've never been so embarrassed. She doesn't say anything and I'm grateful for that.

I do know what I'm like. I can be hard on people, but it's because I have such high standards. I'm not what you would call a cuddly person. Marcia was the nice one. She made the friends, and got the boyfriends. I just tagged along. She was my best friend. My only friend. And now I might have lost Colin and the kids, too, because of my stupid, rigid rules. The Liz Graham code of behaviour. And look where all my rules have got me.

'I'm sorry,' I say, once I can breathe again. I look up at Colin and the kids, standing there looking concerned. 'I'm sorry I was horrible to your mum about coming here. I can see it's a good place.' I snuffle in another breath and hold onto Hattie's hand. 'I just miss her so much, and I wanted someone to blame, even though I know it's no-one's fault.'

'D'you know we do weekend courses, Liz?' says Alice, into the silence that follows my apology.

'Young Callum has asked about learning to play the drums, and Hattie wants to learn about being a Doula - a natural midwife. Maybe there's something you would like to do? Marcia was learning to weave. Come into the barn and let me show you what she was doing.' She pulls me off the chair and we walk into a ramshackle barn, trailed by Colin and the kids.

There, in the corner, are three looms. Two have almost completed pieces of cloth on them. I pick the edge of one up and rub it between my fingers. It is warm with a scratchiness, hidden in the softness.

'All the colours are naturally dyed from fruits and plants we grow on the farm,' says Alice, and I marvel at the yellows, oranges and blues woven into stripes.

The third loom has only a short strip of completed cloth poking out at the bottom. The wools lie in a neat pile next to the machine.

'This is the one Marcia was working on before she became too ill to continue. It was going to be a throw for your sofa,' she says to Colin.

Nobody speaks. Dust dances in the fingers of weak sunlight. There is a stillness here, a watchfulness. Colin touches the cloth. He picks up the end and puts it next to his cheek. Can he feel her too? She's here. I feel her presence, smell her perfume. It's the scent of violets. Flowers she loved.

In the rafters, a grey collared-dove rustles its wings, and swoops up through a hole in the roof. I take it as a sign that Marcia has gone, too. Happy to leave us now.

Taking a breath of new spring air, I find a watery smile: for my family and for me, and for what might yet be.

'Yes, Alice, I think I'd like to learn to weave. I'd also like it if you would teach me.'

DEBS RICCIO

Consequences

This is the worst part. Actually, on a scale of one to ten, this is nine. Ten is when I have to bring them back.

The woman who answers the door on the second ring of the bell is, as always, beautifully dressed. A cream outfit, probably designer, I don't know; I'm not a dedicated follower of fashion, but Fran is. Her hair is smoothed back from her face and her skin is shining with health. She could be a model. And she knows it.

'Harry, Georgia, Daddy's here!' she announces into the immaculate hallway.

There's a gold clasp at the nape of her neck as she turns her head and, for a moment, the Twenty-Year-Old Me is tempted to lean over the terracotta step and discard it, freeing the heavy chestnut waves to fall around her shoulders the way they used to: should do.

I take in a deep breath, smile and rock back on my trainers for the wait. They never stampede to the door to greet me. They're not allowed to run in the house - something about damaging the weft of the pile on the carpets. She never used to worry about the runner in the hallway where we used to live. But that was before. Before the Mums and Tums, before the Pre-school Nursery, and before Max stepped in with his size elevens, and showed Frannie how much more she could have with him. And you can't argue with an estate agent; they've had training.

Half of me didn't even blame her at the time. We were struggling to keep up with the mortgage repayments on the house in Margate Road and, even though I was working all the hours I could, a carpenter's wage was never going to be enough to cover four mouths and a mortgage. That's what you get for having too much to drink one birthday, abandoning the rules of protection 'just this once' and then finding out it's produced not just one little mistake, but mistakes *twinned*.

We did this stupid little dance the day Fran did the test. I say *dance*, because it was like a psychological tango. The line on the indicator couldn't have been a deeper shade and, for a moment, we both avoided each other's eyes. I looked up first.

'It's positive,' I said needlessly.

'I'm pregnant.' She turned then. Her eyes had filled with tears and I wasn't sure if she was upset or pleased. Wasn't sure whether I was either, to be truthful.

'I don't know if I'm ready.' She frowned. 'I'm not even twenty yet. It's not on my radar. I don't think I can…'

I took her hands. 'We don't have to make a

decision yet. We don't have to do anything yet. Let's just play it by ear, see how we feel about it. See where our thoughts take us and decide another day. OK? We're in this together. We'll decide together and, if either one of us isn't happy, then that's when we have to make a choice.'

She didn't say anything.

'OK?' I tried. 'Nothing has gone wrong - nothing terrible has happened. It's just one of those things, that's all. Fate. Maybe it was meant to happen.'

'Fate,' she repeated. 'Do you think so? Do you think we were meant to have a baby before we're both twenty three? What will our parents say? What will I do about work? What will you do about work? What about the house? We've literally only just signed the mortgage papers. What if we can't manage - what if we can't afford to?'

I'd squeezed her hands. 'That's a lot of *'what ifs'*. Here's another - what if we just get rid of it? If we hadn't been so drunk and ignored the chance of pregnancy then we wouldn't be sitting here having this discussion. That baby would have been safe inside a condom and flushed down the loo by morning. Maybe we should think about it like that. Pretend we *did* do it the right way and this isn't happening?'

'You mean take a morning after pill.'

'I suppose.'

'And kill it.'

I'd winced then. I never imagined ever having a

conversation like this. Ever.

'I don't think you can look at it like that. It's not really *killing*, is it? You can't be more than two weeks, three tops. I think it's just a cluster of cells, right now - not even the size of a pinhead.'

'You know a lot about foetuses, all of a sudden.'

'I've read stuff, seen it on the telly, I guess.'

'Yes, well.'

'Let's forget it,' I tried. 'Let's just see how -'

'Forget it? How can I forget that there's something growing inside me - there's an alien creature, getting bigger and bigger inside my stomach, and the longer I try to forget about it, the bigger it's getting? How? Could you forget something like that, Matt? Could you?'

'It's not actually growing inside your stomach, Fran. It's your womb -'

'Oh, right - so now you're my bloody gynaecologist, are you? Brilliant. You have it then - go on - if you're so bloody informed - YOU have it!'

We didn't often not speak to one another but, that night, Fran had slept on the sofa and she didn't even say goodbye before she left for work the next morning. I felt like I'd done something wrong; it was all my fault. I was sure it couldn't have been. Two to tango, and all that. She could just as easily have grabbed a condom as me, couldn't she? Weren't we both to blame - if *blame* was the right word for this situation?

'Daa-adddyyy!'

Georgia squeals as she drops from the bottom stair. She half-heartedly checks her mother's expression, but continues regardless, launching her eager nine-year-old body at my frame; I catch her full force as she slams into my stomach.

'Where's your brother, darling?'

Fran flicks her eyes towards the bannister railings which curl around the stairwell and stop like a question mark at the landing. 'Isn't he ready yet? I thought Nanny Phoebe sorted your bags out this morning?'

'Harry's not coming,' Georgie says, matter-of-factly. 'He's up to level eight and he can't leave it. He says the drones will get him if he logs out.'

I start to laugh and that sets Georgie off. Harry and his computer games; he's so funny. I can just picture him up there, belly-down on the end of his bed, his list of 'cheats' lying beside him; pencil behind his ear, just like daddy; determined to sort the baddies out and not be distracted by real life. I suppose, to a nine-year-old, this *is* real life.

'Well, we can't have that, can we?' Fran takes a breath and smoothes down her dress. She doesn't have a stomach anymore; she has a personal trainer instead. 'Georgia, wait here with your father and I'll just go and -'

'It doesn't matter, Frannie.' I stop her. 'Let him enjoy his game. You can drop him off later, if you like, when he's ready. Georgie and me'll be okay, won't we, cherub?'

'*Cherub...* Daa-aaaad!' She swipes me with her backpack.

I notice it's a new one. Purple with silver stars. The pink phase seems to be waning now. I make a mental note. You have to be switched on when you're not around them all the time. I bought Harry a Manchester United strip a couple of birthdays ago and can still feel the blow of exclusion as I watched his face fall when he opened it.

'Man U?' Max had smirked. 'Oh dear, Matthew, somebody didn't keep their eye on the ball, did they?'

If I hadn't felt so utterly miserable about getting Harry the wrong team strip, I'd have swung for the arrogant, smarmy bastard. Oh, the punches I've withheld. You've no idea.

'No, darling, that can't happen.' Fran directs the reply to my question at our daughter. She's good at doing that. Maybe she has a personal... Personal trainer. You know what I mean.

'Mummy and Max have got things to do, haven't we? Remember? Max is getting his award this evening - remember we talked about this? We can't take Harry with us and we can't leave him here. He has to go with you - to Daddy's for the weekend. That's how it works. Every other weekend, you know the routine.'

Fran lifts her eyes from Georgie and gives me one of her unyielding, pleading smiles.

'I could always...' I begin breezily, waving a hand towards the stairs Georgie appeared down.

'Oh no.' Fran's eyebrows fly and her voice takes on another level.

I like that I can still have some effect on her.

'Yeeeesss! Daddy can stay here until you get back - that's a bri-illiant idea, Daddy - come on, come on.'

She drags me over the threshold and, momentarily, I am the closest I've been to Frannie since she pecked me on the cheek following our 'formal separation' at the courthouse. Georgie has already flung her backpack down in the hallway and is pulling me towards a coat stand.

'You have to use this, here, look - to wipe your shoes on, and you have to hang your jacket up over - oh, you haven't got one. Never mind. And through here - come on, Daddy, come on. I want you to see my roo-oom!'

Fran is frantic. 'Georgia. This isn't - Georgie! Listen to me, this is not a good idea - we can telephone Nanny Phoebe or get Granny Nichol round to babysit you, but Daddy cannot be here when Max gets back. He can't!'

Suddenly, there is quiet. Georgie stills, her head lifts, her bottom lip sticks out and her hand starts to hot up around mine as she turns towards her mother.

'Why can't he be here? He's my daddy. And it's Daddy's weekend.'

'Well... because Daddy isn't supposed - I mean, he shouldn't... Look... it's not Daddy's house, it's Max's and because he doesn't know that Daddy is here, then he might not be very happy about it and... Well...'

Again, she turns her eyes to mine and tilts her head imploringly. She gets a wink and a grin for her trouble. Her nostrils flare angrily in response.

'So, what's your room like then, swee'pea?' I goad more for Fran's sake than Georgie's. 'Is it all PINK?'

I poke her gently in the ribs. She squeals like a piglet and shoots off up the stairs, taking them two at a time the way she does back at mine. At the top of the stairs, she stops and yells, 'Come o-on!'

Fran's face is a picture. She's wide-eyed and open-mouthed and, for some reason, speech and the power to move eludes her. I don't know what *will* happen when Max gets home. All I know is that it's my weekend for the kids and I'm going to spend my time with them as planned. Or un-planned, as the case appears to be.

Oh, this carpet really *is* quite luxurious.

We stop at Harry's bedroom first. It's bigger than the living room at my place. And that's got a table and chairs at the back of it too. He's even got a double bed -I didn't have one of those until Fran and I moved in together. He does a double take as we approach, grins, and then his eyes flick straight back to the screen.

He's in exactly the position I imagined him to be. Flat out on his stomach. Head at the end of the bed, in front of the game. His cheats book is open, curled at the edges, and I slide it away as I sit down beside him. He rolls his weight over towards me and back again, like a wolf greeting an alpha male, and I smile back.

He really is doing very well with this game.

'Daaa-aaad, come on, let's go and see *my* room. Come o-on.'

Just as we're padding across the landing towards a door which has a purple star with 'Georgia' splashed across it in silver, I hear the front door open and low, mumbling sounds begin to creep up through from the hallway below.

'Daddy, you're not loo-ooking!'

Georgie is in the middle of showing me her enormous collection of stuffed toys. They are arranged over two shelves above her bed and appear to be in height and colour order. I am momentarily distracted from trying to make out what Fran is telling Max and move to take a closer look at her display.

'You *do* this, Gee?' I ask her.

She frowns.

'You colour code them and put them in height order?'

'Oh no, Nanny Phoebe does that. Mummy says it has to look neat and tidy. Max likes everything to be neat.'

'Nanny Phoebe does it?'

'She has to do it every day!' Georgie is delighted. 'She says I can mess them up as much as I like and she'll still do it - it's her job.'

'Is it? No, no, I suppose it is. Ah well …'

'Don't you like them, Daddy?'

'Yes, no, of course I do, I just think they look a

little... I don't know... regimented sitting up there like that, you know?'

'Reggie-dent-wha?'

'Regimented - like soldiers. Like rows in an army.'

Georgia looks worried so I poke her to make her giggle.

'But the most colourful army I've ever seen!'

'And the fluffiest!' she adds.

From downstairs, I can hear voices turning from low and measured into impatient and angry. Half of me feels bad for getting Fran into this impossible situation; the other half couldn't give a toss. Not after how they left me high and dry when she went with the twins.

'I'm afraid, Mr Berriman, there's not a great deal I can do for you,' the young solicitor had told me. 'The law will always side with the mother in cases like this and the fact you're not married does make bargaining that much more difficult. I'm sorry I can't say anything that will make you feel any better. Have you and your partner... Have you discussed mediation?'

'Mediation? What for? So she can tell me again she's met somebody else and that's it? He can afford to give her and my children everything they need and I can't. How do you suppose that would help?'

'We have to suggest mediation as a matter of course,' she smiled nicely.

'Right. And I suppose there's no point in asking how I'm supposed to afford to pay child maintenance on top of the mortgage is there?'

'Let me just see.' She leafed through the paperwork and sucked on a pen.

Irrationally, I hoped it would leak all over the file, preventing it from leaving her office.

'Mrs - I mean Miss - um... Your partner is not pressing for child maintenance. I believe her new partner isn't... er...'

'Short of a few bob. No, he's not. Well, that puts me in my place then, doesn't it? I suppose that means I've got no rights with my children either then, does it?'

'Your rights as father to your two children remain unaffected. There will be a legal agreement between the both of you and if you can't agree on contact arrangements then a contact order will be arranged through the court.'

'Right.' I bet Fran loved all this law and order crap.

'Really, Mr Berriman, I must say that this is one of the more straightforward cases I've dealt with in a long time. Your partner appears a very reasonable woman.'

'Oh, she is. That's why she's taken my children away from me, from their *home* and moved them in with a slimeball estate agent who reckons he's better than everybody else. You don't get more reasonable than that, do you?'

I had every right to be bitter and twisted. That's how I felt.

But, now? Lying on my little girl's bed, staring at the ordered line-up of multi-coloured soft toys and marvelling at how well their hues are matched with the next one, I feel a stab of pity. Not just for Georgie and Harry and the way they're being brought up by a man who isn't their father, but for Fran too, because this wasn't the Fran I knew back then.

I'm covered in little toys, balanced on my head, my shoulders and the length of both legs, a silver-grey elephant making its laboured way up my mountainside left arm when Georgie's bedroom door opens and Fran appears.

'We're off,' she says.

She's lost her vibrancy. Her eyes have taken on that same veneer of resignation that they did the time we did the pregnancy test; she's not good when she's out of control and I suppose that's what happened when I walked through the door this evening.

'OK then,' I say nonchalantly. 'Have fun.'

'Daddy's Mount Verucca, Mummy - look!' Georgie balances a white bear on my knee.

'Vesuvius,' I correct her.

'And when he erupts, all the animals will have to take cover over there in the forest.'

Fran's eyes nervously take in the makeshift forest we've built from her desk and chair and all manner of other childish accoutrements. Something else for Nanny Phoebe to get her teeth into come morning, no doubt.

'I'll see you both Sunday then,' Fran says. 'I've said goodbye to your brother. Now be good for Daddy, won't you?'

'We're always good for Daddy, aren't we, Daddy?'

Georgie clambers off the bed. She circles Fran with her arms and sighs happily. 'And Daddy's always good for us.'

I see Fran's eyes cloud over. 'And don't forget to set the alarm and lock both doors before you go, OK?'

Georgie and I nod in unison.

'Before we go back home with Daddy,' she says, and I need nothing more.

SAL PAGE

Patricia

Tricia's in the staff room. She's had her coffee in the mug with the pansies on and she's washing it up, with all the other mugs and plates she's found lying around. It's still a novelty being here, still gives her a thrill that someone has given her a chance after all this time. To spend all day, organising the beautiful objects in what had always been her favourite shop. It was her dream job.

Pat's wedged at one end of the sofa leaning on a tower of newspapers and eating instant noodles. Every now and again, she spots something on one of the piles around the room and wonders where it came from. A little yellow pot of artificial flowers – did she really buy that? The wicker magazine rack – empty. A pile of jackets and blouses on hangers - tags still attached. She ought to sort them through. See which fit and which don't.

'You always line everything up so neatly, Tricia.' Kate looks impressed.

Marianne nudges Kate as they sit, elbow-to-elbow, with their mugs of tea. 'Bet her kitchen cupboards are immaculate.'

Tricia smiles and continues to stack the teaspoons in the cutlery drawer. She picks up a cloth and a bottle of antibacterial spray and moves along the work surface, wiping at the tea and coffee rings.

Kate stands up. 'You don't have to do that, love.'

'I don't mind. I enjoy it.'

'Come round at the weekend and do mine, if you like. The place is a right tip.' Marianne laughs as she puts her mug in the sink. She and Kate head back to work.

Tricia dries the last few mugs. Placing them in the cupboard, she makes sure all the handles are angled in the same direction.

A box of sewing fabrics for the quilt Pat keeps meaning to start. And she will start it. One day. Once she can make some space. And where did she last see her sewing box? The dining room? Beyond the doorway, she can just see through. No, that's all Graham's stuff through there. His collections in plastic boxes. She told him those cups and saucers would be worth something one day. And the ugly Toby jugs. There were three or four ukuleles, and a pile of music, somewhere in there too. Not that he ever played them. Said he'd get back to it once Pat got things a bit tidier in the house.

In a quiet moment towards the end of the afternoon, Kate comes to Tricia's counter with some boxes of stock.

'These are yours I think, love.'

'Thanks, I'll put them away now.'

'Your displays look great.'

Tricia grins at her and pulls one of the boxes open.

Kate peers into the box. 'I love all this storage stuff. Perfect department for you, I reckon.'

Kate leaves her as she unwraps jewelled trinket boxes of varying sizes and colours and arranges them artistically on a glass shelf. Yes, she is rather good at this.

A proper tidy, that's all the house needs. Pat is sure there's space for everything. Somehow, it had all ended up in the wrong room. She gets up from the sofa and picks at a pile of books on the floor. One of the titles catches her eye. This was her mother's. There was a whole set in this series once. Weren't they all in the wooden bookcase with the glass front? She hasn't seen that bookcase in years. She sits back down and opens the book.

Tricia serves her last customers, a couple buying faux leather shoeboxes with little see-through windows.

'We're moving in together next weekend.'

'Our first real home. We want to be organised.'

'A place for everything and -'

' - everything in its place!'

They look at each other and laugh. Tricia laughs along with them. She looks at the man, all blond floppy fringe and white teeth. This young woman will find out soon enough that he may finish her sentences but he won't pick his clothes up off the floor.

'There you are. All packed up for you. Thank you.'

Tricia watches them walk away, arm-in-arm, with a bagful of boxes each. She liked those shoeboxes. Maybe she could use her staff discount to get some for her shoes.

On the bus, she stares at herself in the window. Raindrop reflections scatter across her face, lit by flickering red and orange lights from passing traffic. That's me, she thinks. That's Tricia, the lady who's obsessively neat and organised. She smiles at herself but her stomach is churning. After stopping at the garage to pick up some supplies, she hurries along the road and up the driveway. As she pushes her front door, something falls behind it and she has to put her shopping down and give the door a good shove to get it to open enough to squeeze through.

She steps over the bulging boxes – mostly newspapers, with two framed prints of Venice and a pale blue teddy bear balanced on top - and shuffles sideways towards the foot of the stairs. She stubs her toe, yet again, on one of the bicycles and catches her reflection in the tiny piece of hallway mirror that's still visible between all the stuff.

Tricia glares at herself and Pat glares back. That's me. That's Pat, the woman who can't throw anything away. The woman who's had two bicycles, languishing in her hallway for years. Graham said they'd go on bike rides to country pubs, or beside the river once the house was sorted, but instead he left to live in a neat little house with a neat little woman who puts out her rubbish and recycling every week without fail. A woman who hoovers every day and never buys anything she doesn't need.

As she edges her way up the stairs, placing her feet carefully on the few inches of spare space on each step, a book falls from higher up and slaps Pat on the head. At least it was only a paperback this time.

She clambers over some tins of paint and a box with a foot spa in it, crab-walks into the bedroom and sits on her quarter-of-bed, among clothes, shoes and bags that slither towards her, collecting at her back. She pulls out a suede boot. Tricia could wear these for work. Where's the other one? Pat looks round helplessly for a few seconds then gives up and chucks it on top of a pile over the other side of the room.

She leans forward and switches on the television. It peeps out from among the piles, only the dusty screen visible. She opens her carrier bag. She takes out a couple of magazines and a newspaper then unwraps the tiny plastic straw and stabs into the juice carton. She pulls the egg and cress sandwich from its triangular box, bites a corner and wedges the box with the other sandwich-half behind the alarm clock on top of a slippery pile of magazines and unopened mail.

Pat stares at the TV. A man is demonstrating a new kind of food mixer. It looks really useful. She can make that chocolate mousse once she can get further into her kitchen than a few feet. She finishes the sandwich then curls up on the edge of her bed, pulls a blanket and her mum's old fox fur coat over her and looks out across the room.

She'll sort things out tomorrow. One bag for the rubbish. One bag for the charity shop. That's what her neighbour suggests, just to get started. Well-meaning advice, Pat knows, but starting is difficult. Where had she seen that roll of bin bags?

Pat sighs. She's so tired. Every shoe and coat they ever wore, every magazine or book they ever read or didn't read, each ornament or vase picked up in a charity shop. Bags of unopened shopping, brief, exciting purchases once, the contents now a mystery. An ironing board, jutting out from the heaps of stuff. Even from here she can see two irons, their cables tangled together. On top of the ironing board is a pile of free newspapers, a brand new garden hose, a six-pack of Y-fronts – '3 for 2' - and a toy boat still in the box. She bought the boat for her nephew's ninth birthday. How old is he now?

It's Pat's day off tomorrow. She'll go out. Have lunch in a café and a look round the shops. Perhaps Tricia can stop her from buying anything.

NICOLA TERVIT

Onions

That night, I shoplifted some onions. Crammed into my pocket, wrinkled orbs of pointlessness, the thrill driving me out of the supermarket. I was invincible, untouchable, sailing past the security guard.

The cold air of October at 11.00pm bit into me and I enjoyed feeling something, anything. Part of me wished for rain or snow, something that would awaken my senses and make me remember that I was still in my body.

A bus pulled up at the stop and I got onto it without looking at the destination. I counted out five dull silver coins into the bus driver's hand and he printed me a ticket for as far as it would get me.

My nose was still bleeding as we pulled out of Newcastle. A steady stream of scarlet, tracing down my face. At this time of night, there were no helpful old dears to fuss over me and offer me carefully laundered handkerchiefs to mop it up. A man sat opposite, looking oddly at me. He could probably smell the onions, sweating in my pocket from the bus's heater. He was about my age, just a couple of years away from thirty. The arms of his coat weren't quite long enough for him, leaving his wrists exposed and vulnerable.

'Hi,' I said.

'Drink?' He held out a bottle of vodka to me, mostly empty.

I moved beside him and gulped down the alcohol, burning into my empty stomach. The sting reminded me that it had been days since I had eaten anything. I thought of my onions. I hadn't even considered them as edible.

'The thing about onions,' I told him without being asked, 'is that they have layers. Like people.'

'Funny, I think the thing about onions is that they make me cry.'

'That too.'

Another gulp of vodka. The challenge was not letting it make me retch, keeping it inside of me, a liquid secret.

He didn't talk after that and I liked that about him. I liked that he was comfortable in silence, didn't need to make small talk about the weather, or how dark it was, or how work had been. Work, a distant memory to me now. With time, I had forgotten how to hold these conversations, the polite back-and-forth. They seemed so pointless now.

When he got off the bus, he didn't say goodbye or take his bottle away from me. I realised this was because I had emptied it. I hadn't even thanked him for this gift, of the alcohol and of his time, taking the edge off for just a few minutes.

I slipped my hand into my pocket and pulled out the onions. There were four, different shapes and sizes. My onions. They had become friends to me, pets. I considered naming them. I turned them over in my hands, noting with disinterest that my knuckles were covered in blood from my nosebleed.

'This is your stop, love,' the bus driver called.

I was the only person left on the bus so he must have been talking to me. I climbed out, not sure where I was.

There was a convenience store on the corner, still open. I wandered in, browsing for a few minutes, running my hands over the Mars bars and cereal boxes, hesitating over a bottle of Lucozade before I put it back. The woman behind the counter looked exhausted, propping herself up on her elbow. I made my way over to her and took her in for a minute, another human being, considering her.

'I killed a man.'

Her face blanched, taking me in, my unbrushed hair and wild eyes. No bag, no coat. The blood covering my jumper and knuckles.

'Why don't you sit down?'

I sat down.

She picked up the phone and spoke in hushed tones, too quiet for me to hear. I caught one word, 'hurry', and they did.

I rode in the back of the police car. They took my

onions off me before my interview and I never got them back.

In the end, the policeman who interviewed me was kind, after he had brought my record up.

'You didn't really kill a man.'

I turned away from the pity in his eyes and shook my head. He pressed leaflets into my hand and insisted on driving me home.

He dropped me off at my flat and I walked inside. It was after midnight.

'Happy anniversary,' I whispered to the photograph on the mantelpiece.

ISABEL COSTELLO
Half of Everything

Sandy was going to make landfall within twenty-four hours, they said. I spent the afternoon bringing stuff in from the veranda: boots, planters, patio furniture that wasn't too heavy to lift. It would all have to go soon enough. As my neighbours were doing the same, we joked that our precautions were probably unnecessary, raising our voices against the wind. We all had torch batteries in abundance. The grocery stores had a run on canned soup. There was the kind of happy, cosy atmosphere I'd always liked about our little dead-end street, cut in half by the B and Q lines. The kids opposite had already decorated for Halloween, three days away. The exact same time last year, a hurricane was predicted to batter New York City but blew out to sea once it reached the Carolinas.

Since then, I'd had my own personal hurricane. It was too soon to say if I'd survived.

As it started to get dark, everyone went inside, wishing each other good luck and 'See you on the other side.' When friends invited me to sit with them, I lied, saying Amy was due home. One by one, bay windows lit up in our big wooden houses which were tightly packed together. Nobody used the narrow shared driveways in between, except in severe weather, when they were good to shelter cars from the hundred-year-old trees the neighbourhood was known for. There was one right outside our house.

You never know.

I went along with these things because it was expected of me and, when I'd finished my pre-emptive salvage operation, I stood in the middle of the road, twice as wide without the cars, and took a good look at 42 Vandemar Court, the family home that no longer was. We'd have had to downsize eventually, with Amy leaving for college next year, the boys long gone.

Twenty-five years we lived here - such a neat, round number. A quarter century. Half my life. The age of our eldest son.

The length of a marriage.

Soon, some other family would greet my neighbours, bake banana bread for new mothers and sit on the stoop, handing out candy on Halloween. The veranda looked oddly tidy now and the realtor's FOR SALE board was already swinging out on its hinges. Part of me wanted to lie down right there in the street and take my chances. Bring it on, Sandy, God, whoever the fuck's in charge! Anything else you'd like to throw at me?

I delivered a sharp kick to the sign as I went back inside, thinking about the listing: *Brooklyn Victorian in need of light refreshment*, my ass. I'd settle for a stiff drink. Maybe it'd ease the pain in my toe – that's right, I can't even inflict damage on a flimsy wooden post without it hurting me more. Good thing the younger me wasn't here to judge me, the girl who ignored Rick's protests and insisted on carrying boxes in from the U-Haul, balancing them on her pregnant belly. Lucky we didn't have much back then. It was only when the truck was empty, I let him carry me over the threshold, teasing him for being so corny.

I went inside and uncorked a bottle of red, which was getting to be something of a habit. The way I looked at it was, if I was going to do the whole lonely, abandoned, middle-aged woman thing, I may as well go the whole hog. Maybe I'd get a cat when the house sold and I had to move to an apartment in a bad neighbourhood where nobody knew me. There's no way I could stay here on my share of the spoils and a lousy teacher's salary.

Skipping dinner, I settled in for an evening on the couch, grading a pile of papers on Newton's Laws. The TV channels were full of *Countdown to Sandy* coverage and something about my situation really made me feel for the people being told to leave their homes, some only a couple miles away in Brighton Beach. We'd be all right here where most things - electric, cable, etc - were under the surface. The house itself had weathered all kinds of storms: when Amy was accused of bullying in middle school; when Danny cut his face open on the subway railings;

Joel getting that girl pregnant. And, of course, there was the time Rick was sued by a client who wasn't happy with his teeth. The only one who'd never been the lead player in any drama was me, and I'd never even noticed.

Time passed. It does that. I was halfway down the bottle of wine when I thought I heard the doorbell, and dismissed it. It sounded again, and this time it was insistent, unmistakable. The only reason I hauled myself off the couch was in case it was Amy, who was forever losing her keys. I'd told her to stay put at Joshua's but, as a rule, Amy did as Amy pleased.

'What are *you* doing here?'

Rick stood on the veranda, shivering and stamping his feet. I hadn't laid eyes on him since he made good on his New Year's resolution to leave me and, because the kids were grown, we had no need to talk. The divorce papers, including the instruction to sell the house, had come through his attorney. Pretty shabby.

'Hi, Jessica,' he said, without looking at me. He sounded like a nervous acquaintance wanting to ask a favour. 'I was about to drive back to Westchester and I thought maybe Amy would feel safer there ...'

Amy had taken our break-up the way she took most things – as an excuse to act out. I wasn't totally sure how she felt – although she'd certainly shown me no mercy, she'd declared her father a forbidden subject, right down to the mention of his name.

I crossed my arms. 'I doubt that very much. She's at her boyfriend's. Why would you come all the way over here without calling?'

Before Rick could reply, a gust of wind unbalanced him, making him look over both shoulders, like there was someone behind who meant him harm. He looked older, thinner in the face, greyer around the temples.

'Listen, could I possibly come in for a moment? The traffic's going to be hell and I could really use a cup of coffee before I get going.'

A big ask, but it was so clear he expected me to say no that I couldn't give him the satisfaction.

'Help yourself,' I said, turning my back, glad to get back into the warm house.

I could only imagine the look on my face when, five minutes later, Rick wandered into the living room, holding an empty wineglass which he proceeded to fill with Zinfandel before sinking into what had always been his chair.

'Sorry, is this OK? I saw you had some open,' he said, raising his glass to me out of habit then hurriedly placing it on the coffee table.

Nothing to celebrate here.

'The place looks different,' he continued. 'I can't work out what you changed.'

'I got rid of a lot of stuff. You have to, when you sell a house you've lived in so long. Clutter, according to the realtor.'

'But what about the kids' photos, the ones on the fridge door?'

Prints from ten or fifteen years ago, pre-digital.

Stained and dog-eared, some of them the only copy. All gone, nothing left but fingerprints. You can always rely on stainless steel for that.

'Of course, I kept the kids' photos. Jesus, what do you take me for?'

'It seems huge with so little furniture,' he said, looking through to the dining room. 'It reminds me ...' His mouth contorted. 'Do you remember?'

He wasn't thinking of the boxes and the U-Haul truck. He was thinking how we laid the mattress down in front of the fireplace because we couldn't wait to bring it upstairs.

What gives you the right? I wanted to say, but I stayed silent, not knowing what sound might escape me: a deranged Halloween scream. A mournful prairie dog howl. By tilting my head, I made my hair hide my face.

'So, where's Marcia?' I said.

'*Maria.*'

'OK then, where's Maria?'

'She's visiting her mother in Escondido.'

'You know what? You never told me what she looks like,' I said, relishing his discomfort. There hadn't been a lot of talking before, and there wasn't any after. 'Is she beautiful?'

Rick was deliberating, as if he didn't know the answer. 'Don't do this, Jessica.'

'I'm just asking a simple question.'

'I take no pleasure -' said Rick.

'You take no pleasure?' I laughed. 'That's classic.

You take *no pleasure* in leaving me for a thirty-five-year-old? Isn't that precisely what you're doing?'

His eyes shone weirdly in the reflection from the TV. We were both distracted by a map of the eastern seaboard on the screen, complete with sweeping arrows and alarming wind speed predictions. It zoomed in first on New York City and then Brooklyn, with talk of power outages and flooding.

'Holy crap, I'm actually starting to believe this thing's coming our way.'

'The timing is terrible,' said Rick. 'I'm booked solid all day tomorrow.'

He actually thought anyone would be worrying about orthodontics! That was him all over, that refusal to acknowledge what was going on. I almost wanted the house to be blown to pieces to teach him a lesson.

Then I remembered; he didn't live here anymore.

'Will you listen to what they're saying already? *Stay home until it's over*.' A horrible thought occurred to me. 'You should really hit the road.'

When he made no sign of moving, I swept up my papers to leave the room. 'Let yourself out,' I said, 'I have work to do.'

Later, I could still hear the TV in the living room and went to turn it off. I nearly freaked out when I saw Rick, slumped in his armchair, fast asleep. I went over and put my hand on his shoulder, about to wake him, when I spotted he'd polished off the Zinfandel. Not good. I went to bed, spooked by the absence of the subway rumbling and vibrating now the system had been shut down.

A lot of things you don't think of as comforting, until they're not there.

The day Sandy struck, I stayed upstairs as long as I could, hunger devouring me until I simply had to eat something. It was darker than normal for the time of day. From my bedroom window, I could see Rick had a new car – the only one still braving it by the kerb in our deserted street. After all the years he dreamed of owning a Miata when we were young, now he was single, he'd gone for the most boring, unadventurous sedan imaginable, and I kind of resented that. For God's sake, one of us was supposed to be having a good time out of all this.

'So now you're here for the duration?' I said as I came down the stairs, catching the end of a bulletin about all the bridges being closed.

Still in his chair, Rick looked crumpled and exhausted. I guessed he hadn't moved from the living room, except to take a piss and make coffee. The sheer fact of his presence made me so antsy, I could hardly bear it.

'I don't appreciate that you've put me in this position. Now I can't even ask you to leave.'

The official message was clear enough: *Do not venture outside for any reason.*

Sandy had made landfall and Atlantic City was being destroyed by enormous waves. I could hardly stand to watch the news anchors in rain gear, being battered by gales and drenched with spray, their voices blown away in the inch between mouth and microphone. They couldn't hide it; they were terrified.

As I made myself a grilled cheese sandwich, I could feel in the bones of the house that the storm was moving in. Everything that had ever rattled, creaked or groaned was doing it now. The sound of the wind was high-pitched, hysterical. As rain lashed the side of the house, I realised I'd forgotten to tape up the basement windows that always leaked. I went back to the living room and glared at Rick.

'If all this is about the divorce papers, you should know that I signed them last week. As a matter of fact, I hand delivered them to your attorney's office on Friday.'

I'd sat in traffic for over an hour to save $8.75 in registered mail charges.

'It's not that,' he said. 'I told you, I wanted to bring Amy to Westchester.'

'I've just been speaking with Amy. She told you she was staying in Brooklyn before you even left work.'

Rick sagged. He opened his hands in a gesture that was half defeat, half relief.

'What is it you want from me exactly?' I asked. 'I signed your goddamn papers, the house is on the market, I'm not standing in the way of you and Maria. It's all going your way, Rick. You should be happy.'

'I know you signed the papers,' he said. 'And you're right - Amy refused to come with me. She's been giving me a really hard time. She told me again yesterday how sad you are. I'm here because it doesn't feel right to leave it this way.'

'Amy said that? Wow.' That threw me so much I didn't even deny the rest. Then suddenly it came to me. 'Did Maria leave you? Is that why she's in Escondido?'

Rick sighed. 'I don't know where she is, Jessica. We broke up months ago. This was never about Maria - I was looking for an easy way out. I'm not proud of that.'

'Wow,' I said again. *Easy way out*.

'You know, some of what's making this so hard would have happened anyway,' he said softly. 'The kids leaving home, us getting older. Did you really think we'd stay in this big house, rattling around for the rest of our lives?'

'I'm going outside,' I said, the weight of the front door almost pulling my arm off. Every leaf and branch of the old trees, every blade of grass was in violent motion; forgotten objects from the yards made it the entire length of the street without touching down. The rain pelted my face as I gripped the railings of the veranda just to stay in one place. The big tree was still standing – for now.

After a while, I sensed Rick was out there with me.

'I don't get why it matters so much on top of everything else, but it kills me to leave this place,' I said. 'To leave this way.'

'I know,' he said. 'I never thought it would be like

this for us. I'm sorry.'

If only we'd noticed when we stopped talking. Where once we were like magnets locked together, we'd turned to face in other directions. From then on, everything pushed us further apart.

But I'd figure out a way of dealing with it - I had to. Maybe, one day, Rick and I would be the kind of people who could find it in themselves to sit together at their children's weddings and be civil about it.

'I'm selling the practice,' he said. 'I can't do it another day. I'm going to move back to Colorado, try and work out what I want. You'll get half of everything, after Amy's college fees.'

I turned to look at him.

'Half of everything,' he said again. 'You always were half of everything.'

He touched my face, and I covered his hand with mine.

'There'll be other Marias,' I said.

'That's what I'm afraid of.'

We both jumped back, shielding our heads as the FOR SALE sign rose up out of the ground and hurtled toward us, before changing course and soaring up over the rooftops, out of sight.

AMANDA BLOCK

Unsettled

The cat stretches itself out on top of the stove, its claws unsheathed, its body lengthening like a concertina.

'Get down!'

The broom narrowly misses the creature's ears, which flatten against its head in irritation.

'Shoo,' says the broom's owner, now prodding at the cat with the bristly end. 'It's hot as Hell when it gets going, as you're well aware.'

Taking its time, the animal rolls off the warming stove, landing on its paws with a soft thump, and then leaps past the sink onto the windowsill. She wishes it wouldn't sit up there either. All but its yellow gaze seeps into the silhouette of branches knocking against the other side of the glass in the wind - *tap tap tap* - as though the forest is trying to get in.

She turns her back on it, returning to her bowl, gathering up the sticky dough between her fingers, throws it roughly upon the flour-strewn tabletop. She begins to flatten it out, her skinny forearms growing pink beneath the liver spots, her breath coming in short puffs with every thrust of the rolling pin. The cat whines softly.

'Don't start,' she pants. 'I'm doing it, and that's that.'

She can't remember when she started it all, or why. Ingredients have always been hard to come by this deep, and even harder for her. She used to haggle with the few who still trusted her, the ones who had known her from the beginning: a bag of flour for a clump of stomach-settling roots; two pots of ginger for advice on a tickly cough. Now, she mostly relies on her store cupboard, no longer daring to venture far from the house - not since the children began to disappear.

Choosing a knife with a long, wide blade, she scores a series of straight grooves into the dough until it parts into flat squares. Carefully, she peels them from the table and lays them onto a tray, before glazing them with a layer of egg white.

The flames are skittish at the back of the stove, but part obediently as she pushes the tray inside. The cat hops onto the table, tiptoeing hopefully towards the warmth, and then dashes away at the clunk of the stove door closing, leaving behind it a trail of floury footprints.

Tap tap, go the branches at the window, *tap tap tap*.

She needs to cut them back, trim all of the trees that are creeping up on her house. In the early days, the young men used to help her, grumbling all the while about the decision to move so far in. It had been wise at the time: everyone had been running from something, everyone wanted to lose themselves between the branches. It wasn't until they had built up the little settlement that they realised they weren't the only ones hiding in the forest.

'Doesn't need long,' she tells the cat. 'I mustn't fall asleep.'

It ignores her, continuing to lick at its dusty paws, its tail ticking from side to side. Only when it seems completely satisfied its feet are flour-free, does it look up at her, its face splitting into a yawn that displays long white teeth.

When the first child disappeared, they said the boy must have lost his way. But then a girl vanished, and another two boys, so their minds turned to wolves. The men went out, scoured the forest, and found a sickly old creature that they nailed to the settlement's gate. She remembers how it looked, strung up for all to see: mangy, underfed, clearly an old pack member left to die, not a child-killer caught on the hunt. Nevertheless, the night after the wolf was brought in, they all came together to celebrate, singing and dancing to the old songs and drinking mead around a great fire in the square. Three days later, another child was gone.

Tap tap tap.

It had to be wolves, they had told one another. So they hunted and hunted, but aside from that decrepit beast, no wolves were found. Nor was anything of the missing children: no tracks, no clothes, no blood, no bones. The forest had swallowed them whole.

Outside, the trees' skeletal limbs sway back and

forth beyond the glass, as though checking she is still paying attention. She watches them for a while, hypnotised by the movement, and then gives a yelp of surprise as something dark darts past the window.

'It's not them,' she says, clutching at her chest, 'not this close.'

Nevertheless, she longs to draw the curtains, shut out the possibility of seeing them. But she won't cower in the dark, so she lowers her gaze and begins to wipe the flour from the tabletop.

In the absence of wolves, a witch was found. A poor, mad girl with a squint and a twitch whose parents had perished in the settlement's first winter. She was dragged before the elders, questioned, tortured, and then pushed into the brook for the final test. She passed, but drowned anyway.

'Curse them!'

The children continued to vanish, more and more, and now she cannot recall most of their faces: she thinks there was a freckly girl, twin brothers, a boy who was only just walking, but she isn't sure. It is only the little girl with the two plaits who she remembers – who she wishes she could forget.

Long ago, she warned the elders it wasn't right: folk weren't supposed to live this deep. But they had made their plans, were already packed, and she could only follow. She told herself she would look after them, be their wise woman – but really, she had nowhere else to go. Perhaps it was because they built her little house on the edge, its windows looking out from the settlement and into the darkness that she saw, she sees: there are worse things in the forest than wolves and witches.

Tap tap. Tap. Tap tap tap.

As she pulls the tray from the stove, a sweet, spicy scent overwhelms her. She's almost tempted to go outside, inhale the damp, dark terror of the trees, just so she can return and wrap herself once more in this other smell, the forest's opposite: warm and comforting and good.

'That's why I have to keep making them,' she informs the cat, 'for the ones that are left. So they have something.'

She doesn't go outside anymore, not if she can help it. For she has seen them, the worst in the forest, and knows now why folk weren't meant to live this deep. Something ungodly is breeding here. The sunlight cannot reach the spaces between all the overlapping branches and so, down, down, down, shadows cross shadows cross shadows. Until, on the forest floor, near where they so foolishly settled, shadows are no longer shackled and lifeless.

They have never taken an adult, but she is still afraid; for the children, the settlement and – she won't even admit it to the cat – for herself too. Because shadows can't be caught and punished, nailed to a gate or drowned in a brook. Not like wolves. Not like witches.

She forces herself to keep busy: cutting at the cooling dough, painting onto it, sticking it together.

Only, the whistling of the wind and the creaking of the trees outside is growing louder and louder, her heart is ticking faster and faster, and then, suddenly -

TAP TAP TAP

- two hands are reaching through the branches, rattling at her window.

With a cry of alarm, she stumbles backwards.

'No,' she moans, shutting her eyes, pressing her palms against her ears.

But with sight and sound removed, she is back there at once; in the dark and quiet of a few months' past, when her firewood ran low and, since the men had stopped bringing her any, she ventured out. Clutching a sack in one hand, drawing her shawls tightly around her with the other, she began to trudge further from the settlement and deeper into the forest.

At first, she collected twigs from the ground, sweating from the effort, trembling from the cold, and from the fact that - out of the corner of her eye - she could see movement. Then she turned her attention on the thick, tall bodies of the trees.

'I'm not afraid.'

Taking out her knife, she began to saw at the lowest branches, twisting at the last green tendons until they tore. Then she dared herself to look up, to face them, and that was when she saw her: standing a little way away, in silhouette against the feeble forest light, the little girl with two plaits was watching.

'You!' She staggered forward. 'No – wait! Come back!'

The sack and the knife dropped from her hands as she hobbled after the child. The branches pulled away one of her shawls, slapped at her hands and face, tried to stop her, but on she went, her mind running as fast as her feet: *she's alive and how can this be and are there any others and she disappeared months ago and why is she running and what does this mean for me?*

She didn't see the upturned root. As her thin body smacked against the ground, she felt her bones knock against one another. Blood filled her mouth. 'I'll take you home!'

Struggling to get up, she saw the girl again, peeping out at her from behind a tree, still cast in darkness from the vast canopy above.

'Come on,' she told the child, 'I'll get the stove on, make you something good to –'

Her words became a whimper. She fell back onto her knees.

The girl had skipped into a tiny clearing, where the dim light from far above had managed to reach the forest floor. There, the darkness should have slipped off, been snagged on the branches, just like the lost shawl. But it remained. The figure was an empty space, a void of light, and as it turned round and round in the bright clearing like a dancer, the old woman saw: this was no child.

Before, when she had only caught glimpses of the shadows, she had imagined them to be sharp-edged, spindly creatures, like the branches from which they were birthed. Now she had seen one clearly, now she was stumbling away as fast as she could, her thoughts echoed with the terrible truth the others would never believe: the shadows were the dark images of those they had taken.

TAP TAP TAP.

Something brushes at her legs and she shrieks, trying to kick it away. But it is just the cat. The hands at the window are gone, and only the branches are beating against the glass now.

Turning its reproachful gaze from her to the door, the cat hisses. Outside, she can hear children's voices. With a last look at her handiwork, she hobbles over, pulls at the latch, and finds two of them, pink and real, standing on her doorstep.

'We saw you at the window,' says the girl, looking at her shoes, 'We tried to knock.'

'We're not supposed to be out,' mumbles the boy. He is hovering behind his sister, gazing at the warm room beyond.

'Well, you're here now,' says the witch, standing aside to let them in.

The cat yowls in protest as they come tumbling through the doorway. The branches too, having been whipped up by the wind, are clattering and crashing against the walls as hard as ever, as though trying to shake the place from its foundations.

The children, two of the last few in the forest, notice none of this. They have sat themselves down, pulled their chairs close, rested their elbows on the table, and only have eyes for the gingerbread house.

AMANDA SAINT
Am I Too Late?

As the plane circles Heathrow and Sinead O'Connor's voice pours into Hannah's ears through her iPod, she re-writes the lyrics in her head. *It's been two years, one month and nineteen days, since I went away.* She'd thought she'd never want to come back but now, as the rising sun turns the sky a dirty pink and the plane begins its final descent, the sparkly lights below slowly turn into cars zooming around and houses filled with people, and a swell of longing brings unexpected tears to her eyes. What will it be like to be here again?

Nobody knows she is coming. There is no-one waiting at arrivals to welcome her back after so long. The plane has landed at the new Terminal 5. It's very shiny. That won't last. She heads for the bus that will take her one step nearer to home but, at the last moment, changes direction and gets on a tube train instead. The Piccadilly line. Perhaps she'll get off in the West End, hide in the crowds for a few days while she gets used to being in England again.

The rocking of the train lulls her into a doze.

'Excuse me. Do you know the best way to get to Waterloo?' An American voice.

Hannah opens her eyes. Blinks twice. 'Um, no. Sorry.'

A tube map is thrust in her face. 'Where is it on here?'

Hannah wants to push the map back in the man's big, looming face but she sits up and takes it from him. She doesn't know London well. Where is Waterloo? Near the river? She finds it, points it out.

'Change here, Green Park, then get the Jubilee line to Waterloo.'

The man thanks her and turns back to his wife, shows her the way, then they both look back at Hannah and smile. She doesn't smile back but closes her eyes again and tucks her backpack more tightly against the seat with her legs. Please don't start talking to me.

'Apologies, ladies and gents, this train is being held here due to a signal failure at Acton Town. As soon as I have an update I'll let you know.'

The announcement wakes Hannah and she looks out of the train window. Northfields. She's never heard of it. The doors re-open and the fresh air and birdsong that enter the carriage bring her to her feet. When she alights onto the platform, the sun is warm and there are flowers everywhere. She likes the feel of it. She'll find somewhere to stay while she decides what to do.

At the top of the stairs, there's a man in a London Underground uniform with a wet look perm. She hasn't seen one of those in a very long time.

'Hi,' she says as she approaches him, 'Is there a backpackers' or a cheap B&B anywhere near here?'

His eyebrows raise as he takes in her grey hair, her wrinkled skin. But he smiles and takes her to the map on the wall. Shows her the way to a YMCA.

'It's quite a long walk. You should have stayed on to the next stop.'

'Thanks. I'll be fine.' Hannah smiles and walks out into the street.

There's a flower stall to her left, the cheery colours glowing extra bright in the sunshine. People are smiling at strangers. The sun always does that to people in England.

She turns right, hefting her backpack into a more comfortable position as she heads off down the road. A stench of boiled oil and old chicken bones wafts across the street from a ropey-looking takeaway shop. Perhaps it's not going to be as nice as she'd expected. Once she gets further down the road though, pleasant cafes and restaurants sit side-by-side with expensive fishmongers and gift shops whose windows are filled with Cath Kidston-style trinkets. The road widens and the green of the park she has been told to walk through spills out onto the pavement. Hannah smiles at the sight of a very proper English park after so long looking at dusty roads and palm trees.

As she strolls along, relishing the soft yet tangy smell of newly mown grass, commuters and school runs hurry past her. Some of them tut at how slow she is going, how much space she takes up on the path.

This makes her smile too. Londoners, both old and new, are well known for their impatience. The pace she has got used to in her time away really is not suitable for London on a weekday morning so Hannah veers onto the grass. She sits down by a large tree stump, just outside the play park. Empty now as harassed mothers herd older children to school, before bringing younger ones here to run and scream, burn off steam. While they sit, stunned, on benches. No one told them it would be like this.

'Is that lady dead, Mummy?'

'Shush, no. Come away. She's sleeping.'

'Why is she sleeping there?'

Hannah doesn't hear the reply as the voices that woke her move away. Her eyes open and all she can see is blue sky. All she can feel is grass beneath her back and a tightness in her face from too much sun. London. She got off the plane then came to London. Slowly, she is getting nearer to home. When she'd left, her anger had driven her as far away as she could get – New Zealand. She's been slowly getting closer with every move since: Australia, Malaysia, Thailand, India, Turkey. Now she's very nearly all the way home.

After stretching her arms above her head and then down to her toes, Hannah reaches into a side pocket of her backpack and retrieves a pot of moisturiser. She rubs it into her sun-scorched face then leans back against the tree stump. Judging by the position of the sun, she must have been sleeping for hours. It's busier now – people playing ball and lying in the sun, small children filling the play park.

A boy in the sandpit has his tongue sticking out as he concentrates on transferring sand from one bucket to another. He is about the same age as Sam would have been now. Hannah waits for the familiar surge of anger to wash through her as she remembers her grandson. But instead she feels a gentle yearning, a sweet nostalgia. A smile creeps up on her as she remembers his fingers gripping tightly around her own, sees his chunky legs kicking the air, his blue eyes going brown then learning to focus on the world.

Hannah reaches for her backpack again. Digs down deep beneath the dirty clothes and the crumpled paperbacks, until her hand closes on the battered and crumpled envelope with the photos in. She'd looked at them every hour of every day to start with but she'd slowly weaned herself off them. Now, it must be a few months since she last saw him. Saw them.

The photographs spill out over her lap and onto the grass as she tips the envelope upside down. Big smiles, shiny eyes, cradling arms, laughs and kisses, are all around her as she gathers them back together. Amelia, exhausted in the hospital bed, Sam, wrinkled and red-faced, lying on her chest. Amelia, Grant and Sam home as a family for the first time, cuddled on the sofa. As her fingers trace the contours of her daughter's happy face, Hannah realises her anger is all gone. It's not fair and she should have gone before them, would have gone before them but for a stranger's momentary lapse of concentration on a wet road, but she's no longer mad at the world.

Where's the other photo? The one of them all together that was taken just a few days before the accident. Hannah picks the envelope back up from the grass and there it is inside. The fold had kept it in there. As Hannah unfolds the photo, Ed's face appears and a small moan escapes her. Eddie. Her body suddenly aches for him as she remembers his touch. How could she have left him? It wasn't his fault. Quickly, she stuffs the photos back into her bag.

Back at the train station, she takes a deep breath as she picks up the pay phone and dials the number that was hers for twenty-five years. Will he still be there? The ringing tone starts in her ear and her breath catches in her throat as it's answered almost immediately.

'Hello?'

Eddie. He sounds older, smaller. What has she done? Her breath hasn't returned. She can't speak.

'Hello? Who's there?'

Hannah tries to form the words she wants to say but the only sound she can make is a small croak. It's enough.

'Hannah. It's you. I know it's you.'

The sound of her name on his lips releases her breath in a sob.

'It is. It is me. Am I too late?'

ALAN GILLESPIE

Issues

Benny calls out, whether someone's walking past or not. 'Bigishoooo! Err yer bigishoo.' He stands nestled beneath a sandstone archway, and winks at me, his magazines held out like a dowsing rod. 'Ta very much, Godblessye hen.' 'Much obliged sur, huvagoodday.'

His clothes are shabby but clean, frayed cuffs and wet shoes. Four magazines sell between 8.00am and 10.00am, earning him six pounds and eighty pence. The street falls quiet after the morning rush of office and shop workers. You're not supposed to move around, he tells me, but you have to keep moving. There's another patch near the train station that should get some traffic.

I'm shadowing Benny for the day. Tomorrow, it'll be just me, with my own bundle of magazines and a laminated tag around my neck. He's showing me the ropes by which I'll be tied. You need to be careful, he tells me. Can't trespass on someone else's territory. Can't stand on another man's toes. He's not specific about consequences.

The magazines are a precious commodity, Benny

says. They're a form of currency. Take care nobody pinches them. And if someone's got something you want, swap them for it. He winks again.

'Bigishoooo! Err yer bigishoo.' Benny bows and scrapes when someone pushes a cold coin into his palm. 'Yass,' he says, counting the metal discs. 'Atz enuff furra bed the night.'

One of the hotels will take him for a few pounds. I've got something sorted as well, free temporary accommodation at Hope House. They don't let you stay long. I'm supposed to get my name on a housing list. It's good for their statistics, apparently.

A single bed for a single night, and then I'll be out on my own.

That night, stuck in limbo between sleep and nausea, I wrap my legs around the sheets and imagine I'm far away, with Harold again.

Harold always had the best taste in beds. It was impeccable.

I close my eyes and we're chug chug chugging, aboard the Orient Express, wrapped up in embroidered quilts that scratch my skin. Or we're spread out in a four poster at the Ritz, giggling like schoolchildren, eating purple cherries with dollops of yoghurt. Or we're sinking into waterbeds and gripping wrought-iron frames, and roll, roll, rolling through the night on an Arctic cruise. Harold was wonderful. He told me bed was like a stage. I always thought it was more like a canvas.

Not that we spent all our time together on a

mattress. There were black tie evenings in art galleries, VIP rooms in cocktail bars, rooftop terraces sipping Hendrick's and tonic with cubes of cucumber, driving his Porsche in Italian shoes, splattering each other with paint in my studio, cufflink shopping at Tiffany's, first class flights, my penthouse apartment, walk-in wardrobe, balcony overlooking the river. Harold always left the rent money for me in an envelope on the dressing table.

I fall asleep on a stiff board in Hope House, wishing that he had never died.

'Big Issue! Who wants a Big Issue?'

I don't have Benny's talent for salesmanship yet. He comes along to say hello, on his way to a promising patch outside the new shopping centre. He tells me to relax. Tells me I'll get used to the life after a day or two. Tells me to stay away from the shopping centre or he'll do me.

No wink.

I become invisible. Men walk past, smelling divine, ignoring me completely. Mothers push prams, facing straight ahead while their children stare. I sell one magazine, to a pensioner. She drops two grubby coins into my hand and I pat my pockets, even though I know I don't have change. Not to worry, she says. Just you keep it, son. I thank her very much and resist the urge to throw up. The way she looks at me, the way she looks through me, makes me loathe myself.

'Bigishoooo! Get your bigishoo.'

I'm getting the hang of this. At least I think so. Two

more copies sell. Nobody takes their change, but I should get some from the supermarket, just in case. Although that means I'll have to buy something.

When Harold died, I had some money to keep me going. When it began running out, I would shop at night, buying all the produce that was going off at a reduced price. And when I could no longer afford that, I went round the back, through the bins. Peeling open stale sandwiches. Relieved and revolted.

I haven't really lived since Harold died. We were together for years. He knew every fancy and fetish and I was never disappointed. He spoiled me, of course he did. Because I loved him and he loved me. But when he died, all the wealth and comfort and security went to his wife.

I wasn't welcome at the funeral. I wasn't mentioned in the will. I didn't get a penny. Friends who'd known all about us, feigned ignorance and sidled up to her. Wiped her tears, held her hand, accepted her invitations to supper. If she ever knew about her husband's secret boyfriend, she never let on. Harold never mentioned it, but I'm sure she knew. She must have.

When I was evicted from my flat, three months in arrears with the rent, it had been transformed. All the clean lines were gone. The minimalist, Swedish decor had been covered up. Blame it on artistic temperament.

I consider it my masterpiece. My homage to Harold. Onto every surface of the home he'd kept me in went layer upon layer of thick oil paint, swabbed on in dank tan and cold slate and sooty bistre, a whirlpool of everything I couldn't say. Onto the wooden floorboards I painted a swirling, turbulent vortex. The ceiling became a stratus of foggy cloud, like bottled exhaust fumes. I made the bath sheer black. Likewise the toilet.

I did the windows last: plum and cobalt, crimson and carrot, in thin brushstrokes portraying broken glass and dead sunflowers. Stroke by stroke, the daylight faded, replaced by gloom, backlit like stained glass.

If this seems dramatic, well, I'm a painter. Always have been. A writer might have tortured himself with obscure verses. A musician might have sung ballads with tears in his eyes. It was just my way of mourning. Of trying to mourn.

'Bigishoooo! Get yer bigishoo.'

It's raining and I've ended up in a rotten spot with no shelter. I'm scared to move because I've been warned, by a chin-scarred thug, that if he sees me near his plot again he'll have me. He's claimed the stairs outside the Church of Scotland for his own, been there seven years, find your own bloody patch. His clothes are new and his cheeks are plump. A middle-class tramp, of all things. I bet they bring him tea and polythene bags full of old stuff every Sunday.

My feet are sodden, breached by the rain, and my magazines wrinkle up. I wrap them in cellophane but it's useless. The drizzle's getting everywhere.

A policeman stops to check my ID. He's clean shaven, clothes neatly pressed. Big black shoes jutting out from flawless trousers. I want to cling onto his arm and bury my face in his chest. Want him to hold me. Someone tried to sell me drugs last night, I tell him. He's not interested. Maybe if I steal his hat he'll arrest me, take me in the back of his van, throw me in a cell for the night. But he's marching away, long legs, square shoulders.

The people walking past stare from beneath umbrellas. Eyes shifting over me. They're wondering how someone manages to ruin their life so much they end up like this. Wondering what I did to deserve it. Wondering where I'll sleep tonight.

I wonder too.

It's all my own fault. That's the worst thing. This was avoidable. I just wasn't looking where I was going.

After I graduated from art school, I sold a few paintings. My debts were deep but a list of contacts kept me ticking over for a while. I made money from time to time. When I sold a piece, I spoiled myself until the funds ran out, spending months in Paris, in Athens, in Venice.

I got by on youth and enthusiasm and bursaries and the contents of other men's pockets. And then I met Harold. It was all different with him.

I told him I was his and that I wasn't going anywhere. He told me he was mine and that he would give me anything. And then Harold died.

It's been years since I painted anything worth more than the cost of the materials. I've no pension. No income. No assets. My buttocks have sunk down low and my arms have deflated. I used to be a package, a catch, a trophy boyfriend. I never thought the day would come when I couldn't cling onto the coattails of a repressed homosexual with money.

You'd be amazed how many men are married with children, driving the Land Rover, holidaying in Mallorca, celebrating anniversaries, double dating, dinner partying, sleeping in queen-sized marital beds, all the time denying their instinct. And it's because gay relationships just aren't the same. It's cruel but they don't have that gravitas; not in the real world, where prejudice and phobias are much more commonplace than the BBC lets you believe.

In a gay relationship you rely on each other as best friends as well as partners. You've got yourself a friend/lover/partner hybrid. And when he's gone, you're isolated.

Alone.

Fucked.

The magazines aren't shifting and my nose starts to drip. I pack it in and go to the underground station. For the price of a single journey, I can stay down there for hours, ten feet under, going round and round the wet city in circles.

I flick through one of my magazines on the train, trying to blend in. Trying to look like a normal man who's just bought one, rather than an outsider trying to hawk them off. One page catches my eye. It's the kind of article I once would've read from back to front.

Says there's a Van Gogh exhibit opening at Kelvingrove Museum. The Starry Night's going up for all of Glasgow to see. Says it's worth a hundred million dollars.

That much for one painting. It baffles me. Makes me question all those years when I stuck my nose up in the air and ooh-ed and aah-ed at things hanging from walls.

The train stops at a station. It's late afternoon and people are going home, thousands of clockwork mice following their routine. A girl sits next to me, long legs crossed, a defensive pose. I glance at her perfect skin, can't stop looking. I'm making her uncomfortable.

Soon it'll be dark and I'll be alone in the streets. I think that maybe I'll go along to the Van Gogh exhibition this weekend.

Maybe I'll run into one of the old crowd. One of Harold's business associates. A friendly face. They might want to take me for a coffee. Maybe lunch. Who knows where it could lead?

The girl gets off at her stop. I wonder who's waiting for her on the other side of the barriers. The pleats of her skirt brush my hand.

I've ended up right on the fucking lip of society. I'm clinging on with fingertips but I've seen people who've been chewed up and spat out the system altogether. No passport, no P60, no state pension. Nameless people that can't even get an NHS doctor. Some receptionist saying, 'What's yer name?' and, 'What's yer address?' and that's that.

Can't get a house if you've no job. Can't get a job if you've no address.

Best place to end up is jail. You're still outside society, removed from the civilised structure, but at least you get a roof. At least you're not a nothing.

When I leave the underground station, it's night. In a supermarket, I buy Grant's gin and value tonic water. No food. I walk over the Clyde, on a footbridge, swigging from both bottles, one after the other. It slips down my throat like heartburn.

Shuffling footsteps to my left and Benny appears, of all people, crazy-eyed and unsteady. 'Magine findin yoo here,' he says. 'Howzitgaun? A wee drink wid be magic, ta.'

I never noticed before, but he's toothless. Pink gums between dark chops. He looks at me, scuffs his feet. Sips from the bottle and looks up and down the road. No traffic. Sips again. Kicks me in the balls and rips the scarf from my neck, twisting me to the ground. Then he's running away, scarf flapping loose and gin slopping from the bottle, over his knuckles, into the gutter.

I hold onto the railing and pull myself up. Below, the water is inky, churning currents and frothy spit, reflected streetlights dancing in the dark. I lean over the edge, see my breath catching and crystallising in the cold air. I close my eyes. Harold, I whisper. Harold, for fuck's sake.

The Starry Night's twenty nine inches by thirty six. Big. But not too big. I know every corner of the Kelvingrove, every doorway and crevice. Used to go there all the time. Exhibitions, opening nights, fundraisers. Even a few weddings – me and Harold sitting, side-by-side in the pews, hands folded across our laps, ankles intertwined.

Prison's not a place someone normally desires to be. And there's people would rather live in a bin than behind bars, but that's them, not me. I'm not used to this. I hate the cold. I miss walls and roofs. I miss interaction. If it's a question of survival, sheer survival, some people can handle living on the streets, but I can't. I need the system. I need society, even if it's one running behind prison walls.

Getting in the door's the hard part, I reckon. Once you're inside it you can kick up a fuss, cause some trouble and make sure you're not released. But how to get there in the first place? I can't murder. I couldn't handle being in a wing surrounded by killers. Besides, it seems unnecessary.

Theft it is then. And what better to steal than the medium I've spent my life pretending to appreciate, pretending to create? A thousand and forty four square inches of canvas and oil. A hundred million dollars. Dutch fingerprints melted into the sky. That's the curious thing about paint: you use it wet, have a slim window of time to mould and spread it just the way you like, and then it sets, and it's solid, for the rest of your days and many more besides.

You need to get things in order when you've got the chance, because, if you leave it too long, the game's a bogey.

So I'll steal the painting, get caught, and go to jail. Or steal the painting, get away with it, and sell it. I can't really see a downside to either option.

I pick a cigarette butt out the bin and light up. Feel the smoke curling down my throat. Walk up and down the path alongside the museum. It's closing time. The lights inside flicker and fade. The staff leave. Someone's left a window open.

The sky's dark blue and the lights from the city drown out the stars, swirling about in a yellow-orange haze. The university tower's bold against the backdrop, reaching up and out with boughs of brick. Rain falls, oily and black.

'Bigishoooo! Err yer bigishoo.'

But there's nobody around. And even if there was, I'm invisible, remember? I merge into the shadows and slip inside.

MIKEY JACKSON
Funny How Things Turn Out

Funny how things turn out. Emma had returned to her hometown for one reason only, to make her peace with her mother. But she never expected what would happen next.

The train was pulling into the station. Emma didn't want to miss her stop. She'd suffered nightmares all week about falling asleep on the train and ending up in Outer Mongolia, or whatever faraway places were called these days. That would never do.

Emma rose hastily from her seat and almost bowled over the passing woman. A quick apology, a steadying of posture, then bang! Realisation. Recognition. That moment of silent, wide-eyed, rabbit-in-headlights stillness. And then –

'Kate!'

'Emma!'

A high-pitched double helping of, 'Oh, my God.' And the animated hug of two people who hadn't laid eyes on each other for ...

Gosh! Had it really been that long?

They both alighted from the train. For the first few seconds, the two of them stood like statues on the station platform, enveloped in a concoction of disbelief, amazement and glowing warmth. This was much to the annoyance of the storm of passengers behind them, all hastily attempting to vacate the carriage. Awareness, however, (and a rather rude station worker) promptly forced them to move aside in order to ease the congestion.

A lot of time had passed. Had it really been that long? It certainly had. Nigh on ten years had elapsed since Emma last stood at this very station. She could picture that final afternoon so vividly. Emma, laden with a beaten-up suitcase and one-way ticket. Kate, in tears, begging her not to leave.

'I can't stay,' was Emma's pained response. 'Not now. Not after this.'

Emma had been offered lucrative employment in a city six hundred miles away. It couldn't possibly be turned down. She was on her way to a better life. A career move like no other. A fresh start. A new beginning. A brand new Emma.

She had promised Kate wholeheartedly that she would write regularly. A few letters were scribed, but her brand spanking new life was soon to become a hectic one. Busy. Demanding. And very eventful. No time to put pen to paper, and thus no further communication in that medium or any other. Of course, she'd often think, 'Oh, I must write that letter,' but 'must write' never quite evolved into 'did write.' Birthday and Christmas cards were exchanged, but even those customs ceased after a few years. Emma wasn't too sure who had stopped sending them first. Probably her. Actually, most likely her.

Making peace with Mum had been this week's grand plan. Train ride here. Massive grovel. Heart-to-heart. Peace restored between them. Stay a few days. Plenty of home-made cake. And then the long train ride home again. But could this also be a chance to heal the rather ugly and gaping wound she shared with Kate? She certainly hoped so.

And now here they were. Emma and Kate. Together again. Two women who had grown up with each other. Mates ever since they were so high. The best of friends. Soul mates. Inseparable. Nothing could possibly come between them. But of course, something had. Or rather somebody.

Alan.

It was Emma who had first dated handsome, funny, sexy Alan. The decision to move in with him came after only three short months.

'Emma, it's way too soon,' warned a worried Kate. 'For God's sake, get to know the guy inside out first.'

But did Emma take any notice? No, siree. When you're in love, you quit listening to your head. And that's when the problems began.

Alan's drunkenness. Alan's jealousy. Alan's anger. Alan's fist.

A completely different side to the man who, before cohabiting, was fun, friendly and happy-go-lucky. Kate advised her friend to fight back, but the man was burly and intimidating when he'd been drinking.

Emma's petite and nimble frame was no match for such alcohol-fuelled rage.

However, Emma soon saw sense. She escaped from the relationship before the violence became too intense. If she'd stayed much longer, the bruises she endured every drunken weekend would have undoubtedly escalated to broken bones. Or worse. One lonely Friday night, she packed some clothes, adequate cosmetics – and what was left of her dignity – into a weekend bag and left.

Emma crashed a few nights at Kate's place. At first, she lived in fear of reprisals, but mercifully, aside from a couple of spates of late-night repentant begging on the cold side of a heavily bolted front door, Alan caused no further strife. In no time at all, she sorted herself out with suitable accommodation and made the best of a life alone.

Kate shacking up with Alan was the shock of the century. In fact, an absolute bombshell. Emma was totally knocked back by the revelation. What the hell was the stupid girl thinking? This was barely a few weeks after Emma had been forced to flee for her life. Just over a month since Emma had last warmed the monster's bed and taken his punches. Now it seemed as though Kate was next in line to share the same fate: an heir to his fist. But, alas, the stubborn girl's mind was made up. She was not prepared to give up her new boyfriend. Kate had made her bed and Alan was going to lie in it.

'All right, fine, I'll change the record,' sighed

Emma, giving in, 'But if he ever tries to do the same to you, make sure you fight back.'

'There's no need to worry,' Kate reassured her. 'Alan says he's changed. And I believe him.'

Emma knew better, of course. It would only be a matter of time before the soft fingertips Alan placed on Kate's body would be substituted by something far worse. But Kate was adamant. This lady was not for turning. She dismissed such caution with an indifferent wave of the hand.

'Shut up, Emma. You're just jealous.'

What? Wham! The worst female sin of all time. Kate had chosen a man over her best friend.

The falling-out occurred around the same time as the job offer. Emma and Kate were never going to be the same again – and her former joke of a relationship with Alan had caused untold friction between herself and her mother – so she accepted the post without the slightest hesitation. Kate accused her of running away from her troubles and walking out on their friendship. Emma had denied it with vigour at the time but, on reflection, maybe Kate had been right after all. So much time had elapsed since, and there was little point now in fretting over the past.

'Hey, let's hit a coffee shop and catch up on the last ten years,' suggested Kate.

Emma accepted and off they went.

Over a peace-making coffee and a guilty slice of carrot cake, Emma shared her experiences, including the fact that her busy and chaotic life left no time for love or relationships. Instead, she'd acquired a few male friends with the added bonus of no-strings bedroom-bonanza every now and then. After all, like every woman, she had needs. Kate revealed that she had finally landed herself a job lucrative enough to afford a decent life. She was on her way up. Emma was happy for her.

The subject of Alan was inevitable.

'Me and Alan? Oh, we're still together.'

Initially, Emma found herself walking on eggshells during such a delicate conversation, just in case Kate had become nothing more than his personal punch bag. But, no. This was not the case. Emma was surprised to discover that Kate and Alan had been married for the last nine years. Emma was genuinely pleased for her. Maybe she had been wrong after all. Maybe Alan had indeed changed for the better. However, there was something Kate wanted to show her. Something really important.

They took a bus to the other side of town and walked the rest of the way, eventually arriving at a large and lavish house. Emma was undeniably impressed. The couple had done well for themselves. Upon entering the house, Emma found herself intrigued by the presence of a live-in carer. Not the usual au pair one might expect in a well-to-do household. This young woman was a trained nurse.

Kate led Emma up the stairs to the master bedroom. There lay Alan in the bed. Awake, yet essentially lifeless. No recognition. No movement. No indication of thought. Just empty, staring eyes.

Kate placed a comforting arm around Emma. An explanation was in order. It had happened late one night, just over eight years ago. Alan's drunken return. A fight. A struggle.

And a crystal ornament smashed against his skull.

It had been self-defence. But now Alan was doomed to life in a vegetative state, with Kate condemned to the lifelong burden of caring for him.

'And as you can see, Emma,' concluded Kate solemnly. 'I took your advice. I did fight back. Funny how things turn out.'

DEBBIE ASH-CLARKE

No Longer Home

'I'm going home now.' Lily stubbed out her cigarette on the side of the bench and picked up her school bag. Then she hesitated. 'Are you OK?'

'Doesn't really feel like home now my mum has gone,' I said, twisting my hair round and round my fingers.

'Your hair'll split if you do that.' Lily took a stick of lip gloss from her pocket and smeared it onto her lips; offered me a wine gum. 'Guess you haven't much choice.'

'No.' I sighed. I got up, and we traipsed back across the park towards the estate, our socks wet from the long grass.

It was the saddest October I'd known in my fifteen years. Mum had died three weeks ago. We'd had the funeral; I'd cried 'til my eyes were sore and my face went puffy. She'd wanted to be buried, but Les had decided.

'Cremation's cheaper,' he'd told me. 'No point spending money on her when she's dead.'

It had been pointless to argue. Les, always the control freak, now had no-one to calm him. I was stuck with him. And him with me.

Mum was special. I know most people would say that about their mum, but she really was. She had presence; she made everybody smile. And she'd made this shithole of a house inviting - like a show home, but real and warm, relaxed and lived in. She'd pick things up cheap - a rug here, a vase there, a scented candle - when she'd saved a little from the grocery bill or sold some stuff on eBay. Curtains to brighten that sunless room. Finding the right things without spending much was a gift she had.

And when she was home from work, delicious smells would seep from the kitchen up the stairs to my room - a spicy dinner, or a cake. I'd offer to help sometimes; not as often as I should have.

Two days after she died, I found Les in their room, stuffing her jumpers and dresses into an old bin bag, creased and rejected. I glared at him, my cheeks wet.

'Don't do it now, Les. Please. Can't it wait? Maybe in a few weeks -'

'Charity shop can use these. You've got to face it, Beth - she's gone.' He opened a drawer in the chest and silky undies followed the jumpers into the bag.

'She was my mum, Les!' I picked up an aqua sundress that reminded me of her: her warm skin, her big smile. I remembered being cuddled when she was wearing that. She'd had it for years.

'We've got to move on. It's unhealthy not to, eh?' He stood up and cuffed me playfully round the head like I was his. I ducked away.

Then he started on the house stuff: the cushions, the ornaments, everything she'd done. He didn't tell me. Things disappeared, and I'd look for them in the wheelie bin hours later or the next day, and there they were, stinking of fish bones and cabbage. Unrescuable. My heart burst with sadness.

It was as if he'd hated her. He was removing all traces. The house was dull and bare now. A bachelor's house. Not the home my mum had made.

A week later, he started pausing outside my room when he went to the loo in the night. I'd hear the footsteps, plod plod plod plod, the bathroom door opening and closing, the sound of pee in the bowl, and then the door again, plod plod. And he'd stop, right outside my room.

Was he listening? What for? He knew I was alone.

Was he thinking of coming in? He'd always been the pervert, touching my arm a little too long, putting his arm round my waist for a photo, making it look friendly like, but it wasn't. I knew his game. I knew the way he looked at me when my mum was turned away.

I wanted to tell someone, but who? Nobody'd believe me. Well, Lily would, but I just couldn't. It was as if telling someone'd make it real, make it true. And maybe it was all in my head?

Lily and I would sit in her kitchen, drinking tea and spreading peanut butter on toast. Then my mobile would ring and it'd be him, Les, moaning at me to come home and make dinner. I always had to cook. He didn't. Not ever. Apparently 'cos he was working, I should cook. But I was fifteen and he was an adult, and I had school.

'It's women's work, innit?'

I scowled at him as I stood at the sink, peeling potatoes and carrots to go with a Fray Bentos pie. Fucking chauvinist pig. Like someone from a hundred years ago.

Twenty-two days after Mum died, he went to the loo as usual in the middle of the night. It was 3.00am, his normal time. But, this time, the footsteps paused for longer than ever. I thought he'd died on the spot. I wished he had.

Then my worst fear. The doorknob turned. The door pushed open. His ugly face above burgundy pyjamas, the fly hanging open, his dick falling out.

He had a semi. I turned away, rolling myself in the duvet, hiding in it. But he sat on the edge of the bed and pulled it away from me. Pulled it down. Pressed his hand against my breasts as I wriggled to get away, turning onto my front so he couldn't get at me.

'You owe me, girl,' he said. 'You're costing me money. And now I haven't got your mum - you're gonna have to meet me halfway. You get what I'm saying?'

Then he got up and left. Left me alone again in my bed, but in no doubt now.

Next morning, I got up as usual, showered and dressed, laid out breakfast for him. I couldn't force down the corn flakes I usually ate, so I went to my room to pack my books. Not just text books and exercise books this time. I took some extra things. Some money I'd got saved. Loads of pants. Some polo tops for school. Some socks and a pair of tights. I squeezed them all into my rucksack and went downstairs.

He was eating his breakfast when I left. Toast with marmalade dangling from his mouth.

'I'll see you later, girl,' he said.

His eyes gleamed. He'd never been pleased to see me before. I had to do this, and I had to do it now.

By the time I got to school, I felt hot and my face felt sweaty. I'd walked faster than usual. No reason, no point. I just couldn't wait to get away.

Lily was standing on the corner of the playground where we always met. She held her ciggie behind her so the teachers wouldn't see, but they'd have to have been blind. Truth is, they knew half the kids did it, but they didn't care.

Lily exhaled smoky breath and looked me up and down. 'What's up?'

'What d'you mean?'

'You just look ... funny.'

I shrugged.

'C'mon, tell me.'

'I'm not going back there,' I said. 'He's a pervert.' I dropped my voice. 'He came into my room last night.'

Lily dropped the ciggie on the ground and stubbed it out. She stood right in front of me, leaning towards me. 'What? He didn't -?'

'He touched me here!' I gestured. 'And he said ... He said I owed him. I'm not going back, Lily. Never.'

'What are you gonna do?'

I opened my bag and showed her. It was stuffed full of clothes.

'You can come to mine. My mum'll let you. I know she will. I'll ring her.'

'Put your bag down, Beth,' Sharon said. 'But you know, we haven't got a spare room, so it'll have to be the sofa. And it can't be for long. You need to sort something out.'

'She can't go back to Les's, Mum.'

Sharon plumped the cushions and tidied the TV mags. 'I'm sure it will blow over,' she said. 'You're just upset, love, after your mum dying and all. Come here, have a hug.'

I let myself be hugged, but it didn't feel real. Sharon was playing a part, going through the motions. She didn't get it.

'He touched her, Mum. In her bed. She can't go back. That's not gonna blow over.'

My cheeks burned. I hated that Lily was telling her mum that, but I had nowhere else to go.

'Well, we'll see. I expect he was just giving her a night night hug to make her feel loved now Anne's gone. No point making a fuss.'

'Mum!'

'Bangers, beans and mash this evening, OK? And no more than two nights, Beth. OK?' Sharon gave me a narrow-eyed stare. 'I haven't got money to be paying for your dinner every night. Hard enough with my own two. I am a single parent, you know.'

Yes, I did know. Everyone knew. Lily was cool, but her mum was a slapper. Been round the block a good few times from what I'd heard.

'Thanks, Sharon. Can I help?' I asked.

The sofa was uncomfortable, so I put the cushions on the floor to lie on, and wrapped the blanket round me that Lily had found upstairs. I woke stiff and cold in the morning, and Sharon, who came down first, was in a foul mood.

'My good sofa and you're messing around with it, putting it all on the floor where god knows what has been. This can't go on, Beth. It can't.'

Only one night and I was already unwelcome.

Lily came down, clean and washed. I sprayed deodorant in my pits and pulled on a clean polo top. I felt manky, but never mind. I didn't dare ask to get washed properly. Lily's brother Nate was in the kitchen, slopping milk from his cereal onto the floor. Sharon didn't seem to notice or care. A few minutes later, Lily bent and mopped the floor with a dishcloth.

'Take all your stuff, Beth, when you leave for school,' Sharon said.

'Mum!' Lily tried, but Sharon was adamant.

'I don't want to get in trouble with the benefits for sub-letting.'

'It's not bloody sub-letting, Mum. Letting a friend stay. I thought you said two nights?'

'Changed me mind, ain't I? Go on, kid - go back to

Les. He's okay. I had a thing with him once, you know?'

No, I hadn't known. But it was no surprise.

Lily slammed the front door behind us as we left.

'I'm sorry,' she said. 'I did try. So what are you gonna do tonight?'

The day at school dragged on. I couldn't concentrate. It was hard thinking about adverbs and metaphors, amps and volts, when I was worrying about where I was gonna sleep. A few times, the teachers caught me miles away, not listening, and they didn't seem pleased.

'You're usually a good student, Beth! What's got into you today?'

Lily and I weren't together in all the classes, but in the last class of the day, maths, we always sat together.

'I've thought what you should do,' she whispered to me as Mrs Khan explained how to solve an equation on the board.

'What?'

'Tell her. She's nice. She'll understand.'

'What she's supposed to do about it?'

'Beth. Lily. No talking. Have you been paying attention?' Mrs Khan frowned.

'Yes, miss,' we chorused.

'Come on then, Lily. Come up here and show us how to do the next one.'

Lily hesitated, then stood and glanced back at me. Her face blamed me. She stood, useless, at the board.

'You weren't listening, were you? I've a mind to give you both detention.'

Lily pulled a face and sat down again. We didn't whisper any more. Mrs Khan's eyes were on us.

At the end of the lesson, Lily didn't pack her stuff. She went up to Mrs Khan and spoke to her as our classmates headed noisily for the door. I couldn't hear what she was saying. I packed away my stuff.

Then Mrs Khan came over. 'Is this true, Beth? Is it true that you feel unsafe at home because of your stepfather?'

I swallowed hard. How many people did I have to tell?

'Yes, miss.'

'Gather your things up, Beth. You're coming with me. Lily, leave it with me, OK? I'll make sure she's safe. Thanks for what you've done.'

Mrs Khan put a reassuring hand on my shoulder as she steered me out of the room. I looked back at Lily, her face full of sadness, but also hope.

Hope. Did I have any?

It felt strange being shown to a room in a stranger's house. It was past ten o'clock and I was exhausted. It'd taken hours. Questions in the staff room, then a social worker had arrived. More questions. Cups of tea. Packets of sandwiches brought by the deputy head. More questions. Eventually, the social worker told me she'd found somewhere for me for that night.

'Emergency accommodation,' she explained. 'A nice family. They'll look after you 'til we can find you a proper home.'

'What are they like?'

'They're really kind, love. Come on.'

She drove me there. It was ten minutes away. We rang the doorbell and a woman answered. A bit podgy, with a cornflower blue jumper. A big smile. Straggly hair.

'Come in, my lovely,' she gushed. 'I'm Sam. I'll show you to your room.'

I glanced back at the social worker, and she urged me on.

'I'll be in touch,' she said. 'Sleep well.'

The bedroom was tiny, but cosy. Bed pushed next to the radiator. I liked the way the window looked out on the cul-de-sac, and I could see a patch of green by the bus stop. I liked that the woman made me feel safe. Perhaps, after all, I could one day feel at home again somewhere.

MICHELE SHELDON

Shirley

You shouted, Shirley, Shirl! It's me!

And then just stood in front of me, arms open wide, inviting me to hug you.

The weight of your expectation, your keenness for me to be her, trapped me in that street.

So I said, I'm fine, followed by a squeak of thanks.

We stood like that, Saturday morning shoppers bustling around us, your elderly friend alternately glancing at you and then me. I could feel my daughter's green eyes boring into me. I daren't look. But I needn't. I could imagine her face all right, all crumpled up, trying to understand who I was: her mother or this Shirl.

It's been a long time, too long, you said.

And then you shook your head as if we should never have let that time slip between us.

I stared at the faded yellow and blue tattoo on your forearm, trying to work out whether it was a flower, or some kind of monster.

I stepped back. You stepped forward.

You said, I tried ringing. I did try ringing. Why didn't you get back to me, Shirl? It's not like Shirl, I said to mum, didn't I, mum?

The elderly lady behind you nodded and said, No, I said it's not like Shirl not to get back to you. Not like her at all.

Then you turned back to me.

This your little one?

I nodded.

She's just like you, Shirl, when you was her age.

The spit, said your mum.

I'm going to Claire's, my daughter said, tugging at my sleeve like I always tell her not to.

Teenagers, you said, and I shrugged apologetically, though she wasn't even 12 years old.

I'll meet you in there, I called after her, pleased she was so impatient, for the first and last time.

Anyway, Shirl, where you been? You just disappeared. Vanished into thin air, you said, and clicked your fingers.

The sound was sudden and violent, despite the traffic growling past and the chit-chat of shoppers. I could feel everything speed up, my heartbeat, my breathing. As if the past were being fast-forwarded. Everything had changed so much since I lived here - what? Fourteen, fifteen years ago? Well before Katie was born. It was the same but not the same; like a dream when everyday places are mixed up with the unfamiliar. The old bakery had turned into a Costa, the shoe shop was transformed into a smart Italian restaurant, the key-cutting place a charity shop and someone, presumably the council, had erected a large bronze statue of a woman with a hare's head and her arm around a horse. The seagulls had fouled the hare lady's giant ears and breasts. But they'd left the horse alone, as if they were making a point; they disapproved of this chimera. The street was getting busier and shoppers were having to push past us now. A young woman with a baby in a buggy and a toddler in tow said, excuse me, excuse me, I can't get past. But you didn't hear her and you didn't move. Neither did I. You were watching me, waiting for a reply, and she went around us, tutting.

Just here and there, I mumbled.

Oh, I tried ringing so many times, didn't I, Mum? you said, arms crossed in front of you.

Your mum nodded and said, yeah, loads of times. She rang you loads of times, Shirl. But you was never in.

You said, I gave up in the end, didn't I, mum? I thought she must have just packed up and gone. Left town. And I thought to myself, well, I can't blame her, really. I'd probably do the same.

Sorry, I whispered.

You uncrossed your arms then and opened them wide again and said, No, Shirl, don't you dare go apologising. It ain't your fault. I wanted to see if you was all right, that's all.

And then you pulled a face as if something terrible had happened to this Shirl. I could feel your pity like a solid thing. It hit me hard in the stomach just before you filled the empty space and flung your arms around me. Shoppers were now keeping their distance, going right around us, ogling us as they passed from a safe distance. We were no longer a blocking-the-pavement-pain-in–the-arse, but a spectacle, like those pan-pipers that no-one wants to listen to, or someone begging.

I caught the eye of an elderly man. He was bent over, walking slowly with a battered walking stick, like a stereotype of an old person. He had come out of the opticians opposite. I don't know why but he smiled at me like a conspirator, as if he could tell I was trapped in that street. I smiled back, temporarily mesmerised by a flash of how he'd looked years ago when he'd once been handsome.

Then I noticed my arms. They felt heavy and useless just hanging there, so I lifted them and patted your back hesitantly. I felt like a child: only comforting an upset friend out of politeness when, in fact, you just want them to shut up and get back to playing.

And in my ear you whispered, we heard you was sleeping on the streets. We looked for you everywhere. Weeks and weeks we spent.

I closed my eyes, willing you to let go. I didn't want to come here. We'd only stopped because I remembered the town had a Claire's. Katie had been seduced by its spinning displays of glittery nail varnish, make-up, sparkly necklaces, rings and bracelets, coloured hair extensions, and promises of a glamorous other self for a couple of quid. Just ten minutes, I'd said. Yes, just ten minutes, Katie had promised. I know exactly what I want, she'd said.

And then, when you did let go, you looked right in my face and said, you look different, Shirl.

I breathed in your breath of tea and stale fags and whispered, really? How?

Because I wanted to know what this Shirl, with an old person's name, looked like. Because I'm not meant to be old like that yet; maybe to toddlers, teenagers and to my daughter, but not to middle-aged people like this woman and her mum.

Older, I said. I must look older?

Well, we all look older, Shirl, but no, just different, you said.

I caught a glimpse of my daughter. She was standing in her you-promised-me-a-special-treat-hands-on-hips-stance, next to the doorway of Claire's. Even her red curls looked impatient as the wind tossed them around. I wondered what I'd tell her. Whether I'd make it into a joke afterwards. What to do? I wondered if anyone else had seen me.

I've got to go, I said. My daughter, I said.

Well, you take good care of yourself, Shirl. Any time you want a chat, you just ring or come round. We're still at the same house.

Ok, I said, bye then, take care. And I hurried away, not turning back, each step taking me further away from this Shirl you'd known so well. And when I reached my daughter, she said, what was all that about, mum? She totally thought you were that Shirl.

Shirl indeed, I said, trying to laugh.

And as she vanished behind the display stands of last season's scarves, I quickly wiped my eyes with the corner of my own.

NEIL CAMPBELL
The Rainbow Snooker Club

Two people were having sex behind the back of The Hacienda. Tom continued past them along the towpath and came out near The Peveril of the Peak. He tried the locked doors of the Briton's Protection. He looked through the frosted glass at the drinkers sat at the bar and then wandered towards Whitworth Street. In the shadow of Oxford Road Station there was a girl sitting on the steps of The Rainbow Snooker Club.

'Spare some change,' she said, holding out an empty plastic cup.

He reached into his trouser pocket, pulled out a fistful of heavy change and passed her some pound coins. 'I recognize you. You're Gillian Brown. Don Brown's sister.'

'So what?'

'Well, what are you doing here?'

'Spare some change?' she said, as a man in a suit walked past.

'Do you want to go in for a game of snooker?'

'Don't be daft.'

'Is there a bar in there?'

'Of course there is.'

'Can I buy you a drink?'

'Come on then.'

Smoke carried across the tables from the barman's cigarette but nobody played snooker. The old man was reading a *Manchester Evening News*, the newspaper spread out across the bar.

Tom stood with Gillian. The barman eventually looked up. Gillian looked at Tom.

'What do you want?' Tom said.

'Jack Daniels and coke.'

'Jack Daniels and coke? OK, mate, two of those.'

She drank hers in one. Then she told Tom she was going.

'Why? Where to? Come on, let me get you another. I've got plenty of money, don't worry about that.'

'George, can you do us a cup of tea?' she said to the barman.

'Tea?' said Tom.

'Yeah, tea.'

When George passed her the tea, she took the mug in two hands and brought it close to her chest. Tom had a Jack Daniels with ice.

'Let's have a game,' he said.

'What?'

'Let's have a game of snooker.'

'You're too pissed.'

'I'm not,' he said. 'I'll get a lager. Sure you don't want one?'

'Sure.'

He passed her a cue and she stood there, watching as he tried to get the reds in the triangle. He put the green on the yellow spot but, apart from that, it was right. When he broke off, he completely missed the pack. He walked over to the scoreboard on the wall and slid it to 4.

She walked to the table. But she couldn't hold the cue properly and with her first shot, she brushed the side of the white with the cue tip, moving it a few inches and not hitting any other ball. George carried on reading the paper.

'Stupid game this,' she said, after missing another shot.

'You are useless,' he said, laughing at her.

'Get yourself another drink.'

'I will. And you drink your tea.'

He managed a decent break. Then she missed and he made another break to take the frame. He was getting into it and wanted to play more but she was bored.

After a frame on his own, he got himself another lager. They left the snooker club and trailed around the Manchester streets, before spending some time in a café on Piccadilly Approach, around the corner from The Waldorf. She had more tea, and he had some too, but it made him feel sick. He wanted another drink and she told him where they could get one if he just followed her.

He couldn't remember finishing that last drink. He didn't remember what had happened to the girl, or the money in his pockets, but he supposed there was a connection. He had a vague memory of being on Temperance Street.

As a kid, he'd played snooker at Don's house. It was a six-foot table, with a slate bed that was stored upright in the front room. To play, they rested the table on two armchairs and it was surprisingly level, though you could slide pots down the rail. When he and Don played, he enjoyed seeing a glimpse of Don's sister as she got herself ready for a night out. Then her friend would come round. She was really fit. Tom enjoyed seeing the two of them, all dressed up for a night out in Ashton-under-Lyne.

When they were old enough, Tom and Don went out into Ashton-under-Lyne, but Tom was so shy that he never spoke to girls until he was drunk. He would make eye contact with them, but if they waited for him to walk over, they were disappointed. He didn't feel like he had anything to offer. He had a shit job and he didn't have a car and he didn't have anything to say. And it seemed such an unnatural environment. He had a quiet voice and it would be a massive effort to be heard above the music. So he got drunk and on the way home, smashed his fists into shutters.

Gillian was fit then. She seemed happy, and he wondered how she could have ended up on the streets. Don's mum and dad were really nice people, and he remembered that Don's dad liked Elvis and, sometimes, when they played snooker, they'd put some of the Elvis cassettes on and listen to them as they played. Don was a funny lad. He could hum the theme tune to the snooker.

At a certain point, Tom didn't see Don anymore. He couldn't remember why. When he was older and stopped drinking, he thought maybe that he should have carried on with the snooker, instead of playing team sports all those years. Individual sport, snooker or golf, would have been better for him. Nobody let you down. He could have practised on his own. He made some pretty good breaks during those games with Don, and that was without any practice at all.

At first, he shouted at the stone walls. Then he vomited in to the toilet next to him. Later in the night, he pulled the blue plastic mat on top of himself. In the morning, as he waited, he laughed hysterically at the interaction between a drunken prostitute and the desk sergeant. They seemed to be entertaining him. A little later, Tom had his DNA and fingerprints taken, all the time talking to the police staff, some of whom seemed too small and young.

Walking out of Longsight Station and sitting down at a bus stop to put his shoelaces back in, he had a vague memory of repeatedly swearing at a young policeman on Oxford Road. This memory relaxed him.

He suddenly felt hungry and went into a McDonald's near Kingsway, and joined the line of people there before getting a cheeseburger and sitting with it among families. He watched the orderly way in which people queued for their meals and shook his head at them. He sat down and looked at the oil stains on his knees.

After half of the cheeseburger, he made his way back to Plymouth Grove, and ended up in a park off Upper Brook Street called Gartside Gardens, where he sat on a bench in the cold sun near a concrete basketball court. He thought about the desk sergeant's words to him as his belongings were emptied out of a plastic bag onto the desk. As Tom picked up his shoelaces the man had said, 'We'll see you next time.'

On the following Friday night, he walked through the city centre. At first, he thought all the people were on drugs. They walked around like zombies and talked in strange voices. Or they were really loud, vulgar and stupid. He wondered how civilization had reached such a point. But he checked himself for hypocrisy, sanctimony.

He walked down Portland Street, past The Circus Tavern and The Old Monkey and then cut down Oxford Road on his way to The Rainbow Snooker Club. He waited on the steps for a while before joining the long line outside The Ritz.

DAN MAITLAND
Idle Hands

It would normally be at least 11.30 before Jesus would even consider retiring to his allotment. Actually, it wasn't really his allotment and, in fact, belonged to a Mr Frederick Archibald Duffy, who had conveniently died three years prior. His then, by default.

Thing was, the place was fine in the summer. Nothing better than sitting on an old packing case, watching the carrot tops as the evening sun goes down, a nice mug of tea from the ex-Mr Duffy's Silver Jubilee mug. Nothing better. But in the winter, most people (and this was something that had perhaps not occurred to Jesus) come to their little brown strips, hoe and rake, drink tea, organise their tools on hooks and shelves in their neat wooden sheds, share philosophies with fellow members of the local Round Table or the Ex-Servicemen's Club - and then, and this is the crux, they go home. To their wives. Who have been frittering away their days, paying bills, shopping, sanitising toilets, washing things (clothes, kitchens etc) and perhaps even raising a couple of children. These men don't *live* in the tidy little huts.

They don't unroll a thin, leaky mattress onto the threadbare carpet, barely cushioning the wooden floor. They don't keep their mattress wrapped in a polythene sheet, propped against the driest, least knackered wall to minimise damp. They don't pull a tatty, green sleeping bag out from inside a large, plastic plant pot, then suddenly throw open the rickety door to sling their last empty can of Tennent's into Mr Smithfield's military French bean display; or slip out into the night in a crouched, coughing run, chuckling between grunts, to bury it under Mr Smithfield's prize-winning marrow. They don't lie down upon the damp mattress, inside the raggedy-baggedy sleeping bag, in a state of undress that is entirely dependent on the season, and put a careful flame to a blackened oil lamp. Then pull out the Dostoevsky, or the Proust (or even the W B Yeats on a more romantic night) from its hallowed space upon the once-seedling-now-book shelf. And, with a sigh of contentment, lay their greasy, old head upon their rolled-up, greasy old jumper and read enraptured, until the oil runs out. Or Mr Sun puts a kindly eye to the cracked glass of the window and says, 'Hey, Jesus. Come on now. Even you need sleep.' But then, of course, *they* have somewhere else to go. And, of course, *they* are prepared to pay for it. The women.

It was midnight before Jesus arrived back at the shed. And for the first time in ten years, he wasn't drunk. Of course, he had drunk. He just wasn't drunk. He'd been looking for Danny. Not much goes unnoticed in a town like Shillingworth and he'd heard, through eavesdropped tail-ends and then deliberate questioning, about the boy's disappearance. He was worried. He had even gone round to see Danny's mum, but she had coldly seen him off.

All over town he'd looked. Starting with the most obvious: the Rec - round by the paint-flaking swings, where Danny would sometimes hide out when being an adult became too much for him. Then Jesus went down by the river, amongst the UB40 fishermen, where Danny was not allowed to play but, in rare moments of small defiance, would sometimes wander - briefly, before the maternal yoke pulled him back into line. He looked down the small, unkempt streets and crumbling, corner shops of Shillingworth old town, where the friends would sometimes stroll - swigging aluminium-flavoured lemonade and beer respectively. Danny was lost. And Jesus had a horrible feeling, amongst the egg, chips, sweet tea and beer in the pit of his stomach, that something was wrong. He'd had this feeling before.

As he walked towards his hut, careful, even now, to rest his heavy tread upon a Smithfield veg row, he could make out the warm glow of his little oil lamp coming through the cracked glass windows. He was grateful for its welcome. Philosophically, he didn't need a home, an anchor, a material weight. But, tonight, he was tired and sad, and he felt old without the booze to hold him up. And he briefly understood the need for a small thing of one's own: a buttress against the cold and the wind and the rudeness and the envy. And the sorrow. Then he remembered that he was nearly out of oil and was pissed off at himself for being so careless as to leave the bloody thing burning. And all understanding vanished, washed away by an angry trickle of self-recrimination. This was what he shared with Danny: the world was too complicated; 'Real Life' was too painful, frightening, time-consuming. He stupefied himself with booze to drown out its angry clamour. Danny was lucky, he was born that way.

Jesus reached the door and pushed it open. It went too easily. He normally set up a little barricade on the other side, so it would wedge itself shut if pushed the wrong way. Much like himself.

'Hello, Danny,' he said, even before he saw Danny's weary figure, hunched in teeth-chattering coldness upon his summer carrots crate.

'Hello, Jesus.'

The boy looked awful, truly awful. Jesus hurried over to the big pot, pulled out the still reasonably-quilted bag and wrapped it around Danny's shivering shoulders. Danny made no move to draw it around himself and Jesus had to do it for him.

'Was I supposed to see you today?'

Jesus took a moment to answer, puzzled and disconcerted by the state of his friend.

'You can see me any time, old son,' he offered eventually. 'But I don't believe we had a definite appointment. Hold on, I'll check with my secretary. Miss Knockers, would you -'

He didn't bother continuing with the joke. Danny didn't get them anyway. And now was not the time for a long exposition into why he was such a funny geezer.

'Are you sure?'

What was wrong with the kid? Even *he* wasn't this dumb! Jesus struck a match and, reaching over Danny's immobile form, put it to a small Gaz camping ring. He then filled his blackened kettle with two cups-worth of water from a plastic bottle.

'Everyone's been looking for you, you know.'

'Have they?'

'Oh yes, boy, they have. I saw your mum this afternoon. Very worried, she was. Didn't know where you were. Didn't turn up for work, evidently.'

'I always tell mum where I'm going.'

'Well, you do usually, son. Not today though, apparently.'

The sleeping bag had slipped from around Danny's shoulders and Jesus reached over again to pull it in.

'Watch y'self, son,' he said. 'Catch yer fuckin' death, won't you. Gotta keep warm, you know. Human beings die if they don't keep warm.'

'Do you think I was supposed to be at work then?'

'Well, reading between the lines, old son ...'

'Doing what?'

'Jesus H! What's wrong with you, boy? You're not

this fuckin' stupid!'

The kettle had boiled. He pulled it, steaming and whistling, from the burner - which he left on for the heat, then went to the door and sloshed out the Jubilee mug and an enamel-coated camping mug.

'What's going on, son?' Again, kindly.

'What's going on?' Danny echoed.

Jesus sighed, and turned his attention to finishing the tea ritual.

'Look, how about *I* ask a couple of questions now, and *you* try to answer them, eh? How about that, eh, Danny? There you go. Get that down ya. Jesus' miracle dumbness cure.' He handed the boy the larger, cleaner mug.

'Is it?'

'What?'

'A miracle something cure?'

Jesus reached over and tousled Danny's hair. It was damp and greasy. There was a graze on his forehead.

'No, it's just tea, you plonker.' He raised a hand to Danny's forehead, and brushed the graze with his dirt-grained fingers. 'How d'ya do that, son?' he asked gently.

'What?'

'Your head, Numbnuts. You've cut it.'

'Have I?'

'For God's sake boy, what's happened to you?'

'I don't know. I was supposed to be somewhere?'

'That's right, lad, work.'

Danny tried that on for size. 'Work ... Yeah, maybe work. Where was I supposed to work, Jesus?'

Jesus ran a hand over his face. Then tried again. 'Fucked if I know, son. I'm afraid that's the sort of information a chap's supposed to carry around in his own head.' He tapped his scalp. 'I mean how would it be if -' He stopped. Again, pointless.

'It was a lovely day.'

'Was it, son?'

'Oh yes, Jesus. But I had to walk a really long way.'

'Walk? What about your van?'

'What van?'

'What van? Uuh, the little white one? The van you haven't stopped talking about since you got it?'

Blank.

'The bloody Trumpton van! You know: small, white, SSWR on the side in big black letters!' His voice became harsh suddenly.

'Oh yes, I remember.'

'Well, thank her majesty for that.' Then softened. 'And what about it?'

'Eh?'

'Where is it, boy?'

'Oh, that wasn't my van.'

'It wasn't?'

'Oh no, I found it.'

'I don't think so, son. I think those nice people at -' Sarcastic now.

'No.' Firmly. 'I found it.'

Jesus was beginning to get really worried. Maybe

the boy was concussed. Maybe he'd crashed. But the scratch on his head didn't look serious enough.

'*Where* did you find it, Dan?' Softly again, coaxing a nut into a frightened squirrel.

'On the road.'

Jesus nodded. 'Uh huh?'

'It had stopped. And I was walking.' Danny's voice became animated. 'It really was a lovely day, Jesus. There were all the birds and the sky was so blue. Just like summer. Do you think Mum will take me to the beach? Is it summer, Jesus?'

Summer? Jesus shook his head. At the question, rather than in answer to it.

'Oh.' Danny took him at face value as always. 'I thought it was. Are you sure?'

'Are you tired, Danny?'

'I don't know, am I? I walked a very long way, Jesus.'

'Yes you did, son, yes you did. I'll tell you what, I think you are tired. You walked a very long way. How about having a little nap?'

Jesus stood up from his crouched position on the thinly carpeted floor and began to manoeuvre the mattress out of its plastic sheeting, taking care not to disturb Danny, who was sitting on his packing case, oblivious, sipping his tea.

Jesus gently took the mug from his friend's hands and also the sleeping bag from his shoulders. 'There you go, son. All lovely and warm.'

Danny stood up and began to take off his overalls.

'No, no, no, son. Not that warm. How about you keep them on, eh? And get into the bed as you are.'

'But that's dirty. Mum says -'

'I know what Mum says, but you're staying at my house tonight, aren't you?'

Danny nodded.

'And in my house you have to do what I say. And I say you get into bed with your clothes on.'

Danny opened his mouth to speak.

'And no, you don't have to brush your teeth.'

'But -'

'Or wash your face and hands. Now come on, son, in you get.' Jesus held the sleeping bag open while Danny obediently clambered in.

'Now I'm just going to pop out.'

Danny looked up in slight alarm.

'It's alright, son. I'm just gonna pop out and see yer mum. She'll be worried. I won't be long. And as a special treat, you can keep the light on.'

Danny settled back in contentment. Mum never let him leave the light on. 'OK, Jesus. Na night, Jesus' - resting his weary head upon the jumper-pillow

'Goodnight, son. Back soon.'

Jesus set up his little wedge trap and stepped out into the cloudless night: a prophet amongst the spotless stars. He trudged across the frosting ground of Smithfieldville, and on into the street-lit shell of the town. Where only drunks and ghosts and madmen now walked. On his way to Danny's Mum. With a head full of questions. And a belly full of fear.

WENDY OGDEN

The Importance of Singing

London, 2041

The women are all standing in doorways - nothing changes. The men are indoors, playing with their crystals and reading old war books. The family at number 13 got a newspaper yesterday, but it will be a week old when it's my old man's turn to read.

Still, I gets to know what's going on in the world because my girl, Diane, like me she's thirteen, well, her Mum is the landlady of The Queen's Head. We already know that *Who Wants to Win Ten Quid?* is going to be on the radio tonight. It's the last show ever, Harry the landlord says, and he's got two big speakers for his crystal radio in the pub.

It's one hell of a time since the old man could afford a pint. Di likes me to call him Dad, but I sometimes forget. Dad says I'm punching above my weight with Di, but who is he to talk? Anyways, Dad's always saying how different beer tasted when he was a kid, and there's no way he'll be putting any vegetables Harry's way. Dad says he'll never barter food for half a glass of water, boiled with pearl barley, whosoever's brewed it.

My old man and Di's mum were talking in the alley the other night about the programme on the radio tonight. They were giggling together about how people used to watch the programme, *watch* the programme, on something called ITV. I've seen old TVs down the dump but don't know what the 'I' stands for.

In the alleyway, they talked about what they would do with the money if they could get on the radio and win ten quid. Di's mum wants to live in the country, she said, and the old man reckoned ten quid would get her a farmhouse, no problem. Then he told her he couldn't leave Mum and all us lot in this slum. Next, she's crying so loud he has to kiss her to get the noise down. I've heard him telling Mum that if he won, he would get her one of those old converted warehouses on the Thames. The old man thinks higher-up homes will get us further from the rats. Mum said we could clip the chickens' wing feathers but pigs might fly.

Everyone knows that competition is a fix anyway, because the people who get on the radio always seem to come from Barnet. How random is that selection? I've thought about moving to Barnet, but then again, with no phone signals left on the planet, how you going to call if you know the answer? I found an old book on *Ghostbusters* but if you can't even call them you're finished. I suppose I might be lucky and get a question on *Ghostbusters* but that's a long shot. This is probably why they're shutting the radio show down.

They say when stuff was on the box, people had more hope.

Dad told me about when people used to watch shows, instead of listen. A film was actually made about the TV show. I don't really get what films were about, not having ever watched a TV show, but Dad said length was the thing, and seeing the bigger picture. This film was about slum people, and their dogs, and how they got so hopeful about winning ten quid.

I just don't get this sense of hope about anything nowadays and can't imagine what was so interesting about life on the East India Dock Road. Slum people wouldn't waste food on dogs now, either, so it seems daft to me, what people got up to in the past, or even made films about. It's no wonder the world went broke.

Trades are always going up. The old man tells us all the time. Fourteen carrots used to get him some lamb neck, but now people are looking for onions, and even potatoes when the weather's been bad. Pig trotters used to get us flour, but now they are looking for ears as well. We're lucky to have a garden, Mum says, but she wouldn't say that if she heard what the old man was getting up to in his potting shed.

If I went to Barnet, I'd take my Diane with me. We're both sick and tired of vegetable-picking. They grow all sorts on the railway lines but it's mostly greens this time of year. She dug up a silver coin last week. You're supposed to hand stuff in but Di kissed the face on the coin then put it in her shoe. I make her right on that. After work, we walked along the underground tunnels home and looked at it under the candlelight.

Seems so weird that people just swapped coins, or bits of paper, and not that long ago. My dad even remembers banks. Then again, trains used to run underground, along tunnels perfect for mushroom growing and rhubarb. The trains made decent homes, so the old man says nothing was wasted in the long run. Di reckons there are some people around that do still use money so she's going to save her coin. Like she says, the radio show must have ten quid, or they wouldn't put the show on the radio.

Di's mum thinks it was a nice idea, money, but it was just like a river that dried up. Maybe that's what my old man sees in her. She likes walking along the Thames, and sometimes they sneak off together and eat jellied eels. How they pay for them, I don't know. My mum tried eating the eels once, but gagged so many times it even put her off walking along the riverbank. Dad moans she won't let him boil his eels in her kitchen now.

Mum reckons if you can't eat money, or smoke it, or wear it to work, then what's the point? Dad'll never leave her though. See, he feeds the hens and she collects the eggs. Apart from that, they both know all the words of *Send in the Clowns*.

My Diane doesn't even know this song. I never told her about my old man and her mum but she found out by chance. Now she thinks everything's gonna fall apart. I always found it odd how her parents could run a pub without singing together, but there's Royals for you.

LINDSAY FISHER

Herschel and a Handful of Silver Fish Tales

He has a New York studio apartment. High in the sky and one of those seeming-big numbers on all his mail: 6255 Shore Street, Manhattan. He looks out over the water, all the way to where his father and mother disembarked, years back, the word 'liberty' on their lips and, as if in answer to their call, she was there, and Liberty seemed to nod her starburst head and bid them welcome to their new home. That's how they afterwards told it to Herschel, and he believed that's how it was.

'This is our story,' they said.

They'd left behind everything they could not carry. A whole different path they took, and they woke one sudden morning to find themselves in this city on the other side of the world. The new world, they called it. Herschel heard them through all the years of his childhood and beyond, talking over what they had lost, raking through the ashes of a life that was gone forever, swapping stories with their neighbours, comparing scars.

And there were scars. Herschel's father had

slipped that first day and that was another story he told. Trying to leap from off the small boat that had at last brought them ashore from Ellis Island, he lost his footing, like the ground shifted under his feet, and he slipped on the spilled silver of small fish. And Herschel's father fell, face to the ground. When he told it, there was something like a dance in his falling again. Kissing the carpet in their front room is what it looked like, as he would have kissed the ground of this new place anyway, but he did not thank God in that fish-silver fall nor bless the ground beneath him; Herschel's father cursed instead.

That first morning in the new world, Herschel's father cut his hand on broken glass. He rubbed the scar when he told that and something was in his eyes, for the story reminded Herschel's father of another glass-breaking time. Not the stamping on a wine-glass at his wedding, but something bigger and more dark, something behind them. The skin on Herschel's father's palm was ever afterwards white and puckered, like cloth when a thread is pulled. He might have been a tailor, but for that fall, though there were tailors enough that stepped ashore before and after him. Instead, Herschel's father dealt in bolts of cloth and reels of thread and packets of pins and buttons.

Herschel's mother was marked too. She had a soreness in her bones, all her days in this new place. She said it was from sleeping crooked in a bed with three other women, a hard, wooden bed, big enough for one, except there were three curled together in a ship's bunk and Herschel's mother curled there too, and that for the long time of a sea-journey that took them from there to here. And her back was never really straight again and her bones ached.

'You are lucky,' they said to Herschel. 'You should feel lucky.'

Then they started again with their stories of how it had been before, stories of the place they'd left, the place they'd once called home: cats in porcelain sitting on small tables, and silver candelabra, and a library of books all bound in red and black leather, and paintings hanging on the walls, and a bed that had belonged to his father's father and the mattress stuffed with eiderdown, so that their dreams were always dreams of flying, and the women sitting, drinking sweet tea from small glasses and watching the grass grow and counting the fruit in the trees, and the men, working hard and becoming rich, and ginger candies in the hands of all the children. All their stories were like that, polished like pebbles that are turned in a river, over and over, and a little smoother for each turning.

So it was that Herschel yearned too for the things they had no more, the things he'd never had except through their stories. His first boyish dreams were of going back, of escaping the place where they were to journey, back to the place that was closer to home. But he knew that could never be. That other life was no more. He could see it was gone in the looks that passed between his parents whenever a story was ended.

That world they spoke of so fondly, only existed now in what was said at family gatherings where uncles and aunts laughed and kissed and cried and shook their heads, remembering what was so completely lost. Herschel noted how the stories that were told shifted from the truth a little more and more with each telling, just in the way a pebble is far from where it began when it is found and lifted out of the water. And they said that Herschel should feel blessed.

For Rachel, it was the same, and they both had the need to free themselves of all that 'lucky' they should be feeling. She was the same age as Herschel. He remembers the first sight he had of her at the Feldshuh's wedding: Sisel and Schmuel joined together as one, under the one prayer shawl, Rabbi Kupner, crumbs of titzkebroidt in his beard and laughing at nothing all the day, and Herschel's mother, crying for the wooden jewellery box she had left behind, a wedding gift from her mother that she had not thought about 'til then. Rachel was there that day, at the Feldshuh's house, dressed in white, like she was the bride, or an angel, or a ghost. The collar of her dress was high and her hair like a black veil to hide her blushes. Only, she was never as innocent as she appeared.

It was Rachel who kissed Herschel, the tip of her ten-year-old tongue in his mouth. He remembers that too, her hair falling across his face and smelling of havdalah spice. He remembers sitting on the roof of a Brooklyn apartment block and the sound of Rachel's feet dancing on the metal stairs as she came to him with that kiss. Herschel sat on his haunches waiting, curled into himself, his lips sewn shut, and she came to soften him. A kiss on the cheek at first and Rachel calling Herschel 'cousin' when he wasn't. She stripped down to her underclothes, so as to keep her dress clean and against the stickiness of summer, and she sat beside him, staring out at the brick buildings that hemmed them in and hemmed in the stars too.

'Do you ever wonder?' she said. 'What it would have been to have stayed?'

Herschel nodded. At least, he afterwards imagined that he did.

'Some stayed,' she told him. 'There are names my parents use and they whisper when they say them and they call on God to bless their souls in heaven. So many names. And a star falling from the sky for every one that died.'

Herschel did not know why she was telling him this, why she was speaking to him like his mother, like his father. Herschel did not know what Rachel wanted him to say. He kept quiet, did not tell her the thoughts that were running through his head, stayed blocked and not speaking.

Rachel just talked anyway. And Herschel listened. Stories she told him, stories of her school-days and her homework-nights and her dreams of another place that she had never seen and that might have been home instead of the place they had been born to. Herschel has them all recorded, the stories she told, scribbles he made in an exercise book when he got home that night, written by the yellow light of an oil-lamp, and Herschel trying to make sense of what she said. Afterwards, those stories were read over and over whenever he thought of Rachel, which was often.

Years later, Herschel showed her what he had written. She said she did not recognize the stories on the paper. She said he'd made them up. They were not her words, and she pouted as one who is cross, or pretending to be.

Herschel had to admit that he had not kept to what she had said, not precisely, not the words she had spoken. Herschel had used all available words. He understood about stories and pebbles turning and truth being a shifting thing. But the stories he had written were hers, he insisted, even though the words were changed.

'Too real,' she protested.

The stories he said were hers were too real. Or too fantastical, for stories can be both at the same time. All the little detail that he had added - she recognized the detail, but not herself in the stories. Stars fell out of a Brooklyn sky, he'd written, all the stars. And it came true, for there were no more stars to be seen in the city sky above them. And he'd written of a rooftop angel, and she undressed for him, and her hair smelled of faraway places, and she kissed his cheek and kissed his lips and spoke straight into his mouth as if passing words from her tongue to his.

'Do words taste of anything?' Rachel said.

Herschel thought they must.

And there, in his sky-high apartment, 6255 Shore Street, Manhattan, Rachel kissed him again, like on the roof that first ten-year-old night. And in the middle of that kiss, she said she was sorry and Herschel tasted salt. She said she was sorry to be so late. Something about an accident on the subway, and a person under the rails, and people squeezing forward to see, and Rachel knocked this way and that, snatching glimpses of the dead person through the legs of those in front of her. Rachel said that she noticed the dead woman's print dress was torn, had been torn before and held together by a bent pin. It was the pin she remembered, shaped like a fish with one eye.

Rachael stripped off then, like that rooftop meeting when she was a girl of ten. Down to her underwear again, and her clothes laid as neat as neat over the back of a chair. Then she climbed into Herschel's bed.

'Do you believe in fate?' she said. She was shaking when she said it.

Herschel thought he didn't.

'Or chance?'

'I do not take any risks,' he said. But that wasn't what she meant.

She was crying, held there in Herschel's arms, and maybe it was the shock. She kept saying about the pin, like a fish. In Herschel's head the fish took shape and he was there at the subway station, craning his neck to see a woman looking like she was asleep, her feet under the train and a small kicking silver fish sucking its last breath on the sleeve of her torn print dress. Men in black felt hats, and faces all aglower, lifted the woman high above their heads and carried her out into the light. Like Orpheus bringing Eurydice back to the living and back home, Herschel thought. Only Orpheus never did, for the dead stay dead no matter how often the story is told.

When Rachel was asleep and Herschel felt like he was alone in the daylight dim of his studio apartment, he wrote down that subway story of Rachel's, and it was different from the way Rachel had told it. He did not use her words, but used his own, and so the story was different and more like his dream, with the men in dark hats pushing their way aggressively out into the New York bright street, and the fish flicking and flicking its silver tale.

Of course, Herschel meant to write 'tail' and when he read what he'd written instead he thought he had made a joke and he laughed out loud, his laughter making a small disturbance in the air, and then nothing.

He wrote, too, about Rachel falling asleep in his bed, and how he watched her dream, hoping that it was not blood that she dreamed of. And home is where the heart is, he wrote and he did not know why. He wrote down what Rachel had said about her stories not being hers, even though they had been – just the words changed. And he thought of the stories his parents told, over and over, stories belonging to Herschel now they had both gone, or maybe it was Hershel who belonged to the stories. Belonging and not belonging; that's what he felt.

He also wrote down the questions Rachel had asked, about chance and fate, and he thought about these things too, considered all the small and bigger collisions that had brought them to this moment and this place high in the sky and looking out over the water towards a statue that announced freedom in her name. It's the working of God, his parents would have said. He could see his father's raised hands and the scar on one palm. God's will in bringing them here, he would have said. God's will in saving them when so many others had not been saved. God's will in everything. That did not make sense to Herschel, that God had not saved the others too, when this new place was big enough it could have been home to them all and they could all have been saved. Luck or fate, Herschel could not decide, had no great thing to say about life – just stories to tell.

There was a river on the edge of where Herschel's father lived when he was a boy. Wider than a road that river was, and clear as glass so you could see the fish coming out from the dark under the bridge. Herschel's father was there with a tin bucket and a cloth net, scooping only pebbles from the water and throwing them back again, throwing them further downstream, helping them on their way to where they were going. Then, on the bridge, was a girl in a summer dress, the sun behind her so Herschel's father could not see her face, could see only the outline of her through the white cloth.

'Try again,' the girl urged.

So Herschel's father did. He stretched the full reach of one arm and scooped once more. This time in his net, when he looked, there was a surprise fish, long as a finger, all silver and small rainbows. Herschel crooked and crooked his own finger in imitation of his father telling the story. The girl on the bridge was Herschel's mother, and she kept insisting that he put the caught fish back in the precise place where he had found it: 'Otherwise it would be lost and forever looking for the place that was its home.'

Herschel believed in silver fish and stars falling and angels dancing up stairs and undressing for him on all the roofs in Brooklyn. They seemed real, as stories can. But he could not decide between chance or fate and, when Rachel woke, he thought that he would tell her that. He'd also tell her the story of his father catching pebbles and a single silver fish and his mother just a girl then in a white dress and standing on a bridge with the sun behind her. Then Herschel thought he'd ask Rachel to stay in his bed. Not just for a night, but for all the nights, 'til years turned over and they'd tell their own children stories about tailors in Brooklyn and stars in the spaces between the buildings when you looked up and angel-kisses on rooftops and grandparents grown too quickly old and buried in Brooklyn's Mount Hope Cemetery – stories rooted in where they had been and blossoming now in where they were. And maybe, for these children at least, Herschel thought, maybe for them this still seeming-new place would feel like home.

MAX DUNBAR
Land of Little Black Ghosts

Sunday. The busiest day of the week. He got up before dawn and began picking litter on the Transpennine Trail. Took a wheelbarrow with a roll of industrial plackeys and a litter spear. He speared empty Dixy Chicken boxes, tubs of White Lightning, flyers for the Warehouse Project or the Ram or Trof Salutation, cans of John Smith's, paper and polystyrene from a thousand nameless Fallowfield takeaways. He picked up shards of glass from between bridges, a pile of it under the Kingsway tunnel, spread out from the tunnel's curve as if someone had hurled a pint glass against the wall, very hard: once, an edge pierced his skin through the rubber gloves and he tied it with an antiseptic bandage. Sometimes, people thought him a barman, from the plasters on his fingers and hands; even the best ones drop a glass.

He found a woman's shoe. He found a black, wide-brimmed hat. He found needles. He found pipes. Sometimes, there were wallets, or mobiles, which he handed in to Withington police station. On occasion, he found dead animals on the verge, necessitating a call to the street-cleaning team, which would come out and dispose of the corpse to government standards. This time, there was nothing interesting but a piece of paper, covered margin-to-margin in Parker scribbles, completely legible but it made no sense: *I am going to write a book called CRAZY and I will make a film called CRAZY and start a band called CRAZY and our big tune will be called CRAZY and you will be my CRAZY QUEEN* was about as far as he got. By now, his clothes were soaked up to the knees in drink discards and his jeans were covered in stray leaves from ploughing through gradients of overgrowth, spear-bobbing for lingerie or crisp packets caught on some high, splintered branch.

The day spread out and he began to see people. At first, an isolated dog walker or morning jogger. The odd group, still on the go from the night before. He saw a couple pushing a shopping trolley full of metal and wood. Mountain bikers swished past, encased in pink and yellow. Then the familiar pattern of cyclists, skateboarders, rollerbladers, scallies, cut-throats and families. The sun was bright and heavy in the sky.

One of the cyclists hailed him: 'Hey, do you want help with that?'

'You sure?' He tossed the man a bag and a spear.

They walked on. The cyclist picked it up easy. Sounds of metal on plastic, metal on aluminium, brash and abrasive.

'So what do you do?' the cyclist asked.

'I work part time, B&Q.'

Except that wasn't all he did.

They called him The Volunteer.

Monday, he worked a shift at the CAB in the Northern Quarter.

Tuesday, he cycled over to Swinton to work at the Welfare Rights.

On Wednesdays, he used to work at Manchester Debt Advice, except that got cut, so now he cycled over to Stockport to work at the Debt Advice there.

Thursdays, Rochdale Law Centre.

Fridays and Saturdays, he helped out at the church on Burnage Lane.

Friday and Saturday nights, he worked at the Samaritans.

Nothing skilled, nothing unsupervised, just a presence, the listener, the apologist, veteran of CRBs and suspicious looks, there to offer comfort if not action to a parade of broken men and women: bitter and self-righteous workless families, asylum seekers who still bore the electro scars from Evin or New Bell, depressives, obsessives, products of the care and prison system, victims of character and circumstance who negotiated in angry bewilderment the pathways of a state that didn't care about them. The infrastructure was falling apart, this new government, but it didn't do good to get on a *high horse* about anything, you can only do what you can.

He talked on with the cyclist. The feeling of awkwardness began to fade.

By the time they reached the Yew Tree Bridge,

another couple of people had joined them – a Spanish woman and her partner from Sale. They reached Princess Parkway as a group of around ten people, including a couple of student hipsters and an eighty-year-old Malay veteran. At the Chorlton tramlines, the group had swelled to over twenty, and the wheelbarrow was almost full.

The atmosphere had become noisy and unsettled, with wild, happy chatter bouncing in his ears, when he saw the man. He had clearly just dismounted St Werburgh's Steps, and had locked his knuckles behind his head, swaying with a ferocious urgency: hard to miss, but seemingly possible, as no one else had even noticed this guy. The Volunteer sprinted over just as the man collapsed, and not an exhausted topple but a full-scale surrender to the floor.

This man had grey hair, a red face, tracksuit, shell-suit even, probably a drinker, younger than he looked, older than he felt. The Volunteer had his phone on and had got through to the ambulance before he even reached the old man. Guy couldn't stand, a stroke maybe or something. Everyone had been having such a jolly time picking litter in the sunshine that it took a while for the new reality to sink in, the pretence of solemnity, hanging around and the vague proffer of practical information. The dispatcher kept asking questions, which he relayed to the old man. Stroke a few years ago, he had been right. The old man kept asking for cigarettes.

An FRU was on the scene in moments. The old

man still could not stand, so they had to load him onto a stretcher and take him over the tramlines and, carefully, up the steps to the bridge where the ambo drew up. The paramedics thanked him for stopping and calling. Not everyone would, the guy said.

With the departure of the old man, the atmosphere lightened again. The cyclist suggested a trip to the pub, so they went to the Spread Eagle. There was a lot of drink and laughter and conversation. It had a scary lightness on it. People said things to him, but it was hard to get a grip on what was said.

He headed at last orders. It was a warm and boneless night. He got the last bus back to Gorton. The house. Thing is, when you work, you don't think, and when you stop, it all comes back in. Shapes gathered on the drive. He put the key in the lock. Darkness closed around him.

SARAH EVANS

Between the Gaps

The phone rings in the midst of a busy morning.

'Hello?' I query, only to be met with silence. 'Hello?'

'Is that Marilyn?'

It's been ten years, but I recognise the voice instantly. 'Doreen?'

'Yes.'

We pause and my mind floods with apologies and questions.

'How are you?' we say simultaneously.

'I ... Look ... Could we meet?' she says.

'Yes, of course.'

'I was thinking of coming up to London. One weekend.'

'Come to the house. I mean, if it's convenient. Just twenty minutes on the District Line. Come for lunch.'

'No - I mean I won't stay long. But I'd like to see where you've settled.'

Only afterwards do the questions start up. *Why?*

Pete asks exactly that when I explain. 'So why now?'

'I don't know.'

He looks at me in that thoughtful way he has. 'You've never really said why you never go and see them.'

'I don't know. It just sort of happened.'

When I moved to London, my life filled up with work and friends. The one time I did visit, well, it wasn't the same. Another child had taken my place, and I thought - not because Doreen wasn't warm, in her tussled, distracted way - I thought that, after all, fostering a child was only supposed to be a temporary measure and she and Jim did of course get paid to do it.

The day arrives and I've cleaned the house specially, though I don't quite know why I've bothered. I think back to the cosy chaos of Doreen's house. Doreen and Jim's.

Pete cradles my face gently between his hands as he kisses me.

'Hope it goes well,' he says.

I stand at the window and watch as he cycles off and, though it was me who asked him not to be here, now I'm wishing he wasn't going after all. Because standing here like this, I feel unexpectedly nervous. I watch people pass. I keep thinking that I see her and it turns out not to be, nothing like.

But then - this time the certainty is instant. Her green raincoat is an exact match for the one she always wore, though it can't be the same one, surely. Her hair has turned grey and her shoulders stoop a little. But it's her. My substitute mum for four years.

A better mum than my own. I wonder how I can possibly have let time slip the way it has, how I could have failed to keep in touch, letting old affections slip through the cracks.

I go to the door and open it before she knocks. She smiles, but there's an anxious pleat between her eyes. She always did have a worried air, concerned for her charges, wanting to do right by us. I smile back and I probably look anxious too. We embrace awkwardly; she feels thinner than before and I've lost my puppy fat, so our bones rub up against each other. I usher her in and listen to her exclamations of *just look at you, looking so well, so grown-up.*

I show her through to the living room and she says, 'Doesn't this look nice.' I maintain the stretch of my smile and hold back from saying that it's only temporary, we hope to move somewhere bigger soon.

'I'll make tea.'

'Oh, don't bother.'

'It isn't any bother.'

Doreen. Tea. I picture how she always had a mug to hand, and how I never saw her finish a cup, because there were always distractions, important things needing to get done. I tell her to sit on the sofa, but she follows me through to the kitchen anyway and says, once again, how nice everything is. I see how it's out of date, but clean. I wonder if her kitchen has been updated in the ten years since I last sat, enfolded within its baked-bread warmth and fragrance. It feels rude to ask directly.

'Have you made any changes?' I ask. 'To the house?'

She looks at me, her smile faltering. 'We sold the house.'

It's a second or two before I realise that I'm standing with my mouth open, my eyes wide. 'Oh,' is all I manage.

'It got too big.'

'Yes.'

I feel outrage. Though I haven't even visited for ten years. *It was my home,* I want to say; I feel I should have been consulted.

I think of the small, dusk-pink room, right up at the top with the sloping ceiling, the room that I called mine.

Not that it was mine. Not really.

I remind myself how many others will have slept in that narrow bed, peered out of the skylight at the stars, kept shells and conkers on the wonky shelf, stored secrets underneath the loose floorboard in the corner, pushed pennies between the cracks, 'til nothing remained but a glinted edge.

'So where do the two of you live now?' My voice emerges false and perky.

'We ... I mean, I ... I didn't move far. A small flat, just the other side of town.'

My face creases, first in puzzlement, then in dread. 'Jim?' I ask, my voice unexpectedly hoarse.

'Oh, he's fine,' she says brusquely. 'He moved away. What else could I do - in the circumstances?'

Circumstances?

It occurs to me that it might be better if we're sitting down.

'I'll just finish,' I say as my hands busy themselves with making tea and putting out biscuits.

We sit across from each other at the tiny circular table, which just fits into the corner of the kitchen and which Pete and I never actually use. The table wobbles a little as she places her elbows on it and then she tucks her elbows away.

I raise my mug and pretend to sip. It's too hot anyway.

'So,' I say slowly, my expression set for offering sympathy. 'What happened? I mean you and Jim?'

My mind fails to wrap itself around the fact that they're no longer together; perhaps I don't want it to. They have been my ideal of devoted coupledom all my life. Not like my real family.

She stares fixedly down at the plastic tablecloth, as if the answer lies there in the yellow flowers. Until I think she isn't going to answer.

Then she looks at me, her eyes narrowed and sharp as steel. 'Did he ever touch you?' she asks.

The question makes no sense. Of course he touched me. Affectionate cuffs to the shoulder and chucks to the chin and all-encompassing hugs. But the sick feeling in my stomach has already gripped, while my mind is slowly catching up with what she means.

'*Inappropriately,*' she adds.

'No.' I sound angry and I'm not sure who with.

'Why?'

She seems to sag, a beach ball that's been punctured. Her eyes are wide and hurt and tired and they don't meet mine. Her hands flutter and fall. 'There've been …' she says, '… allegations.'

'Who?'

'Boys. It seems it was the boys.'

'And it's been proved?'

'Not enough evidence for prosecutions. Not after all this time. And he's sticking to his story. Denies it all.'

'Well, perhaps -'

'Three of them have come forward.'

'You believe them?'

'Not at first. But three. From different times. They didn't know each other.'

My mind is a wasp's nest of questions but, looking at her, I don't have the heart to ask any of them. She wouldn't be here, if she wasn't sure.

I think of the boys from my time there. Little Matt, who always wet the bed. Tim, who pulled my hair. I want to ask for names, but don't.

She pushes her mug of tea away, untouched. She starts to stand, leaning heavily on the table, which wobbles and sets the tea spilling.

'I'm sorry,' she says.

'It's all right.' Except it isn't. 'You don't have to go.'

'I did wonder,' she says. 'What with you not coming back, not keeping in touch. I can't face following up with all of them. I just wanted to know.'

When she's gone, I sit back down and my finger traces curling lines in the spilt tea. I think how when I'm asked about my family, I tell people unflinchingly how, aged thirteen, I was taken into care. When people mumble *sorry*, I look them in the eye and say it wasn't so bad, not really. *I had wonderful foster parents, providing a wonderful home.*

I think how I had some sort of teenage crush on Jim. And how the one time I visited, I was put out by the attention he was giving a little boy and the way he almost ignored me being there. I think of things I might have noticed and did not, a glint of unwanted knowledge slipping through, getting lost. Did I know? Did I choose not to?

Two hours later, Pete finds me still sitting here. He smiles easily.

'How did it go?'

I stand and let him put his arms around me, burying my face in his neck, grateful he can't see my face.

'It was fine,' I say. 'It was good to catch up.'

JILLY WOOD
Home Advantage

Suzanne Wilson stood in the marbled lobby and prayed for patience as her nineteen-year-old meal-ticket squared up to a man more than twice his age. The job should have been easy. Show the kid (sorry, client) a selection of the best rental properties in the area. Wait for him to choose the one he liked. Send humungous invoice to his management company. Receive payment, placate bank manager, high fives all round.

The building was brand new, but the concierge was old-school, suited and booted, with shining shoes, ramrod posture, and a military-standard haircut. His face was professionally blank, but his feelings about her client as a potential tenant were crystal clear.

Johan Moore gave the old soldier a final scowl and spun round on his good leg. His sweat pants fell even lower on his hips, showing a good three inches of underwear bearing his name on the waistband. He hitched them up, and they slid back down.

'Let's go.'

'Go where? You haven't even seen the place.'

'Don't need to.' He chewed ostentatiously,

snapping his gum half a dozen times; she gritted her teeth and reminded herself that he was not her son. 'I don't like it here.'

'Mr Moore -'

'Jo,' he corrected. 'Or JoMo.'

'Jo. This is the tenth place we've seen today.' Unlike him, she was wearing formal shoes and, after two days, her feet were screaming for relief. 'We viewed ten yesterday. Perhaps we should discuss why you didn't like any of those before I waste your time showing you another ten tomorrow.'

'I don't like this neighbourhood.' He flicked a glance back at the concierge. 'It's all fancy restaurants and old lady salons.' He reached up to groom his hair, shaved close and dark to somewhere high above his ears, where a tight tangle of custard-yellow curls clustered improbably. 'I need somewhere more me. Clerkenwell, or Shoreditch.'

Clurkenwell or Sure Ditch. His biography said he'd been born in Yorkshire, but he'd grown up in Florida, and his accent was pure Sunshine State.

'Unfortunately, Jo, neither of those areas is within fifteen minutes' drive of the National Tennis Centre.' She tapped the client questionnaire on her clipboard. It was the only thing he'd been clear about. 'Shoreditch to Roehampton would take you more than an hour on a good day.'

He muttered something that made the concierge stiffen even further, and stomped outside. He was favouring his good leg, which spoiled the effect.

'Sorry about that,' she said over her shoulder as she hurried after him.

'Best of luck, ma'am,' followed her through the double doors.

He was sitting on the bench in the manicured gardens, hunched moodily over his phone. She sat carefully on the other end, slipped her feet out of her shoes, and waited for him to finish tweeting his displeasure to his many thousands of followers.

'What's on the list for tomorrow?' he asked, without looking up.

She flipped through the remaining options. 'Two double bedrooms, both en suite, own entrance, a few streets from here?'

'No way.'

'Beautiful loft-style apartment with fantastic kitchen?'

'Pointless. Don't cook.'

'River view?'

'I'll be in the gym. I won't see it. And I bet it stinks in summer.'

'Spectacular penthouse?'

'Don't like heights.'

'You don't want a garden. You don't want a house. You don't like old buildings because the floorboards creak.' She listed yesterday's disasters. 'I have to ask you, JoMo,' she gave full weight to his ridiculous nickname and he slanted her a sideways look, 'What do you want? Please tell me and put us both out of our misery.'

His eyes slid away from hers and he turned back to his phone. 'I'll know it when I see it.'

'Frankly, I'm not sure it exists,' she said.

'Why do you care?' he muttered. 'You're getting paid anyway.'

Not until you sign on the dotted line, JoMo.

This was getting them nowhere. Her feet rebelled at the idea of further torture, but the prospect of facing Mr Brown at NatWest empty-handed was far, far worse.

'Tell me something, Jo,' she said. 'You're the next great hope of British tennis, right?'

'I'll be top 50 soon.' Good grief, the kid actually cracked a smile, and his face didn't break. 'I'm going to be top 10 before I'm 21.' He stretched his leg out, and his expression clouded over again. 'As soon as I rehab my knee.'

'What do you do when you're playing somebody for the first time?'

He shrugged. 'Do my homework. Make a plan. Play to my strengths. Exploit the other guy's weak points.'

'What if your plan doesn't work?'

'Change the game,' he said automatically. 'Try something else.'

'What if you've tried everything you can think of and you're still not getting anywhere?'

'Never, ever give up,' he said. 'Keep trying to make him do things your way. If all else fails, attack.'

Out of the mouths of kids and clients.

'Thank you, Jo.' She reached over, confiscated his phone, and dropped it in her bag.

'Heyyyy,' he said, outraged. 'What are you doing?'

'Taking your advice,' she said. 'You can have your phone back when you tell me ...'

She thought for a minute. 'Five things you want from your new home.'

'I'll complain,' he said.

'If you want to look ridiculous.' She zipped her bag and tucked it under her arm. 'It would be easier to answer the question.'

He folded his arms, scowling. 'Wi-fi.'

'One.' She raised a single finger.

'A big bed with an orthopaedic mattress.'

'Two.' He was well over six feet tall, with broad shoulders and long limbs, so that made sense.

'Plenty of noise.'

'Sorry?'

'I'm used to lots of people around.' He fidgeted on the bench. 'I can't sleep when it's quiet.'

That was unexpected. Somewhere with hustle and bustle. It ruled out most of the other places on her list but, finally, they were making progress. 'Two more things and you can have your phone back.'

He frowned. 'A bathroom with a proper shower and loads of hot water. And restaurants,' he said eventually. 'Not fancy places. Somewhere I can get home-cooked food. Pasta. Or chicken.'

'Any particular kind of pasta?'

'Spaghetti. With tomato and basil.' To-may-do and

bay-sil. 'Nothing with cream. Clams are good. Or meat sauce.'

Bingo.

'I love pasta.' Suzanne unzipped her bag and handed his phone back. 'In fact, we're having spaghetti bolognese for dinner tonight.'

'Oh. Wow.' He swallowed hard, and she actually heard his stomach rumble. 'I don't suppose ...'

Exploit his weak points. Never give up.

'I'd invite you to join us, but I need to go through the database and see if I can find some places that might be more suitable for you.' He looked so crestfallen, she almost laughed out loud. 'Unless, maybe, you do that whilst I make supper?'

It seemed as though every neighbour in the street was out in their front garden as Suzanne directed JoMo to park his testosterone rocket. The next available parking space was two streets away, and he was leaning on his car, soaking up the attention, by the time she hobbled back.

Suddenly, this didn't seem like such a good idea. He followed her up the path, looking around with great interest, and she was horribly aware of the weeds choking the handkerchief-sized front garden and the peeling paint on the door.

'Hi, Mum.' As usual, Alex was at the table, head buried in his homework. 'Did you find a pad for the Great White Hope?'

'Not yet,' Jo said from behind her. 'Your mom's taken me to twenty places, and they all sucked.'

Alex's head shot up as Jo sauntered into the kitchen, pulled up a chair, and planted his elbows on the table.

'All of them?'

'Yeah. That's why she's bribing me with pasta.'

'Jo, this is my son, Alex. Alex, this is Jo.'

She should have saved her breath. Neither was listening, as her son and her client eyeballed one another across the debris of textbooks and notes. Jo was a couple of years older and nearly a foot taller, but Alex was a force of nature.

'What was wrong with the places you saw?'

'I didn't like them.' Jo's lip curled. The 'doh' was silent, but it was definitely there.

'Well, obviously. I was asking why.' Clearly translated as 'Doh to you, too.'

'Because they weren't right, OK?'

'Can you be more specific?'

Jo's coffee-coloured skin darkened to a deep, rich brown. 'I told your mom, I'll know it when I see it.'

'That's ridiculously imprecise.' Alex put down his pen and treated Jo to the scrutiny he normally reserved for his natural history projects. 'How do you expect Mum to find you somewhere if you don't give her any data to work with?'

'Because that's her job?' Jo drawled, slouching, and Alex, bless him, bristled.

'She's not a mind-reader. She can't find you what you want if you don't tell her what to look for.'

Jo had no idea what he was up against. *I'll rescue*

319

him in a minute, Suzanne told herself guiltily. Or maybe not.

'What about your questionnaire, Mum?' In Alex's world she was close to infallible, and she did her best not to disillusion him. 'Your clipboard has more firepower than Harry Potter's wand.'

'It does,' she said. 'But it needs fuel. If you put nothing in, there's a pretty good chance you'll get nothing out.'

Alex frowned, and Jo looked over at Suzanne, nonplussed. She should have helped him out, but she simply couldn't make herself do it. She pulled up the remaining chair, kicked off her shoes, put her head in her hands, and laughed. Go, Alex.

'But why -'

'OK, OK, OK.' Jo lifted his hands up. 'My bad. I did not answer the questions.'

'But -'

'Give me a break, will you?' He pushed his chair back from the table and stood up, banging his head on the light fitting. 'I couldn't do them. *I don't know what I want.*'

Suzanne stopped laughing. For two days, she'd been fantasizing about putting him over her knee. Not for a moment had it occurred to her that his brattishness might be bravado.

'Sorry.' He sat down again. 'The last three years, I've been on a court or in a plane or a hotel room. I see the same people over and over, but half the time I don't know what city or even what time zone I'm in.

Before that, I lived at an academy with a couple of hundred other kids.'

He stretched out an arm, lifted Suzanne's clipboard from the kitchen counter, and started to read.

'Do I prefer a south-facing property? Do I require a separate entrance? Do I prefer lateral space? Must I be close to public transport?' He put his hands on the table, palms up. 'How am I supposed to know these things?'

Alex looked at Jo for a long moment. Her son's face was screwed into the expression that usually indicated a really juicy physics or chemistry problem. 'Mum, will you log us in after dinner?' he said. 'I think Jo and I need to talk.'

Suzanne washed the dishes, worked through her entire ironing pile and, finally, sat down with a glass of wine and her laptop. There was loud laughter coming from the spare bedroom that doubled as her study, so they clearly weren't killing one another in there, but her database wasn't that funny, nor should it have taken them nearly two hours to put together a short list of places.

Eventually, they emerged, looking ridiculously pleased with themselves. Jo looked down at Alex, who handed over one of her spare clipboards with a single piece of paper attached.

'I told Jo you're the best,' he said. 'You just need good data to work with.'

Suzanne looked down at the board and shook her head. It was her questionnaire all right, but not so much revised as ripped up and reinvented. She took a sip of wine and started to think.

Jo put one huge hand on Alex's shoulder. 'If I get this, Alex, I'll owe you big time.'

'Good.' Alex's face broke out into a satisfied grin that broadcast 'problem solved'. 'When you get this, I'm coming to visit.'

Nightingale Lodge.

Jo looked dubiously up at the water-damaged brickwork. It had clearly been a fine place in its day, but that day had most likely been well before he was born.

'OK, I could walk to the Centre from here, or buy a bike. What else does it have going for it?'

Suzanne let them into the building and he stood back to make room for a couple of young women heading the other way. They did a double-take as they passed, nudged one another, and then stopped again half-way down the path and looked back. Jo straightened his shoulders and smiled back, and Suzanne bit back her own smile, hoping this would turn out to be the brilliant idea it had seemed two days ago.

'There's only one bedroom, but it's quite a good size,' she said, opening the door to the flat and showing him inside. 'The building has wi-fi but you should probably think about having your own broadband installed.'

The main room was reasonably spacious with nice, high ceilings. There was a strong smell of paint but, thank goodness, the place was pristine. Unfortunately, the sound insulation was not great, and she winced as a muffled thump-thump-thump from upstairs made the walls vibrate.

'Kanye West.' He listened for a moment, and then his head started to nod.

She opened the internal doors. Win or lose, this was not going to be a lengthy viewing. 'The bathroom's rather basic, but there's an excellent hot water supply.'

'Mmm.'

'The kitchen's fully equipped and it works, though the appliances aren't as high a quality as I'd like.'

'Whatever.' He was still nodding. Footsteps clattered down the stairs and the front door slammed.

'I don't suppose you'll use it much anyway. Shall we go for a coffee and talk about it?'

'Don't drink hot drinks,' he said. 'I'll have water and you can explain.'

She locked up behind him, crossed the lobby and pushed open the battered wooden doors to the small in-house cafe. The place was heaving, and the noise level was so high she doubted they'd be having much of a conversation, but her client looked around and broke into a beam that transformed him from surly to shockingly handsome. The sound stopped for a moment and then resumed at an even greater volume.

Suzanne looked around and shook her head, feeling every one of her forty years. Policemen weren't the only ones getting younger every day.

He followed her to the counter, still looking back over his shoulder, and she had to tap his arm a couple of times to get his attention.

'Jo, meet my friend Donna. Her spaghetti bolognese is even better than mine.'

The kid had nice manners, when he chose to use them. He held his hand out. Donna took one look up at him, nipped round to the customer side and kissed his cheek instead.

'Must be good,' he said politely.

'Wait 'til you taste it,' Donna said. 'I grill a mean chicken breast, too.'

He looked at Suzanne and she patted her clipboard. 'Data,' she said. 'Tell me what home means to you, and I'll make it happen.'

'We're open early 'til late,' Donna continued. 'Have to, with people coming and going at all hours of the day and night.'

Jo looked from one to the other. 'What is this place?'

'It's historic,' Suzanne said. 'You could Google it.' He waited. 'It was the gift of a wealthy Londoner after Queen Mary's Hospital saved his daughter's life.'

'So -'

'When he died, he left it to be used as accommodation for nurses, and that's what it's been ever since,' Donna chimed in. 'The current caretaker prefers to live with his family, so his flat has been sitting empty. We suggested to the Trust that they should consider letting it out, and they agreed, if a suitable tenant could be found.'

'You may have to pay a little over the asking price to secure it right away,' Suzanne said. 'It's still far cheaper than any of the other places we looked at.' She paused. 'That's assuming it meets your -'

'Excuse me.' The speaker was dark and petite, probably in her early twenties. She looked back to where a group of friends nodded and waved and called encouragement. 'Are you JoMo? I'm Kathy. My friends and I were wondering if you'd like to join us. There's a spare seat at our table.'

'One moment, Kathy.' He bent and folded Suzanne into a hug. 'Alex was right,' he said. 'You're the best. Please tell my agent to make it happen. Longest lease he can get.' He grinned at her and kissed Donna's cheek again. 'That's Suzanne,' she heard him say as he followed Kathy to the table. 'She finds homes for people.'

Once they'd figured out what was what important, the job was easy. High fives all round and everyone was happy, even Mr Brown at NatWest. JoMo's getting closer to his goal of becoming the first Englishman to win Wimbledon since Fred Perry in 1936. And when anyone asks his secret, he just smiles and says, 'Home advantage.'

ALICE CUNINGHAME
Tunnels

It is January and, even in the centre of my house full of tunnels, the cold seeps in from outside. I realise I need new gloves; the ones I am wearing are too frayed. They catch on things in the tunnels, leaving broken wool on them, stuck to chipped plastic and worn metal. I will look for new gloves when I go out; when I go searching through all the things the others don't want. I go to skips and dumps and bins, taking the detritus of other people's lives and building with it. Other people think my house is chaos and dirty sickness. I know they're wrong. The neighbours want me to leave; they threaten me with the council. I just keep moving and replacing and squashing, making the tunnels. I have systems, places for different things, so I can find them. I suppose they're not really tunnels that I make, but alleyways, walls of my things that reach to the ceiling. I call them tunnels because that's what they feel like - warm and deep.

I find my thickest coat, and leave the house. The sky is deep grey, pressing on the roofs. I listen as my steps scrape the pavement. I am heading for the council tip, forty minutes away. That's where I mostly get things, although there is more pleasure in the little finds on pavements, driveways, parks, the back alleys of industrial estates. I like things that look as if they once meant something, that were once central and loved, but whose meaning had become scattered, forgotten. The outgrown dress, the worn cushion, the cracked jewellery box.

As I walk, I think about Sara. I think about how, in summer, we would sit in the garden, with the night coming up around us as the suburban lights clicked out. Twigs, black against twilight blue, and pale flowers, stark bright in darkness. Soft hair, long fingers on my arm. Grey curls from our cigarettes. I keep memories like these; I like the way they feel dense but can still be kept distant, unbroken. I remember the stage, in the club, 1968. Vibrations from the saxophone, languid smoke under a low ceiling. The notes and the people and Sara at the front of the stage, the way her body seemed to glide with the music as she sang. The jazz and the darkness and Sara. It felt like everything.

When we first met, she walked into the club and sat, purposeful, at the bar. She waited, after we had finished playing and her friends had left, crossed legs in black stockings, and long fingers. Everything exact, organised and just as it needed to be. Sara got what she needed, what she wanted, from this effortless sleekness of presence. Letting me buy her drinks with her half-smile. She captivated the band as she had me, and then she started to sing with us. Her voice was only just above average, but nobody cared. Sara was not just a singer. Sara was red lipstick that never wiped off; she was rustling dresses, perfect curls in her hair that fell out in the sweat without caring, their sheen bright in the smoky musical dark. She was just there, absorbed into my life. There were no decisions. Life was jazz and whisky chasers, dark rooms and morning taxis, sex and cheap speed. Grimy Soho rooms. All tangled and pretty and relentless.

Later, 6.00am, snorting drugs and drinking shots became 6.00am, watching deep grey rain hit the dawn pavement. And Sara pretending to sleep. Our bed, too wide. A white cot in the corner. Two people in a room containing two empty beds. We had tried to have a child for three years, feeling that, alone, we were not enough for ourselves. Our little world of youth and music had begun to flag; gigs were less exciting, and everything was drifting into a strange haze of unknown change. Marriage, children: suddenly, these were not far off abstractions; they were what we needed to do next. She stopped her pill a few months after the wedding and miscarried for the first time a year after. Twice more, and then we were there, in that room, not sleeping and not talking on an early Sunday morning. I remember how my stomach felt twisted, eating itself from inside when I remembered what we were.

I've reached the dump, and I go for my usual search. I haven't thought about Sara like this for a long time, and I don't want to start to think about what happened. I don't know. I only remember a ball of argument, stairs, blood, lights, sirens, white noise. There are different places for different things, categories of rubbish. It is busy, people coming in their cars, unloading everything from their boots, men in orange jackets directing it all. I never speak to them, but they know me, giving me sly glances of inquisitive recognition. I search the general section. This is where I look; the other sections are assigned to certain things and are unexciting: fridges, televisions, recyclables. I find a couple of things I might keep, stuff them down into my rucksack. An old picture frame, wood with worn-off gold paint, greenish. A plastic bag of broken paperback books with cracking spines. I think about taking the mahogany cabinet door I find them under, but decide it's too big. Then this saxophone box. I know it feels heavy enough to have the instrument in it. I haven't played since Sara.

I take it home quickly, walking against the bite of the wind. The clouds are darkening. Inside, I go to my usual chair next to the kitchen door. I look at the black box on my lap, it is barely marked. I open it. The saxophone is perfect, smooth cold metal in soft lining. There are reeds and a cleaning cloth with it. I wonder why this was on the dump. It's not rubbish. Was it there because of some rage? An unthinking punishment? Some argument gone too far? Or a prized possession, thrown out as a bad memory? I slip into the garden with the sax and my chair, wanting to get into the air. A chair leg catches in bindweed. I pull it off, shakily.

The sax feels heavy, slippery, as if it might leap from my fingers. It is after four o'clock now and the winter's early dark and deep clouds are turning the garden to night. My hands shake as I attach a reed. I play for the first time in nearly four decades, thinly at first, the vibrations dull and unfamiliar on my lips. Dim lit winter jasmine shines through dark brambles as the snow begins to fall, soft and large. The notes I play get fuller in the air. They thicken and fly with the snow. I am back in the club with Sara, and this, again, feels like everything.

Stories for Homes

IAIN MALONEY
A Cityscape, At Night

Where do you usually start? With a cityscape, at night. The camera rises from behind a building – typically a Parisian apartment with those quintessential, slanted, slate roofs – and gives you the whole city smack in the face. You get the tower, Sacre Coeur, everything spread out with potential: the street, the building, the room, the window of the ex- or soon-to-be lover, gazing forlornly out onto the city, trying to see into the bedroom of The One.

Of course, it doesn't have to be Paris. Any city will do. Find me a city and I'll find you an occupied window.

Let's take Edinburgh. I know it better than Paris and happen to think the castle is much more impressive than the tower and, when this is made into the Hollywood-blockbusting-rom-com it's destined to become, you will surely agree with me as …

The camera rises from behind a Georgian town house, probably looking from Stockbridge, climbing the hill at an angle and, suddenly, you get the castle and the monument, the ridge of the Royal Mile, the hotel, Saints Andrew and Giles, all spread out with potential, and we zoom in on a specific street, on number 14, top left, on the window where he stands, gazing forlornly out onto the city, trying to see … Well, he doesn't know yet. That's the problem.

What shall we call him?

I've never been very good at naming people. You know those conversations you have, the 'what will you call your children?' conversations that you have to change to 'what would you call your children, were you to have any?' because there's always one person who tries to spoil the party by saying, 'oh, I'm not going to have kids. I hate children' and it's always the person who ends up spurting out an entire regiment by the time they're 30 that says this. At least, it has been in my experience. Maybe that's just my friends. Maybe that's just me.

Anyway.

I could never think of anything. Names? My mind would go blank, apart from boring names like Nigel, Norman, Kevin, Steven, Stuart, Claire, Jane, Anne, Diane and Margaret. You don't get many Margarets now, do you? Old fashioned, I guess. Or I'd think of the most ridiculous names, the kind that would guarantee a playground kicking: Maxwell, Tarquin, Anastasia, Michelangelo. But nothing I would ever actually choose. It always worried me, still does, that when I finally hear the tiny patter of the little heart-attack that follows the words 'I'm pregnant', I will spend nine months unable to think of all but the most boring or ridiculous names and end up blurting out some nonsense at the registry office.

That's not true.

Well, not strictly. I could think of some girls' names. I liked Sylvia for a while. Around about the time I was angsty and obsessed with Sylvia Plath. You don't get many Sylvias now either, do you? Maybe the conversation: 'Who was I named after?' 'A woman who put her head in a gas oven' puts people off. I liked Eilidh for a while. I still have a thing for Gaelic spellings. Scandinavian, as well. I liked Astrid until I met a complete twannock called Astrid. Boys' names, however. No chance.

So, after all that ...

What shall we call him?

I glance up from the computer, looking for inspiration. The *Complete Blackadder* DVD set sits on the shelf to my right. Edmund and Baldrick, I ignore, but Rowan catches my fancy. Apparently, Hemmingway used to get book titles by flicking through a book of poetry and stopping at random. Hence *For Whom the Bell Tolls* and *A Farewell to Arms*. Rowan it is.

Rowan is looking out of the window. Now, the flats on this street are nice but they aren't massive, especially on the top floor, so the window isn't the biggest. It's not one of those huge tenement ones, like in Glasgow. Nor is it a gorgeous bay window you can fit a sofa in, or an entire dining table, like my father had after he moved out and bought that flat in Aberdeen. It's an average-sized window, jutting out from the sloping roof. I can't remember what they're called, that style of window, but his head is half an inch off the ceiling and, if he were to stand on his tiptoes, as he does now to see if anything is happening down below, his head would push into the faded, white artex and cause him some pain.

They are sash windows, sliding up or down and, apparently, swivelling round, so you can clean them without risking life and limb by climbing out onto the foot wide ledge outside. They've seen better days though - as has Rowan, if we're being honest - and could do with a good once-over with a damp sand-blaster. They don't quite close at the top and a draught constantly whistles through, like an old kettle coming to the boil and being hit by Stevenson's Rocket with the horn blasting. When there's any heat in the flat - anything from the shower being on, to a moth causing friction by flapping - condensation collects on the glass, blocking the view, and on the top of the frame, where it builds into huge drops and then drips onto whatever is below. In this case, Rowan's glass of cheap Bulgarian red, bought three for ten from Asda earlier in the day. The condensation/temperature problem is also causing mould to grow on the walls around the window and for black gunk to collect in any available crevice. The only time any of this is ever cleaned is when he tries to balance his clapped-out laptop on the tiny window-sill and steal wi-fi from the neighbours and doesn't want his pride-and-joy piece-of-junk dripped on.

Rowan's looking out of the window because he has

been dumped. I know I said he didn't know which window he was looking for but that's not strictly true. I also know that that's the second time in as many pages that I've used the phrase 'that's not strictly true' but you'll just have to get used to that. If truth be told, a large part of Rowan's brain is just hoping that he catches a glimpse of a beautiful woman changing with her curtains not fully drawn, but you can't build a story around a bored man vaguely hoping to see some tits. Well, you can, but it wouldn't be a very romantic story and that's what I'm aiming for. That's what sells.

He was dumped some time in the morning and now he's standing at the window drinking three for ten Bulgarian red from Asda. Can you guess what he's listening to on his Cambridge Audio separates? Stevie Wonder's, *I Believe (When I Fall in Love with You It'll Be Forever)*. Why? Because it's the saddest song from the High Fidelity soundtrack and, yes, Rowan has that little imagination. Quite frankly, he's not that cut up, he's just going through what he assumes to be the motions of a break-up. He's been dumped that many times that he has become a pastiche of a man-who-has-been-dumped. In fact, let's imagine that this is an Alan Warner novel and call him Man-Who-Has-Been-Dumped and dispense with this whole Rowan thing. Atkinson can have his first name back.

Man-Who-Has-Been-Dumped is not very good at relationships. He's too honest. His naïve honesty gets him into bed. It also gets him thrown out again, pretty damn fast. Honesty is all right, as long as you think she's beautiful and you'll do anything to bed her. Honesty isn't all right when you've come to your senses and discovered that, rather than looking like Marilyn Monroe, she does, in fact, look like Marilyn Manson.

The girl. Woman. When do you stop saying girlfriend? His womanfriend. Her name? Doesn't matter really, since she's gone. You know her though, know the type. Still, got to jump through the hoops. After all, that's my job, isn't it? Providing pegs to hang your imagination on, a join-the-dots that leads to … what? A picture of the modern psyche is the expected outcome. Well, Man-Who-Has-Been-Dumped's most recent protagonist was … Drum roll. A Guardian reader. Post-grad. Long skirts and Manu Chao CDs. Cultural History with the lighter side of feminism. Feels guilty about saying Merry Christmas to non-Christians and has fifteen LiveJournal posts about *The Cove*. Our man doesn't get a mention, except as a non-specific we.

Man-Who-Has-Been-Dumped has a dilemma. Stevie Wonder's *I Believe (When I Fall in Love with You It'll Be Forever)* is the last song on the High Fidelity soundtrack, which means he's finished listening to his Top Five Break-Up Original Movie Soundtracks Of All Time As Suggested By Nick Hornby In The Sunday Papers and therefore can't think of what to play next. He's heard that Dylan's *Blood On The Tracks* is about a break-up but, every time he's picked it up in Fopp, he's thought, 'Do I really want to be the kind of person who buys a Dylan album?' and gone for some Belle and Sebastian instead, because this is Scotland and that's what you do.

He looks at his CD rack: thirty seven discs, stacked vertically in alphabetical order from top to bottom. If he owns more than one disc by the same band then they are in chronological order of release, from top to bottom. He scans through them, imagining that his life is a film and that he has to choose the perfect music for this scene. Eventually, he lands on The Divine Comedy, *A Short Album about Love* and plays it.

Now that the soundtrack is sorted (although he did choose an album that only lasts thirty one minutes and a handful of seconds so we'll be back over to the stereo soon enough) he refills his glass and resumes his position at the window.

If you hadn't guessed it already, Man-Who-Has-Been-Dumped is a student. Worse, he's a philosophy student. Worse still, he's a philosophy post-grad, who is working under the delusion that he can change the world. The world, despite its best efforts, using a variety of women and banking regulations, has yet to break him. It will, one day. In a few years, Man-Who-Is-Still-Being-Dumped-Regularly will find himself sitting at his desk at 1.43pm with a recently emptied bottle of wine between him and his laptop and will suddenly realise, with piercing clarity, that nothing he does will ever matter. There will be no fanfare to greet this momentous moment. No fireworks, no applause. His shoulders will merely slump forward slightly, as if making a vague attempt to protect his heart. His head will hang heavier and his eye-line will drop another notch towards the floor. His spirit will have been broken. He will see his dreams for what they are - cobwebs cluttering his mind, no use but to remind him that life once held promise but now holds only time. His bright future will be behind him.

But that is a few years away. Just now, he still believes that the contents of his notebook and hard drive can, when combined and turned from scattered fragments into a coherent whole, change the world. Change it for the better. Make every one happier. Solve problems. Maybe all problems. War. Stop war. His notebook and hard drive contain the embryo of nothing less than World Peace.

He may be right. His ideas are good. Insightful. Sharp. Simple. What he lacks in personal relationships, he more than makes up for in ideas. The problem is they will never become a coherent whole. The closest he will ever get to presenting World Peace to a grateful planet will be drunkenly expounding to a diminishing group of friends between rounds at the pub quiz on a Tuesday night.

Nothing is happening outside the window. Edinburgh has emptied itself in preparation for the onslaught of the Radio 4-listening Guardian-reading ciabatta-baking hordes that descend every August for the annual celebration of ways of passing time. Man-

Who-Has-Been-Dumped still goes to a few comedy shows, Fringe Sunday, the latest Eastern European rep company's sequel to Godot, but the whole month makes him feel sad and empty. He is always sad and empty and it's only the crowds that make him realise it.

JOHN TAYLOR
Trust Not Optional

Dozing in the minibus after a long day at the centre. A day full of voices and lights and colours and people pushing past, and loving people and funny people and scary people and angry people. And me stuck in the middle, no way to move my wheelchair. In the way, waiting. Needing out, needing to get away. Waiting, always waiting.

Audrey will be there.

Now I'm wide awake, wishing I could stop the bus, but it swings into the gateway. Too fast, and my head rolls across the headrest, jolts back again and hits the frame.

The pain blurs the voices around me, but I hear, *Don't forget Joe's bag!* That's me, Joe.

I hate the next bit. My chair wobbling on the tail lift. Nothing I can do but wait for the bump at the bottom, the moment my whole body tenses up. Then it's Audrey's voice, complaining. And she's pushing my chair too fast, and my toes are hanging over the footrest, waiting to hurt.

You need toileting. That's an Audrey word: *toileting.* Hell.

I'm tensed up before we're even in the bathroom. Audrey leans right over me, smelling of soap, and all I can see is bulging green and yellow dress. Fastens the straps of my hoist while she's ordering the new carer around. Gill must be upstairs, helping Peter – I need her here, now.

I'm on the changing bed, helpless, and Audrey sends the girl off to get some wipes. Makes sure we're alone, as usual. Grabs me where it hurts and calls me an old rogue. Rubs around with her rough fingers, sending feelings I don't want through my body. Lets go before the girl comes back. Tapes up my pad so tight, it hurts.

Then she's jerking me around in the hoist. Into the chair, and she never gets me straight. Leaning right over again, feeling around and under me for the straps, pulling and tugging, strapping me in. Too much Audrey, too close.

Now I'm back in the front room. Waiting. This isn't where I want to be. I'm not safe here. Waiting for more Audrey nightmare. Why can't Gill come and sort Audrey out? I hate this room, with the TV in the corner, always on. People on the TV. Little, trapped people in the box. Trapped people who can't get out. Trapped like me. Can't get out. Can't get away from Audrey.

I'm looking the other way, trying to block out the TV, the edge of my headrest rubbing the sore place on my chin. The edge I hate, all soggy and smelly with my dribble. But I have to look this way. Can't look at the trapped people in the TV. They don't smell of anything, and I can't touch them. People stuck in a box in the corner.

Susan isn't stuck. She's right here, with her comfortable, sweaty smell. Spinning round next to me, smiling at her hand, holding it up in a shaft of sunlight. A slim hand that's been in her mouth – soggy, with white and pink chew marks.

Susan is free – nothing can trap her like those TV people. Free with her magical hand in the magic circle she spins – her centre, her home.

Has she been toileted?

I freeze.

Audrey doesn't wait, doesn't ask Susan, doesn't let her finish her circle. She just grabs her arm.

Susan's precious hand flops, the spell is broken, and she tries to bite the big fat hand that stopped her.

Her teeth don't get there. Audrey doesn't shout – someone might notice. She grabs Susan's hair, and pulls her to the floor.

I can't look away, can't even move – I'm right here. In spasm with Susan's terror and pain.

All I can see is Audrey's back – heaving green and yellow patterns, smothering Susan.

Teeth! Audrey whispers. *Teeth, is it? You little bitch!*

Teeth. I would get my teeth into green-and-yellow Audrey. Bite Audrey hard, for Susan.

Some hope. My teeth don't work when I need them. They only work when Audrey shoves that goo down my throat.

She's still down there. I can't see Susan. I can hear her sputtering, like her mouth is squashed. No magic circle for Susan down there.

Then I hear Gill coming downstairs with Peter. Gill, the manager. *Come on, Gill!* If I could shout, scream – anything to make her notice. Stupid mouth won't work.

Audrey gets up quick, panting, straightening her dress. Leaves Susan crying on the floor.

Peter says, *Cup of tea – cup of tea – cup of tea!* Like nothing's happening.

Susan – what's wrong? says Gill, dashing over to her. I don't hear any more – Susan can scream now. Loud.

Gill sends Audrey off with Peter, and kneels down next to Susan. And she just waits.

I'm waiting too. Waiting for hurting Susan. Waiting for Gill. Waiting for everyone safe. Waiting to be safe. Waiting.

Susan twists her head from side to side, her pale blue eyes looking everywhere, frantic. Needing to be safe, needing comfort, needing her hand, needing an anchor.

Her eyes stop. They focus on Gill. Susan stops screaming, with her mouth wide open, her face red. She lies back, and tears flow into her hair. Her wonderful hand rises towards Gill, who cups it in her own hands, ever so gently. She knows how special and magical that hand is for Susan. Her centre, her only home.

Gill doesn't speak, she just gives Susan time. And she glances over her shoulder and smiles at me. A hurting smile. Gill knows.

Susan reaches out her other hand and gets up, unsteady, leaning on Gill. There's a puddle of pee, but all Gill says is, *Poor Susan.*

Gill reaches out to me. *You saw, didn't you, Joe?*

I'm working at it, and manage a hiss.

Joe, did Audrey grab her when she was spinning?

I know some of the sounds she's making, the words. I know what she means. And I have to work, really work, breathing hard to make another hiss.

I'll check for bruises. This is stopping now. Thank you, Joe.

Gill takes Susan to the bathroom. At least Susan's safe.

And I'm waiting again.

I can hear Audrey laughing in the kitchen with Peter, and she's talking at that new carer, Rosie. *You'll learn how to handle them. Don't worry what Gill says – she's not the one who has to do all the changing.*

And the girl is talking, but I can't hear.

Then it's Audrey's loud voice again. *They don't know, do they? I feel a right prat, talking to them.*

They don't know, she says. Audrey doesn't know my anger.

I'm not safe. She might come in here. Susan's safe – I'm not. I want, need … Need to feel …

They call this place a home.

A home.

Peter and Susan and me live here. In a home. Helen did too, but she's dead-in-the-sky. That's what Mum tells me, but I saw them put Helen in the ground in a box. Gill made sure I was there – said it mattered.

Helen and me used to smile a lot. And I miss her not-working smile. Mine never works either, but Helen always knew. Knew the real smiles and the mistake smiles. And sometimes Gill put our chairs so close together, Helen could lean her head on my arm.

I'm missing those warm feelings, those Helen feelings.

We have nice carers who chat with us: gentle people, all of them.

All but Audrey.

And I'm still waiting, and Audrey's still in the kitchen.

I used to live with Mum. Not sure about Mum, now. No one takes me to see her – I don't think she wants me there. She comes here and watches TV every Sunday afternoon. Sits on the sofa and doesn't talk. Gives me hello and goodbye kisses. Dry kisses, like Mum's run out of love.

I'm still waiting. Where's Gill?

Then Audrey's here: up close, big, staring down at me. Angry, hands on hips. Says, *What are you looking at?* Grabs my handles and now she's leaning over the back of my chair – the monster in my dreams with her bright red lipstick and make-up like a mask.

Not telling anyone, are you, Joe? she says, and shakes

the chair.

I knew that was coming. Audrey's shake. Just enough to jolt me into spasm. Just enough to make her smile. Audrey's smile, like a big wet slash across her lipstick. And she's gone, back in the kitchen before Gill comes back.

I hear Gill's quiet voice in the kitchen, and Audrey's angry voice. A door slams, and I'm in spasm again.

It's quiet. No voices. Waiting. Frightened.

Gill walks in, with Susan in pink pyjamas.

Susan is smiling now, holding on to Gill's arm. She takes one graceful step away from Gill, into the middle of the room, and starts to spin her magic circle. One step, two steps, swivelling around, arms out, head back, dancing with an invisible partner. Making a place for herself, a place to love her magic hand. A safe place; her home.

Gill pulls a chair up next to me, where I can see without twisting my head. She asks with her eyebrows, and then gently rubs my arms, first one and then the other, loosening all my cramped-up muscles. She gets out her picture board in case I need help understanding – but Gill knows I don't need it much.

Joe, I've suspended Audrey, she says. *It wasn't just Susan. I saw how frightened you looked. It's not the first time she's lied to me – she's had her warnings. If she comes back at all, it won't be in this house. No Audrey – do you understand, Joe?*

I try a hiss, and it's easier this time.

I wish I knew how long it's been going on. You know, don't you, Joe?

And I do that hiss again.

Was it from the start?

I try to hold her eyes with mine. Deep breath. Hiss.

Gill says, *Look at my pictures – the next bit matters.* And she draws, and I understand. *Joe, were those hisses a mistake?*

I mustn't make a sound, and I try so hard, my eyes shut.

Thank you, Joe, she says, and lays her hand on mine. *I'm sorry, Joe. We took her on because she was experienced. I really am sorry.*

I try a smile, and I think it works, because Gill's eyes go all soft.

Joe, we must tell people how you say yes and no. I've guessed the yes before, but not the no. She takes the book that hangs on the back of my chair, and asks the new girl, Rosie, to come and sit with us while she's busy.

Rosie has a warm smile and gentle fingers that rest on my hand when she says hello. And she gives Susan her drink, one sip at a time, waiting while Susan spins a few more circles, never interrupting.

Then she fetches my mug of tea. She doesn't stand over me like Audrey, she looks into my eyes. And the tea is just how I like it, not too yucky and tepid. Rosie is so careful, I don't choke once, and she asks me before she wipes my chin, softly. I like Rosie already.

Gill brings my book back. *I've written it on the cover,*

Joe, she says. *Underneath your picture.* She points at the words. *Joe can say YES and NO. If Joe is giving you eye contact, a hiss means YES. If he concentrates and closes his eyes, that means NO. Take care to double-check. Joe also makes involuntary sounds and movements.*

And I give her a big hiss.

Gill knows I can't help hissing at other times when I don't mean yes. Audrey calls me Hissing Sid. But I'm Joe, and Gill always calls me Joe. Green-and-yellow Audrey isn't coming back. Maybe she'll be in a box like those TV people who don't touch and smell.

Rosie asks me if I want some time in my room, and I don't even need to hiss, because she knows. Gill comes along to show her my favourite music and stuff.

She puts the light on low, behind me, not in my eyes. And I can smell the soothing lavender oil and hear the quiet, rippling piano music.

All right if we leave you for a bit, Joe? Gill says.

Easy hiss.

You're safe now, Joe.

Another easy hiss.

We're off to take Susan to bed. I'll tell her a story – that might help. Gill does her story sign.

A big hiss. Susan loves Gill's voice.

I'm glad you approve, Joe, Gill says with a smile, and they leave me on my own.

I'm not waiting any more. Not waiting for anything.

I'm here, safe. Losing myself in the music and the

scent and the safeness and the feeling that nearly everything is right.

And later on, everything is right.

Gill helps Rosie change me, carefully, gently. And they hoist me into bed without any bumps. Now I can stretch out and relax.

It's easy now – I can lift up my arms. And they're reaching out, reaching for Gill.

She knows what I want, and her arms are round me in the soft cuddle I've needed all day. The hug no one manages when I'm stuck in my chair. The hug that holds me together. The safe hug, helping me feel that I matter. I'm not one of those little people in the TV box with no smell and no touch.

Rosie looks worried. *Is it allowed? Hugging?*

If Joe asks, and you're comfortable with it, Gill says.

Really?

Joe has no control of his own space, Rosie. Respecting Joe means making choices that he physically cannot. To deprive him of touch is neglect, and wrong. Wrong in just the same way that inappropriate touch is wrong. It's abuse.

Rosie looks into my eyes, and turns to Gill, even more worried now. *Then how do I judge what's appropriate and what isn't?*

Gill smiles. *You've made that judgement, Rosie. You need to offer Joe a hug. He might accept it – you'll know.*

I can feel it. I can feel that hug before Rosie opens her arms.

Before Rosie even hugs me, Gill says, *Can you feel the trust in your choice, Rosie? Joe hasn't got much option but to trust you. But you can make the difference, and trust him.*

And Rosie does.

With Gill and Rosie, I'm feeling as if all the good people in the world are holding me safe. It's as if Susan is holding me, but Susan never would. And Helen is holding me, but alive Helen never could. All holding me, loving me, caring for me, and I'm loving them back.

I'm not in a home, like they tell me. This is my home.

JANE ROBERTS

The Gift

I give you a home.

Fee. Simple. Absolute. In possession.

This is the gift of ownership, of belonging. And I give it to you. For always. Forever. No selected years on lease, just freehold. No rent charge. No mortgage. No tenancy at will, in common, or at sufferance. No overriding interests. No liabilities. No restrictive covenants – no strictures full stop.

There will be no adverse possession.

Whether this gift is legal or equitable – it makes no difference. I give you licence to do anything, to be yourself. Every easement and profit is yours. The only trust is exactly that – our common bond.

This home is registered to you alone. You will feel it, hear it beating all around you. I am yours.

WILLIAM ANGELO
Daniel's Gift

It upsets me when John reads the Bible these days. As I arrive, he is slumped back in his wheelchair with the Bible on the kitchen counter, splayed out under his hand. He mouths the words. His lips move, until his belly prevents him breathing in any more and then they move again after the gasp of his breath rushing out. I wonder whether his thoughts stop there as well; if his mind is in thrall to the wreck that his body is becoming.

'What are you reading, John?' I ask.

'The Bastard Isaiah!' He spits the words at me.

'Don't say that, John. You love the Bible - especially the prophets - especially Isaiah.'

'It's claptrap. It's shit!'

'If you really believed that, John, you wouldn't read it every day. You must get something from it. I think you curse it because you're depressed.'

I should have stopped sooner. When he's in this black mood there's no shifting him.

'Depressed, my arse. Somewhere in this, in here,' he slaps the book, 'there's an explanation. What's so special about these lies and fairy tales? How can people believe this rubbish?'

And he's done it again. He's hooked me.

'John, your favourite psalm, Psalm 14.1, the fool hath said -'

'- in his heart, there is no God!' His voice rages over mine, drowning me out. 'So, I'm a fool am I, Daniel? *I'm* the fool. Well, tell me, Mr Know-it-All, who was it spent two years in the nut house? Who's the one who had a certificate to prove he was a fool? Eh?'

The only way to go from here would be to drag it all out again: my attempt to kill myself, my incarceration, the death of our parents, how John brought me up, his stroke. John would shout and froth and swear at me. He would wave his fists, impotently. I would shrink and fall silent. Inside, my heart would break over what was happening to my beloved brother. So I take a deep breath and wait until the rant blows itself out.

'What was the work you wanted me to look at, John?'

John grunts. He pats the counter by the sink. 'It's rocking. If you put any pressure on it, it tips back.'

With great difficulty, he pulls himself out of his wheelchair and shuffles round behind it. I know better than to offer any assistance. With one hand on the back of the chair for support, he puts his other hand on the oak work top and pushes down. It sags under his weight, leaving the strip of quadrant behind on the wall. There's a gap of three quarters of an inch.

He drags himself and the chair clear so that I can take a look. It doesn't take long. The cold water pipe has a loose joint right up against the wall. Judging from the stain and build-up of scale, it has been leaking for years. I reach around and down. The boards are soaking wet and soft. I can push my finger into them. Straightening up, I wipe the mould from my hand with a paper towel.

'It's a mess, John. There's a leak. I can fix that easily enough, but I have to replace the boards under the units, which means disconnecting everything and pulling them out. I'm almost certain that the joists underneath will be rotten too, so I'll have to cut them out and put in a new support frame.'

He frowns and nods. 'When will you start?'

'I'll come over at the weekend. It'll take three or four days.'

I run my hand over the counter, feeling the swollen grain of the oak behind the sink.

'I'll plane and sand the top, and oil it when I've finished.'

Back in my workshop, I allow the stillness to soothe me. I love the softness of sawdust under my feet on the concrete floor, the tools - clean, ready, and in their allotted place. Most of all, I love the smell of wood. The good pine boards I set aside for John's kitchen are brash, raw, impetuous. The scent will overpower me if I allow it. Set out on the bench are the pieces of a mahogany bookcase that I am repairing. It is old and silent. A mortise joint at the back has broken and I have had to cut out a section of timber and replace it with a new piece. The saw cut has brought life out of the bookcase. The perfume released is subtle and complex, bitter resins that were locked away a hundred years ago or more. I take the pieces and put them away while the glue hardens.

Now, with my mind clear, I can turn to the gift that I am building for John. It is by far the most complicated piece of joinery I have attempted - ever.

I enjoy all of my work. Most of it is basic carpentry: skirting boards, stud walls, door frames, roof timbers. Sometimes, there is a little more skill required. I had a full oak kitchen to build a few months ago but, yes, I enjoy it all. And I like to do things properly. The other chippies laugh at me. They'll punch a screw straight through a door frame into the softwood upright, sending the screw head below the surface level so that it pulls the wood into a little dip around it. For a day or so, this is fine but, as the wood relaxes, it bulges back. Anybody following on will find it difficult to sand out for filling and painting. For the sake of half a minute, I drill and countersink every screw hole.

'Come on, slow-coach,' they say, 'You're not building the Taj Mahal, you know.'

So I work for a while on the gift for John, and I work properly. The cuts are clean, made with fine quality back-saws that I have kept sharp. One hand on the saw, one hand on the timber, just as I was taught. The dovetails are tight. I'm pleased when I see them, not out of vanity, but because they are exactly how they should be.

I made the casing for the hidden mechanism from merbau because I needed a very hard wood. I had never used it before and, when I had completed the boxes, sanded and polished them, I was astonished by the way they sparkled, as though they were sprinkled with flecks of gold. I sat and stared at them, turning them around in the light for nearly an hour. Then they went into the assembly, out of sight forever.

It's Friday and I have a call to make. Mrs Cooper hands me a cup of tea, milky and sweet. I prefer it black without sugar, but it's a kindness from her, and I repay her with a broad smile and my thanks.

She has an excellent pine table with one leg loose. She says, 'It was my mother's,' and I can see from the way it is made that it's old. Most modern pine tables have the legs braced with a steel strap. They are pierced with a threaded rod and a butterfly nut holds the leg in place. This table is all timber. The square top of the leg fits snugly into the corner and is held in place with a two inch diameter dowel joint.

'Mrs Cooper, you know that you shouldn't keep this beautiful table in your conservatory?'

She smiles sadly and says, 'I know, but it's so big. I have nowhere else.'

'Look here.' I show her the dowel. 'The whole top of the leg has dried out and shrunk in the heat over the years. Only a tiny fraction of an inch, but enough so that the glue has failed.'

'Oh, Daniel, can it be mended?'

'Yes. I can pack it with an epoxy resin, or cut back the dowel, drill the leg out and put a new dowel in.'

'Which is better?'

'Both ways will produce a repair. The resin will last for many years. The right way is to replace the dowel.'

'Which way is cheaper?'

'I won't charge you for this, Mrs Cooper.'

'Oh, but you must.' Her face is filled with concern, but I can hear her relief.

'Well, all right, you can pay me with another cup of your good tea when I bring the leg back. And flowers; fill the conservatory with flowers, Mrs Cooper. Bring some life into the room and the table will fare much better.'

In the afternoon, as I build stud walls on the new estate, my mind wanders back to childhood. I played in these fields. I played with John, who looked after me as well as any parent. Our father was a kind man, but serious, particularly when we read the Bible together. To him, there was a great beauty in the ceremony and ritual of the word. The readings had to be done as they had always been done.

When our parents were dead, John and I still read from the Bible, but it was very different. It was a joyous affair, filled with fun and mystery and adventure. John would stop, half way through a passage, and drag me out into the fields.

'Don't you see, Daniel, it's like this. Look at the life in the trees, and the birds, and the sky, and in you.

This is God's word, echoing today. This is what the book means.' And he'd whirl me around until we both collapsed, laughing and happy.

We were inseparable. I can hardly believe how hard he worked to keep our tiny family together. And then, later, we worked together. John was the light; I was always more like our father.

At first I hardly noticed the changes in John. The Bible was such a major part of our lives that when he was too tired to read with me, I thought nothing of it; John would never be parted from the book.

In the evening, I continue working on the gift for John. I have such high hopes for it. Sometimes, I worry that I'm wrong, but I love him so much, and I pray that this might help, in some small way, to bring the joy of the book back to him.

The next stage is crucial. I have to fit the core mechanism and it must work. It took me a long time to find just what I needed. The mechanism has to be strong, but not so strong that it breaks the timber. In the end, by sheer chance, I found a spring-set, manufactured by an American four-wheel-drive truck company. The springs are intended to raise and lower an additional step at the rear of a vehicle, so that you can climb in, but they are perfect in every way for my purpose. You might even say that the Lord provides!

John is more cheerful when I call on him at the weekend. I fill the kettle and a couple of pans then I set to work, disconnecting the supply to the taps. He watches me from his chair. After half an hour has passed, he says, 'Daniel, is there nothing I can do?'

I say, 'Not really - not at the moment, anyway. When I start to move the units back I'll need you to support one end. You can do that from your chair.'

I don't really need him for that, but I can see he wants to help.

On Sunday morning I take John to church.

Monday is breath-taking. I swing open the doors of my workshop and gaze at the mist rolling off the hills beyond the town. The sun is just above the horizon and it sends shafts of light between the houses in front of me. There is birdsong - the promise of new life. I try to open myself, to take in as much as I can of the wonder; imprint it on my soul. John's gift is complete now.

By Tuesday evening, the work in the house is done. I have sanded and oiled the oak counter and persuaded John not to use it for a day or two. He nods and pats the worktop. I can see that he is pleased with the work. I feel more contented, more at peace, now that it is done.

'John, is there anything else I can do for you?'

'No, Daniel.'

It is Friday. This is the day that I must deliver the gift to John. The sky is dark and the air is unsettled. There is no birdsong yet, just the howl of the wind and spatter of rain. There is a terrible fear in my heart and yet I know I must be strong. I load the parts into the back of my van and set off for John's house.

I see a light on in the town. Somebody is up as

early as me. They will be warm - I imagine them making tea, perhaps. I had so hoped for another bright Spring day instead of this dreadful gloom. I put these thoughts out of my mind. It is, as it is intended to be; it is right.

The road winds out of town to the terrace where John lives. I stop the van and unload the cargo. The timber parts clip together precisely in moments. I have prepared a slot in the grassy bank opposite John's house and the main post is inserted and raised high. It seems sturdy. I settle myself. I pray for strength one more time.

I hoist myself up to the footrest and clip the belt around my waist. Fields to the right, with the light of dawn just penetrating the rolling clouds, houses to my left, shut tight against the weather, rain in my face.

This is the day that the Lord hath made; let us rejoice and be glad in it.

I reach out to either side and trigger the mechanism.

Pain.

Pain.

Pain.

The bolts are through my hands and feet.

I had not realised - so much pain.

I had not known - so much blood and I cannot support my body. I hang.

I am crying and hanging. A cry comes from within me.

'My God, my God, why hast thou forsaken me?'

But John will see. Through my screams and tears, I know. He will remember that the word is true; he will return to the book; he will see me rise again as we were promised.

As did the risen Lord.

SUSAN CHADWICK
A Ticket Home

Will you come back with me? I've bought you a ticket. I'm on my way to meet you and I hope you'll come home.

I haven't seen you for half my lifetime, so why search for you now? Well, maybe the aunts were right and you were The One. If you were The One then, could you be The One, now? Have I wasted all this time without you? I missed you. I still miss you. Oh yes.

You've been so long in that other world. I long to see you again, and find out if my memories serve me well. I want us to make new memories, to move things along. I want to laugh like I mean it.

I packed little for my visit, and so I skipped out of the taxi at the airport and danced to the check-in queue without a trolley. In the aeroplane with no baggage wedging me in, I stretched out, gleeful in my seat, then wriggled. I could barely sit still. I'm going to see you once more, after all this too-long time. I was twenty-six when you left twenty-six years ago, so there's a symmetry about our reunion: the same number of my years, either side of that pivotal point of your departure. It's time.

The funny thing is, I don't remember arriving at all. I don't know if you met me, or if anyone did. But the next moment, I was there, in a hotel lobby with you, unable to look away; I couldn't read whether you were pleased to see me or not.

The years have been kind to you. You haven't aged, whilst I am twenty-six years older, older than you were when you died, and my youth has faded. I stopped eating after you went on alone; I just forgot. I withered and dried. I didn't stint on the red wine though, nor the cigarettes and the mournful ballad music turned up to full volume into my endless night.

Back then, our cats kept me alive instead of you; they nuzzled me awake, they insisted I got out of bed to feed them, and off to the shops to buy their food. They played with leaves in front of me and made me smile. They'd stare for ages at a moth so that I stared too; they made me notice life outside of myself.

My friends came round with pies and listened in the darkness while I bored them with incoherent memories and spilled red wine down my front. Those same friends who found me somewhere else to live that I could afford on my own; who borrowed a truck to load our furniture which became my furniture and who helped me clean my new, spiritless home-for-one.

Now, now I see you again. I don't know what I feel, beyond anxiety. A white-out in my brain.

Do you want me? Still? You are concave on a low

chair in that hotel lobby, laughing with someone next to you and glancing at me often.

Why don't you talk to me instead of him? Are you nervous to be alone with me? I don't know, I can't tell.

How dare you die. Do you know how angry I was? You robbed me. You left me; left me to face the rest of my life alone. You *should* be nervous with me; you did wrong and I'm furious.

I hate you, I love you, I despise you. I am hollow with aching for you.

I'm a different person now. So is everybody, except you. You've been pickled, walled up in my head, suspended, outside time.

I want to touch you and feel your skin on my skin but I'm afraid I'll explode open like a ripe flower if you touch me. I want your arms around me, so tight I can barely breathe. Engulf me, let me feel precious and safe, let me soak up your smell, let it seep into me, let me come home to you. Then fear engulfs me before you can. Please, no. Was it all illusion-delusion, grown wild in my head?

You look at me again. Your eyes still melt me; I can barely hold your gaze; my bones are dissolving.

Then we are alone in the hotel bedroom, our pores are weeping with yearning; we're drenched. The body has a memory too.

The vision sways, light through fire.

I am unclothed on the bed. The white sheets are tumbled, daylight billows through the voile curtains. You're walking around the room, naked. I reach for you and miss. You haven't noticed my grasping need.

I am wearied by life but you are not.

Don't look at me.

There's another woman in your life now – in your death. I knew her before, but I can't place her. You've told everybody that you've only recently met her but I know differently. She's from way back, from before me. I don't like you having a life before me. Or after me. Send her away.

We are on a jetty, being social with the crowd. The sun shines and the drinks keep coming. People say how nice it is to see me after all this time. I've no idea what they're doing here, these people from my life after you. They ask what I know of this other woman. I tell them you lied. Is she The One for you, or a stopgap until I arrived? Were you waiting for me to catch up? Do you still want me? Do you want *me*?

We sit in the hotel lobby holding hands. You are playing with my fingers and we're thinking our own thoughts. It's a stretching moment, so right. I've been longing to belong for so long; I'm home.

I look at the clock. Our flight is at eleven! How could I have forgotten? The week has gone so quickly. You're coming back, too. Aren't you?

We rush out into the bright sun to hail a cab to the airport. My little luggage left behind in our room doesn't matter. I have what's important, right here and the tickets in my handbag are enough for us. You always travelled light, barely anchored to that life. We run, hand in hand, smiling.

We sit in the airport cart as it speeds past dozens of entrance gates. I don't know which is the right one. I scrabble through my bag for the ticket information to tell us but I can't find it. It is nearly eleven. If we could just get to the right desk before the plane leaves – but I don't know where to go. Time is running out and there are so many gates. I don't want to tell the driver that I don't know which one is right. You are right here beside me; I know you're coming with me. At long last. Aren't you? I can't tell you either, that I've lost the tickets; not now, not when I know you're coming home with me. I think you are. Please don't change your mind; please don't leave me again. We're scanning the gates as they flash past. Our thighs are rubbing against each other, the friction frying our bodies, bonding them together with liquid fire. You are here, close. I can't find the tickets. We're going to miss the plane.

I know that I'll never leave now, I can't leave, I never did leave. How can I leave when I've found you? I know I'll stay here with you now; it's the only place I want to be. I relax into you; let the plane go, it's all right. Why do we need tickets when we're already home?

JACQUELINE WARD
Brick Heart

Sitting here, waiting for the taxi, I can't help but look up the hallway and think about how I came to be here. I'll be away in no time, and it doesn't seem two minutes since I was dragging my cases into the pokey bedroom. But time moves faster when you're getting on a bit. Or so they say. They also say that lightning never strikes twice but, once again, I'm being forced to move out.

Not that I mind so much this time. This place never felt like home. Well, maybe a small part of it that I brought with me did, but not really. I told Ettie Clark, the day I moved in. We were sitting on the bottom stair, all out of breath and she lit a cigarette.

'What'll you do now, Annie? Now it's all over?'

I took the cigarette and had a quick drag. I'd stopped smoking years ago, but this was something different. This was life-changing.

'Don't know, love. Probably go and help out somewhere, you know. Keep myself busy.'

'Yeah. I'm going to work at the charity shop. The one in the high street. That way, I get the pick of the clothes.'

There she was, Ettie Clark, always with a plan. Always thinking up a new strategy. It was she who came up with the plan for 23 Harlequin Street. The plan that got me into all that trouble.

It all started about a year after Jim died. Poor bugger died in the back bedroom before they could get him to the hospice; at least he had his family near him. I held his hand. We'd lived there all our married life, and brought up three sons and a daughter there. The lads were long gone, living on the other side of town, but our Debbie was still at home. Even then, anyone could see she was going to be a handful and, sure enough, she brought this posh bloke home two years after Jim died and said she was marrying him and going to live in Chelsea. I was pleased at first, 'til I realised I'd have to pay for the wedding. She knew, that one, she knew her Dad had left me some money. Then there was the insurance.

'You could always re-mortgage, Mum. You and Dad didn't have a mortgage on this house, did you?'

She'd looked around, like there was a bad smell, and pulled a funny face, like she had peed her pants. He just stood there, all gold cuff-links and hair gel.

'That won't be happening, Debbie. You'll get what you're given. This is my home.'

So that was the last I saw of her for a while. She went off to the Bahamas and got married on the beach, then had a big party for his family, one that I wasn't invited to. Two days after the wedding, I got the letter. It was in a brown envelope and, just as I picked it up off the mat, Ettie knocked on the door. She lived at number 19. She had one as well.

We sat on the doorstep and opened them. Compulsory Purchase Orders. Numbers 3–37 Harlequin Street were being knocked down to make way for a new estate. There'd been rumours, but we hadn't believed them. Who'd take away our homes? Who'd do that to me and Ettie and Mad George? We read the order over and over again and, that morning, I felt the first corner of my heart crumble. They were going to throw me out of the house where I'd raised my kids and watched my husband die. Eight cats and four dogs were buried in that back yard. And two budgies. Countless gerbils. I'd watched my children's tears for their dead pets falling into the turned soil. We couldn't believe we'd have to give up our homes.

It didn't matter what we believed because, within a week, we'd all been offered alternative accommodation. Ettie was going to live with her daughter and Mad George was going into a one-bedroom flat. I rang the boys, but I knew I couldn't go to them because they all had kiddies.

Andrew summed up the situation perfectly. 'Well, Mam, there's always our Debbie. If you don't want to go into the flat they've offered you, go and live with our Debbie in that big house she's got.'

It was a good job we were on the phone and he couldn't see my face. I think I decided what I was going to do there and then, but I needed to discuss it with Ettie.

The next day, me and Ettie sat in the back and talked about it in hushed voices. The sit-in. I wasn't going anywhere and Ettie was going to help me stay. We'd heard that they couldn't throw you out of your home if you were still living there and you didn't let them in, so that was what we would do. Make sure someone was there at all times. We whispered our way into a protest. For Ettie, it was the next thing to plan, the next strategy. She had an active mind, did Ettie; she used to work at the GPO. But me, I was more of a home bird, and my protest wasn't just about 23 Harlequin Street. It was about not getting my heart broken. I belonged there and I wasn't about to leave anytime soon.

It's about belonging, isn't it, home? Knowing where you are. I read this article about muscle memory, where your body just knows where to go, and that's what it was like for me. I could have navigated every inch of that house with my eyes shut. I did, in a way, when the babies wanted feeding in the night and I had to go downstairs. Carrying a baby in the dark isn't the best thing to do, but I trusted the house; it was part of me and I was part of it.

So me and Ettie sat there. For weeks and weeks. Months.

The local papers came and took photos, and the Co-op drove our shopping round. Every day, the site manager came and looked in on us, checking the premises weren't empty. We'd pass him some tea and cake out of the back window and watch as they carted everyone's belongings out of the empty houses that surrounded us. It felt like the war, where every day there was some kind of truce in no-man's land. They'd try to catch us out but Ettie was too quick for them.

When Debbie saw it in the papers, she came up, husband in tow.

'Mother. How could you do this? Don't you know I've got my reputation to think of?'

Ettie smiled. 'You weren't thinking much about that down the park when you were fifteen, were you, Debbie, pet?'

'Deborah, to you. Deborah Preston-Mawes.'

I bit my lip, trying not to laugh, and Ettie had to turn away. The way she said it sounded like 'mouse'. Deborah Preston-Mouse.

Debbie was bright red. 'None of this is funny. You're going to get yourself in trouble. And we don't want any convictions, do we?'

I looked her straight in the eye. When I stood up I was five foot nothing and a good five inches smaller than her. She had her dad's height. But she backed away, all the same.

'Forgot about you getting done for underage drinking and nicking those shoes from the market, have you, Miss La-de-da? Now bugger off down South and take that lump of lard with you.'

He trotted off behind her and I haven't seen her again to this day. But she was right. It did all end in trouble. One day, I'd gone out back to water my begonias and, not realising, Ettie went to fetch the milk in at the front. She left the door open. When we got back in the front room, the site manager was there with a bailiff and a court order. It was a fair cop. I knew it had to come to an end one day. I stood outside while they moved my furniture into a van. Another piece of my heart crumbled that day, as I turned my back on number 23. But Ettie wasn't finished yet. The day I moved in here, we hatched a plan to stop them from knocking that row of terraced houses down. We dressed up every night in dark trews and jumpers and went down there and poured muck in the petrol tanks of all the trucks and diggers.

It all took me away from the fact that I was devastated. I felt like I'd left Jim there, with my favourite dog, Bumper. I tried to settle into this one-bedroom place they'd moved me to; it's a perfectly nice little flat and it's easy to keep tidy. But it was never home. Little pieces of my heart were still scattered around number 23 and I couldn't rest until I'd got them back. I went there every day at first, just to gawp at my house. Me and Ettie went on our covert missions of an evening and, for a time, we did hold the job up. Until we got caught.

We were just pouring a handful of dirt into the tank of a mini digger when I felt a hand on my shoulder. Ettie screamed and I knew it was trouble. They only kept us in the cells for a couple of hours. Then the site manager came and said they wouldn't press charges if we'd accept an injunction. We weren't to go within 500 yards of number 23.

I looked at the policeman. I was dog tired. 'I can't agree to that. How will I get my heart back?'

They all looked at each other.

'Your heart, Annie? How do you mean?'

'Well, I left it in number 23 with Jim and Bumper. I need to get it back.'

I expect it was then that I first came to the attention of the dementia team. It did sound like rubbish, what I'd said, but I knew what I meant. Ettie did too, but when her daughter came to fetch her, muttering something about angina, she gave me a look that made me think Ettie wouldn't be joining me on any more covert missions, heart or no heart.

So I was released. Ten days later, when the coast was clear, I hid round the corner of Mortimer Street and watched as the wrecking ball smashed my home to bits. I felt every crash and bang in my bones, and I thought, at first, that this was the end of me. I sat there all night, in the ginnel, waiting for first light. I crossed over, knowing that if I got caught breaking the injunction I'd go to prison, but I did it anyway. I picked through the rubble, familiar flashes of wallpaper making me tear up, a bit of tile off the fireplace, blinking up at me, half the toilet I had cleaned every day since I was eighteen, smashed and discarded.

I had to move quickly, because later on they would dig it all over, dig up my Bumper and my lovely cats, all the gerbils and my children's tears with them. I looked around for something to keep, something precious. Then I saw it. Jim and I had always kept our room nice, and he'd put up new wallpaper every time I wanted it. And there it was. A brick, with layers upon layers of wallpaper on it, peeling away to reveal all the years of our lives, all the love, all the dreams, all the tenderness. I had it all there in my hand.

I heaved it into my Co-op bag and hurried away before anyone caught me. When I got back to the flat, I put the brick in a pillowcase and took it to bed with me and slept for the first time since I had moved here. Someone told me once that the best way to get to sleep is to think about somewhere you love and imagine that you are there again, visiting all the rooms. It made me wonder where the past goes, where all those things that were once real are kept safe, so we can go back there in our minds. Even when they are really gone.

The next day, I woke up and I felt much better. I took my brick down to the charity shop to show Ettie and she understood. She was pleased that I had found it. It was a little heavy to carry around, but not as heavy as my heart had been. I knew it was too good to be true though, and when I heard a knock on the front door, about a year later, I could sense it. Two women stood there, looking officious.

'Hello, Annie. We're from social services. We've just come to do an assessment.'

I knew straight away it was about that business at the police station. I'd been waiting for them to come busy-bodying around.

'Took you long enough.'

They came in and the blonde one looked around.

'So, Annie, you got an injunction, did you? You were arrested and the officers said you were a little bit confused.'

I nodded. 'Mmm. I'd just been evicted.'

'But you were rehoused. This is very nice.'

I watched them as their eyes scanned the tiny living room and rested on my brick.

'Why have you got a brick on your mantelpiece, Annie? A house brick?'

I could see the other one tick a box, probably something about dementia or Alzheimer's. Or mental health issues. No point, I thought, you've already put me in a box. I laughed and they began to look more worried. The blonde one got up and walked over to my brick.

'Don't touch it!'

They both looked startled and I rushed over and grabbed it, hugging it tight to my chest. I'd taken it out of the pillowcase so I could see it all the time, to remind me of where I belonged, to place myself there, and now I was beginning to regret it. They looked at each other and the blonde one shook her head.

'Right, Annie. We're going to try to sort out some sheltered housing for you, somewhere you can be looked after properly.'

I stood there with my brick. I must have looked a right tata. Ettie laughed when I told her later on, but

I'd done it again: I'd managed to get myself moved.

'So you had hold of the brick like they were going to take it? Bloody hell, Annie, I bet they think you're touched.' She patted my arm. Ettie had been a good friend and I was grateful for her. She was looking all conspiratorial now, like she had a plan. Ettie always had a plan. 'Thing is, if they come back, they might try and take your brick.'

I nodded. 'They can't, Ettie love. It's all I have left that's home.'

She laughed. 'Never mind all that soppy stuff. We have to act now. We have to make it look less like ... well, a brick. Disguise it as ... something. Ideas?'

It was like being on *Mastermind*. We tried to think of something heavy and square that wasn't a brick. We thought of a thousand things, staying up all night and me smoking Ettie's cigs because I'd given up years ago. Finally, we came up with it. First thing in the morning, we went to the charity shop. We stuck shells onto the three sides of my brick that didn't have wallpaper on and then, on top, Ettie stuck a shell ornament of a dolphin with a clock in the middle of it. It was grotesque but it no longer looked like a brick.

Ettie sat back and laughed. 'Well, that's it. No one can say that it's a brick now. It's in there somewhere, buried under layers of shit.'

I nodded and poured her a tot of rum. 'Yeah. Like any feelings of belonging I've got left – they're in there somewhere, like you say.'

She drank the rum and laughed louder. 'Wherever

I lay my brick, that's my home.'

I sniggered. 'Absence makes the brick grow fonder.'

But now it's time to go and I'm sitting here, waiting for the taxi, with my little case. The busybodies came yesterday and packed everything up for me. They'd looked around when they came in.

'Not taking that brick, are you, Annie? No room for it at Ash Place.'

Ash Place. They'd shown me a brochure. Sounded very exciting.

'No. Long gone, that.'

They'd gone away then and I'd hoped they wouldn't come back today, but now I can see their outlines through the glass door and I get up and open it before they knock.

'Keen, aren't you? We've taken your things to Ash Place now. I bet you're pleased your mate's moving in, aren't you? Ettie Clarke. You know, Annie, your partner in crime? She's a lot better after her heart attack. And George Summers, you know, Mad George? He's there too.'

Me and Ettie. Both broken-hearted one way or another. And George. A proper little reunion. I start to pick up my little bag but she stops me.

'Let me take that. Goodness, Annie, that's really heavy. What've you got in here?'

She opens it, and I hope on Jim and Bumper and all the gerbils that she doesn't guess. 'It's a clock my deceased husband bought me. At Torquay.'

Our eyes meet. Then she sees the shells and the dolphin and the tin clock.

She sighs. 'OK, Annie. Whatever you say.'

So it seems that you are supposed to belong wherever they put you, call it home, as long as you keep your past covered up and pretend you're happy. When we arrive, Ettie's waiting, and she helps me to carry my heavy heart to where hers is mending. She looks like she has a plan.

SOPHIE WELLSTOOD

Say Good Morning to the Stars

My mother wasn't always drunk, but that's like saying it doesn't always rain in a rainforest, or it's not always snowing in Alaska. More often than not, we'd get home from school or from playing out, and find something had changed somewhere about the house - a new animal sleeping or pacing around in the sitting room, or a half-painted chair in the garden; perhaps a new lodger moved into one of the bedrooms or a pan of pig food boiled dry, the kitchen full of greasy smoke and whatever animal or animals were in there, whining and snorting and freaking out.

Somewhere within a one or two mile radius, my mother would be lying face up to the sky, as if she had been doing star jumps and had frozen as she fell - in the garden, in the paddock, a barn or anywhere around our village. Then came the regular kind of hide-and-seek we played, where two of us three kids - usually me and my younger brother - would go off and find her, shake her until she stopped snoring, get her to stand and do the wobbling walk back to the house, while the other one - usually my older sister -

would get tea, clean up and feed whatever animal or animals needed feeding. Then we would all disappear to our separate rooms. The nights would fall and, during the dark hours, we would inevitably hear our mother get up from her bed, or from watching the TV, and go to whichever cupboard or drawer or handbag or wellington boot or sack of animal food she kept her whisky hidden in.

By the time I was fifteen, I'd developed a serious pot habit, scoring from anyone I could find, always putting word out that I was interested in whatever there was on offer, smoke, powder or pills, it didn't matter. I spent many sick days and nights with a weasly man out of town who sold rotten gear to all the bikers and punks. Surprisingly, he never tried anything on with me but, after a bad twenty-four hours of mushrooms where we had melting walls and sharks coming out of the toilet, I gave him a wide berth and started looking to score elsewhere.

I had an older cousin, Vanessa, from a good side of our family, who was in her final year at university in Oxford. We wrote a lot; she made time to ask how things were going in my house and with my mother, and sent me wild, beautiful drawings of trees and flowers. She said the gear in Oxford was superb; it was what made life worth living so, early one morning during the summer holidays, I took my mother a cup of tea in bed and told her I would be going away for an indefinite break to recharge my batteries. My mother held the mug with trembling hands and I could see the top of a whisky bottle tucked down between the side of her bed and the table.

'All right then, darling,' she said, with a voice as shaky as her hands.

I packed a rucksack with clothes, soap, toothpaste, food, my best tapes, my Sylvia Plath anthology and my writing notebooks. I took two pounds out of my mother's purse, ripped up an old sack of pony nuts and made a sign saying: 'Oxford please'. I kissed the various animals, especially my dog.

It took me all day to hitch to Oxford. I had rides with two lorry drivers and an elderly businessman, who stopped at a café to get me tea and a sandwich. He took me straight to the address I had for Nessa - a cold, damp terrace on the Cowley Road with a large buddleia in the front garden and a couple of bikes leaning against the rotting wooden fence. The businessman patted me on the knee and gave me five pounds, saying he wanted me to get the bus back home straight away with it. I promised him that I would, and thanked him very much for his kindness.

A poster saying *'Nuclear Power? No Thanks!'* was stuck in the front room window, facing the street, along with one of a peace symbol and another of a clenched black fist. Nessa opened the door, looking much thinner than when I'd seen her the Christmas before. Her hair was cut very short, almost shaved, her arms bare and blotchy. I waved goodbye to the businessman.

I had never seen so much dope in my life. Nessa lived with her boyfriend, Marcus, and two other guys - two skinny art degree dropouts, called Martin and Chris, who were starting an anarchy magazine. Martin and Chris rolled joints for breakfast then spent the days writing, playing guitars, boiling brown rice and frying up eggs and bean sprouts. Every day, the kitchen was filled with hash smoke and the smell of the gas from the cooker, and the boiling rice steamed up all the windows until we joked that we were in a submarine. We made up songs about kelpies and sirens and mermen calling us away from the oppression of the establishment and into a new silent, salty universe.

We were sick and tired of it all - Ness's dissertation deadlines, my repressive, sexist school and all the idiots in it, the whole oppressive culture of exams, the Falklands war, nuclear power, terrible pop music, fascist Thatcher. We needed the freedom to express ourselves, to explore our ideologies, away from hierarchical, Orwellian institutions. But our anger had nothing substantial to cling to; we raged into smoky air, our furious words gathering a curious sort of form but then sliding uselessly away like the condensation on the kitchen windows. I knew it had to be more than gravity keeping us flattened and impotent, and it especially seemed to me that the simple possession of a white skin, a greater age and a penis was all it took to properly control and oppress.

Vanessa had been given a car for her 21st birthday

and, after three or four days in the house, we decided to drive to Cornwall to a holiday cabin belonging to Marcus's family and take some acid. I'd read a lot of Aldous Huxley and Carlos Castaneda and was convinced that psychedelics were the key to unlocking the true power and magic of the mind and therefore the solution to all that was wrong and evil with Western so-called civilisation. This wild, isolated hut would be the perfect place to journey into the depths of our psyches and fully connect with the power of nature. Nessa called up her dealer friend and, by the end of the evening, we had an ounce of Moroccan hash, a cap of thick Lebanese oil and five small tabs of blotting paper, each with a tiny sunshine imprinted onto it.

For once, we were all up early. We squeezed food and bedding into the boot of Nessa's Renault. Marcus claimed boyfriend rights to the passenger seat and said he would read the map. I was squashed in the back with Martin and Chris. Nessa was the only one with a real licence, and it was her car after all, so she drove all the way, peering through the windscreen with bloodshot eyes. Marcus wanted to listen to Duran Duran or the Bee Gees but he was outvoted by the rest of us so we played Patti Smith and The Cure and my Dave Brubeck tapes and we smoked and shouted out of the windows at all the normals and their pathetic bourgeois lives.

The hut sat deep in some tangled hazel and beech woods, a couple of miles inland from the North

Cornish coast. We got there, ragged and tetchy, in the late afternoon and had to park half a mile away at the end of a bridleway as it was only accessible by foot. We hauled all the bags of bedding and food over our shoulders and set off into the trees. The air and the birdsong felt very good after the smoky mess of the car journey. Marcus and Nessa were tense with each other, and more than once she turned to me and raised her eyebrows at something he'd said. I hadn't brought any proper boots of course, preferring always to wear sandals or flip flops, so my feet became covered in mud. Martin and Chris went barefoot as it was more natural, but Chris stubbed his toe, so put his shoes and socks back on again. Martin kept his shoes off and said he felt really connected with the earth.

We reached the hut after twenty minutes. Marcus retrieved the key from its hiding place in a log pile. There were just two rooms – a kitchen with a wooden table, a few mismatched chairs and stools, a wood burning stove and an old settee. There was a gas bottle, attached to a couple of rings for cooking, plus a few blackened pans and a tin kettle. The adjacent room had two bunk beds and a double bed. Outside, there was a makeshift lean-to shed and a toilet with some sort of chemical bucket, plus a water butt and buckets for washing.

It took a while but, eventually, we had the wood burning stove alight and a version of a meal in front of us. After eating, we rolled and smoked, rolled and smoked. I began to feel my thoughts existing as separate to me; I could visualise them floating around the cobwebby beams, then flying away and linking with all the other thoughts that had ever existed, from Shakespeare to Sylvia, Proust to Patti, Cornish caveman to Quentin Crisp. Martin and Chris played their guitars, improvising Django Reinhardt licks around Bob Marley riffs. Marcus tried to do a hundred press-ups, but lost count. Nessa sat silently at the table with her sketchpad and pencils, drawing her hands, left, right, left, right.

Tomorrow, we would have breakfast, then go deep into the woods and take the acid. Nessa had it stashed in her little baccy tin, the small white blots carefully wrapped in tissue paper and Clingfilm. I lit candles around the hut, closed the windows and door to keep the moths out, and made everyone tea. I watched their faces in the candlelight. Four humans around a table, their skins waxy in the unsettled light, their eyes puffy and unfocused.

Marcus squabbled briefly with Chris and Martin about who should get the double bed then agreed that they would take it in turns. I laid my sleeping bag on the lumpy settee and crashed out.

Sometime during the night, I felt a weight by my feet and opened my eyes. Marcus was sitting there, smoking a cigarette. He didn't say anything for a minute, just stared through the candlelight, the red tip of the cigarette glowing stronger with each drag he took. I turned over in my bag, pretending to be asleep.

'She's completely frigid. Stupid cunt. Won't let me near her.' His words were slow-motion bullets. I felt him shift his weight and move closer. 'Why are girls like that? Huh? Why are you such prick teases?' I stayed silent. 'I know you're awake,' he said.

I pulled the sleeping bag up higher over my shoulders. 'Don't know what you mean,' I muttered, and deliberately yawned loudly and extendedly.

My mouth was dry from all the joints, and I knew I must still be stoned. My thoughts were thick and gluey, and a fluttering bird of panic was beginning to awaken in my chest.

'You know exactly what I mean,' he said, and leaned right over my face.

I could smell the sour tobacco on his breath, plus sweat and something else. Something male, unpleasant.

'You're a dyke, aren't you?' he laughed.

The truth was, I had never heard that word back then, and I honestly didn't know if I was or wasn't. I guessed it was an insult, though, so I denied it. He laughed even louder, a silly, squeaky laugh, and I was scared he would wake the others.

'How old are you, really?'

'Fifteen. So what?'

'Have you ever given a blow job?'

I knew full well what a blow job was, and no, I had never given one nor had any intention of ever giving one. 'None of your business.'

'Wanna learn how?'

'No.'

'Don't your parents mind you not being at home, dykey?'

This time, it was my turn to laugh, but not because he'd said anything funny. The idea that my parents, as a twosome, a couple, a united front, Mr and Mrs Normal, might know or care about my whereabouts, was something I'd long learned to live without. I pulled one of the cushions over my head. It stank of mould and damp.

'Goodnight, Marcus.'

He whispered *bitch* and squeezed my backside hard through my sleeping bag, then the settee bounced a little as he got up. My heart was still banging behind my ribs and I forced myself to think happy thoughts to make it slow down. I took myself to the fields behind my farm on an early summer's morning. I ran my fingers over banks of cow parsley, picked a sprig and held it against my cheek. The soft, creamy petals tickled and soothed me. A few minutes later, I heard Nessa making little *nuh nuh nuh* sounds, followed by Marcus grunting. Then silence.

The candles flickered into pools of melted wax then, one by one, they turned into thin twists of smoke and died. Time was impossible to measure, inconsequential. Sleep was beyond me now, the roof above my head, heavy and full of webs, and I longed for open space, air, the universe. As quiet as a ghost, I pulled on my clothes, filled my rucksack with as much food as I could fit in, took the baccy tin from the table and wrapped my sleeping bag around me.

The Milky Way peppered the sky, the blackest tangles of branches and leaves shot through with distant silver. I walked deeper into the woods, stumbling, cracking twigs underfoot and hearing my dad's voice reading me Hansel and Gretel. I know nothing about navigation but I recognised the North Star when it appeared between the treetops, high above the bucket of the Plough: the one constant, immovable star, the most ancient, the one true guide. I smiled and tipped my head back, breathing in the night, the damp, the brambles and moss. I carried on walking. When finally I heard the sweet, tumbling call of a lone blackbird, and the North Star was slipping away into a new pink sky, I lay my rucksack down on the ground, slid into my sleeping bag and closed my eyes.

JULIE GLENNIE
A Cold Snap

Alexis rubbed a peephole on the misted windowpane in her bedroom. Outside, the farm was small in a landscape of windswept snow like frozen dunes. The house was an oasis in a desert; or more like a gulag in Siberia, freezing her breath despite the droning pump of the radiators. The shrunken tail of mercury on the thermometer hovered just above zero. Thank God, she'd put antifreeze in the Land Rover yesterday and Rob had lagged the pipes.

On her way to the landing, Alexis stepped over an open suitcase and a sprawl of clothes on the bedroom floor. Rob's mobile blinked at her from under his Calvin Klein boxers. Downstairs, she took a fleece from the hallway, shuffled into the kitchen, and popped toast under the grill. The kettle hissed to a climax, and she poured boiling water onto a teabag. Steam whirled into her face; she inhaled heat, and gripped the mug's warmth like a tramp. She spread butter on her toast, watching the oil slick melt into the bread, smelling the nutty saltiness.

A ray of sunshine crossed the table and cast a wafer of tepid warmth over her numb skin. Her wedding ring glinted in the blue, glacial light. *I'm going to survive*, she thought.

After breakfast, she slipped on fur-lined boots and wrapped Rob's scarf round her neck. She had bought it for him last Christmas, something thick and woolly to protect him from the winds that ravaged the hillsides. It carried his scent.

Five years ago, Rob had grabbed her hands and begged her to leave the city. 'I hate the saccharine taste it leaves in your mouth. I want to touch and feel real things, not look at screens all day.'

She had blinked, wide-eyed at him. 'But, Rob, we've only just got the flat.'

'We can sell, and buy something else. You get more for your money in the country.'

Alexis was in line for promotion at Citibank. 'What about my job?' she wailed. 'What about your job?

'I can feel the countryside in my bones. It's calling me.'

Rob was like a Rottweiler with a new toy. He pestered and moaned, persuaded and cajoled, until she was dizzy with it. There was no show-down, no ultimatum. She couldn't mark the moment of capitulation, but capitulate she did, in the way that a boulder, battered by currents, eventually washes downstream. This was where she had landed, this solitary farm in the heart of the Welsh countryside, miles from Harrods and Harvey Nicks, and wearing fur-lined boots instead of stilettos.

The first year they arrived, it had snowed. Fleeced

and booted, she and Rob had walked out, hand in hand. He had tripped over some half-buried tree roots; she had laughed, and he had pulled her sharply down. They had rolled like bear cubs in the snow. Rob was halfway to being a bully but didn't mean it.

'Doesn't know his own strength,' his mother used to say with an indulgent smile.

Friends had warned Alexis against Rob, but she liked the element of threat, the idea that her big, burly man could snap her in two.

She pushed open the door onto the back yard, and sniffed the air, coughing as the chafing cold hit the membranes of her nostrils and throat. There was no smell - he pungent farm aroma locked in by ice.

In the cowshed, she moved between the plush, brown flanks, golden warmth seeping into her. Rob had insisted on a small herd, manageable for beginners. It turned out that Rob wasn't good at mornings, so she had taken on milking duties. She swabbed the udders, attached tubing, and watched as the white liquid bubbled up through plastic. It would be impossible to get her churns to the end of the drive for the milk truck, but cows needed milking.

Afterwards, she crossed the yard to let out the horses. Moist clouds flared from their nostrils as they dipped their heads and scraped at the snow with their hooves. In the stables, she shoveled droppings into a wheelbarrow and tipped them onto the profiterole-like pyramid of the dung heap. She yanked against the frozen stiffness of the tap. No water came - she would have to fill the buckets in the house and ferry them down.

Back at the house, she sliced vegetables for the chickens: carrot, cabbage and apple. They were the most spoiled chickens in the world.

Rob used to say, 'You love them more than me.'

Hands on hips, comically indignant - 'I've been slaving over a hot stove all day for you,' setting down a plate of rich beef stew, or plump herby sausages - good rustic fare.

He had patted his stomach. 'All this home cooking's making me fat.'

'More cuddly,' she had said, snuggling into his arms.

A tremor ran through her as she reminisced, as if he were in the room, his breath against her neck, his hand round her waist.

On the local radio station, the presenter asked a town councillor why the emergency services weren't coping, and why gritting lorries weren't getting down country roads; people had been trapped in their cars, and some people had been trapped in their houses. Alexis had told Rob it wasn't safe to go. But when she discovered his secret mobile, there hadn't been a lot of choice.

In the garden, the bird table's extended arm was silhouetted against white. The cold halted the flow of sap in plants. Fish froze in the pond, suspended in layers of dreary green ice. In the garden, dead birds morphed into ice-cubes - you could have chipped bits off them with an ice pick. The world was trapped in a vice of cold, separating living things from the business of living. But she was a trail of gunpowder, a current of electricity zipping round a circuit board, zapping life into her animals. Better get out there to bed-down, feed and water - make everything warm and snug - another day complete.

Rattling her bucket, she crunched down the garden path. It felt as if the sky had fallen as she walked through slurring, falling white. Snowflakes settled on her nose and over her dark, fleeced shoulders - a shroud of white ash. Snow drifted down her neck and turned into needles on red, raw skin.

After feeding the chickens, she could avoid it no longer. Before the Big Freeze, Rob had felled dead trees in the woods, and she'd driven up with the tractor and trailer to collect them. With the radiators struggling, she would have to split logs for the log burner.

She rounded the stables at the end of the yard. The chopping block pierced through the snow, blunt-edged and wide like a truncated thumb, gangrene black. All around, lay amputated tree branches, good ash with clustered rings signifying carbon density. Rob had said they would give a slow burn, each log lasting hours.

Barns loomed dark against the churning whiteness. Chickens clucked and fussed. Time crawled beneath the blinding sky. The axe was propped against the stable wall. She seized a stump of wood and placed it on the block. Swinging back, she aimed at the bulls-eye of rings, letting the axe-head choose its arc, just as Rob had shown her. It cleaved the log with an explosive crack.

A memory tore through her head: a dream of Rob leaving this home of theirs, leaving her lost in a wilderness. Her dream-self discovered his other phone, hiding under the bed like a murderer. The dream-self listened to voicemails, her heart quickening, her breath coming in spasms.

Rob had walked into the room - his shocked yet angry expression that of a man caught in the act.

'This isn't what you think. It's a mad woman, a stalker. I was going to tell you.'

But how would a stalker know this phone number that even she didn't know? How did the stalker know that he was bored with country life? *Dying in slow motion* was what she had said - how he had put it. The stalker had texted thanks to Rob for the best night of her life - kiss, kiss, kiss followed by a smiley face.

Rob told her, 'I want to go back home to London.'

She was crying, but trying not to beg. 'I thought this was home.'

'I put on a brave face, for your sake, but I haven't been happy here for a long time.'

'But you were the one who wanted to live here.'

He was stern, like a schoolmaster losing patience with a naughty child. 'Alexis, I'm sick of pretending. I'm leaving.'

His coldness sliced through her like the cut of an

ice-cold blade. He had tethered her like a dog to this country life - and now he was abandoning her.

'You're not leaving me in the cold,' she said, 'With the central heating not working.'

'Don't worry,' he said, sounding relieved to be doing something for her. 'I'll chop some firewood before I go; you'll be OK. You like it here, don't you? This is your home.'

It was only home because you were here.

In the dream, she'd followed him through the kitchen and into the yard, picking up the axe propped by the back door. Once round the corner, out of sight of the horses and the chickens, she'd interlocked her fingers round the handle, and swung the axe behind her. His thickset shoulders marched in front, the head bobbing up and down. The axe fell, almost of its own accord, onto a patch of hair at the back of his head and halfway between his ears.

It was just a dream - a nightmare. She shuddered and wrapped Rob's scarf tighter round her neck, grappling for reality, the feeling of coarse wool against her skin, snow trapped beneath like a rim of fire. Her breath in tatters, she needed action to banish weird drifting feelings - another stroke of the axe would do it. She swung the blade above her head, and then stopped. Her arms strained and wobbled. She dropped the axe without knowing she had done so. Her eyes fixed on a place in the snow, beyond the chopping block.

There was a hand, the pink flesh frosted as if

wearing a glove made from icing sugar. She looked at it, and then at the axe. The blade was dark with blood. A scream rang out. The sound splintered the crystal world.

She dropped to her knees and scraped at the snow with her bare hands, slowly at first, and then with frantic sweeps. A wrist appeared, and a fleeced arm. A memory of sand sculptures on the beach at a Spanish resort - horses and mermaids, swimming out of the waves. It had felt as if the artists had unearthed something already there. Now she was the sculptor, shaping flesh from snow. Another arm emerged, outstretched with a checked shirt cuff poking from under the fleece. A man, sleeping under a white blanket, the rise of his alabaster chest not moving. Her hands, like rudders, pushed aside frozen currents and revealed the broad planes of a beloved face, enveloped by a powder of frost - Rob lay against a blood-red pillow of snow.

JENNIFER HARVEY
Ten Stories High

One

Somewhere out there, someone else is sitting at a window, thinking the same thing.

It was probability. All those people, packed in tight together. Experiencing the same things, at the same time, in the same place. Some of them were going to start thinking the same.

Collective consciousness. He'd read about that someplace.

Most likely in one of those magazines they keep in the waiting room.

He always takes a few of them. Just to help pass the night away.

And it had always struck him that the contents seemed better suited to the night, and he wondered if anyone ever read them during the day.

Something else he'd read, again in one of those magazines, was that people have a circadian rhythm.

Circadian.

When he first saw that word, he'd thought of a beetle. Some chirping insect that buzzed you awake in the morning then lulled you to sleep at night.

And he'd been pleased to discover that the idea had not been so far from the truth.

Nightshift work, the article went on to explain, disturbed this natural rhythm. And it turned out this was not good. The human body was not equipped for it. The cardiovascular system in particular.

Which was true. He had felt it. His heart pumping out a complaint. Go to sleep. Go to sleep. Go to sleep. His blood vessels straining and stretching, trying to stay awake.

The night, transforming him.

And he saw them all then, sitting at their windows, dreaming their collective dream.

One by one they go. Out into the night. A flap of tawny wings lifting them upwards.

Metamorphosis.

Two

Metamorphosis!

That was the word she'd been looking for.

Although perhaps that wouldn't really have been so appropriate, now she thought of it. That story. What was it again? The man that wakes up as an insect?

Helen might have thought she was insulting her. She could be sensitive that way.

Still, there was no doubt about it. The transformation was astounding.

There were four stones of Helen that simply didn't exist anymore.

She'd last seen her a year or so ago. Back when Helen was still fat. Because that was the only word you could really use to describe her. There was nothing cruel in it. It was simply true.

Anything else would have just been being polite.

She'd always thought that Helen was OK with it. Her size. She seemed confident. Strident even. Determined to be herself and to hell with what anyone else thought.

In many ways, she'd admired it. Helen's feisty independence.

Not that she could ever allow herself to get so fat. I mean, it wasn't healthy for a start.

But it was good that there were women like Helen out there. Not giving a damn. Letting the world see that being thin wasn't the be all and end all, just because you happened to be a girl.

Only now it seemed that it was. After all, there was Helen standing in the street, smiling away at her. Proud even at her achievement. Talking to her about how much she was enjoying 'wearing nice clothes like everybody else.'

She had nodded. 'What a difference!'

And they'd said their goodbyes and laughed at how nice it was to bump into one another and how they really had to meet up soon. And she had watched as Helen turned and walked down the high street, toting her bags of new clothes.

There was still a slight sway to her hips, and she had smiled at that and thought to herself.

'I'm still thinner.'

Three

'I'm still thinner.'

Jocelyn had come up with that one. And we'd all agreed. 'Brilliant!'

I'd dropped the note in her bag. She saw it when she took out her books.

And you could see her welling up when she read it and we'd all sat there and sniggered.

She'd gone on a diet after Suzy and me had caught her eating chips in the canteen.

'I wouldn't eat those if I were you,' Suzy had sniped as we walked past. And the others at the table had all laughed.

She was just that kind of girl. Soft-looking. Always holding back. When she laughed, a little trickle of saliva always formed in the corners of her mouth.

So she always had it coming. Nobody liked her.

They spoke to us all, of course. Afterwards. Trying to figure out why she had done it. But nobody said anything. I mean, it's not like you can see a thing like that coming, is it?

For a while though, a counsellor was made available.

'Just in case anyone needs to talk through any of this.'

And Jocelyn and me had looked at one another and shrugged. I did think though that maybe I should tell her mum one thing.

They had found her with a little pile of money beside her and no-one could figure it out.

Lunch money. I knew that's what it was.

A tidy sum too.

Twenty-four quid.

Four

'Twenty-four quid.'

She holds out her hand to him so he can count it for himself.

'Shit. Is that really it?'

'Yup.'

She doesn't even try to work it out. Five into twenty-four. The sum of it is pretty simple after all. Five into twenty-four equals: not enough.

She makes neat little piles of coins on the table. As if ordering them like that will deprive them of some of their power.

But the facts remain the same and she sighs. 'Listen, I'm closer so I can walk. You get the bus.'

He doesn't say a word. Just nods.

She thought to say more. 'All this walking will keep me fit.'

But now is not the moment for something glib because she can see he is doing the arithmetic in his head. The return fare, four-pounds eighty, times five.

Twenty-four. Exactly twenty-four.

The 'beg, borrow and steal weeks' is what she calls days like these.

She has begged a few quid from her mother. 'I'll pay you back next week.' Though they both know this is not true.

She has borrowed a dozen eggs from next door, and is hoping they won't come knocking, asking for them back, because she hasn't told him about it, knowing how it would make him feel.

She has stolen biscuits at work from the jar in the kitchen. Which is enough to keep you going.

But there are five more days of this and she's not sure this time how they're going to make it.

'What's for tea?' he asks.

And they both smile, because what else is there to do?

'Guess?'

'Steak and chips?'

'Got it in one.'

It's become their little joke, though with every telling of it, it is wearing thin.

She leaves him sitting there, re-arranging the piles of coins and heads to the kitchen.

The eggs sit in their box in the almost empty fridge.

Carefully, she opens it and takes out two.

'Scrambled or fried?' she shouts to him.

'You decide.'

And, for a moment, she doesn't know what to do.

The eggs in her hands, slightly chilled, feel so light. As if they hold nothing inside and are no more nourishing than air.

'I know! Omelette.'

She cracks the eggs, one by one, into the bowl.

Five

She cracks the eggs, one by one, into the bowl. Six perfect yellow suns float in their own viscous universe. It seems a shame to whisk them up and destroy the peaceful symmetry that has formed inside the bowl.

And so she measures out the sugar, sprinkles it slowly onto the eggs, watching as they collapse in on themselves and are submerged under a mountain of silver crystals.

Before taking the whisk to the lot and beating furiously.

Words from the night before are thrashing inside her head.

'I think we should call it quits.'

Call it quits. It was the casualness of it that pricked the most.

The whisk clangs against the bowl. She tuts. 'No, Janice. Not like this. Gently. That's the way.'

And she relaxes and folds the mixture together. The slow rhythm comforting her. Her sigh somewhere between ache and desire, she sways with it and thinks of him, even though she knows she shouldn't.

The flour has been sifted, the chocolate melted without her being aware of it, and she pours the sweet smelling unguent into the tin, then sets it down gently in the oven.

Is this what it takes? she wonders. Is this where comfort comes from? Is this what soothes?

The smell of warm, soon to be forgotten days wafts through the room.

She will take tea, alone. With a fine china cup that lets the light shine through, and a delicate plate that rings when the fork is set down on it.

And she will eat. Every crumb. Licking her fingers and her lips until it is gone.

Savouring the sweet taste of it. She smiles.

And so the forgetting begins.

Six

And so the forgetting begins. But not the way he thought it would.

He thought it would be slow. There would be things in the way. Far too many things. Things he would bump up against. Expectedly, at first. Then less and less so. Taken by surprise, some days, at the sight of her there, in some small thing. A hair clasp lost in the sofa. A shopping list crumpled in a pocket. Things like that.

That was what he had expected.

She had tried to prepare him for it. And he had let

her believe that such a thing was possible. That she could protect him somehow from all that was to come, just by thinking about it in advance.

The two of them together, hunched up close, making plans for when she would no longer be there.

'When I no longer exist.' That was how she liked to put it.

And he had hated it, that phrase, but never said so. Something about it made him think about how long that lack of existence actually was. Infinitesimal.

As if she had never really been there at all.

She had looked him in the eye, time and time again, checking his reaction to be sure he understood she meant it. 'Find someone else.'

Which left him wanting to yell out loud. 'But I found you!'

Mia had been an urge. A physical need that required addressing.

Nothing more than that, was what he told himself. Though he never said it to her.

Together, they never talk about Lisa.

Mostly, they laugh. And it is always Mia that starts it.

The morning sun pours in and falls on her face and her eyelids flicker but do not open. First, she smiles.

This is always how she does it. How she moves from sleep to wakefulness. With that smile.

And it is this that has filled him. Something that he did not expect.

He brushes a kiss on her lips, on that smile, and

her eyes open.

'What time is it?'

Seven

'What time is it?'

Danny pulls at his sleeve, trying to find his watch. Each time the elastic on his cuff pings back at his wrist, he sniffs. 'Shit. Did I lose my watch?'

'Dunno.'

He unzips his jacket and fumbles to get it off. 'C'mon Janey, help me with this will you?'

I tug at it too hard and fall backwards onto the grass as it comes away from his arms. Then I lie there, staring up at the sky and the black bulk of the tower as it looms over us.

'Four o'clock,' Danny eventually manages.

'What, in the morning?'

He looks at me as if I'm daft.

'You see that light up there?' I point up at some vague piece of sky.

'What, the stars you mean?'

'Not the sky! There, that light that's on up there.'

Danny squints up into the darkness then gives up. 'Where?'

'Just count up the floors until you get to seven.' He points at the tower and starts to count upwards, floor by floor, really slowly, like a kid that has just learned to read. One sniff per floor. Until he gets to seven.

'Oh, yeah. What about it?'

'That'll be my dad waiting up for me.'

'Whoa!' is all he can manage to that.

And I agree. 'Yeah. Whoa.'

Danny comes and lies beside me in the grass.

Overhead, the lights begin to swirl and dance and the sky darkens and lightens, darkens and lightens. Retreating and expanding. A huge whirling carousel.

Somewhere, I hear Danny giggle.

Then he prods me. 'Maybe you should wait a bit before going up?'

'Yeah, maybe.'

And so we lie there in the damp grass. The sun rising. Illuminating everything.

And it's mesmerising the way the colours are changing.

Eight

It's mesmerising the way the colours are changing.

Gone now are the aubergine purples, the claret reds, the damson blues. In their place comes pale lilac blossom, magnolia yellow, sage green.

Soothing colours but still tender to the touch.

I tap my finger there, just below the eyelid, and wince.

My face had always been a no-go zone for his fists. So when the blow arrived, he stopped and cursed himself.

Then, as my flesh swelled and the colours screamed at him like an accusation, he issued his edict. 'Best you don't go out for a few days. Don't open the door. I'll ring the bell so you know it's me.'

The orders coming, quick and easy, as if he had thought of them long ago.

No apologies. No promises. Because he knows, as well as I, that when the tenderness has gone and the blemishes have faded, he will strike again.

But in less visible places because a damaged face is inconvenient.

Footsteps echo in the corridor. Keys rattle. And again, I wince.

The bell rings twice, letting me know it's him at the door.

Nine

The bell rings twice letting me know it's him at the door. Followed by the usual unnecessary greeting.

'It's only me, Mrs Ogilvy!'

'I know it's you, Mike, no need to shout.'

It's our standard greeting ever since I told him there was no need to announce himself like that. I know it's him from the bell.

'But I can't just walk straight in on you, Mrs Ogilvy. What if you hadn't heard the bell and I just showed up all of a sudden in your living room? You'd die of fright.'

Quite where he gets that idea from is anyone's guess. But people think so many stupid things about you when you're old that you give up keeping track of them.

He puts the shopping down and sits beside me, already poised in full-on concerned mode. This means I'm in for a lecture. Because it's the third time this week that the lift's been out and left me stuck here, 'vulnerable and in need of assistance' as he puts it. And he thinks it's time I thought about leaving and getting myself into some place 'better suited' to my 'needs'.

But what does he know about what I need? What does he know of home? All the years it takes to call a place by that name?

He clasps my hands in his, ready to begin, but I snatch them away, and actually hear him gasp as I do so.

'Please, no lectures today, Mike, OK?'

He sighs and stands up, placing a hand on my shoulder. 'Right, well you let me know if you need me then, Mrs Ogilvy.'

And I pat his hand as it rests there on my shoulder, to let him know that I do appreciate it, all he does. But that it's all I want from him. Advice is not on my list of 'needs'.

He gently clicks the door shut behind him. I listen out for it, then head to the window and take my seat there, ready to watch the day begin.

From up here, you can see it all. All the comings and goings. You never get tired of looking at it.

Ten

You never get tired of looking at it. It's a funny thing that.

At ground level, all you notice is the chaos. Down there, it can seem ugly.

It's only up high that the patterns emerge. The beauty. The way it's been laid out. The network of streets, woven like a grid. All those angles, measured precisely at ninety degrees. The whole place controlled and fitted together with a purpose and a plan. A vision someone had years ago that had no doubt looked good on paper.

The tower blocks rise up amid the order but don't disturb it. Simply mimic, vertically, what's below.

From this vantage point, it is impressive and strangely comforting. Floating high above it all, you get the impression that perhaps things really can be ordered, planned out, fitted together just so.

And at night, the place twinkles and glows against the deepening purple of the darkened sky. And I wonder: do the people sitting there, inside all those tiny droplets of yellow light, realise just how beautiful it is? And sometimes another thought will enter my head; though it is one I always try to push away.

Somewhere out there, someone else is sitting at a window, thinking the same thing.

KATE LORD BROWN

Company

The sign above the door read 'Mes Amis'. The hard edges of the neon words were softened by the rain, which dripped over its twisting tubes like quick tongues around candy canes.

'Mes Amis. What a misnomer,' I thought as the notoriously aggressive landlord threw another drunk out onto the pavement outside.

I watched as the man lay there, talking to his own reflection in the window. A car drove past, sending a shower of water from the gutter over him. He didn't skip a beat, just went right on talking to himself, the street lights washing away on the glassy pavement around him.

I forced my attention back to the cast meeting. Margot was sitting at the head of the table, waving her arms as she spoke. I sat at the other end, the actors in our company between us. Margot insisted on the usual symmetry, as if we were still married, rather than just director and producer.

'Did she choose this place deliberately?' I thought as I swirled the ice around in the base of my heavy tumbler, the condensation cool against my fingertips.

She knew I'd hate it. It was times like this I could really do with a proper drink. I glanced at the window again, and then at my watch.

'She's late,' I thought. 'Boris has probably taken the long route from the airport. I know I would have done if I'd had the chance.'

My eyes flickered over Margot's face. I can hardly bear to look at her these days. She's a constant reminder of everything that's gone. Behind her was the reflection of a man. It took me a moment to realize it was my own image floating wretchedly in the gloom. The lighting in the bar accentuated the heavy lines on my tanned face. I ran my hand through my hair as I looked away. I felt tired, and old. I needed a haircut.

'Boris must be around the same age as Eva,' I thought. It bothered me, the thought of her with him. 'Eva can handle him though,' I told myself. 'She can take care of herself if he ever ... But he's a good-looking guy. Any woman would be flattered. Who am I kidding?'

Distantly, I heard Margot still chattering on and on about the production.

'Why did she insist on a meeting, tonight of all nights?' I thought. 'She knew Eva was flying back into London.'

I glanced over at Margot. As she smiled at one of the cast, her eyes bulged like a panting Pekinese. She had cerise lipstick smeared across her teeth, I saw with distaste. God, how that stuff used to cling to the glasses at home. The last time I kissed Eva goodbye, she had just eaten a slice of a Cox's apple, and she smelt sweet and clear. I love apples too.

I beckoned to the waitress. 'Same again,' I said, placing the empty glass on her tray. My voice sounded alien to me, as if someone else had spoken.

'Sure thing. Get you anything else?' she asked, giving me the eye.

Maybe she had recognised me. It happens a lot.

'Pascal, what do you think about Act II?' Margot asked loudly, her voice cutting through my appreciation of the waitress like an unseen gull screeching in fog. She glared at the waitress as she spoke.

The girl was pretty in a bland way. Not beautiful, not like Eva, though she was around the same age. I shook my head and smiled as she shrugged her shoulders, then looked at Margot.

'Act II? What do I think of Act II,' I mused.

I stood and put my hands in my pockets. Through the hole in the left one, my fingertips brushed my inner thigh. It felt illicit somehow, to be touching myself so intimately, but I kept my hand there all the same.

'Perhaps you should ask your leading man,' I said, leaning on the table with the other hand.

The shadow I cast across them lengthened as I leaned closer to Margot.

She sensed my mood immediately and backed

down. 'When he turns up, of course I will,' she said quietly.

'Boris can't be much longer,' one of the company giggled, and Margot glared at her furiously.

I sat down again when the waitress brought my drink over. Just then, some guy came in at the door, shaking the rain from his hair. I caught Margot looking up at exactly the same time as me, and we both looked away disappointed. She shuffled her papers, and began to discuss the casting again.

I sipped my drink. 'What I wouldn't give for a shot of bourbon,' I thought. 'Just the one. But Eva hates how I get when I drink.'

'Maybe I'll take a part this time,' I said suddenly, and the whole table turned to look at me.

I hadn't meant to say it; I had just been thinking it to myself. If it hadn't been for the shock on their faces, I would have questioned if I'd said it out loud. You know how sometimes you say something and then can't remember five minutes later if you'd actually said it or if you were just wondering about it, but you don't want to run the risk of repeating yourself and end up looking like an idiot? That happens a lot to me lately.

'But you haven't acted for years, not since Eva left, in fact,' Margot said with a clipped tone to her voice.

'Well, maybe it's about time I did,' I said, swaggering slightly.

'But who would produce the show then?' she said, her eyes narrowing.

'I would, as usual,' I said, squaring up to her. 'I didn't say I wanted the lead, did I? Just a small part, that's all I want in anything, now that Eva's gone.'

Margot looked away. 'I don't know how Boris would feel about being on the same stage as you,' she muttered, shuffling the pages of the script. 'Even in a minor role, you would completely overshadow any attention paid to him.'

'Poor Boris,' I said sarcastically.

'What is it with you? What have you got against him?' she said, scattering her pages on the table.

Everyone seemed to be receding until it was just the two of us there. It seemed like she was very close to me. I felt too hot. The smoke and the noise made my head swim.

'It's Eva, isn't it?' Margot laughed finally, folding her arms. 'You're jealous about Eva.'

'Don't be ridiculous,' I said too quickly.

'Jealous?' I thought, 'Of course I'm jealous. Eva. That was always my favourite name. Now I hardly ever get the chance to say it aloud, although I think about her all the time. I want to jump up on the table and yell her name until she comes running to me again. Right now, Boris is no doubt chattering away as he drives her here. Eva this and Eva that. It's come to this. Now I'm jealous even of her name.'

'Eva!' Margot said suddenly, and I turned to see their figures in the doorway.

Eva was handing Boris the jacket that he'd given to her as shelter from the rain.

'How chivalrous,' I thought dryly, and had to fight the urge to run to her and take her in my arms. There was a time when she would have run to me.

'Hi, everyone!' she called brightly.

She had grown thinner, I thought. 'Everyone' leapt up to kiss them both and I hung back as Margot fussed around them. I saw Eva glance at me once or twice, uncomfortably, the way I look at Margot sometimes now. How did it come to this? How did all those years of loving her come down to this, more awkward than strangers who at least give one another the benefit of the doubt?

'I think we're about done,' I heard Margot say. 'The ballet starts at 8.00,' Eva said to Margot. 'We'd better hurry or we'll be late.'

I saw Boris' face fall. She turned her body into him and spoke quietly. As she did so, I saw his stupid handsome face light up like a Christmas tree. I made a mental note to play poker with him sometime. It would give me the greatest pleasure to take him to the cleaners. So Boris was going to see her later. What about me? As they turned to go, Margot took pity on me. She spoke quickly to Eva. I was too disappointed to come forward. Eva walked towards me. She looked so beautiful, she took my breath away. There were so many questions I wanted to ask her: was she happy? Did she like living in the south? Did she still like cinnamon toast for breakfast?

She looked at me with those sad eyes of hers, and smiled, nervously. 'Hi,' she said, and kissed me gently on the cheek.

'Eva,' I said, and I squeezed her hand. It fell like a wounded animal at her side.

'I've got to dash,' she said, her voice disjointed. 'We booked these tickets months ago. Perhaps I'll see you over the weekend.'

'When are you leaving?'

'Sunday night.' Her eyes flickered to her mother and the door.

'So soon?'

'I have to work!' she laughed, backing away. 'I've got to go. Bye, Dad.' She turned and I watched them walk away.

The breath caught in my throat as I waited for her to turn to me once more, to smile and wave, but I found myself, one hand still raised, no longer waving, staring at the door as it closed softly behind them. The rain still slicked down the panes. Was that it? Was that what I had been looking forward to for weeks? My baby and her mother. The women I love more than any other in the world, walking away again. I am alone, again. How did it happen? How did it come to this? All for one minor indiscretion; some waitress whose name I can't even remember. Yes, I betrayed them, but at least it was quick and sharp, and they moved on. Their betrayal is more treacherous. They wield the enduring disappointment that has covered my life like a cape of pale fog, deadening my senses, killing every pleasure in my life.

'Forgive me,' I said. 'I'm sorry,' I said.

Even then, they turned and walked away, leaving my sorrow to drift on and on. Perhaps we betrayed each other, in our ways. I was weak, but they were strong. Lost in the fog of my own life, lost in blind misery, lost without them, I sensed that Boris had been hovering at my side for some time, and I pulled my attention back to the surface, and the noise of the bar flooded in.

'Buy you a drink?' he asked cautiously.

I nodded dumbly, and joined him at the bar. His question was a relief. I thought for one dreadful moment that he was going to ask my permission to marry Eva. It seemed appropriate somehow; two disappointed men together while two bright, happy women went off into the night. I envy them, their easy relationship. I miss the company of my women. I miss the colour they brought to my life. There are too many bars and too many waitresses like this one.

'Bourbon, on the rocks.'

They are only attractive when you have a home to go to. I miss my life, my home, my wife, but more than that I miss my child, my baby bird, my Eva. Eva, Eva, Eva, like a sigh. Where did you go?

MIKE SCOTT THOMSON

Green Door

'At the very least,' I tell Steve before leaving for work, 'just try to get those three things done. Please?'

'Sure thing, Katie,' he says, not even looking at me, as he squats within a helix of cardboard boxes stacked upon the floor.

I'm not certain what he expects to gain from unpacking now. We don't yet have any furniture. No shelves, seats or anything. All we have is the telly plugged in one corner of the room, and the hi-fi in another. But that's not stopping Steve, as he rummages inside one of the boxes.

A second or two later, he pulls something out. 'Ta da!'

'And what do you propose to do with that?' I ask, as I regard the TV remote control he's holding aloft like a glittering prize.

He looks at it, and then at me, as if I'm the dumb one here. 'What d'ya think? World Cup. It's the other side of the world. Kick off in two hours.'

I shoot him a withering look. 'So,' I say, 'plenty of time to do - what?'

He rolls his eyes. 'One. Buy contents insurance. Two. Call the landlord and tell him about the busted tap. Three. See our neighbours and introduce myself.'

'And?'

'Tell them to shut the fuck up.'

'But not in so many words, right?'

'OK, OK.' He springs to his feet. 'I'll be polite. Promise.'

'Just see that you do.' I move forward and give him a quick peck on the cheek. 'Enjoy your football. And see you later.'

The slam of the flimsy front door rattles through the house as I tug it closed.

As I commute the longer journey into work, I consider our change of circumstance.

We were, I concede, lucky to get it. Two months' notice to find a new place: no time at all really. Not with rent prices the way they are, and Steve being out of work. Still, we should have seen it coming. The house next to our old place went for two eighty-five. The one opposite, three hundred. Asking price for the one eight doors down is three fifty. So I don't suppose I can blame old Mr Kyriakos. As we shifted the last of our boxes out through the old green door on Saturday afternoon, someone in a white van came round to hammer a new 'For Sale' sign into what had once been our front lawn.

Steve checked the Find-A-Property app on his iPhone. 'Three sixty-five,' he said.

'What's that then?' I asked. 'Pence?'

We laughed but, the thing is, it'll get snapped up.

And now we're here: two suburbs to the south further out, much pricier but only a little larger. We saw it for the first time last week. I made a mental checklist as we were shown around.

Beige-and-cream coloured floral wallpaper from the 1970s. Check.

Pungent stomach-shafting odour as if something small and furry has expired behind the skirting board. Check.

Cold tap on the bath looser than my tongue after one too many vodka martinis. Check.

Paper-thin walls, flimsy enough to hear a gnat fart from three blocks away. Check.

Green door. Ooh! I nudged Steve. I always liked our old front door. Green: the colour of change and renewal.

'Gotta be a sign,' he said.

'But the rest -'

'Nothing that a lick of paint won't fix,' he said.

As if he'd ever lifted a paintbrush in his life.

It was moot, anyway. We were running out of options.

'We'll take it,' we told the estate agent.

We were so exhausted by the Saturday, having carted boxes between our old house and the new one, that not even the neighbours woke us.

No such luck on the Sunday evening. The two of us sat up, propped up on some pillows against the wall, stretched out on the stinking, old mattress left behind in the larger of the two bedrooms.

'Yo yo yo,' went the microphone-enhanced voice from behind the partition wall. 'Word up, y'all.'

Hip-hop beats soundtracked his incessant tuneless

yammer. The occasional 'parp!' of a blast of deep bass sent our duvet and top lips rippling in sync to its rhythm.

'Get yo' ass down to - nah, bro, stop jus' a minute there.'

The noise abated and we sighed with relief.

'Is that it?' I asked Steve.

Silence fell for exactly four-and-a-half seconds.

'Parp!' went the bass from next door. 'Word up, y'all!' barked the guy as the drums started again.

'Go round,' I told Steve.

'Balls to that,' said Steve. 'I ain't getting my head kicked in.'

'Nor,' I said with steel in my voice, 'am I.'

They finally shut up at three in the morning and, boy, am I tired. I am not looking forward to work today.

I arrive back at our new home at 6.30pm, shattered. The telly is on in the far corner of the room. Steve has deemed it necessary to unpack the tin opener from the kitchen utensils box, but nothing else.

'So,' I ask him. 'Did you get those things sorted?'

A brief wave of panic flitters across his face. 'Ah,' he says.

'Oh, bloody hell, Steve.'

'I tried, honest. After the football, I had to go and sign on, right? And then I came back, went next door, but there was no answer. Then I spent two hours trying to fix the tap, but couldn't. So I went to call the landlord, then realised we don't have a landline yet.

So that meant I couldn't phone for insurance either.' He shrugs, pulls his hapless Stan Laurel impression. 'Sorry, babe.'

'Steve,' I say, 'you don't need a landline. You have an iPhone, remember?'

His face twitches. 'Oops,' he says. 'I keep forgetting there's a phone on my phone.'

I stare sharp, pointy daggers at him. 'Tomorrow, right?'

'Right.'

Later that night, the beats start up again.

'Yo yo yo!' reverberates the familiar voice, not muffled one decibel by the plasterboard partition between the two master bedrooms. 'Get yo' ass down to Jam'n'Joint! Wednesday night, get outta sight!'

He must have been working on his rhymes. A bit.

The beats stop again. Steve and I turn to each other, puff our cheeks.

'They're recording,' I say. 'He keeps saying the same thing over and over again.'

'Take four, bro',' says the voice from next door. 'We gotta do the number.' The beats and bass start. My heavy eyelids shudder to the frequency. 'Jam'n'Joint!' says the voice. 'At the Arches. Call 07884 940193 for more info, y'all.'

'What was that?' I ask Steve.

But he doesn't need to answer; the voice repeats it for me.

'Give me your iPhone,' I tell Steve.

I don't need vodka martinis to take *this* on. My

tongue has been loosened by this white-hot ball of wrath burning in my belly. To hell with 'polite'.

I snatch the phone and punch in the number. I hear ringing, from both down the line and, through the partition wall, the tinny ringtone of a surprising 'She'll be Coming Round the Mountain When She Comes', clashing with the hip-hop beats. Both sets of music stop and I hear a click from down the line.

There's a puzzled pause of a few seconds. 'Yeah, hello?'

I stretch my most sarcastic smile across my haggard face, grit my teeth and draw on my four years' experience working in my terrible customer service job.

'Oh, good *evening*, sir. Am I speaking to the managing director, chief operating officer or otherwise esteemed creative controller of the popular box social, "Jam and Joint?"'

There's another confused gap from the other end of the line. 'Er. Yeah.'

'Splendid,' I continue, my Home Counties accent having taken on a cut-glass edge. 'It's *such* a pleasure, believe me, to be conversing with such a doyen of our fair city's fabulous entertainments scene. I can hardly contain my excitement.'

Another pause. 'Who's this?'

'Ah, my dear fellow! Allow me to introduce myself: Lady Katherine Oxberry, at your service. I'm your new *neighbour*! So pleased to make your acquaintance! Perhaps, at an hour more favourable, I can grace your company with the view to the temporary acquisition of a half-pound of fair trade sugar?'

Silence from the other end.

'Oh, come now, my man! You do know what neighbours do?'

'Er,' said the voice from down the line.

'They *look out for each other*. It is with this noble maxim in mind that I have the following request I wish to impart upon your good self.'

'Uh? Wassat then?'

'*Put a fucking sock in it*.' I press the hang-up button and pass it back to Steve. He's looking at me, one eyebrow raised.

'See?' I smirk. 'It's gone quiet. Now let's get some sleep.'

Five minutes later, the beats start again. This time they don't shut up until four.

'I've had it,' I tell Steve, red-eyed and irritable at eight the next morning.

He looks at me, worried. 'What'cha gonna do?'

'Give me your Pan Sonic CD.'

Steve shrugs, but goes to a box and roots around. I go to the hi-fi in the corner of the living room, unplug it and carry it upstairs to the master bedroom. I prop its two speakers against the wall, sound-side inwards, and turn the volume up to eleven. Steve gives me the Pan Sonic CD, I slide it inside and set it on repeat.

'They must sleep during the day,' I say, 'So let's see how they bloody like it.'

'Just as well I have to go out,' mutters Steve, but I barely hear him as I press play, the first super-deep distorted bass notes from Finland's finest musical crazies wobbling its way through the plasterboard. The walls tremble. Not even Sleeping Fucking Beauty will be able to survive this one.

'See you,' I say to Steve with fire in my eyes, 'later.' I turn back as I open the green door and step across the threshold. 'And don't you dare turn it off. This is war.'

I depart for work with grim satisfaction.

I arrive back at 6.30pm to find the front door has been kicked in. Adrenaline bottlenecks in my chest as I freeze, blood draining from my face. My hands buzz with pins and needles as my limbs weaken. With one shaking hand, I push the splintered green door open. It creaks, complaining on its hinges.

'Steve?' I call.

No answer.

'Steve, are you home?'

Nothing.

I set foot in the hallway. My foot squelches into something deep and moist. The carpet. It's wet. More than wet. It's glistening with two inches of water. I gulp.

I look around - at the hallway, kitchen, living room. The whole place is filmed with the iridescent sheen of water. I try a light switch; it doesn't work. Nothing electrical does. Everything's broken. Craning my neck, I see the ceiling. Before, it had been a clean off-white. Now it is lumpy, sunken in four or five places and, in the kitchen, caved in.

All our cardboard boxes are ruined. I dread to think what their contents are like. Our possessions. Clothes, books, CDs. Photos. The telly.

Oh, God. The contents insurance. We still don't have any.

I turn this way and that, panicked. I feel myself hyperventilate. Not this. Not our new house. Not our new*home*.

From behind me, I hear a noise. It's someone coming down the stairs. I swing round, but it isn't Steve. It's a young man, about twenty, wearing a tracksuit and black baseball cap.

With the wounded look of someone with bad news to deliver, worse than his young years know how to deal with, he gives a rueful grimace. 'Hey,' he says. 'You must live here.'

I nod.

'Shit,' he says. 'Something got busted here, big time.'

I look at the front door.

'Kinda had to do that, like,' he says. 'There was this water, see. Seepin' into our living room. From your wall. Daz saw it first. He says to me, shit's fucked up with their plumbin', man, gotta sort this shit out.'

From above us, through the gaping hole in the kitchen ceiling, I hear a voice. Another young lad peers at us upside down from the destroyed bathroom.

'Oh man,' he says. 'Wouldn't wish this on my worst enemy.' He swings himself upright. 'Had to turn the water off at the mains. Needed to break into your loft.' He looks at his hand; it's bandaged and stained red. 'Sorta fucked myself up, but don't worry about it.'

I look at Daz through the ceiling, and his friend next to me in the kitchen. I raise my hand to my face, not knowing what to do, what to say.

Two words eventually come to my lips. 'Thank you,' I say in a small voice.

'Yo, no problem,' says Daz. 'Anytime.'

'That's what neighbours do, right?' says his friend. 'They look out for each other.' He sees my reaction, and winks.

I can't help but smile back. It's only when I see the tin opener on the kitchen surface, the one item on the entire ground floor which has escaped water damage, that the tears come.

The landlord is a greying 60-something by the name of Mr Baldacci and, in the company of the emergency plumber, he takes the news well, all things considered.

'Whoa,' he mutters as he passes through the stricken doorway. 'And you didn't even get to unpack.'

Daz and Will are getting stuck in with brooms and mops in the kitchen and hallway; a white-faced Steve, having arrived back from wherever the hell he was, is piling our ruined items into one far corner of the living room. I'm still holding that damn tin opener and wondering just what on earth we're going to do.

The landlord and plumber trudge upstairs then mutter to themselves in the bathroom. I catch the words 'shoddy workmanship, innit?' from above my head, and hear the clunk and clangs of metal on metal. A few minutes later, the plumber looks down through the hole in the kitchen ceiling.

'The tap in the bathroom. It's been pourin' water through the ceilin' all day. Wasn't that well fixed to begin with, but somethin', I dunno, somethin' shook it loose ...'

He gets up again and leaves the room with the landlord. I pray to God that neither of them see the speakers still stacked against the wall in the bedroom.

Steve and I look at each other in the mottled twilight of our water-sodden living room.

'Six weeks,' I say. 'Six fucking weeks, without a home.'

He stares at me. I don't need to say what else I'm thinking. The insurance that never was. The tap that was never mended. The calls that were never made.

The CD that shouldn't have been played, his expression says back.

I glance up at him. 'Where the hell have you been today, anyway?' I smudge a tear from the corner of my eye. 'Bet you've been watching the bloody World Cup. Of all the things to be doing.'

He sniffs. 'I had an interview, didn't I.' I glance up at him. 'For a plumbing course, ironically enough.'

I frown. 'I didn't know that.'

'No,' he says, 'You didn't. I did tell you this morning, but you were too busy with -'

He cuts himself off as we spot the figures of Daz and Will in the doorway.

'You guys got anywhere to go?' asks Will. 'It's just that, we got a spare room. It's small, like, but there's space -'

'Just until you get sorted here,' says Daz.

'And you can come to our club night,' says Will. 'At the Arches. Tomorrow. It may cheer you up. After this shit, ya know?'

'And after that,' grins Daz, 'We'll be quiet. Right, Will?'

'Right on.'

I give a small smile. I think Steve may be smiling too. 'Thank you so much,' I tell them. 'That would be wonderful.'

We follow them outside into the cool night air, down the driveway and straight back up again on their side. Their place is a mirror image of ours.

Daz reaches for the key with his uninjured hand, and unlocks the door. Will tips his cap. 'Yo yo yo,' he chirps. 'Make yo'self at home!'

I nudge Steve, and point to the front door. 'Look,' I say. 'It's green.'

'Gotta be a sign,' he says.

As we cross the threshold carrying only the clothes on our backs, we both know it's a good time to start over.

GAIL JACK

Henry

I wasn't drunk. No, really, I wasn't. OK, so maybe I'd had a few, but it wasn't Friday's usual heavy session, so I'd say I was more liberated than lubricated. Not a bad way to ease myself into the weekend, in fact. And, with the prospect of the house to myself and a small carry-out to help liberate me further, what more could a man want?

Well, a break in the weather might have been nice. Had the gods been kinder, the rain would have started while I was still in the chippie and I could have stayed in there and watched the rest of the game. True, I might have gone home smelling like a fish supper, but at least I would have been dry. As it was, the deluge started not long after I'd left - and me with no money for a taxi. Sod's law, I suppose. The rain itself wouldn't have bothered me too much if it hadn't been for the lightning. Call me spineless, but I'm no good when it comes to unrestrained high voltage. I legged it to the nearest doorway.

Those older shops with the recessed doorways are great. Dry. And *safe*. I figured I'd eat my chips before the wrapper disintegrated and wait for the rain to ease up. I didn't see the other guy at first because he was sort of tucked into the shadows; he gave me a bit of a start when he stirred. He was older than me and leaning heavily against the wall. It did occur to me that he'd partaken of the same falling-down water that I had, but then I noticed that he had one of those funny walking stick things with feet - and that he was wearing pyjama trousers and a pair of slippers with his shirt and tie.

It seemed only polite to give him a nod. 'Can you believe this weather?' I said.

I held out the soggy paper bag and offered him a chip. I expected a polite refusal but he surprised me with a lop-sided grimace that I took to be a smile, before he slowly extended his arm. He had to let go of his walking stick to do it and his movements were a little jerky, which made me think he'd had a stroke, so I made it easy for him. I picked the biggest chip I could find, slathered in curry sauce, and put it in his fingers.

'Now mind, it's hot,' I said, like I was talking to a five-year-old. I felt like an idiot after I'd said it but, hey, he didn't seem to mind; he kept smiling. Or grimacing.

He managed to find his mouth OK, but then I had a brief moment of panic. What if he choked on the chip? That can happen, right? Or what if he was allergic to the curry sauce? It could have been a real disaster because I had no idea about that Heineken manoeuvre and no life in my phone to call for help. In any case, he seemed to manage OK and his face didn't swell like a football, so I relaxed a bit and gave him another.

We shared the chips in silence. Well, silence except for the rain, of course. It was like one of those freaky rainstorm CDs with the additional *swish* of passing traffic. I could say it was relaxing, but it wouldn't be the truth. My feet were squelching in my trainers every time I moved and there's nothing worse than having cold, wet jeans wrapped around the bottom half of your legs. I couldn't think of anything intelligent to say and my neighbour didn't seem to be much into conversation either so that added to the awkwardness.

I couldn't suss him out. He wasn't wet, so he must have been standing in the doorway before the rain came on, but I couldn't fathom how he'd got there or where he might be going. He didn't look fit enough to walk far - although he wasn't one of those shrunken individuals that a stiff breeze would blow over - and I couldn't think of any old folks' homes in the area, especially not upmarket ones. He had the look of a retired GP or perhaps a lawyer: distinguished, tidy - apart from the pyjama thing, that is. I had him pegged as a Charles ... or maybe a Henry ...

It continued to pour - and I mean, really pour. Puddles were forming across the uneven pavement and, by the look of the clouds, I could tell it wasn't going to let up any time soon. It was early evening, and the streetlights hadn't kicked in yet, so there was no warm orange glow to penetrate the thick grey veil of vertical rain. Pedestrians had trickled down to the foolhardy few and traffic was almost non-existent. I debated becoming one of the foolhardy few but, as luck would have it, lightning cracked the air in front of us and the thunder rolled in almost right behind it. Decision made; I was staying put. And so was Henry, although I noticed that he seemed to be leaning a bit heavier into the side of the doorway. I'm usually not very good at that sort of thing, but it looked like he might be struggling a bit. 'Wait here, Henry,' I said. 'I'll be right back.'

I darted off into the rain and came back with one of those aluminium chairs from the coffee place next door. Hell, it's not like anyone was going to miss it; the place was dead inside as well as out. I wiped the chair down as best I could with the sleeve of my jacket.

'Right,' I said. 'You sit here.'

Getting Henry into the chair was easier said than done. I hadn't figured on his balance being quite so bad. Nor mine, for that matter, and it didn't help that the bloody chair was so light; he was almost on the deck a couple of times. Nevertheless, we managed it, and I definitely think Henry was relieved to be sitting down.

'Now me,' I decided, and ran back for another chair. I found a pack of cigarettes in my pocket and, as I settled down to wait for the rain to let up, I drew one out and set it to my lips.

Henry got a little agitated. 'Elephants,' he said, quite clearly.

It was the first time I'd heard him speak, but what the flaming hell? *Elephants?*

'Elephants,' he said again, and mimicked a smoking motion.

I gave him a tab and lit it for him, then watched as he closed his eyes and inhaled. It was the funniest thing, seeing the pleasure on his face. He grinned and gave me the thumbs up as he settled back in his chair with his legs stretched out in front of him. Honestly, he could have been at a cricket match.

We talked for ages. Well, I talked. Mostly about football but I may have touched on a few other things as well. It's amazing how loose your tongue gets when you're talking to a stranger. It's probably just as well that I don't remember half the stuff that I droned on about. Henry's contribution was limited to the odd thumbs up or thumbs down, with the occasional lop-sided grin and at least one grimace, but he managed to make himself understood; he was more of a rugby man, for instance. I was also witness to another of his linguistic inaccuracies when I cracked open the lager.

'Ah,' he said appreciatively, 'October.'

I don't know how that elephants/October thing works. It didn't seem to bother Henry too much, so I don't know if he knew that his words came out all wrong. Actually, nothing seemed to bother Henry much - not even the fact that I kept calling him Henry - but by the time we'd worked our way through a couple of cans, it was pretty late; I was beginning to wonder what to do next. I had already given Henry my jacket - not that he seemed cold or anything - but I couldn't see that being out in this weather would be good for him at his age. And I couldn't just leave him there when I left. My only other option was to have the police pick him up and see if they could find out where he'd come from. As it was, matters were taken out of my hands.

Henry had begun to take an interest in a silver Audi that had already been up and down the street a few times and then pulled up in front of us. Nice motor. I mean, we're talking top of the range here.

'Motorbike,' he said, and shook his head. His grin had gone.

There seemed to be some kind of domestic going on inside the car because it was ages before the passenger door opened and a woman got out. I wouldn't like to guess how old she was but, if I likened her to Henry's motorbike analogy, I'd say she was definitely built to a high maintenance spec. She carefully picked her way over to us, circumventing the worst of the puddles, and stood in front of Henry. Her gaze took in everything - the seating arrangement, the cigarette ends on the ground, the can in Henry's hand - but I don't think I've ever been ignored quite so thoroughly in all my life. It was almost artistic.

'Dad,' she said. 'Let's get you to the car.'

So that was that. No fussing, no nagging, no

histrionics of any sort - I couldn't tell if that was a good thing or a bad. And I couldn't tell what Henry thought about it because his face was expressionless. I don't know - maybe Henry was in the habit of making a run for it. Or maybe she was just waiting till she got him alone before she gave him a tongue-lashing. In any case, his daughter had him out of the chair, on his feet with walking stick in hand, and ready to go before I had time to process the thought that I wouldn't be seeing him again. I think she would have dragged him off without so much as a second look at me, but Henry dug his heels in and stopped her in her tracks; he wanted to say goodbye and give me back my jacket. I think a little bit of mischief got into me.

'You keep it, Henry,' I said.

I stayed in the doorway until they drove off and then made my way home in the rain, hoping that Henry was the man I thought he was - and that he discovered the contents of my jacket pockets before his daughter did: two cans of October and one pack of elephants. Rations for another rainy day.

SAM SCHLEE
Skeleton House

It hinged on a death. Our house. We bought it last year, and it's ours now – more or less. We share the thing with a bank. Over the next 20 or 30 years, the bank will reluctantly sell the rest of it to us in little monthly packets. We will grit and grind our teeth to meet the repayments.

My girlfriend's rich aunt passed away. No children. My girlfriend's mother inherited a slew of money and gave her a chunk for a deposit. I scraped something together too. And now all our dreams and ambitions are true at once. We can call a house a home, our own.

We are bound to the ground. Beholden to the foundations. We own a piece of land and the things on top of it. The home that always promised to solve every problem there was.

I spent my first night in the house with the smell of fish and chips and cardboard boxes lingering in the air. I felt the house surround me; it seemed unreasonable that so much weight could be my responsibility. What if it fell down?

It was a terrace with two bedrooms and a

bathroom upstairs and a kitchen, study and living room downstairs. As I lay trying to sleep that first night, I could only think about all the things that we owned. Each one, a material responsibility contained only by corrugated card.

I dreamt that night. In my dream every box tore open like a dinosaur egg in a film. Every book and piece of Tupperware burst from the boxes that held them. They flowed like lava and soon filled the bottom floor. I knew that we would be smothered and I woke up to warn Kate. She was not sympathetic to my fears.

We were moving relentlessly towards the perfect home and regressing endlessly towards the mean. We made lists of things we wanted, things we could afford and things we couldn't. We called our parents, and they brought us furniture from their houses that they no longer needed. And everything went on, and everything goes on.

It came from death, and our biggest ever purchase puts us on the road to death. It ties us firmly to our own wills and the inheritance of our inevitable progeny. But there is no doubt that it is essential that you dig yourself in. That you take possession of a piece of land. One with walls. One that you can defend with your very life.

There is a body on the tracks. Don't look back.

You keep jarring your fingers against stones.

A coin. Glossy water.

We'd been there a year when I decided to dig in

my garden. I wanted to burrow into the soil beneath the surface that I owned. I don't know what the law is - how deep is the earth mine for? I wondered whether I might sense when the soil stopped being mine and started belonging to the earth again.

I wore wellington boots. Which is something I can do now that I have a place to dig. I started after breakfast and I dug all day. Kate was at work. I called in sick early in the morning with a bad case of ennui.

Soil and mud clung to my hair. In amongst the grit and grime, I found shards of pottery, pieces of glass. I wanted to find an arrowhead. But they are not as common as I wish they were. Sometimes I would drop the shovel and reach into the soil and push it around with my hands.

My fingernails were dirty.

I swear I felt another hand pushing up when mine was pushing down. I swear that I touched finger tips.

By about lunch time, I had a trench two metres long and a metre wide. I'd already gotten about a metre deep. I really had started early. I really had worked hard. I could tell because there was a lot of soil in a pile outside of the hole.

I was pretty sure that I'd find a way out down there.

Kate came home and it was dark. I was clean and everything inside the house was as it should be. I was too tired to cook. I think, by then, I genuinely was getting ill. I at least looked wan enough to assuage any suspicions she might have had.

We had a quiet evening; we watched television and smiled at each other. I lay my head in Kate's lap and she stroked my hair. Everything was perfect. We drank real ale. And I really did feel poorly.

I decided I wouldn't tell her what I'd found in the hole.

Kate left before I woke. I think she would have said something if she'd noticed the hole in the garden.

I hadn't been surprised to find a skeleton.

The day before, at about 4.00pm, I had seen a flash of cracked yellow - hard and smooth. On my hands and knees, I began to push soil away from what I'd found and saw that it was a skull. My trench had been perfectly placed - as if I was always digging for the body.

I uncovered the skull and took some time to stare into those eye sockets. Before I knew it, it was five o' clock and Kate was heading home. I knew I would have to clean up so I stopped right then.

I had woken up that morning from a dream. The house still felt new to me - you know how much you dream when you're somewhere new? At least, that's the way it is for me.

In the dream, I walked behind the skeleton; I could see right through it. It was an ordinary day, nothing unusual except, everywhere I went, the skeleton was right in front of me.

I woke with a genuine chill. I felt on firmer ground when I called into work sick again. I drank a cup of tea and ate a bowl of muesli while I considered the day ahead. It was already Woman's Hour by the time I left the house for the end of the garden.

I worked diligently - though I was feeling a little poorly, and very tired. My muscles were aching from the day before; I felt every gesture a hundred times over. I started clearing more of the dirt away from the skull. I had a little brush and some water to clean up the bone as best I could. The cloud cleared and the sun shone down on my efforts.

I'm no expert. But I could see breaks fused and marks of fresher violence as I worked along the length of the body. I didn't really anticipate the number of bones that there were to uncover. Who knows how long it had been there? Certainly, this was the first time that the skeleton had been lit by clear, crisp sun. As I said, I worked diligently so it would look its best.

It was difficult to keep the mud from the bones. It seemed to keep creeping over them, even once I'd cleaned them. They were all still sunk into the soil - I didn't want to mess up the positions, the bone that was exposed was bright, slightly yellow, lit well by the sun which was high in the sky. I stood at one end of the trench and admired this body that was not mine.

I climbed down into the trench and lay beside it. We compared the shape of our bodies like lovers do. It seemed smaller, its thigh bone was shorter I think. Also her hips seemed broad - hence the pronoun.

I lay there for a little while, but the trench was deep and, as the sun slipped further away from midday, the shadow was quick to appear. It was cold. I tried to stick it out. I wanted to run my fingers along all them bones (them bones, them bones). But I think I only managed about half before I decided to climb from that damp pit for the last time.

Underground are rivers and rivers.

Bones that will never get sore.

The truth is it's easy to forget.

Anyway. Getting cold, I peered down into the pit at her. I know that I could've called the police and we could have all found out what it is she's doing down there. But I worry that if we took her out, the whole ground would just fall in. She is better left alone.

Everything seems in order down there. I'm pleased that I've seen her. I'm glad I've had the chance to count her bones and clean her up. I decided to bury her again. You shouldn't go digging over old bones. And Kate would only have been angry about the mess.

I pushed the soil back into the hole as quickly as I could, sometimes sort of pushing and scraping it in with my feet and legs. Before long, she was covered. Soon after, all the soil was back in the pit. All the gaps of air meant there was a mound. It was a beautiful tumulus. Is that the singular or the plural?

I knew Kate would be angry - I didn't want anyone to suspect. I had a plank of wood that the scaffolders had left after the repointing was done; I thought it might do to flatten the soil. I put it on top of the mound and walked along it. I kept doing this in different spots until it was more or less level with the ground.

My clothes and skin were caked in mud and I hadn't managed to keep track of time. Dazed, I traipsed through the house and ran myself a bath. I left unmistakeable tracks. Almost an hour later, Kate got home. She found me in the bath, the radio berating me, the temperature maintained by a constant topping up and letting out. I hardly knew the time had passed.

Love, she said, you've left a mess, she said.

The steam and fug matched the slowness of my mind which chugged along.

I've been digging, I said.

I didn't want her to think I'd made it up. So I didn't say about the bones.

At the weekend, I said I was still ill and stayed in bed. I slept a lot. Kate made a vegetable patch. I've put the skeleton out of my mind (back in the ground).

TRACEY ICETON

Home Tomorrow

He's coming home tomorrow.

He's a tiny pink bundle, an armful of warmth. I could carry him home in my pocket. His starfish hand reaches out and grips a lock of my hair, strangles it tight. I clutch him to me. Kiss his wet, gummy mouth. Give him a finger to suck on. Dreams of his life flood my world, quenching the parched landscape.

He's in his uniform. The first he'll wear: navy blazer, grey shorts, white shirt, striped tie. I sent him out early, neatly tucked and fastened. He's home late, wrinkled and messy. He smiles, laughs. I prayed all day for that smile, that laugh. Expected a pout on his perfectly red mouth, dreaded tears. I swoop him up into my arms.

He rushes to the table. Leaves his skateboard, muddy gritted wheels, on the kitchen floor. *Don't leave it there. I'm going out again after tea.* He swallows the mound of mash in two mouthfuls. Some of it smears around his mouth. I grab a tissue and clear the gunk so I can see his smile. *Don't, Mum. I'm not a baby.* Yes you are.

He wakes me with the front door. I was listening

for it anyway; footsteps heavy and sodden with lager on the stairs, his gurgled choking, the flushing of the toilet. I get up to help. He leans on the doorframe, swaying in an imaginary breeze. His lips move in slow motion. The words are slurred. I help him to bed.

He waves the paper triumphantly. It's the first thing I see, after his radiant grin, brighter than June sun. He passed with honours. The tight-jawed, pursed-lipped, chewed-biro nights were not for nothing. I steal a hug. No kiss now, he's too old. A man. All grown-up and ready to go.

He brings Jenny. She's nice. We eat dinner together. They wash up, she offers. I watch through the doorway. He dabs soapsuds on her nose. She retaliates with a full beard and moustache. He pulls her close and kisses her, the foamy beard shared out equally. The twinkling ring on her finger drives ice into my heart. He's hers now, not mine. But still, she is nice.

He marches up the drive in another uniform, the last he'll wear. He salutes us as we open the door. His pale lips are pressed into a stiff line. He takes off the hat and smiles uncertainly. I want to cry. He's leaving us. Jenny holds my hand. She wants to cry too. He kisses us both goodbye. His mouth is not the soft baby pout of long ago.

He's coming home tomorrow. I insisted. Told them every journey he ever went on started here, at home. So this one must too. I refused Wootton Bassett, the folded flag, bugle and salvo. They agreed. They're sending a car. With a box. He won't smile when he sees us this time. He won't even know he's here. But he'll be home.

ANDREW JAMES

For the Boys

Davey

Annie would tell me stories about the house.

The parties they'd had there, the way she'd created a magical haven with strings of lights and swathes of faux silk and brocade, the two rooms she'd decorated for her two sons, pictures she'd bought to hang on the walls, the laughter.

The fights.

And the ghost, the presence she'd tell me about, all wide-eyed and goose-bumped, and how he - always*he* - had removed photographs from hooks and made clocks race to midnight and *yes, killed the fish!* and yet -

And yet his presence was calm, soothing even, watching over her and the boys. Nothing to be scared of. No need to be afraid. Not like now.

The first time I knew anything was wrong, great bullets of rain were ricocheting off the bricks and pounding us as we stood wrapped in each other, her face already wet, distant thunder drowning out the sobs that shook against my shoulder. A neighbour had called, said the house was being boarded up, yellow tape across the garden path, *'and he said it wouldn't happen again, he said he'd sorted it out -'*

And the lane had turned into a river and we'd watched it wash her dreams away.

'He' was Annie's ex. Ex-husband, ex-breadwinner, ex-wife-beater, perpetual bastard and all-round fantasist. Father to the boys, ex-friend of mine and the reason I'd met Annie in the first place. They'd divorced three years earlier; just a year ago, he'd told me that they'd only separated, giving each other a little space. And while she and her children lived with a steady stream of bailiffs and money lenders wandering up the path of the last-known-address, he maintained a rented flat down on the river.

In adversity can be found a hidden resolve, and so it proved. No more rushing back from work to find he'd already picked the kids up from school, treating access agreements and previously made plans as irrelevancies, riding in to play hero to two children he'd long since stopped contributing towards -

And so she and the boys moved out and she somehow borrowed enough money for a deposit and found a place to rent. The rent alone took over half of her salary and, after bills, there was barely any left for food and the fare to work, but they'd be free of the fear of the knock on the door. And for two years they were, and life was good. Except that her ex-husband moved back into the house. As tactical manoeuvres go, that was pretty low.

Paul

The telly's on in my room. I'm keeping the sound low, it's *still early*. It gives me enough light to sort through the chest of drawers for today's clothes and it keeps me company. On top of the chest, my Cheerios are going soggy in the bowl.

I like it when it's half dark. I can see what I need, but colours hide in the shadows. I pull out a sweater, toss it on the bed, close the drawer and open another.

Deep breath -

Under the T-shirts, below the socks, the bright blue of a football jersey from a past I can't let go but don't want to think about too much.

Stay in the shadows, blue -

I need to keep it, he gave it to me. It's my test, see if I can *Deal With It*. That's what Mum said I had to do once. Deal With It. So it's my challenge, otherwise I'll feel his arm around me, feel his whisky lips on my face, smell his sweat, hear him –

I'm sorry, Paul, mate, truly I am, but your mum and me, we're not getting along at the moment, but I'll be back for you, you and Davey, you'll see, I'll be back in no time, I promise –

Except he never did come back.

It's OK, though. Me and Davey and Mum, we got on OK. We Dealt With It. Tough at first, mind. Chucked out the house, we were. But in the end, Mum got a job and we got this flat. And now Davey's got a good job and a flashy car and we look after

Mum, me and Davey, and that's OK.

I pick up my bowl and spoon. Like I thought, soggy. But all right.

On the telly, another blue. The big bear and his friends, singing and dancing in front of his blue house. He makes me laugh and when I do, I feel some milk come out and run onto my chin. I wipe it away with the back of my hand and my face feels rough because I need a shave.

Bear welcomes everyone to his house –

If I concentrate I can push him from my mind.

Bear finds a small blue mouse in his kitchen –

Too many memories –

Bear starts singing a duet with the mouse: 'Home is where the heart is ...'

I agree with the bear. Home is where the heart is -

I've got a job now, too. Part of a team, working the bins. I like it. Out in the wagon with my mates, *my muckers*, emptying the bins, having a laugh. Decent money it is, good tips at Christmas, meant I could buy good presents. And that model car for me, the same one that Davey drives, the Audi.

Bear calls for a shadow to come and play -

I finish my cereal, put the bowl on top of the TV, stretch. Thinking about what Davey said yesterday. It makes me smile. Davey needs me. Said he wanted a favour.

At first I thought he was cross. I told him, not working today, don't work Wednesdays, it's *a day off*, has been since they *changed the rota*. But it was OK because Davey had calmed down and then he didn't sound cross anymore and he said that tomorrow would have to do, no tomorrow would be OK, tomorrow would be fine -

So Davey needs me. Makes me glad.

Davey

Redundancy seeps into lives like a cancer, malignant final demands lying on the doormat like assassins in the shadows.

Annie fought it, month to month, but it became a battle she could only lose. So when her family in Cape Town offered air tickets and time away over Easter, she packed what she could into boxes and begged storage space in attics and garages. Telling the boys only that their latest adventure meant they were going to see grandparents and uncles, they took the train to Heathrow.

It was about three weeks later that I got the message on my phone, telling me she wasn't coming back. A short succession of texts between us revealed that she'd found an apartment, the younger of the two boys had started school, the elder one would be doing so soon and she had the promise of a job.

My phone in hand, thumbs pressing patterns onto the screen: 'Will come visit asap. Promise. You told M?'

M for Michael. The ex.

'Just about to. Wish me luck x'

Around an hour later, my phone buzzed, a green banner across the screen announcing a new message.

'He went mad. Going to the police.'

As charges of abduction were being emailed halfway around the world, I spoke to lawyers in London, arranging representation through legal aid and using money she would borrow to obtain the right advice. Staying put, it seemed, wasn't an option.

Negotiating via satellites, ultimatums and counterclaims, slowly a position emerged: a return to London in exchange for moving back into the house, the family home again for her and the boys. Tickets and barrister booked.

Paul

I can hear the cockerel. Not a real one. Alarm clock. I turn it off, open one eye –

4.45

Next, I hear rain against the window like *gravel being tossed onto a tin roof*. Need to get up.

Davey -

He bursts into my head and I sit up then get out of bed. In the bathroom, I pee, wash my hands, splash water on my face and brush my teeth, then I go to the kitchen and drink cold milk from a plastic carton and scoop a handful of Cheerios into my mouth from the plastic tub.

Back in my room, out of pyjamas, pulling on a pair of dark jeans, a T-shirt, sweatshirt, a woollen jersey.

In the hallway, Davey's door's open. I put my head into his room but it's empty and the bed looks like it's not been slept in. I pull his door shut and quietly open the door to Mum's room. Silver light falls across the bed where she lies sleeping. She looks beautiful. I blow her a kiss and whisper, *Love you, laters, watch out for alligators*, and shut the door again.

I pull on my work boots, take my army surplus coat from a hook by the front door, slip it on, then check my pockets, counting the items -

Front door key, bus pass, wallet, packet of Mentos, lucky golden cat figure, my *Maneki-neko*, a present from Mum. One, two, three, four, five.

All there. I unbolt the door, step out of the flat.

Davey

Annie took him to court and she won. Allowed to return to the family home, a monthly sum and his access to the children to be twice a month, all written up in an Order. Another fresh start.

Yet, as weeks slid from the calendar, she was sucked back into the past. He paid nothing and would turn up unannounced, as would the bailiffs and the money lenders and, one time, the police.

Back at the court, an irritable and unsympathetic judge gave her an ultimatum: live with it or send him to prison for a fortnight, your choice. How to tell her sons that she'd sent their father to prison? And what would it solve?

Three more repossession orders followed. Each time, he said not to worry, it was getting sorted out.

I was at my desk, replying to emails and feeling strangely dislocated, when my phone vibrated beside me.

'In a horrible B&B. 2 weeks. Then we're being moved anywhere in the country. Worst fears and nightmare come true.'

Paul

The rain's lighter, but I reckon it'll pish down later. I jam my hands into my pockets, wrap my coat around myself. I can feel my lucky cat in my fist and I squeeze him tight. Have to, first ten minutes in the fresh air, brings me luck for the day.

At the bus stop, I look up at the information screen and it says two minutes til my bus. It's going to be a good day. I can feel it.

On the bus, I swipe my pass over the reader. My seat's free, lower deck, window side, close to the automatic doors. My breath clouds the wet window, and it makes the streetlights and shop fronts sparkle like distant stars through fog.

When it's nearly my stop, I stand up and press the bell. At the stop, the doors open with a sigh and I jump off, walk down the side street and into the steamy heat of the café. It's where we meet, me and the lads. Men are sitting and eating bacon sandwiches or toast and I see two of my team.

Jimmy, Delroy -

'All right, Paulie?' Jimmy says.

I grin. 'Just getting a tea, some eggs,' I tell him. 'Anyone want anything?'

'No, you're all right, mate.'

Jimmy and Delroy smile.

Up to the counter: tea, strong, three sugars, two hardboiled eggs, two toast.

Same every day; nothing like it.

Back at the table, all cracked Formica and circular stains. I ask, 'Seen Jack?'

Jimmy swallows, shakes his head. 'Not yet. Reckon he fancied another ten minutes in bed with his old lady, given the weather.'

They grin and I nod my head.

Jack Chandler -

Gaffer Jack -

Might need a word with Gaffer Jack -

A word about Davey -

Seeing as how I'm going to need to sneak off, only for a minute, two tops, back in no time -

Doing a favour for Davey.

Davey

The house looks quiet now. I'm sitting at the wheel of the Audi, breathing deeply. Staring out into the blind suburban night. Throwing occasional glances at two yellow lights that gaze out into the dark: alien eyes glinting onto the roof of the old Jaguar parked in the drive.

I wonder if he's looking out. The ghost. Watching over me, like he did over her during those years of separation and shouting and holding it all together. Wondering if he can read my thoughts, see those two other boys, Paul and me, pulled from pillar to post. I had to make it right. For the boys' sake. For hers. Something had to be done. She deserves to be free of him. And now she is. I can give her that, at least. So it's quiet again now, ghost. Peaceful. No more tears.

I remember what it was like -

And something always has to be done -

I pull off my gloves and toss them into the passenger footwell. They slap against the bat as they fall.

I'll need to get rid of it separately; should have put it in the back with the parcel. I've wiped it down but it'll have fragments of bone embedded in it in all likelihood so I need to make sure it can't be found.

Paul

Out in the wagon and the rain's coming down *in torrents*.

Wet weather-gear on and puddles like lakes.

The wheelie bins lining the street look like an identity parade. I look at Jack, wondering whether to say something. The wagon lurches to a wheezing stop and a door opens.

Delroy's out -

Out into the rain -

Dragging bins from the doorsteps to the side of the road.

The lorry hisses, eases its way along the street before stopping again.

We get out -

Jack -

Me -

Just driver Jimmy left inside.

The rumblecrack of thunder overhead -

Bin handles slippery, gloves soaked.

Tension in my stomach as I peer through the rain -

Delroy's down the street, Jack's behind a parked car -

Back up the street, a flash of car headlights -

My heart in my throat -

I glance at Jack, at Delroy, they've both got their backs to me -

I wave an arm in the air.

The headlights flash once more and the car moves slowly towards the wagon.

Now Jack's approaching, dragging a heavy one. 'Give us a hand with this, Paul, will you?'

I'm looking at the car and I hear him say, 'Paul?'

'Yeah, sorry, Gaffer, sure, no problem.'

It's an easy lift for me and Jack together, fixing the bin to the lorry.

Jack smiles, his face wet, the rain glistening on his wet weather cap. 'Cheers, lad.'

I think about saying something, but Jack's gone,

away up the street.

Now, go now -

Lights flash -

Now -

I dash to the kerb, stumble, run, splashing behind a protective row of wheelie bins.

Davey's out of the Audi, its engine throbbing -

'Hey, Paul -'

I ask him where he was last night and he says, 'Had something to do,' and I grin and it's OK.

Then Davey says, 'Come on. We've got work to do.'

I say, 'Yeah, 'course, no problem.'

He smiles at me. 'Come on then. Got to be quick, you said. Remember?'

A look down the street -

'Yeah, need to be quick.'

Davey pops the boot. In the back is something that looks like *a giant black cigar*, bent in the middle.

'That what you need to get rid of?' I say.

'Yeah,' says Davey, reaching in and starting to drag the cigar out of the car. 'Give me a hand.'

Together we drag the package from the boot. The rain sounds like a drum on the plastic wrapper. It's great being with Davey but I don't want to get caught, so I say, 'I'll take it from here. I need to go.'

'You sure?' Davey says. 'It's heavy.'

'It's OK. See you later, Davey.'

'Yeah,' he says. 'I'll - I'll see you later.'

'Can we go for a drive?' Looking at the Audi.

'Yeah, sure. Sure we can.'

This makes me smile. The package is *bloody heavy*, but I manage to get it onto my shoulder. I steady myself then I'm off down the street, back to the wagon, watching for Jack, seeing Delroy pull out the last of the bins ready to take to the lorry. Jack's side's nearly done, the bins pushed back against garden walls, and I start to trot as I get closer to the wagon.

'Paul, what the hell -'

Jack's approaching and I have to summon all my strength to hurl the broken black cigar into the crusher. The plastic catches and tears and I hear something fall from the package and hit the wet road with a metallic sound.

I'm gasping. 'Sorry, Gaffer.' Thinking quickly. 'This woman, she - she said it wouldn't fit into the bin, would I mind taking it -' Panting.

'Bloody hell, Paul, you know we can't do that,' says Jack. 'It's not our job.'

'I know, I know,' I say. 'Sorry, Jack. Stupid of me.'

Jack turns. 'Get the rest of those bins in, eh? And no more knights in shining bloody armour.'

I dip down and grab the thing that fell out, stuff it into my pocket without looking. Then across the road, hauling the bins -

Back at the depot, shift's done. Taking off the wet weather gear, hanging it on pegs, shrugging off my high-vis jacket.

Hearing something.

CLINK -

I reach into the pocket, feel my lucky cat, *my Maneki-neko*, and there's something else, something metal, something metal around something else, soft but not soft -

I take out my hand and there, in my fist, *Maneki-neko* and a gold ring, a gold ring with letters on it, MJP, a gold signet ring still on a finger –

JOHNNY HERIZ
Out of Bounds

Dave says I'm a scrap. I don't call him Dave. I call him David so I can watch him try not to look angry, but the tips of his ears go red.

So I come in to the kitchen, and say, 'David, what do you do about mice, anyway?'

And his brow furrows, and he bites his lip, and says, 'What mice, Celia?'

So I tell him there's a mouse in my room. I was lying in bed listening to a scurrying and a crinkling, then the mouse sat on my bloody face, light and silent as the night, but I swept it off without thinking. Then there was more scurrying and scratching, for ages.

'It's keeping me awake.'

He sighs. 'I'll get you a mousetrap.'

'No', I say, 'You can't kill it, it's murder,' and he says, 'I can and that's what you do, Scrap, soon there'll be two then four then eight then -'

I say, '*I'll* get one,' and I look on Amazon and there's a Multicatch humane mouse trap. I'm not sure what humane means, but it doesn't kill the mouse, and it's only £4.43 Used, so I say to Dave -

'David – I'm going to buy a humane trap, out of

my own pocket money,' cos I know he'll say I have to pay for it myself. I also know what he's going to say next, so I say, 'And then I'll take it round Alhaji's house,' because him and my mum are always talking about Alhaji and her mum, and how they're leaving their house soon, so I don't think they'll mind having a mouse.

I know Dave doesn't want me to go round to Alhaji's because he and Mum said not to anymore.

'I don't want you getting hurt, poppet,' whatever that means, and I wouldn't tell Mum 'cause she looks sad when she talks about Alhaji's mum, and I don't like it when Mum looks sad. Anyway, that's why I stopped going.

Alhaji's mum works in the hospital and I suppose she has a blue uniform and a little watch like in Holby City, but I like seeing her in her big bright wide dresses, and her teeth are like perfectly white and really, really big, and she's just like summer, and singing all the time.

So Dave says it's *not* a good idea, but it is, so I ask Mum if she can get a Multicatch humane trap from the internet, and I'll give her £5, and she just does it without asking.

I've got three days 'til the trap comes, so at school I'm hinting to Alhaji to ask me over again, but in the end I say I'm coming round, and she looks really happy suddenly, and her face looks like her mum's, only she's got gappy teeth.

Her eyes are like hummingbirds.

She says she's seeing someone called a counsellor at school, and she doesn't know what for, but she misses science, but she says this counsellor is very nosy, and she must be sad because she has boxes of tissues everywhere, so Alhaji tries to cheer her up by telling her things she likes about being in England, but the counsellor just looks sadder. I say maybe she wants a hug, because that's what Mum does if I'm sad, but I don't let Dave near me with a bargepole, because he's not my real dad, and Alhaji says her mum hugs her all the time, happy or sad.

So anyway, three days later, I get the Multicatch and it looks complicated, but it isn't, you just put food in it then wait. Dave says mice like running next to walls, so I should put it up against the skirting board, and if I tidied my room it wouldn't have anything to eat in the first place.

I ignore his last remark and say, 'Thanks, David, I'll do that, thanks.'

I ask Mum if I can have some cheese, but she says she read in *Take A Break* that they infinitely prefer chocolate, which makes sense, so I buy some Maltesers, five for Clive (the mouse) and nineteen for me.

Alhaji keeps herself to herself at school, and it would be nice to see her and her mum again, and I really don't think they would hurt me. She says she's going to give the counsellor – who says to call her Karen, so she can't be a teacher - she says she's going to give her a hug like I said, and I give Alhaji one of the Maltesers I've got left in my bag, and say she should give that to Karen too, and if she doesn't like it, we've always got cheese at home.

There's nothing in the Multicatch the next morning, and I know Clive is still around. Mum gives me earplugs to help me sleep, but they're crap. I take them to school, and have them in in Maths, 'cause Mr Higgins is a bit shouty, but it makes Alhaji giggle, and it isn't her fault, but Mr Higgins comes over and confiscates them, and I have to see him after. He says I'm good at Maths, which I am, but it doesn't mean I like Mr Higgins, which I don't, but I get my earplugs back; not that they're any good at cutting out Clive or Mr Higgins from the equation.

Clive never sits on my face again but, the next morning, there he is in the trap, a scrap like me, and he's eaten a little bit off two Maltesers, and he's breathing really quick and big and trying to hide in a corner. Poor little scrap, so I put *Girl Talk* over the lid so he can go back to sleep.

I slip the trap in my bag and blurt out, 'I'm going to Alhaji's after school,' and my mum looked at Dave like, really surprised, and for once Dave keeps his trap shut (ha ha), so I jump up and out the door double quick, and leave the sticky silence behind.

I don't really mind Dave, and Mum really likes him. There's 'Things We Don't Talk About,' like Alhaji's mum – and like my dad, not ever.

They're 'Out of Bounds,' like the teachers' corridor.

Alhaji isn't in science, but I see her at lunch, and

she says Karen wasn't very nice, and kept asking her why she was giving her a Malteser (Alhaji says it had gone a bit soft, so maybe that's why she was upset), and then Alhaji gave her a big hug, and one of her mum's Banana Boat smiles, and Karen started crying, and said Alhaji could leave early now, with one hand in the Kleenex, so Alhaji kept the Malteser.

When we get to Alhaji's, Mrs Mansaray looks surprised.

Alhaji says, 'Hey, Mam. I got Celia here,' in her special home voice, and I shout, 'Hi!' and we run upstairs.

I don't want to tell Alhaji about releasing Clive in her room, in case she says no, and I'm worried he might give the game away, but he doesn't. Then Alhaji goes for a wee, and I get the Multicatch out, and lift the lid, and Clive is off like Usain Bolt behind her wardrobe, and that is that.

I get home and Dave and Mum are weird at tea. There's a loud silence.

Then Dave says, 'You'll be able to sleep properly tonight then, Scrap, eh?' and he does his silly little laugh, and I wish I had my earplugs in.

Only that night, I *don't* sleep properly, because there's another bloody mouse!

Like Dave said, 'Then there'll be two.'

So I get the trap out and shake the Maltesers to the middle, and put it just where it was before. There's scratching all night. The earplugs are no good, so I listen to Goldfrapp instead, though I'm not strictly allowed. But this is an Emergency.

Anyway, so next morning (but it's the same morning) there's Clive The Second, who's even more of a scrap than Clive the First, and running around loads - no wonder he's skinny. Even when I put *Girl Talk* over him he's ten times noisier than he was.

I wrap the trap up in a thick jumper in my bag so no-one can hear him, and ask Alhaji can I come round again, and she says yes and, this time, Mrs Mansaray gives me the biggest, warmest hug, and she smells of wood and spices and soap, and I'm lost somewhere else, but then I'm upstairs letting Clive the Second out to be with his best friend, like I am.

When I get home this time, there's real trouble. Mum isn't sad but angry, and Dave is moving things round in the kitchen. At tea, Dave asks about school. Now, I never answer that one normally, but this isn't normal, so I tell him about Alhaji, Karen the Sad Counsellor, and the Malteser. He looks even more worried now, and Mum is poking food round her plate.

'But what is a counsellor, Dave?'

'Well, Celia, a counsellor is someone who you can talk to when you aren't happy. They can help you be happy.'

'But Alhaji definitely isn't sad. She's my best friend, so I know.'

'Well, she might be sad, you know, having to leave home and everything.'

'Well, she's *not* sad. She's probably happy because

she's going to get a better house, like ours.'

Mum clunks her fork down and looks up at me, and I get that shaky feeling of not being where I really am. She's looking *into* me like only she can. I don't know why I'm crying but I am, and so is my mum, and neither of us can see Dave, not now.

'What is it, Mum? Is Alhaji moving away? I don't mind because I can get on the bus.'

Now Mum really is crying, both barrels.

Barrels of tears.

'Won't I see her again? What is it, Mum? I can still see her, can't I?'

Dave has his hand on Mum's. He says no, I can't when she's gone, and she's going back home. But I don't know what that means, because she's already got a home, and a school, and she's my best friend anyway, both of us without a proper dad – and I didn't know if I said that out loud this time.

'No, sweetheart, her home is a long, long way away, in Sierra Leone.'

Mum's twisting the tablecloth. 'A long way, darling.'

And I'm crying buckets, even though I don't know where Sierra Leone is, but I do know it's not in stupid England; so I go upstairs with the atlas, and Sierra Leone isn't *anywhere* near England. There's all sorts of countries and water between us. England looks like the only real country on earth, and Sierra Leone is tucked into a tiny corner of a big island called Africa.

The night is very still outside; there's no wind and

I've got the window open, and I can hear owls calling, and I'm just lying on my duvet looking at the atlas. Sierra Leone is not anything like as far as Australia, and I'm wondering where Alhaji's new house is, then I hear a sort of quiet squeak. Tiny, it is. Only I can't work out where it is, but there it is again. So I call downstairs in a hush for Mum, and Mum and Dave come up. Mum has sorted her face out.

I put up my hand like a wall, and the three of us stand perfectly still like owls, then we all hear it, and Dave whispers, 'Behind the chair,' and we tiptoe over, and there's nothing there, so Dave pulls out the chair, and there's lots of squeaking, and on the floor in a pile of carpet fluff and crap are two tiny little hairless, pink baby mice.

'Oh shit!' says Dave.

'David!' says Mum.

'All right, Scrap,' and he rolls the chair back over the babies, and we're clueless what to do.

Mum says, 'I'll make a cup of tea,' and then we're all downstairs, and I simply have to tell them there were two mice, Clive the First and Clive the Second, and they're both living at Alhaji's now because Alhaji's going away soon, so it wouldn't bother her, and Dave says, 'Let's call Clive the Second something else like Bonny, seeing as he's probably a girl,' and Bonny and Clive are the babies' Mummy and Daddy, and now we have to think what's best.

Dave says we can't feed the babies. They need their mum.

I took their mum away from them, and now they're going to die of hunger.

Dave looks at Mum. He hasn't said anything, but she just says, 'No, we can't do that. We just can't. They're babies, for fuck's sake.'

'OK,' says David. 'Celia, you need to go round to Alhaji's and say what's happened,' but Mum says, 'We all need to go round,' and that's that - we're in the car driving round to Mrs Mansaray's house on the estate, late at night.

When we get there, they call Mrs Mansaray 'Ramatu' And Mrs Mansaray says, 'Thank you for everything you've all done for me.' And Mum says, 'Well, I'm so sorry it didn't work out the way -' and then runs out of words and looks down at her feet. Mrs Mansaray puts her hand on Mum's arm.

Then Mrs Mansaray wants to know why we're there, and they all look at me, and Alhaji comes down in her pyjamas and looks at everyone, then at me and we're both smiling now.

Dave says we have to have a conference, and I don't know what that is, but we sit round the kitchen table with cups of tea, and I share Alhaji's chair.

'We're just two scraps, it's OK, Mrs Mansaray.'

So then I have to tell the whole story, and Mrs Mansaray says, 'I know all about the mouse. You didn't have to drive all the way here at ten o'clock at night to tell me about the mouse.'

And I say, 'mice,' and finish my story.

'I was trying to do the right thing, Mrs Mansaray,

and I ended up doing completely the wrong thing. Clive the First and Clive the Second are really Clive and Bonny, and they've left two babies under my chair.'

Then Alhaji jumps up with a really loud squeak, and runs out the room, and her mum murmurs, 'Oh My Lord,' and crosses herself and looks at the open door. 'Oh, my sweet Lord. I put two mousetraps out last night,' and I say, 'Were they humane?'

And she shakes her head. 'They were just cheap ones.'

And then I say, 'Cheese or chocolate?'

And we're all looking at the open door, and then there's a loud *Snap!!!* from upstairs, and Mrs Mansaray slaps her mouth. Her glassy rings catch the kitchen light. Then there's another snap, and Mrs Mansaray's lips are moving silently, and her eyes are shut.

Alhaji appears at the door holding up two pens with mousetraps on them, smiling like a piano.

Now I know I should have said about the mice earlier. I make room for Alhaji and I whisper, 'Are we still friends?' And she holds my hand.

I ask her, 'Will your daddy be in your new house in Sierra Leone?'

Alhaji looks at her mum because maybe she doesn't know. Mum and Dave both say, 'Celia.' Mum's looking right into me again, and I think I might cry, but Mrs Mansaray says slowly, 'Alhaji's daddy has been lost. Nobody knows where he is,

Celia. I think he is with God.'

'Will you see him again, Mrs Mansaray?'

She has a soft smile like a curled up cat. 'One day, Celia. One day.'

Alhaji's eyes are wider and wider open, and she says, '*Might* we see Daddy?' and Mrs Mansaray slightly shakes her head, and now Alhaji might cry.

She says, 'So, David, what are we going to do about these two?'

'We couldn't kill them, Ramatu, so we came over here.' That's Dave.

'I see. Now, Celia, I know you're a clever girl, and I see you've brought your satchel (she means my bag) and I'm betting you've brought your special trap, haven't you, girl?'

Yes, I nod.

It's empty, so we go to the fridge for some cheese, but I say I've spoilt them with chocolate, so they won't want her cheese. Alhaji says I saved their lives twice then, and she's still got Karen's Malteser in her lunch box.

Mrs Mansary says, 'What else have you got in your bag, little lady?' and I show her my pyjamas. 'So you'll be sleeping over then?' which I've never, ever done before, and she and Mum *and* Dave go into another room while me and Alhaji put out the Multicatch against the wall upstairs. And then later, I get a hug from Mum and Dave at the same time by the front door, which is OK (just this once). Then I can hear the car going, and me and Alhaji are lying in bed listening out for mousy sounds.

I say, 'Alhaji, don't you like it here in England?' and she says she does, and she doesn't really want to go to Sierra Leone - it's not her home, but her Mum says they have to, and I say, 'Where is your new house?' and she says she doesn't have one and I say, 'That's silly, where will you live? Everyone's got a house,' and she says, 'Not everyone.' So I say, 'Where will you live?' and there's a long, long silence. Then Alhaji says, 'The Lord will provide.'

There's more silence, then Alhaji whispers, 'Where's your Dad, Celia?' and I say, 'He's Out of Bounds, that's all I know.'

Then we go quiet. I think we heard something.

ANDY SZPUK

The Sign Said For Sale

The sign said for sale
And when the people moved out
Removal men came
To heave away the piano
Along with the beds and everything else
Until the house was empty
And standing forlorn
Like a dog without a tail
The letterbox flapped
And deliveries of junk mail
Landed in a pile
Gathering layers of dust
On a worn out, left behind, welcome mat
The doorbell didn't ring
And no footsteps
Ran down the hall to answer it
The doors were all locked and bolted
Lamps left on timer switches
The seashells in the bathroom
Long gone with the goldfish
Now and then, people arrived

To poke around and peek in corners
Until, one day, a ray of sunshine came
And took the for sale sign down
Once again, the house could breathe
The world was returning
It might be two-year old terrors
Making mucky marks on the landing walls
Or people with a taste
For Sky dishes and wallpaper paste
The house opened its doors
And let them in

TANIA HERSHMAN

Something Like a Tree

She pushes the electronic card they gave her into the mouth of the machine. A whir, another whir. She looks around, and as far as she can see, stretching away across the long, long hall, machines whirring and issuing commands at other small women, small men, who don't speak their language, whose English is filled with polite yeses and little else.

'Nine,' commands the voice.

She stares at the machine. 'Nine?'

An arm shoots out of the side of the machine, unfurls into an arrow, and where it points she sees doors, numbers. The electronic card has been ejected. She takes it, pockets it and walks slowly towards the nine. Another machine, a table, a chair.

'Sit,' and where the first voice was her schoolteacher, this voice is more like her grandfather's.

She sits. She smiles. She looks around. Did anyone see her smile? Can this machine see her?

'Why have you come here?' says the grandfather-machine.

'Yes,' she says, and swallows. A tissue, wiping her

forehead. She is from a place of great heat, but this is not the same. The room is chilled, but she sweats.

'Why have you come here?' Grandfather-machine is measured, patient. It has all day.

'Yes,' she says. She recognises the 'why', the 'come'. She tries: 'I come, to work. I come, I help.'

'Your visa is for a family. What will you do for this family?'

'I clean,' she says. 'Yes. Old person. Grand. Mother. Help.'

The grandfather-machine makes a new sound, a series of buzzing clicks. Then: a piece of paper.

'One year,' says grandfather-machine. 'Goodbye.'

She takes the paper, which is covered in words. She stares. One year? Twelve months? But she needs more, much more than that. A daughter going to university, a son in school. Years, it will take.

'But -' she says.

There is no sound. Grandfather-machine is asleep. Is no longer interested. The door swings open. She understands.

The family is kind. Little children who speak too fast, much too fast, leaving her nodding, yessing, smiling, yessing, nodding. Cleaning is something she understands and she can do well, without instruction. They have a machine for this, too, but it stands in a corner and she has pressed some buttons but it seems to have broken. Every day she wants to ask why, every day she begins, in the morning, as the family have breakfast, but every day what comes out of her mouth is wrong.

The children chatter to each other, the mother and father mumble, and the grandmother doesn't speak at all. The grandmother needs cleaning, needs to be lifted, washed, dressed, and all the while the grandmother stares at something across the room. The grandmother's eyes do not move.

'It's very beautiful,' she tells her daughter when they speak through the machine that is fixed to the wall in her cool room in the basement. She can see her daughter's hair, her daughter's eyes, and she has to make herself not cry.

'It's like a palace, it has so many rooms!'

She forces her voice into excitement, forces it to rise at the end as if this was the adventure she always dreamed of, away from her children, her familiars.

A year later, and the mother takes her to an office in the centre of the city. The mother's auto is voice-controlled, something she has never seen, something that hasn't come to her land yet. Her command of the language is improving, but here is a vehicle that speaks better than she does. She looks out of the window. She still has not discovered why the cleaning machine sits in a corner, silent; why she is needed. She still cannot ask.

In the office in the centre of the city, she nods, she says yes, yes, she smiles and smiles. Across the long, long hall, she sees many machines ask questions of many small women and men.

'For work,' she says. 'Yes, yes,' she says.

A new piece of paper.

'We are so lucky!' says the mother, and she sees she has one more year.

'Yes!' she smiles, nods. Only one more year? Her daughter has two more years of university, her son five more years of school, and then.

The grandmother has not changed. She has not begun dribbling, ranting or waving her arms around. The grandmother hasn't even varied the spot on the wall at which she stares when she is lifted, washed and dressed. It is almost as if the grandmother is not getting any older, just staying very old.

The children, shoving each other, run past the open door. She has never seen them come in. She has never seen the mother or the father tell the children, 'Go say hello to your grandmother'. But she has seen the father come sometimes and sit in the chair in the corner. It is his mother, she thinks. He sits, with his hands on his knees, his earcam still in place in case someone should need him. Often, he says things, but so quietly that she, watching from the hallway, can't hear. He stays sometimes for an hour, and then he gets up and leaves, closing the door.

No-one touches the grandmother. Only she touches the grandmother.

She is renewed again, and then again. She speaks to her son and daughter through the machine fixed to the wall. Her son is so tall now. His voice is deep, she almost doesn't understand him and she tries so hard, tries so hard not to cry when she sees him. They used to cry when they saw her, they used to ask why she couldn't just come back, why they couldn't find another way, why did she, why was she, didn't she ...? Now they just chatter and laugh and talk about friends she has never met, new places built since she left where they go to do things, things that she doesn't know but doesn't want to ask.

'They will understand,' her mother had said to her when she told her what she had to do, where she had to go. 'They will understand.'

She does not go out very much. She lifts and washes and cleans the grandmother, cleaning the sores from the sitting, the leakings from the old, old body. She washes and cleans the grandmother carefully, thoroughly, and then she washes and cleans the house. She picks up an object, wipes underneath, and then sometimes she stands for a few moments with it in her hand, looking. Sometimes: a remote control. Sometimes: a discarded earcam. Sometimes: an animatoy. Then she puts it down and goes back to work.

While she works, she hums, melodies without words. She hums to the grandmother too, as she carefully and thoroughly washes and cleans, to make sure the grandmother knows someone is there, to keep the grandmother, to keep her from changing. She does not want anything to change. Not until her years are enough.

But soon, too soon, the grandmother is dying. It seems as though she will not be very, very old for much longer. When the grandmother tries to breathe there is a dark deep knocking from inside as if something wants to leave. Doctors come, scanning with their tools, but still, there is no stopping death. The mother is looking at the father. The father is looking at the doctor. The children are not home much anymore. Finally, the father nods, the doctor nods, and they go into the grandmother's room.

She is not needed. She stands in the hall outside, and then she stands back when they come to take away the grandmother, the grandmother's eyes closed now, no more knocking inside her chest. She reaches out a hand towards the grandmother.

'Yes,' she says. 'Yes.'

The mother is very sorry. The mother says something fast, and then she says it slower, about 'carer allowance', about 'not being able to', about 'so sorry'. Then there is a new machine in the middle of the room, a new cleaning machine, and they are saying, 'Take a few days,' and she is packing up, telling her children through the machine fixed to the wall in her cool room in the basement that she will let them know when, let them know where.

The mother's auto drops her off in the centre of the city. She stands outside the doors to the building which gave her a piece of paper every year, just one more year. She reaches out her hand and the doors slide open towards the long, long hall with the machines and the small women and small men, but her legs take her backwards and she turns and walks away. Walks away with her small bag of nothing in it and her small purse with the electronic card, enough for a few meals, a few days.

She walks down the bright street, and she turns a corner and another corner and she finds herself walking and walking. She walks until there are no more walls and no more screens and no more autos and no more sliding doors or machines with pieces of paper.

She hopes for something like a tree. She hopes for some animals. She hopes for someone to talk to. In her head she speaks to herself in her own language, but after so long, after so many years, it is mixed up. It is filled with yesses and bits that have stuck to her from conversations: 'detergent', 'allowance,' 'earcam', 'my turn,' 'bedsores', 'homework'. Her head is full of these sticky words, and what use is she now?

She stops walking. The road is everywhere, stretching on both sides. There is no grass. There are no animals. She has her small bag of nothing in it and her small purse with the electronic card and her head full of things that aren't hers, and she has no future and her past is dissolving. She sits down, just sits, right there on the road, and waits for someone to come and tell her what to do next.

LANCE CROSS

Not In My Back Yard

Steve forgot to buy toilet paper.

Steve always forgets to buy toilet paper. It's probably deliberate. He's the sort of loser who would keep a hidden stash - probably one of those super-sized rolls stolen from a pub.

It started with me and Jenny sharing. Two people, two bedrooms, one house.

'Can my friend Steve crash on the sofa for a week while he's between flats?'

Flutter, flutter.

I could agree to anything watching those lashes.

Four months later, we were three people, two bedrooms, one house and zero toilet paper.

Steve only left the house to buy cigarettes and lager, so I put the hard word on Jenny one day when he was at the off-licence. She'd been far from happy and wanted rid of him too so promised to broach the subject of leaving. A week passed, and Steve didn't give the impression he'd been broached, so it looked like I would have to confront him myself.

I didn't get the chance.

'There's been an accident,' Jenny said, leaning over

a kitchen chair staring at the floor.

'I was slicing cheese and he sort of fell on my knife.'

I gawked at the puncture marks covering Steve's limp body as it lay, spread-eagled in front of the oven.

'Right,' I said. 'How many times did he fall on the cheese knife?'

'A few.'

Flutter, flutter.

At this point I had a choice. A choice to do the right thing or the stupid thing.

Flutter, flutter.

Hiding a body in a rug only works if the carpet is man-shaped so I suggested using the large rug in Jenny's bedroom but she'd had to visit three *IKEAs* to find it so wouldn't give it up. I would have thought as Jenny was the cheese cutter, she might have considered a minor personal sacrifice was warranted, but she was having none of it.

Steve's corpse, rolled in a hall runner from the bathroom landing, reminded me of the bacon-wrapped cocktail sausages at my company Christmas party. I wouldn't be eating them again.

That wasn't going to work so I wrapped him in my Arsenal duvet. Steve was a Chelsea supporter. He would have hated it.

'And what are we going to do with this?' I said, pointing at Steve.

I tried to sound blasé, as if deciding where to place a lamp or painting, but squawked like a man trying to figure out how to dispose of a body.

'In the back of the car when it's dark then to Epping Forest.' Jenny was remarkably calm.

I scowled at her.

'I'm sorry about this, Mike, it won't happen again.'

'I should hope not.'

That was all I could think to say that didn't involve the words, 'police', 'murder' or 'prison showers'.

We sat opposite each other in the lounge waiting for dark. I thought about asking what had actually happened but Jenny was still clutching the bloody knife and didn't look to be in her calm zone.

'Why don't we bury him in the garden?' I chirped.

'Because we live here, Mike! You don't bury bodies at your own house. Are you mad?'

Yeah, you stabbed someone repeatedly with a cheese knife and I'm the mad one.

'Sorry, I've never done this before.'

It was her first time too, apparently, but she'd watched enough TV to know if you don't own a pie shop or a wood chipper it's a drive to the forest.

'Aren't people going to notice he's missing?'

'Who?' she said, 'The man at *Kings Street Wine and Spirits*?'

I asked about his family.

Jenny shrugged.

She didn't know if he had any. I asked how long she'd known him before he came to stay.

'I met him the night before,' she said.

'The night before!'

Jenny told me I was a glass-half-empty person and that life was too short so I should live a little. I stared at the man-sized lump under my duvet in the middle of the room.

'Walking through a forest at night carrying a dead guy sounds risky. There's that patch behind the shed which would be about the right size,' I said.

'Mike. I am not living somewhere with a body rotting 30 feet from my bedroom.'

'We could move.'

'But I like this house. All the furniture in my bedroom fits the gaps. I'm not going to *IKEA* again, Mike, I'm just not, OK!'

I held a hand up. 'I get it. We're staying but no dead bodies.'

We sat in silence.

'I like this house too.'

No reply.

We sat in more silence.

'We should get rid of his DNA,' I pronounced.

Jenny wasn't the only one who watched TV.

'Yes. You deal with the blood and I'll deal with his stuff,' ordered Jenny before disappearing into the lounge.

Thanks. I'll clean up your gory mess while you stuff two T-shirts and a Pulp Fiction poster into a bin liner.

One thing I've learnt from watching forensic teams in Las Vegas, Miami and New York is that bleach kills everything. Plan A was to douse the house until the fumes became overpowering but we didn't have bleach, so Plan B was to douse everything in a mix of pomegranate dishwashing liquid and citrus burst refreshing shower gel, with a healthy squirt of fresh and minty toothpaste.

When darkness came, we struggled to the car with the duvet and managed to cram Steve into the boot. The street was deserted and there didn't appear to be any curtain twitchers.

Plain sailing.

I sat in the passenger seat and looked about nervously as Jenny put the key in the ignition and turned.

Nothing happened.

She tried again.

Nothing happened.

'Nothing's happening, Jenny.'

She whacked the steering wheel.

'Bloody car! Start, you bastard, start!'

The rusting, yellow Clio refused to be threatened by Jenny's ranting and sat smugly outside the house so we were left sitting in the living room with a corpse on the floor.

'Of all the times for your car to breakdown.'

Jenny shot me a glance.

If looks could kill ...

'Mount Pleasant Road!' I blurted.

'What?'

'There was a fire on Mount Pleasant Road so there's a vacant house.'

'And we just carry Steve through the streets before breaking into a burnt-out wreck to do some midnight gardening?'

Was that sarcasm in Jenny's voice?

'No, we jump over a few back fences,' I explained as I waved in the general direction of Mount Pleasant Road.

It sounded easy once I'd said it.

'So we only have to sneak through people's back gardens with a body?'

'Yes.'

Jenny leapt up and grabbed my collar. No flutter, flutter. She explained that this wasn't a game and if we got caught we'd be toast.

When did it become my responsibility to be the man with the plan? I didn't kill anyone.

I told her we weren't calling a taxi so, unless she wanted to cut him into pieces and eat him, we didn't have many options.

Jenny was silent as she contemplated the hand sticking out from under the duvet pointing towards Mount Pleasant Road.

The first fence was easy. Only three feet high and the back of the Petersen house was obscured by Hammersmith's biggest camellia bush. The second wasn't as straightforward. It was six foot and an abundance of apple trees forced us to sneak to the Thompson's back door for a spot clear enough for cadaver shot putt.

I was pumped on adrenaline. I had superhuman

strength and every sense was heightened.

In the next yard, a bathroom light came on and we had to stand frozen, listening to old man McNairn abusing his toilet.

Another low fence. I repositioned the dead weight on my shoulder when the yappy Chihuahua that belonged to the Welsh couple at number 22 ran straight at us and sunk its teeth into Steve's protruding left foot.

'Let go, you bald rat!' I hissed, trying to shake it loose with my boot.

That was when Jenny smashed it over the head with a shovel.

Excellent. Now we had two corpses to bury.

With four steps and one immense heave, Steve was over the next fence. Jenny followed, carrying a shovel, a torch and a dead dog.

The final fence. A tall one. Jenny swung his legs and I had his shoulders, but we didn't make it on our first attempt and a fuchsia bush paid the price. I balanced Steve's neck on top of the fence and we threw our weight behind his legs, sending him cartwheeling into 13 Mount Pleasant Road.

Jenny casually tossed the canine cadaver over the fence then I boosted her over and, finally, I scrambled up, damaging more of the native flora.

I'd never dug a grave before but the epinephrine was flowing through me like cheap Rioja as I stood wedged between the fence and shed.

I did all the digging. Jenny was supposed to be

acting as lookout but she got bored, and twisted locks of red hair around her finger, while contemplating her feet.

Although she looked upset, I didn't offer any 'It's all right' speeches as she'd killed a man and we were burying the fact as deep as we could on land that didn't belong to us so it really wasn't all right.

Once we'd covered Steve and Sugar Puff (according to the collar), we piled burnt chairs and the remnants of a table next to the shed to impede access to their final resting place.

It only took two minutes and five fences to be in our lounge, sitting in silence amidst a fug of minty pomegranate, as dawn approached.

We've never spoken about that night and no-one has come looking for Steve. I'm OK with being an accessory, 13 Mount Pleasant Road remains a burnt-out ruin and the neighbours have a new Chihuahua.

It's just me and Jenny again.

Two people, two bedrooms, one house.

And toilet paper.

BIOGRAPHIES

Alan Gillespie is twenty-seven-years-old. He lives in Glasgow and works as an English teacher. Say hello on twitter: @afjgillespie

Amanda Block is a graduate of the Creative Writing Masters at the University of Edinburgh. She is a literary consultant for a small Geneva-based publishing house and a freelance ghostwriter.

In her own creative fiction, she is often inspired by myths and fairy tales, frequently using them as a starting point to tell other stories.

Amanda has been shortlisted for the Bridport Prize, the Chapter One Promotions Short Story Competition and the Waterstones Bookseller's Bursary Award. Her writing has been published in Modern Grimmoire: Fairy Tales, Fables and Folklore and Vintage Script. She is currently working on a collection of short stories and thinking about returning to her half-finished novel. Amanda blogs at www.amandawritersblock.blogspot.com and tweets at @ACWritersBlock

Amanda Saint is obsessed with words. She sells them to anyone who will pay in order to make a living and uses them to write fiction with the rest of the time. Her first novel, As If I Were a River, is currently being edited and an extract will be published in an anthology, Collages, in August 2013. Her Saintly Writer blog features in the book of the Festival of Writing 2012, two of her short stories were long-listed in the 2012 Fish Flash Fiction prize and one has been published in Number Eleven Magazine. Amanda also runs Retreat West, which provides writing retreats, workshops and short story competitions. She lives near the sea in Exmoor National Park with her husband, John, and a marmalade cat, Rusty. When she's not reading or writing she likes to bake and eat cakes, then go walking to keep them from expanding her waistline.www.retreatwest.co.uk

Andrew James is a marketing specialist and author whose first novel Blow Your Kiss Hello is a fast-paced urban fantasy thriller, described as being 'uniquely different and thoroughly gripping' and as having 'all the makings of a cult success.' He lives in South West London. @4ndrewjames #BYKH

Andy Szpuk is a novelist, short story writer, memoirist and poet based in Nottingham, UK. His full-length debut, Sliding on the Snow Stone, is the true story of one Ukrainian man's journey through famine, Soviet terrors, and brutal Nazi occupation in World War Two. Andy is also a member of DIY Poets, a performance poetry collective in Nottingham, and regularly participates in spoken word events.

To sample his poetry and other writings, visit his

blog: One Author's Very Own Discovery Channel (andyszpuk.wordpress.com).

He's the author of The History of Rock and Roll in 99 tweets, a unique story in chapters of 140 characters or less: an eBook available from online retailers. Andy is currently working on Fate and Circumstance: a story of the Ukrainian Lemkos in the Carpathian Mountains (south east Poland), and their battles in the years following World War Two to retain their homes and cultural heritage.

Bernie Steadman has recently retired from a long and rewarding career teaching English Language and Literature to students aged 11 to 18 in Manchester and Devon, and developing her pastoral skills in working with troubled and traumatised teenagers. When not bashing away at a keyboard, Bernie likes to walk along the coast or cycle in the Devon countryside with husband Stuart. She's an active member of two choirs and relishes the adrenaline rush of live performances. Rumour has it that she has taken up knitting and has forced several friends to be grateful for hand-knitted presents of unpredictable quality. The freedom to write whatever and whenever she likes continues to inspire Bernie. She has completed her debut novel, Breathe, and is looking for representation. She also enjoys submitting short stories and poems to magazines and competitions. She is currently working on a sequel to Breathe and making notes for a YA novel.

Chris Nickson was born in Leeds and will likely die there, although in between he's spent many years in the US and elsewhere. He's the author of over 30 non-fiction books, six novels and more CD reviews than you can shake a stick at. A few were even perceptive.

Daniel Maitland is a writer and musician. He released his debut solo album, Rumours Of A Nice Day, in 2008. He has written two novels: The Fat Rats of Flatland for children and Idle Hands for adults; an existential, quantum fantasy friend novella, Things Forgotten, and most recently a Kindle collection of short stories called There Was This Bloke Right. His poetry has been featured on Sky TV and in a number of UK magazines, and his bumper collection, Even Bad Dogs do Good Things can be found in the odd good book shop.

Daniel played for ten years with soul legend, Geno Washington, and worked in a number of other writing and performing projects – including the RSC and The Foundations. Re hobbies and relaxation, he has broken seven golf clubs in anger reaching his escalating handicap, and walked away in a sulk from most London poker venues.

He is in love with a cat called Hamish and rejected the advances of another called Stephen Arthur. Links to most of his work can be found at www.danielmaitland.co.uk

Debbie Ash-Clarke studied Physics at Birmingham University, has worked for a Public Analyst and as a writer and sub-editor for computer magazines PC Support Advisor and PC Network Advisor. She has been writing fiction for more than fifteen years, has just finished writing her first novel and is about to seek representation. Debbie lives with her husband and cat in Buckinghamshire.

Debi Alper is the author of six contemporary urban thrillers, set among London's sub-cultures, the first two of which, Nirvana Bites and Trading Tatiana, were published by Orion to critical acclaim. She has also had short stories published in anthologies and online. Over the years, she has worked as a charity finance officer, a photographer, farm labourer, life model and wig maker. An unexpected result of giving up her day job to concentrate on writing is that she spends a lot of time concentrating on helping other writers to perfect their novels through critiques, mentoring, online courses, Book Doctor sessions and creative writing workshops at festivals. Debi edits in all genres and several authors that she has worked with have been signed up with agents and gone on to see their books published. She also has substantial experience as a judge of writing competitions, both large and small. Debi lives in South London with her partner and two teenage sons. She sometimes feels like a tiny island of oestrogen afloat in a sea of testosterone and smelly socks. www.debialper.co.uk

Debs Riccio lives in Bedford. After her three young adult books received rave rejections from agents, she self-published under her maiden name of D A Cooper (Dead Good, Re: Becca and Let's Go Round Again). She recently added her adult book, Reconstructing Jennifer under her current name. She has a short story in the TwitterTitters book sold in aid of Comic Relief and was runner up in the Choc Lit Publishing's 2012 Winter Writing Competition.

She is writing five other books at the moment as she can't decide which one will earn her the publishing deal of which she dreams. She is a regular contributor to the Strictly Writingwebsite and when she's not writing she is reading, sleeping or faffing about on Facebook. She hates housework nearly as much as she hates celery and doesn't always talk about herself in the third person. She thinks that would be weird.

Frances Gapper's flash fiction chapbook The Tiny Key was published in 2009 by Sylph Editions and Absent Kisses, a collection of longer stories, in 2002 by Diva Books.

One of her stories, A Bit of Tragedy, appears in the Summer 2013 issue of Ireland-based magazine The Moth. In the Wild Wood, a 5,000-word piece of hybrid fiction about the year she spent living with and trying to look after her mother, while having a breakdown herself, is to be included in Short Fiction 7 (University of Plymouth Press).

Gail Jack is amazed to find that the overactive imagination she had as a child is clawing its way through the layers of sensible and responsible living. She has already confessed to a fondness for fig rolls and chocolate ice cream and has recently discovered she is partial to home-made chicken tikka.

On a more serious level, Stories for Homes is a project she is proud and happy to support.

Helen Hardy ranks reading and writing alongside breathing and chocolate among life's necessities. She is published in the East Dulwich Writers' Group's Hoovering the Roof anthologies, and won a Brit Writers Award for her short story Crush.

Iain Maloney was born in Aberdeen and currently lives in Japan. A graduate of the University of Glasgow Creative Writing Masters, he was shortlisted for the Dundee International Book Prize 2013. www.iainmaloney.wordpress.com

Ian Shine's short stories have appeared in Scraps, the anthology for National Flash-Fiction Day 2013, and will be appearing in The Fiction Desk's upcoming anthology. He was also short-listed for Stork Press' first mini short story competition. You can follow him on Twitter @ianshine

Isabel Costello lives in London with her husband and two sons. She has completed her first novel set in London and 1970s Brooklyn and a second is in the works. Isabel enjoys sharing her experience of reading and writing on the Literary Sofa blog, a forum for lively debate with other readers and especially writers. Her newly-discovered passion for the short form has led to publication in the Rattle Tales 2 Anthology and short-listings in the Asham Award 2012 and the Short Fiction Journal Prize 2013. Isabel loves writing British and American English and Brooklyn has become a significant place to her in real life and in fiction. Half of Everything is inspired by and dedicated to Donna Zaengle – a wonderful friend in all weathers, hurricanes included.

Jackie Buxton A tour of one of the few working mills in Britain inspired A Life With Additives. Although the effusive patter of the miller had Jackie immediately sold on the benefits of his virtuous flour, when little change came back from a tenner she couldn't help wondering who would buy it on a regular basis. Jackie edits, teaches creative writing and contributes regularly to Chase magazine. She has had some success in first chapter, blogging and short story competitions and A Time to Push is published in the anthology, They Lied. Jackie has recently launched herself into a re-write of her first novel, Glass Houses, following positive feedback from an agent. Occasionally Jackie ventures in to the real world, where she runs, cycles and sings, anything to get out of cleaning, and loves to have a cappucino with friends or spend time with her long-suffering and amusing family.

Visit www.jackiebuxton.blogspot.com and www.jackiebuxton.moonfruit.com to find out more.

Jacqueline Ward is a writer who calls the North West of England home. Her stories have been included in several anthologies and she is working on her second crime novel. A keen blogger, Jacqueline has also contributed to online magazines such as the F-Word and Bea. Jacqueline edits a safety journal and writes for various safety magazines. She is also an inventor, having won a global Innocentive challenge to measure central nervous capacity in children under two years, and is an artist in the style of the Glasgow School.

Jacqueline is a mother of three and grandmother of four. In her spare time she is a Chartered Health Psychologist, writes academic books about identity construction and runs an international charity. She has recently been appointed an MBE for services to vulnerable people.

Jane Roberts is a freelance writer living in Shropshire, UK. She has been published in magazines, ezines and anthologies - including: Subtext (2009), 100 Stories for Haiti (2010), New Sun Rising: Stories for Japan (2012) and Dark Clouds by Collective

Unconscious (2013). Longlisted for Fish Publishing Flash Fiction 2013, winner of Writers and Artists Flash Fiction 2013. Collector of pseudonyms. Twitter @JaneEHRoberts

Jennifer Harvey, originally from Glasgow, now lives in Amsterdam with her six-year-old daughter, her partner and a senile old dog. She used to think that one day she would make it back home to Scotland, but after almost twenty years living below sea level she now realises that this is unlikely. Her stories and other miscellaneous musings can be found online at www.jenharvey.net

Jilly Wood was born in Derbyshire, where Jane Austen wrote Pride & Prejudice and Charlotte Brontë found the inspiration for Jane Eyre. She's always been a bookworm, despite her parents' efforts to strike a healthy balance and get her outside into the fresh air. She loved English at school, but as a pragmatic Northerner she knew she should get a proper job, so she decided to study law.

She went to university in London, where she has lived ever since. She wasn't cut out to be a lawyer, so she became an accountant, working in businesses including advertising, hairdressing, and music. It wasn't all spreadsheets and calculators. She made some good friends, travelled a lot, and got some awesome haircuts, but she never gave up the idea of writing.

In 2012 she took the plunge, and she's having the time of her life. Find Jilly at www.jillywood.com or on Twitter @jillywords.

Jody Klaire started writing in 2011 and although she had been writing music and lyrics for fifteen years, becoming an author had never been something she aspired to. However, the moment that she began to compose the story for her first novel, she was hooked.

Jody has been many things from police officer to singer/songwriter and tries to use her experiences in life to evoke vivid pictures. She aspires for her characters to touch the hearts of the reader. Jody lives with a host of furry friends: her golden retriever, several gerbils, a hamster, some sneaky voles, a delinquent squirrel and a neighbour's cat. She loves writing, sport, music, art and teaching herself new subjects. Jody is also a proud member of the Word Cloud - an online community of authors and is delighted to be a part of the Stories for Homes Project.

Johnny Heriz works as an architect in Glastonbury. He has written poetry since he was tiny. He used to teach paragliding, and has done a lot of rock-climbing. Now he cycles. He has two sons, who have grown up. He can concentrate on his writing now, which is what he wants to do. He is still married.

John Taylor worked with people with learning disabilities for thirty years, specialising in storytelling, painting and music in therapeutic groups. No longer professionally involved, some of his closest friends are former clients.

He divides his time between writing novels, storytelling and being a husband and parent. He writes for all ages, preferring novels that cross genre boundaries and break the rules. John is represented by Juliet Mushens at The Agency Group, and can be found on Twitter as @johnunworded

Jo Lidbetter fell in love with South East Asia when she first moved there from the UK over twenty years ago. She now lives in Laos, a country still badly suffering from the after effects of the bombs dropped on it during the 'Secret War'. Even today, many injuries occur from previously unexploded bombs, often when children pick them up, believing that they are toys. The Blu-3 is a cluster bomblet that is nicknamed The Pineapple because of its appearance which appeals particularly to children.

Jo previously lived with freedom fighters in a bamboo hut, on the edge of the jungle where Thailand and Burma meet, and it was here that she began to understand some of the realities of life on the edge. Today, she has a much simpler life and spends her time teaching, writing and travelling throughout the region.

Jules Anne Ironside started writing as a child, though she is only counting from when her spelling improved enough to be recognizable as English. She grew up in Dorset in a house full of books. After studying genetics and plant biology at the University of Wales, Aberystwyth, she has worked in various roles within the NHS. She was especially surprised to have ended up working in dentistry. Jules is a keen martial artist having studied more than a dozen martial arts. Her great love is Okinawan Goju Ryu which she has been teaching for fifteen years together with traditional weaponry. In her free time, she likes to read and add to her collection of dead or little-used languages. Writing is her true passion and she has recently enjoyed some success with the publication of several short stories in various anthologies.

Julie Glennie was born in Plymouth, and has a BA in English literature from Bristol University. Together with her husband Chris, she ran a garden centre near Weston-Super-Mare for eighteen years. They took a seven year break in Andorra, where she learnt Spanish, skiing and how to be an ex-pat, before remembering her childhood dream to be a writer. She has been immersed in fiction ever since, writing short stories as well as novels. She is an active member of the Writer's Circle of Andorra with whom she self-published The Five Senses, an anthology of short stories and articles. She is currently back in the UK, where she continues to write. Hobbies include yoga, dancing, hiking and eating home-made cake. She has a full time job as slave to two rather superior Burmese cats, and part-time job as wife and mum.

Kate Lord Brown grew up in the wild and beautiful Devon countryside. After studying philosophy at Durham University and art history at the Courtauld Institute of Art, she travelled round the world. She is married to a pilot, and lives with her family in the Middle East. Her 2011 debut novel, The Beauty Chorus, about women aviators, was inspired by the hours she spent on airfields in the UK, and the experiences of pilots in her family during WW2. Her second novel about the Spanish Civil War, The Perfume Garden, draws on the years she lived in Spain, and will be published in eight countries this year. Kate has an MA in Creative Writing from the Manchester Writing School at MMU, and was a finalist in ITV's People's Author contest. She is working on her next novel. www.katelordbrown.com

Katherine Hetzel has been an egg-pickler, weigher-outer of pic'n'mix sweets, bacon-and-cheese-slicer, a microbiologist (the serious job choice, involving looking down a microscope a lot) and a learning assistant at a primary school. At the moment, she's being a writer. She started writing silly songs and daft poems for her children, which gradually grew into longer stories and ended up on paper – like Follow the Yellow Sick Toad and Granny Rainbow and the Black Shadow, both published in Reading is Magic, a collection of short stories for children published in aid of the NSPCC. She's also written short stories for adults, but her real passion is writing for children; her full-length novel, The Ring Seekers – Adventure in Ambak, is in the final stages of editing before being pitched.

She is an active member of the Word Cloud, operating under the name Squidge, and has just begun to blog at Squidge's Scribbles. squidgesscribbles.blogspot.co.uk

Lance Cross became interested in writing short stories when someone said, 'We need short stories for a Shelter anthology', so I'm new to the art. It was fun and easier than writing my unpublished novel, This Land is Not For Sale (not appearing in good bookshops soon). Want to know more about me? Well, you can't. I don't have a website and I don't blog or twit.

It's not that I don't want to, I'm just lazy and telling anonymous people on the internet what I'm doing leaves me less time for doing it. I spend too much time making banana cake, rubbing the cat's stomach, watching series two of Star Trek and writing, so it wouldn't be very interesting anyway. There are loads of other things I should be doing but I am in a Spock-pussy-cake-rut and they're difficult to break out of.

Lindsay Fisher leaks stories and the leaks grow bigger with each passing week and more and more of them spill out into weird or wonderful places. There ain't no rhyme or reason to what is written, at least none that Lindsay can discern. They're just stories. If they are read, then that is an outcome hoped for but never counted on; if they are enjoyed, then that is what it must be to be blessed by God or the touch of an angel's wing on one's cheek. And to think that Lindsay's stories are now making their own way in the world, that is a small miracle. And since stories are like children and are easily bruised, Lindsay wishes them well and wishes them safe and sends them out there with enough love.

Mandy Berriman is a mother, teacher and writer (not always in that order) who lives with her husband, children and dog on the edge of the Peak District. She works two days a week as a primary school music teacher and works the rest of the week as mother to her two young boys. In her spare time (what spare time?) she writes children's ghost novels, short stories, blogs and, since Jesika has decided to take up full-time residence in her head, she is currently writing her first adult novel: an extension of A Home Without Moles.

Mark Arram is fifty, married with two grown up sons. He lives and works in Peckham. Mark has been homeless and knows the pain of being unwanted by one's family. He wrote the poem in this collection quite quickly and is pleased with it.

Max Dunbar was born in London in 1981. He recently finished a full-length novel and his short fiction has appeared in various print and web journals. He also writes criticism for 3:AM and Butterflies and Wheels. He blogs at maxdunbar.wordpress.com and tweets at @MaxDunbar1. Max lives in Leeds.

Michele Sheldon is a journalist and lives in Folkestone, Kent.

Mike Scott Thomson has been a writer since his teenage years. Now in his 30s, and after dabbling in music journalism, blogging and travel writing, he only turned to fiction in 2011. So far his stories have been published by The Fiction Desk, Litro Magazine, Writers' Forum Magazine and various places online. A short story, Me, Robot, was adapted for performance by the theatre group Berko Speakeasy. He was also awarded runner-up prize in the 2012 Ink Tears Short Story Competition. Based in Mitcham, he works in broadcasting and can be found online at www.mikescottthomson.com.

Mikey Jackson is a freelance writer, novelist and scriptwriter from the seaside town of Worthing, near Brighton, on the South Coast of England where the sun sometimes shines, but it mostly rains. Author of the novel Patience Is a Virgin, he writes scripts, novels, short stories, web copy, gags and letters to the milkman. Find him at www.mikeyjackson.com

Neil Campbell had a story in the Best British Short Stories 2012. Two collections of short stories, Pictures from Hopper and Broken Doll, have been published by Salt. Two poetry chapbooks, Bugsworth Diary and Birds, have been published by Knives Forks and Spoons. He recently completed a short story cycle called The Fold.

Nicola Tervit is a librarian and lover of books, who shares her home with bunnies and chinchillas.

Owain Paciuszko writes waffle for a bunch of websites, makes short films and music videos, plays keyboard and 'sings' in the band Giant Burger, performs repeated attempts at stand-up comedy. He was raised in Cornwall, studied in Wales and currently lives in London. When he grows up he wants to be a space captain.
www.kingoftheducks.com

Pete Domican started writing in 2010. His short fiction work features in Pay Attention: A River Of Stones, 100 RPM - One Hundred Stories Inspired By Music, the second Friday Flash anthology, A Blackbird Sings, Flashflood, Planet Paragraph and

Sixwords Online Magazine. He made the longlist for The New Writer Prose and Poetry competition in both 2011 and 2012. He procrastinates on Twitter as @petedomican

Rachael Dunlop is an award-winning writer of both short stories and flash-fiction, and a serial starter of novels - she has an extensive collection of first chapters. Her stories have been published in various anthologies, including 33 West (Limehouse Books) and The Tipping Point (Rubery Press), and on the Ether Books reading app. Despite living in a very big house, she has given up on having a room of her own and seeks the Muse from her kitchen table.

She blogs when she remembers at rachaeldunlop.blogspot.co.uk and can be found on twitter @rachaeldunlop

Rebecca L. Price is an English teacher based in South East London. She originally comes from Wales and is an ardent Welsh rugby fan, though sadly nowadays she has lost the accent. When not writing or teaching, she enjoys growing vegetables, singing, tea-drinking and having conversations with her cats. This is Rebecca's first piece of published writing and she hopes it will be the start of something. Her patient husband hopes so too, as he would happily give up work and live off the proceeds of her potential success.

Homelessness has always been an issue close to

Rebecca's heart as she has been moved throughout her life by the work her mother has done in youth homelessness in South Wales. She would like to dedicate this story to her mum, Paula - a constant inspiration.

Rebecca Swirsky is a London-based writer specialising in short fiction. Her work varies anywhere between 100 and 10,000 words. Competition success includes winning the A.M. Heath Prize, being shortlisted for the Bridport Prize and Fish Short Fiction Prize, and awarded third prize in Ilkley's Literature Festival Short Story Competition. Rebecca has read and had her work read at the London Review Bookshop, Bloomsbury; Ilkley Literature Festival; and Liars League, Central London.

Her stories and criticism have been published in journals including Matter and the online Royal Academy of Arts Magazine. She has been commissioned to write for the forthcoming Royal Society of Literature Review and has short fiction appearing in Ambit journal.

She writes weekly for the Royal Academy of Arts Magazine online and regularly contributes to a blog on acupuncture. Follow her on Twitter @rebexswirsky

Rob Walton was born in Scunthorpe, and is a graduate of Newcastle University's Creative Writing MA. He has written for the Hull Daily Mail, Scunthorpe United's programme, an online schools'

resource for the Tyneside Cinema, books for teachers and numerous articles for education magazines. He has also written several shows for The Big Fun Club, and his play The Bumps was performed in Newcastle in June 2013. He has collaborated on projects such as Parky Tales for Newcastle Gateshead Initiative/Magnetic Events' Enchanted Parks. In 2012, he worked with sculptor Russ Coleman and the local community to write the text for the New Hartley Memorial Pathway. He was commissioned by New Writing North to write a short story, published in Platform, 2012. Two stories were published in Stations by Arachne Press. A Drop of Golden Sun appeared in Positional Vertigo and Crazy Paving appeared in Root from IRON Press (February 2013). His short stories and flash fictions have appeared on Pygmy Giant, Paragraph Planet, National Flash Fiction Day and 1000words. He lives in North Shields with his family.

Sallie Wood lives in the East Midlands with her husband, two children and a semi-longhaired cat called Summer. She works as a Customer Services Advisor for a local authority. Writing is her passion. She is currently working on her first novel. Sallie enjoys reading, travel and is fascinated by all things paranormal. With Hindsight is her first published story.

Sally Swingewood began writing books when she was four. She wrote and directed her first play at six, casting herself in the lead role as the Virgin Mary. Years of journalism intervened and Sally developed a less dictatorial, more collaborative approach to creative projects. Sally has written for local and international newspapers, devised musicals, edited film and theatre scripts and contributed to a number of books.

Sal Page has an MA in Creative Writing from Lancaster University, won the Calderdale Short Story Prize in 2011 and has stories in various places such as Jawbreakers, the National Flash Fiction Day Anthology, 2012 and The Greenacre Writer's Anthology volume 1, as well as online at The Pygmy Giant, 330 Words and Paragraph Planet.

She lives by the sea in Morecambe, is making 2013 the year of finally learning the ukulele and is in the process of looking for an agent for Queen of the World, her tragi-comic magical-realism novel about a woman who believes she can influence the weather.

Sam Schlee tries his best to write short fiction alongside a PhD in urban geography. He spends his time getting angry about housing and curious about gentrification. This is the first story he's had published.

Sarah Evans has had dozens of stories published in magazines and competition anthologies, including: the Bridport Prize, Unthankbooks, Earlyworks Press and Writers' Forum. Recently her story Shadower won the Bloomsbury Short Sentence story competition and Terms and Conditions was published as part of Unthology No.3. She lives Welwyn Garden City with her husband and her interests include walking and opera.

Sonja Price was born in Bristol and now lives in Weimar, Germany. She studied at UEA and has a PhD in English Literature. She taught English at Graz and Mainz Universities and currently teaches at Jena University.

Writing allows her to have adventures in exotic places without actually leaving her desk. Her first novel is set in Kashmir and was longlisted for the Mslexia Novel Competition. www.sonja-price.com.

Sophie Wellstood grew up in the Warwickshire countryside in the sixties. She has worked in theatre, bookselling and education. She now teaches and writes full time. She lives in west London. Blog:www.sophiewellstood.wordpress.com

Susan Chadwick is a Teller of Tales, Word Nerd, Botanist, Chicken Whisperer, Magpie Mum, Guinea Fowl Wrangler, Fox Rescuer, Cat Cuddler. Explorer of real and surreal worlds, and all-round snoozy person. Likes learning; interested in (almost) everything. Contact her @WhisksTweets

Susmita Bhattacharya was born in Mumbai, India. She sailed around the world in oil tankers for three years with her husband, recording her voyages through painting and writing journals and communing with dolphins. She received an MA in Creative Writing from Cardiff University in 2006 and has had several short stories and poems published since. She lives in Plymouth with her husband, two daughters and the neighbour's cat. She teaches creative writing and blogs at susmita-bhattacharya.blogspot.co.uk. Her debut novel, Crossing Borders, will be published by Parthian Books in 2014. She tweets at @Susmitatweets

Tania Hershman is the author of two collections of short fiction, My Mother Was An Upright Piano (Tangent, 2012) and The White Road and Other Stories (Salt 2008), which was commended for the 2009 Orange Award for New Writers. Tania's award-winning short stories have been widely published in print and online and broadcast on Radio 3 and 4, and she is founder and editor of The Short Review, a journal spotlighting short story collections. www.taniahershman.com

Thomas McColl is 42 and lives in London. He's been published in magazines such as the Alarmist, Open Pen, Notes from the Underground and Geeked, and recently came 2nd in 4'33' Magazine's 60 second story contest. He's also been included in this year's official National Flash-Fiction Day anthology, Scraps, and will shortly be published in a new book being brought out by the guys behind Smoke: A London Peculiar, called From the Slopes of Olympus to the Banks of the Lea.

Tracey Iceton is an English teacher and creative writing tutor. She has an MA in creative writing and was recently awarded funding to study for her PhD. She won the Writers' Block NE Home Tomorrow Short Story Competition, was shortlisted for the 2012 Bristol Short Story Competition with Apple Shot and was joint third prize winner in the 2013 Chapter One Promotions Short Story Competition for Diana of the Moon. Her two novels have been long and shortlisted in the Bridge House Publishing Prize and the Cinnamon Press Debut Novel, Irish Novel Fair and Chapter One Children's Novel competitions. Her publication credits include: Litro, Neon, Tears in the Fence, Ride, The Yellow Room and the Brisbane Courier Mail. She is writing her third novel, book two of her trilogy on the Troubles in Ireland while working on publishing book one, Green Dawn at St Enda's, ready for Easter 2016. She can be contacted through the Society of Authors.

Wendy Ogden lives by the sea in East Sussex. Married, with grown children, she has been writing for over ten years. Publications include short stories in small presses and competition wins include a first prize for a flash fiction, and two seconds for fiction judged by Kate Mosse. She has published articles in The Lady, The New Writer and online and completed a novel. Twitter @eastbournewrite Blog: On The Edge

William Angelo writes novels and short stories, usually serious, sometimes with a comic twist. This short story is not comic. He works all day with computers but prefers being away from work and writing about people. His current novel spans forty years in the lives of the characters and he worries that it may take him that long to finish it. Home is in Sussex with his partner and daughter who is about to follow her brother out of the nest. He is a late-starter in the literary game, but he believes that it's better late than never.

Zelazko Polysk was born in Poland and now lives in England. He has been writing fiction for as long as he can remember, but only recently began submitting his stories to publishers and competitions. Zelazko Polysk is not his real name.

2963015R00300

Printed in Germany
by Amazon Distribution
GmbH, Leipzig